RECKLESS: THE SMOKY MOUNTAIN TRIO

SIERRA HILL

PART I

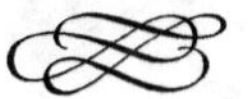

London

CHAPTER 1

I've known Sage Hendricks and Cameron Lucas since we were five years old.

We started out as friends, then grew to be more as the years progressed.

We were a perfect band of misfits – the smarty-pants princess, the angsty punk kid and the Prom King jock. Yet somehow, we worked – most of the time, anyway. Even in grade school, when we first met over their stupid boy antics, they both stole equal parts of my heart, never to return it in the same shape they found it.

The day we met on the playground was the day that changed the direction of my life.

That was the day we became a trio. The Three Amigos.

From that day forward, we were inseparable.

I remember that first day of kindergarten like it was only yester-day. I was the sassy know-it-all, trying to change the world through rules and authority.

"Stop it right this minute you two hooligans," I commanded. My tiny hands at my hips to prove my resolve and seriousness like my momma always did. "Or else I'm gonna tell Miss Lund and then you'll be in big, *big* trouble."

I stood behind the two boys who were fighting over the big yellow bulldozer in the sandbox; my chin up, trying to muster all the bravery I had inside my pixie five-year-old body.

The two boys halted their arguing, each keeping a grasp on the toy and peered up at me. One stocky toe-headed kid with bright blue eyes, and the other a scrappy dark-haired boy with the freckles and eyes so brown they looked like the bottom of Pitney's Pond.

The blond kid sneered, saying with a lisp from his missing teeth, "Nobody likes a tattletale."

The other kid, dirt caked on his face, snorted a giggle, repeating the words of his nemesis. "*Yeah*, nobody likes tattletales."

I crossed my arms over my favorite pink polka dot dress. My momma tried to suggest that I wear something less fancy, but it wasn't her first day – it was *mine*. And I wanted to look pretty and stand out in the crowd, just like my daddy always encouraged me to do.

"I ain't no tattletale," I said with as much bravado as I could muster. "But we're supposed to share. That's what my Sunday school teacher tells us. We're supposed to turn the other cheek and not sin, either."

My voice held a level of authority that typically doesn't come from a little girl and the boys seemed to consider my theological wisdom – *for a second* - until the bigger blond kid yanked the truck from the scrawny kid's hands, sending him flying face first into the sand.

He came up sputtering, as I ran over to lend my hand. Tears streaked down his already dirty cheeks and he tried to hide the fact by wiping at them with the back of his hand. The other kid – looking a bit surprised – began laughing out of spite.

"What'd you go and do that for?" the dark-haired boy asked, pushing himself up off his knees.

I chimed in. "Yeah, you big meanie. You're just a big ol' bully."

My little temper got the best of me, regardless of the fact that I knew fighting was against the rules that Miss Lund had gone over just that very morning. But I couldn't help it. I gave the blond boy a jerking shove to his shoulder, but he was quicker than me and he dodged it by turning his back, as I went sailing into the sand face first.

I landed in the sandbox angrier than a mangy dog and completely humiliated at how I was bested by a bully.

When I moved to get back up, the two boys were already going at each other – like scrappy little bear cubs – throwing punches and slapping at each other's faces. A group of kids formed around us, wanting to see the tussle, all screaming and yelling.

"Hit 'em!"

"Sock it to him!"

"You hit like a girl, sissy!"

That's when I jumped in to break things up. It's was an abomination that they would fight like that. My momma always said there's too much war and hatred in the world and we should love thy neighbor. Which in theory sounded good, but I could never quite understand the rationale, since Mrs. Johnson was our neighbor and she was a mean old witch that yelled at me once for trying to pick up her cat, Luscious.

"You better stop this right now, both of you. You're behaving like…like…*miscreants*."

I had no idea what that word meant, but I'd heard my momma use it many times before with my older brothers, Grady and William. So, whatever the word meant, it wasn't a good one, for that I was sure knowing the headaches my brothers gave my momma.

My commands went completely ignored as the two boys continued to wrestle and kick, knocking each other around, creating a spectacle of themselves in front of our new class-mates. So, I did the only thing that I could think of to break up the fight.

I joined in.

The bigger blond headed boy was on top of the small lanky kid, so I jumped on the back and yanked at the blond boy's hair.

"Ow!" he howled, trying to buck me off his body with a wiggling motion, but I wouldn't give up. I kept at him and his arm came back behind him and he ended up grabbing a piece of my long pony-tail, taking a chunk of it in his sweaty, dirty fist and pulling my head to the side.

While it stung and brought bright tears to my eyes, I wasn't that easily immobilized. I'd fought with my brothers and picked up some good tactics along the way since I was old enough to walk. This was nothing in comparison.

Leaning down over my opponent's head, I bared my teeth, getting a good piece of the earlobe on the boy.

He wailed loudly and we both landed in a heap, his back ending up on top of my chest, crushing me and getting blood on my pretty new dress.

It was then that the teacher finally realized what had been going on and she came running over to the sandbox and wading through the gaggle of kids who were still hooting and hollering over our interesting little scene. Had we been a few years older, the kids probably would've been placing bets, like I'd seen at the illegal cockfights at a neighboring farm.

"What do the three of you think you're doing? This is not how we treat one another or make new friends."

Miss Lund took a giant step into the sandbox, and grabbed hold of tiny, flailing arms, pulling us up to our feet one by one. With a swat to our rear ends, she marched us into the Principals office as the other kids giggled and squawked behind us.

What happened next will forever cement our loyalty and friendship, even though it eventually led us in opposite directions.

The Principal, Mr. Schuler, with his gruff face and graying hair, sat at his desk and eyed us each with pointed stares. I sat in the middle between the two boys, our feet dangling over the chairs above the blue carpet. I still hadn't even learned their names.

"Who would like to tell me what started this fight?"

I glanced side-to-side to each boy to see if they were going to fess up to their actions. When it became clear that neither of them would speak up, based on their bent heads and downcast gazes, I stretched out my hands, grabbing a hand of each boy, holding them tightly as I spoke.

Surprisingly, my voice didn't wobble or shake, and I didn't cry. For some reason, being in the middle of these two boys made me feel strong and confident. Like they propelled me and held me up in some manner.

I had no idea what it really meant when I said what I said, but I'd heard it mentioned before when a man does a solid for a woman.

And at that time, I felt it was my responsibility to speak up for these two rough-necked boys. Something inside me felt a connection worth holding on to. And worth lying about.

"They were defending my honor."

And thus, our friendship began.

Through thick and thin.

Good times and bad.

Until our worlds were ripped apart and they broke my heart in ways that it could never be salvaged. Burnt beyond recognition in a blazing fire too devastating to collect the pieces it left behind.

CHAPTER 2

By seventh grade, our worlds revolved around each other like planets to the sun, and every free moment we were together. It never seemed to matter to Cam and Sage that I was a girl and they were boys.

Until the summer break between seventh and eighth grade. That's when it became more than a little apparent that as a female, I was made different.

At that point, our bodies began developing. I was no longer the skinny, knobby-kneed girl with pigtails. Cam's voice had dropped an octave and his chubby-cheeks and pudgy boy body began to fill out into a more muscular build, especially since he was working out with his junior high football teammates all the time.

And Sage…well, not only did he shoot up a foot to six-foot but the Halloween before, he'd dressed up as Jack Sparrow and found that the smudged eye-liner look appealed to him in many ways. He never wore it around his dad, though, for fear of being smacked around for looking like a "faggot."

As for me, I began trading in my grungy cut-off shorts and baggy t-shirts for more "acceptable" feminine clothing, as my momma called it. Throughout grammar school, I learned that fitting in with the boys was easier if I looked more like one. As I hit puberty, it also helped to conceal my growing breasts. So, momma was happy as a Georgia peach that I was becoming interested in fashion and would take me shopping every chance she got.

One lazy Saturday afternoon, while Cam was off at some football camp, Sage and I moped in my basement, playing video games, when my momma asked us if we wanted to go to the mall. Had it not been for the way Sage's eyes lit up with the opportunity, I would've politely declined. But seeing as he was excited to go, we all piled in my momma's red sedan and drove the thirty miles to the one shopping mall in the county.

She dropped us off in front of Dillard's, giving us each a crisp one-hundred-dollar bill. The look on Sage's face was one of appreciation and mortification.

Trying to hand it back to her, he said, "Thank you, Mrs. Moriety, but I can't take this from you."

Momma waved him off. "Now, Sage, honey. Of course, you can. This is my gift to you since I didn't get you anything for your birthday."

He knew it was all a bullshit lie, because my momma made the best cake this side of Texas for him, knowing full-well that his father would undoubtedly forget his son's birthday. That was my momma. Compassionate and caring. It didn't matter that she had three of her own children, my friends always had a place in our home and in her heart.

Shooing us off in the opposite direction, she sent us on our merry way.

Walking side-by-side, I bumped his shoulder with mine.

"What do you think you're gonna buy?"

I'd only asked the question to hear him say it out loud because truthfully, I already knew. I just wanted to see his face light up with the desire that he'd kept hidden deep inside him.

There was a music store in the mall, full of instruments and all kinds of musical equipment, amps, songbooks, tuning apparatuses. And I knew Sage like the back of my hand. He had been eying a guitar for the last year, looking at it wistfully every time we passed the store window, although he'd tried to hide his yearning.

Sage had always been interested in music and knew every song on the radio. He'd sing along, with a pretend mic in hand, belting out the tunes at the top of his lungs. And he was good.

He could also write lyrics and had notebooks filled with words and poems. In fact, that's what I got him for his fourteenth birthday a month earlier, a beautiful, handcrafted leather-bound notebook so he could write down his thoughts and feelings and turn them into music.

"I'm going to get that guitar," he said, pointing to the window where a shiny acoustic six-string guitar was prominently displaced.

He might have stood there all day long staring longingly at that instrument had I not grabbed his wrist and pulled him inside the store. When we stepped in, a salesperson came toward us from behind the counter.

"May I help you two today?" His nametag said Clarence and he smiled at us politely.

Sage moved toward the guitar, hesitantly stopping himself from reaching for it.

"Yes, sir," I replied. "He'd like to buy that guitar. How much is it?"

The man nodded and plucked it off the stand, the tag dangling from one of the pegs.

"This one here is one-hundred and seventy-two dollars."

Sage's body jerked as if he'd been shot and he slowly turned back to me, an expression of sorrow and defeat written across his face.

Knowing he wanted nothing more in the world than that guitar, I did what any good friend would do in that case, I gave him some of my money as a loan. He could pay me back when he earned enough through odd neighborhood jobs that summer.

He was never one to smile a lot, but a huge grin overtook his face and he hugged me tight.

"Thank you, London. I'll pay you back, okay? Don't you worry about it."

"I'm not worried a bit. But the least you can do is write a song for me someday, okay?"

And from that moment on, he was rarely ever seen without that guitar in his hands. He'd keep it in his locker while we were at school, telling me once that he was worried his dad would hock it for booze money if he didn't keep it away from him.

That summer was when it became glaringly obvious that Sage had a talent so incredible that he was destined for big things someday.

One night, as we laid next to one another out in my backyard under the stars, Sage began to play a song he'd written that day just for me.

It may have been rudimentary at the time and needed some polishing, but it was still the most beautiful song I'd ever heard because it was filled with all the things that he couldn't say but felt to the bottom of his soul.

I climb into bed each night,

Closing my eyes tight.

Hoping to wake with something different

Than what I've been giving in my life.

I thank the good Lord for my friends,

Although sometimes I'm desperate

For something I can't have.

And alone in my feelings and worried that it'll end.

It wasn't the last time he'd write a song about heartbreak and despair. Of confusion over who he was and what he meant to the world.

As he finished the song, our gazes snagged, and I reached for his hand. I was scared to ask the question, but the opportunity was there. So, I took the chance.

"Sage, can I ask you a question?"

"Of course."

I heaved in a breath. "Are you gay?"

He swiveled his head in my direction, his eyes wide as he stared at me in the dark. Because I was nervous, I continued to babble.

"It's okay if you are. I mean, a lot of people are. It's cool if you are and if you like other boys. It doesn't change how I feel about you or anything."

I stopped to take a breath and he started to laugh. In fact, he nearly doubled over laughing like I'd said the funniest thing he'd ever heard in his life. My feistiness got the best of me, along with my embarrassment, so I shoved him hard on his shoulder. He fell to his side with a grunt-snort.

"You jerk. I was trying to be a good friend. Geesh."

When he finally finished laughing, he sat back up and hiccupped. And then there was silence.

I waited, quietly fuming over his audacity to laugh at me when I was trying to be serious and hopefully open the door for him to come out. My wait continued until he finally spoke.

"I don't think I'm gay. Maybe bisexual. I don't really know 'cause I've never kissed a boy. But sometimes…I want to."

His admission to kissing – alluding to the fact that he had kissed a girl – threw me for a loop and I gasped.

"What? Does that mean you've kissed a girl? Who? How dare you keep something like that from me! I'm supposed to be your best friend."

The tone of my voice was teasing, but inside I was a tad bit hurt that I didn't know about this development until now.

Sage lifted a shoulder nonchalantly. "Happened a few weeks ago at Wendy Conner's birthday party, the one you couldn't go to 'cause you were in Atlanta for that dance thing. It was one of those *Truth or Dare* games. I chose the dare."

When I gave him the look that said, "*And?*" he wiggled his eyebrows and continued.

He smiled but spoke with indifference. "And I slipped her the tongue."

"Sage Hendricks, you little devil," I teased, but my eyes dropped to his parted mouth. It made me wonder what it felt like to kiss him.

In fact, the previous school year, my friend Chloe casually inquired about whether I'd kissed either Cam or Sage yet or slept with them. I was appalled at the time that she'd even think that of me or of us. They were my friends, and let's face it, I was fourteen and didn't have those desires at that point in my life.

But now, not even a half year later, sitting here in the dark summer evening talking about such things, had me considering Sage with a different perspective. I was seeing him for the first time as a cute boy who had experienced French kissing other girls.

And it made me jealous.

Tossing the thought away, I asked him the next question on my mind.

"Would you ever want to kiss me? Or Cam?"

The answer I received wasn't anything I had expected. But certainly, changed things in the years to come.

"Maybe."

CHAPTER 3

The summer between our Junior and Senior year was one of the best, and the worst summers, I'd ever known. It had brought friction, jealousy, and desire into our friendship.

And made me long for things that I knew were impossible.

While things changed ever-so-slightly as we entered our sophomore year in high school, those two remained my constants. There wasn't a day that went by where I didn't see them, speak with one of them or spend time with them in some capacity.

That fall, if Cam was off at football practice, I was studying with Sage – who, for the record, was the world's worst studier. He hadn't been diagnosed, but I was fairly certain he had ADHD or ADD because that boy would never sit still. Not for a single minute.

He was always tapping a pen, drumming his fingernails on the table or playing video games instead of focusing on his homework. It always made me curious about what was going on inside that mind of his and what made him tick.

And when Sage was working a shift at the grocery store or writing music on his guitar, I could be found hanging with Cam. We'd kick the soccer ball out in the backyard, watch movies or go for horseback rides along the many trails on our property. And if I was busy with dance, the boys could likely be found at Cam's house playing video games.

When the three of us had downtime and were all together, we were at my house on the farm, swimming in the river or hiking in the woods near my property. It was an idyllic childhood that swiftly and without warning blended into young adulthood; fraught with new and turbulent feelings.

And no matter how innocent our bond was, no one could seem to comprehend how the three of us could be as close as we were and not be more than just friends.

That changed the summer I turned seventeen. I finally noticed what all the other girls in our class saw when they looked at either Cam or Sage. Especially after their growth spurts that year.

"What are you waiting for? Are you chicken?" Sage's voice rang out from the river below me where he kicked and circled in the water like a barracuda in wait.

I was standing on the high river bank, my feet sunk low in the mossy, cool grass, hanging on to the rope for dear life. The strong, twisted fibers of the swing rope were tethered to the large tree limb overlooking the river bank on the edge of my parents' property.

The boys dragged the old, tattered rope from my barn a few weeks earlier and today was the first time we'd had an opportunity to use it. Having two older brothers to pick on me in all manner of ways and being best friends with Cam and Sage my entire life, there were very few things I was actually scared of or that terrified me.

Snakes? *Nope.*

Frogs and insects? *Not even.*

Gunshots and hunting rifles? *No fear.*

But heights? *No thank you, ma'am.*

I'd kept my fear of heights successfully hidden from Cam and Sage for years. When we'd gone to the carnival a few years earlier and while they went on all the tall, looping rides, I feigned a headache and stuck to the carrousel. The only person that knew about my stomach-clenching fear was my momma.

My palms were clammy as I held tightly to the rope, fist-over-fist, as I slowly shuffled to the lip of the overhang. Sage waved from down below, smiling that smile he reserved for me and Cam and no one else, giving me the encouragement I needed to jump.

"Come on, London! Get your ass down here now."

I swallowed the boulder that stuck in my throat, panic lodged deep in my belly. My willowy figure trembled in trepidation as I took a few steps backwards, only to find something blocking my way.

Startling, I jolted and let go of the rope, which through the laws of physics and gravity swung like a pendulum out over the river. The solid mass behind me wrapped an arm around my waist, reaching with his other arm to grab the rope as it made its return journey toward us.

"I've gotchya, London," Cam's deep voice whispered in my ear as my hand landed on the thick, sinewy arm that held me close. "We can do it together if you want."

I stood immobilized and unable to move, my body firing off strange signals to my brain for the first time ever. A different and new kind of energy sizzled and heated between us. Maybe it was a combination of my fear, his sweet gesture, or the warm masculine scent of Cam that seemed to envelop me, but I was caught in an electrifying thought.

It wasn't just comfort I felt in his arms. Against Cam's chest.

It was the beginnings of desire and it shook me to the core. My breasts heaved in a heavy inhale, my brain muddled from the dizzying effects of his voice and his broad, naked chest pressed against my back. My tummy did somersaults, and I felt tingles in the V between my legs where I'd never felt them before around Cam.

Leaning my bikini-clad body against his towering mass, I relaxed. Cameron was my rock. He was my protector. If there was anyone I trusted with my life outside of my family to have my back, it was Cameron Lucas.

His tall frame had bulked up and filled out over the last year as he left boyhood on the cusp of manhood. His broad shoulders and lean, trim waist were a sight to behold. Cam's blond hair was always a tousled mess that was made only worse by the way he constantly worried his fingers through it. The girls at school giggled and blushed when he'd walk by in the hallways, casting his '*come hither*' gaze at them, at the same time he'd lazily run his hand through his shaggy do.

And then there were Cam's eyes. When his eyes connected with you, it was near impossible to look away. His deep-set blue eyes could melt you on the spot with their warmth and character. They held a deep well of compassion and reverence for such a big boy. Most of the time Cam was all business; raised to take life seriously, just like his father, a retired Air Force officer.

His arm tightened around my belly, making it difficult to breathe.

"Are you ready for this?"

In that moment, I wasn't sure what he meant. All I could feel was the way his fingers splayed across my stomach, his pinky grazing the top of my bikini bottoms, and the solid muscle of his thigh pressed against my bare legs.

I nodded uncertainly. "I think I am."

The moment was a blur, held on by short snippets of time. The brief kiss he placed on top of my head. The feeling of jumping, falling and then flying into the unknown.

Something foreign took up residence in my bloodstream, spinning me like a top upside down as he held me against him as we fell together toward the water below.

"I've got you," he repeated gently against my ear. "I'll never let you go."

CHAPTER 4

O nce Cam and I had landed in a splashing, laughing, joyous heap in the depths of the river, with Sage swimming over to us, splashing us even more, we climbed the steep embankment and swam for hours on end. Until the sun began to dip just past the tops of the tall, weeping willows that lined the river bank and dusk was quick to follow.

Sage had to get home before his father did in order to do his chores and begin dinner, otherwise, a punishment was sure to follow. Cam, however, seemed to linger, in no particular hurry to leave. As the day progressed into late afternoon, the crazy, tingly feeling had intensified and dropped low in my belly; they climbed up my spine any time he touched me – however play-fully or unintentional he meant them to be.

It was this strange and familiar, yet unfamiliar, dance we did with one another. We'd horseplay around, joking and splashing one another, our bodies magnetized, pulling closer together in proximity. As if being drawn toward each other in a strong undertow. But the minute our limbs touched or brushed underneath the water, Cam would push away as if he'd been bitten by a water snake.

Yet as the day drew on and the afternoon sun began to drop over the top of the tall Willow trees along the embankment, the innocence of our friendship seemed to dip and drown into the murk of the river. Every touch dawned a new realization that there was something happening between us. A sensual tension began to emerge – whether a lustful look, bite of a lip, or flick of a tongue.

I was both petrified, but curiously excited, and didn't know how to escape the odd sensation growing within my body, taking over like the vining weeds against the water's edge.

I wasn't Cam's first kiss, but he was mine.

Just like that perfect summer day, and the hot July sun glistening off the river that weaved its way along the boundary of my parents' property; the moment leading up to my first kiss was everything that love poems and sonnets are written of.

And then as if in slow motion, like a gravitational pull too strong to keep us apart, wrapping its invisible hold around us, drawing our bodies closer and closer together; keeping only a modicum of space between us. We stood toe to toe, talking about nothing in particular until we got around to the inevitable question that only best friends ask one another in times like these.

Who did we have a crush on?

I watched Cam as he dunked his head backward, the sun sparkling off the water droplets over his broad shoulders. As he stood again, he swiped the hair out of his eyes, slicking it away from his handsome face, the formerly round and chubby cheeks now carved out to accentuate a chiseled jawline of a man.

I copied his move, dipping backward, coming up sputtering water out of my mouth and licking it away off my lips. When I opened my eyes, I found him staring at me in a fascinated, yet lustful gaze.

"Do you still have a thing for Baylor Reynolds?" he asked with reservation.

Baylor and I had barely dated our freshman year and he hadn't even tried to kiss me. He took me to a dance because our mothers were part of the church bazaar committee and thought we'd make a good couple. Baylor was only doing his mother a favor however, because we later found out it was Johnny Fellows that he really liked. And Lord have mercy, was that something for town gossip.

I guffawed incredulously. "Are you kidding me? He smelled like pickled beets. No way."

Cam tipped his head back, roaring with laughter, his grin wide and beautiful when his gaze returned to mine.

"Then who do you like?"

Feeling all sorts of uncomfortable, I shrugged a shoulder. Curiously I watched his eyes roam over the skin of my shoulder blade, then drop to the tops of my breasts that were like buoys above the water, and then returning to meet mine.

I shivered gloriously, goose pimples forming over my flesh. Just from the tracking of his gaze.

"Are you cold, London?"

No, I'm too warm with you so close.

He stepped in closer, our chests brushing against each other. I could feel the tips of my breasts harden and pebble against the Lycra of my bikini. Cam raised both hands to touch my exposed shoulders and arms, then dragged them down and back up again. He did this several times and I reveled in the exquisite feel of his rough palms on my virgin skin.

"If not Baylor, who then? Who do you like?"

Before this, I'd never even thought about an attraction to a boy. I'd never had reason to allow my affections to deepen toward anyone and couldn't even date until I was seventeen. Even if there had been someone that caught my eye, how could they ever measure up to the two boys in my life?

The gentle, humid breeze swept over us, clinging to our wet skin and permeating the air with the sweet, lilac scent of summertime. That is the way I'll always remember my first kiss with Cameron. It'll be etched in my soul and memory for as long as I live.

With a gentle sweep of his hand, he brushed a wayward hair from my eye and tucked it neatly behind my ear, the warmth of my blush rolling over my neck and face.

His breath was warm as he leaned in a fraction of an inch closer. Cam's eyes latched on to my lips, as he dragged the pad of his thumb over my bottom lip. It stirred something inside my belly. My momma always said I had cupid lips, but I always found them to be too big and too plump. But in that moment, the way he looked at me – *like he wanted to devour me* - and stroked my lip, I couldn't have been happier.

Cam's other hand drifted to my waist, as his fingers curled into the feminine curve of my body, sending a rippling shockwave down to my toes.

"I like *you*…" I said in a heated whisper that was carried out into the summer air, as I closed my eyes and lowered my head to avoid the rejection that was sure to come.

It wasn't unusual that I had feelings for Cam. Why wouldn't I? I'd spent over twelve years of my life with him, day after day, summer after summer. I rarely did anything without him and Sage.

Sage.

That thought had my shoulders stiffening under the weight of Cam's presence. The mere idea that something was about to occur between Cam and me, leaving Sage out and unaware, made me feel guilt-ridden. Because it wasn't just Cam and me. Part of us would always include Sage, and I didn't want to ruin it. Or deny my feelings for them both.

As if he recognized this, the corner of Cam's mouth crooked up. "And you like Sage, too."

I nodded, appreciative of his acknowledgment and acceptance of me and my feelings toward the three of us.

"It's okay to like both of us," he reassured, continuing a light brush across my cheek. "We're okay with that."

My forehead furrowed. "Have you guys talked about this?"

I didn't have to explain what I meant. Cam knew what *this* was. The he, me, him and us. Our friendship and connection. The way our hearts blended together, each a different color and size, creating one beautiful masterpiece.

Cam cupped my cheeks and his sky-blue eyes, dark now with something deeper, and answered honestly.

"Not really. But I know Sage likes you, too."

My gasp was stolen when Cam's smile disappeared, and his lips touched mine.

Once.

Twice.

Until I felt like I was melting into the depths of the river, being swept away with the current from the delicious feel of Cam's mouth against mine. He tasted like watermelon and sunlight.

Cam's kiss was like the campfires he would start when we camped together in the Smoky Mountains. It started with the tiniest of sparks, the kindling crackling and snapping to life, which soon builds to a deafening roar. Exactly what was going on inside my head as his lips brushed over mine, pulling me deeper and deeper.

My mouth opened on its own accord, as I tilted my head to the side to provide him better access. I had no idea what I was doing or what I was supposed to do, but Cam's experience and all-consuming method took away my uncertainty and bashfulness and formed it into a ball of need.

My belly clenched in response to the movement of his tongue inside my mouth. The mixture of surprise and lust that laced through my veins, paralyzing me with pleasure. My lips moved in response to his, opening and breathing in his essence.

The sudden rush of wet warmth that flooded between my legs, the ache of something I'd never felt before, emboldened me as I wrapped my arms around his neck and pulled him in closer. His masculine rumble gave me a glowing gratification over my decision.

Never having kissed or been with a boy in this manner, I wasn't ready for the jolt of pleasure that came when he pressed his hardened length against the V of my legs, my bikini bottoms and his swim trunks the only barriers between us.

My body screamed for something it didn't understand it wanted or needed. Every muscle and cell came alive with need - tensing and tightening, flashing with desire. Especially when his tongue swept over my lips, over my teeth with deep, probing flicks. He sucked on my tongue – the sensation zinging low in my belly.

The kiss may have lasted for five minutes. Or forever. I had no idea and lost all sense of time, but we were reluctantly pulled apart by the sing-song voice of my momma calling for me from the house.

"London! It's time to wash up for supper."

I let go of a breath I'd been holding in and I stared wide-eyed into his hungry gaze. I'd never seen Cam wear such an expression and it both scared and thrilled me at the same time.

"You best be going in," he drawled, licking his lip and flashing a lazy grin. "Wouldn't want your momma to think I was doing anything to corrupt her baby girl."

But I want to be corrupted by you, I silently pleaded.

My fingers brushed over my sensitive lips, left puffy and tingly from his impressive kissing skills. Now I understood why the girls in our class went cross-eyed over Cam. Especially the girls he'd been with.

"Yes, I guess I should go." I tried to convince myself to leave, but instead, raised myself up on tiptoe and took his mouth with mine again.

Cam chuckled into my mouth but was silenced just as quickly.

The kiss wasn't long, but it was wholly satisfying and left me reeling from the emotional consequences that this would certainly have on us going forward.

I turned to swim back to the bank but was stopped abruptly as his hand snatched my wrist and yanked me back to him. Water surged and pooled between us but didn't stop him from kissing me one last time. A lingering kiss to let me know he was mine. And I, his.

"London," he muttered, his voice more raspy than usual. "I've wanted to do that for a really long time."

My eyes formed wide circles from his confession. I've never even considered it before now. Cam has always been my best friend. The one I told all my secrets to and shared all my hopes and dreams.

Now I was left with confusion over what would happen next. How would this kiss change us? Would we remain friends? Would we keep this a secret from Sage? Would we kiss again soon?

Sage.

There he was again, always on my mind even when being consumed by Cam, his name at the tip of my tongue.

Surely, Cam and I wouldn't let this happen again, because I couldn't stand hurting Sage. We were family to him and he needed us, just like I needed him.

I'm not sure how Cam felt about any of that, but we'd have to talk about it at some point.

My mother's voice now a little more irritated, came again, and I jumped out of the water and wrapped myself in the towel I'd brought with me earlier in the day.

When I looked back down at Cam, he was still wading in the water with a tight-lipped smile and his eyes were glazed over with a tortured look.

"Are you getting out?" I asked, curious as to why he was just standing there.

Cam waved me along. "You go on. I'll call you later."

I lifted a shoulder with a '*suit yourself*' shrug and tucked the towel flap in between my breasts. My nipples were distended from the excitement that coursed through me. I nearly floated across the backyard and poppy-filled field to my back door where momma was waiting for me.

Waiting for her little girl that at seventeen had just received her first kiss and was on the verge of womanhood.

A young woman now uncertain about where she stood with her best friend. And what it would all mean to her other best friend.

CHAPTER 5

Over the next three weeks, Cam and I never had another opportunity to be alone together. As we waited out the heat of July and moved into the hot, sticky August nights, it was always the three of us together.

In fact, it was as if the kiss between us had never even happened. Either that or Cam hadn't enjoyed it at all, because he made it perfectly clear that he'd rather be anywhere else but alone with me. Anytime that Sage was busy, Cam chose to stay away and made excuses to avoid being alone with me.

It filled me with confusion and made me regret that moment in the river with Cam.

You shouldn't have done it.

Although it stung, I wasn't going to press Cam and embarrass myself any further, so I became good at avoiding the topic and left well enough alone. Everything else remained the same; we regularly texted, but only discussing random things and safe topics.

One starry-night in August, Sage and I had gone to one of the latest hero blockbusters in town. Cam was out of town with his parents on a college scouting trip.

Sage and I walked home from the theater hand in hand, talking about the movie and our rating of the performances of the very hot list of actors when he stopped and stared at me with a very serious expression.

"How come you never go out with anyone other than me and Cam?" he'd asked, surprising me by the topic of conversation.

"What do you mean? Like date? I don't know. Why don't you? You could date anyone you wanted."

He scoffed, kicking at a rock in the dirt road where we stood, only a quarter-mile from my house.

"What about Daniella Delgado? She was always looking at you and flirting with you in Chemistry last year. I know for a fact she has a crush on you because Lottie Harrison told me."

Sage scrunched his nose. "Nah, not my type."

Tilting my head, I squinted at him. "Oh yeah? Who exactly is your type? Emo girls and boys with coal-rimmed eyes and piercings?" I teased.

Sage was my dark-haired, freckle-faced, black clothes-wearing musician boy. My momma had mentioned once that Sage just naturally carried a dark aura about him and that the whole town thought he was troubled; but in reality, if you knew him like I did, you knew Sage was a sweet, loving soul. Although he downplayed that to the rest of the world; the Sage I knew was thoughtful, considerate and loved those that loved him with all his heart.

Those on that list included me, Cam and my momma. Sage's own mother had passed away when he was three. And his father…well, I'd never once seen his father sober. He was the town drunk and was constantly in and out of trouble with the law. Sometimes, he'd be gone for long stretches of time on the road doing lord knows what.

Sage had admitted to me once that he liked it when his father was gone because at least he was alone and unbothered.

It hurt my own heart that this boy, who was growing into a tall, beautiful man and such a talented musician, was so easily cast aside and mistreated by his own father. I couldn't imagine wanting to be alone rather than be in the company of my own family.

Sage bumped my shoulder with his as we continued walking, squeezing my hand tightly against his palm. We always held hands whenever we were alone together. Like we weren't whole if we weren't connected to one another physically. As if Sage craved human touch so much that he needed to be connected to me in some way and needed that in order to survive.

"Nah…I kind of prefer annoying, green-eyed, freckle-nosed, blonde bombshells that disguise themselves as bookworms."

I laughed at Sage's obviously humorous description of me.

"I'm not a bombshell," I whined, looking down at my body in observation. "My boobs aren't nearly as big as Hallie Cunningham's."

Sage stopped, turned to face me, pulling my arms out to the side like I was flying. He cocked his head to the left and then to right, then held his chin as if in deep concentration as he leered at me.

"Turn around," he commanded, circling his finger toward me.

I gave him a WTH scrunchy-face, but complied, hamming it up by wiggling my butt as I turned in a circle at his command.

"Mmm-hmm. Like I said, bombshell. And might I add, your boobs are way better than hers. Her tits are wonky and lopsided."

My mouth dropped open and I squealed. "What? Have you…do you have first-hand experience with them, Sage Hendricks?"

Sage was never one to kiss and tell when it came to girls. Or boys, for that matter. He'd dated, but never more than once and it was usually a drunken hookup at a kegger or river party. It was at Justin Lancer's party a month ago where I noticed Sage going out into the woods with Hallie.

"Maybe…" he smirked. "I guess I'd have to see yours to do any real comparison."

I swatted at his chest with a loud gasp. "Sage Crenshaw Hendricks. How dare you!"

"What? I'm just saying…"

We both laughed as he hooked an arm around my shoulder as he pulled me into a skip down the remainder of the road.

When we neared my house and slowed to a stop at the top of my porch, the porch light illuminated his face in just the right angle for me to notice a subtle bruising under his cheekbone. Oddly, I hadn't noticed it before then, likely because we'd been in a dark theater and that side of his face had been obscured and away from me.

I gasped and lifted my hand to his cheekbone, feathering my fingers over his soft, alabaster skin.

"My God, Sage. What happened?"

He swung my arm away and turned his head to face the opposite direction.

"Nothing. Just the usual. Old man got a bee in his drunk bonnet and decided to take it out on me."

I closed my eyes, the tears of frustration and anger spilling over and down my face. I'd never known hate until I first heard of the physical violence Sage had been subjected to while under his father's roof. I just couldn't fathom how anyone could do that to his son. I was so lucky to have the parents that I did, who loved me and protected me from harm.

"Oh Sage, I'm so sorry. Come inside so we can put some ice on it."

Opening the screen door, I tugged on his hand for him to follow me in. He hesitated only for a moment until I glared at him with a look that told him not to argue; I would win this war.

"Really, it's okay, London. It doesn't even hurt anymore."

I was so angry I could spit nails. I ground my teeth together to keep from saying something that would probably send him away. I opened the freezer and pulled out a bag of frozen peas, wrapping it in a kitchen towel. Grabbing two Cokes out of the fridge next, I nodded toward the basement stairs.

My parents were home and already in their bedroom watching a late-night show by the sounds of muffled laughter and light coming from their doorway. After getting Sage settled on the couch, I made a quick stop in the bathroom and then knocked on my parents' door.

"Momma? You awake?" I whispered, peering through the cracked doorway.

The TV light cast shadows across the darkened room to where my dad was already asleep on his side facing away from me, snoring like a log. He worked hard on the ranch and was normally asleep by nine every night. My momma, however, would remain up watching TV, knitting or reading.

"Hey baby, you're home."

Padding barefoot across the thick carpet, I stopped at her bedside and leaned in to kiss the top of her head.

"Yeah. Sage is with me downstairs. Is it okay if he stays the night?"

Momma adjusted her posture and straightened to a sitting position against her pillows. She heaved a knowing sigh.

"Honey, you know I love Sage, but I don't think it's a good idea that he sleeps over. It's just not appropriate anymore."

I rolled my eyes. "Momma, you know it's not like that between us."

She smiled and shook her head. "It might not be that way now, but I see the way he looks at you, sweetheart."

"Momma," I groaned, not wanting a repeat of our birds and bee's conversation from a few years earlier. Although to be fair, I think she was more embarrassed than I was, considering she couldn't even get herself to say 'blowjob' and dismissed that part entirely.

That's where it's always helpful to have two older brothers and also two male best friends who mentioned those things on the regular. I may not have ever done it, but I sure did know all about it and how much boys loved getting head.

She patted my hand and wrapped me in a hug. "Honey, just know that your feelings may someday change. I just want you to be careful so that no one gets hurt. I'm okay with Sage staying around until midnight, but then he needs to go home."

I was about to argue and state my case but decided it was useless. If I told momma about Sage's bruise and that he might not be safe going home tonight – *or any night* – she would do something drastic, like call the Sherriff to investigate. And I couldn't have that on my conscience. Sage would never forgive me.

We only had one more year of high school and I didn't want something to happen that might take Sage away from me. That happened to Melinda Crumsberry last year. She was raised by her grandmother and when she died unexpectedly, Melinda had no other family to take her in and she was sent with Child Services to live in a foster home the next county over.

Last I heard, Melinda had run away and was possibly living on the streets of Nashville.

"Okay, momma. I'll make sure he leaves at a decent hour. Thank you. G'night."

Bending down, I kissed her softly on the top of her head and left her room. When I returned downstairs, I found Sage already watching a funny movie.

Plopping down next to him, I draped the blanket over my lap. It may have been ninety-five degrees outside, but the basement was always cold from the air conditioning.

"Hey, blanket hog. Give me that," Sage grunted, yanking some of the material off my lap and covering his bare, hairy legs.

I'd marveled at how much hair both Sage and Cam had seemed to accumulate since just last summer. Before, Sage was lanky and scrawny, with knobby knees and spindly arms and legs. But over the past year, he's matured, and his body had transformed right alongside Cam's into something more masculine.

He'd told me he started to shave, and when we were swimming, I noticed that he'd developed a trail of dark, wispy hair, bisecting his stomach from his navel down to his ill-fitting cut-off shorts.

He'd also grown a crop of dark, curly hair underneath his armpits and a light dusting over his pecs. His entire physique had changed; although not as big as Cam, Sage worked out. I got the feeling Sage wanted to bulk up in order to protect himself.

Sitting so close next to Sage, I could feel the bunched muscle of his thigh, tapping against me playfully. *Always moving.* The curly hairs on his legs teased the smooth, bare skin of my own leg. It felt…*intimate*. And sent zings of electric currents racing up and down my spine.

The exact feeling I'd had with Cam several weeks ago in the river.

I swallowed nervously.

What was happening to me all of a sudden? We used to do this all the time as kids, but now it covered us like an invisible weight that made it feel awkward and wrong.

Hunkering further under the blanket, I tried to pay attention to the movie, but I soon grew sleepy and my heavy-lids began to sag and droop.

An hour later, I woke up entangled in the body heat radiating from Sage, who had his arm wrapped securely around my middle and his head resting on my lap.

And that now all-too-familiar feeling between my thighs.

CHAPTER 6

Being careful not to jostle him awake, I removed the blanket from under my chin; the heat became too oppressive and much too hot.

I stared down at the top of Sage's head of thick, dark, messy hair. It was always floppy, but the mass of feathery softness called to me and I weaved my fingers through the silky strands. His moan stopped me short and I held my breath, hoping I didn't wake him with my greedy hands. It wasn't unusual for me to touch him – but this felt different.

Maybe it was just me and my crazy teenage hormones, but it felt almost naughty.

Illicit.

Sensual.

Sage moaned again and then spoke. "*Mmm*. That feels good. Don't stop."

It seemed like I'd put him in a state of euphoria, so I continued my ministrations. I reassured myself that it was okay for me to do this to him because he had no one else who provided him the affection that he deserved. No mother at home to hug him when he was hurt or feeling down. No father who patted him on the back to congratulate him when he'd done something to make him proud.

No, my sweet Sage had no one else but me and Cam to make him feel loved. And that's what I wanted to do.

I continued my gentle combing, sometimes brushing over the tip of his ear, tugging on his lobe, curling my fingers at the nape of his neck. I'd doodle a little on his back and he'd nearly come unglued, purring like a cat. I grinned as I looked down upon the beautiful, burdened boy in my lap.

We were both getting warm, so he shifted and sat up, removing his shirt so that I had better access. My hand trailed over the dips and valleys of his backside, over the smooth shoulders, and the carved cut of his bicep. I traced the inlay of his tapered waist, stopping to tickle at the rib where I knew he was ticklish. It felt good touching him in this way. Making him sigh with satisfaction and laugh with happiness.

His life was so complicated. I just wanted to wrap him up in all the love that I had to give.

When my finger ended up at the waistband of his shorts, I stalled for a moment, noticing the way his body tightened and flexed. His own breath became choppy and anxious as I played with the skin underneath. It was so soft and warm there, I couldn't stop myself.

In the end, I didn't have to stop myself because he did it for me. Practically catapulting upright, he took the blanket with him as it fell to the floor in a heap.

Sage sat at the edge of the couch, his back to me, as I watched his sharp exhalation and ragged breaths, his shoulders rising and falling in rapid succession. My hand instinctively ran down his smooth, muscular back, drifting over the cluster of freckles that created a crescent moon shape above his shoulder blades.

Goose pimples broke out over his skin as I fluttered my fingertips over that expanse of flesh.

His voice was low; a warning. "*London*."

Our knees bumped as he shifted around to face me, but didn't look me in the eye, his lips pressed into a firm frown.

The current that ran between us sparked and sizzled, like the sound of June bugs lighting up the air.

His touch was both welcome, and unfamiliar, as he laid his hand on my thigh, his thumb stroking the peach fuzz on the inside of my bare leg. My eyes closed as I luxuriated in the simple pleasure of his touch.

I felt him shift forward, his palm sliding inward and upwards, as I clenched my legs together; to either stop him or keep him there, I'm not sure.

"London, open your eyes and look at me."

I complied with his request and when I did, he was a breath away from my face.

"I need to kiss you," he said as if it pained him.

Need. Not want.

"Yes."

Slowly, ever so slowly, he leaned forward, cupping my face in his hands, and then covered my lips with his to kiss me. If I were to compare the way Cam first kissed me with Sage's kiss, they were as opposite as the sun and the moon; yet both equally as vital to life.

Cam had a reserve about him that he could control. A gentling factor.

Sage was all passion. All-consuming. Completely unforgiving and demanding, as if to say, *"You're mine. You were made for me."* He took what he wanted from me and only wanted more. And I loved it.

I. Loved. It.

The kiss didn't slow down or wane but instead intensified as his fingers curled into my loose hair, tugging me and keeping me there with him. His movements were stealthy, as he somehow managed to lift me onto his lap, sitting back against the couch cushion with me straddling him like I was riding my horse, Abby.

With Sage's hands under my butt, I lifted my own hands to his bare shoulders and squeezed, my fingers wandering down his arms, the crisp curly hair on his arm tickling me as I went.

Soon, it wasn't enough. The building pressure between our legs grew and intensified. I knew he was excited because his breathing increased, and his length hardened under me, placing pressure where I ached for him. For something just out of reach.

Just as it had when I was with Cam, my panties grew wet and the throb intensified. Without even realizing it, I began to rut against his erection, seeking that elusive friction.

We moaned in unison as Sage's hand burrowed underneath my shirt, sliding up my back as I arched into him, deepening our kiss, our tongues flicking and warring with one another. I couldn't tell if we were being quiet or if our kissing was noisy, but we both grunted and groaned into each other's mouths as we each sought pleasure from the other.

Over the previous winter, I'd become more self-aware and shall we say, developed a fondness for touching myself as I experimented with finding ways to get myself off. Sometimes at night, I'd slide my fingers through the wet, soft curls covering my lower lips and would wiggle them over the hardened nub of my clit until an explosion occurred.

Other times, I'd wake up with my pillow between my legs, clenching my thighs together and writhing in mindless need as I came, uncertain of what brought me to that state of arousal.

None of those experiences had prepared me for the feel of Sage bucking up against me. We were on a mission to learn how fast and how much pressure we could endure.

In one swift movement, Sage flipped me over onto my back and unhooked my bra. Wedged between my now open legs, one hand placed near my head, he hovered over me, staring into my eyes as he lifted my shirt to expose my breasts.

We'd seen each other naked when we were kids, darting through sprinklers and jumping into the lakes and river in the summertime. I'd even seen Cam's naked butt once on a camping trip last year when he jumped out of his tent and ran to the edge of the woods in a crazed hurry to take a leak.

But this was the first time any boy would see my developed boobs. The first of anyone to touch me there and taste me.

His finger thrummed over my achingly hard nipple, eliciting a shooting spark response down below. I arched into him just at the same time he took the hardened peak into his mouth. He suckled and used the flat of his tongue to lick it, as his hand plumped the flesh, squeezing it and making me want to scream out in pleasure for more.

But it wasn't enough. I needed something more, I just didn't have the words for what it was, and having no clue how to ask for it. What I did know was that we had far too many clothes on between us.

"Sage, I need you to touch me…*down there.*"

He stopped playing with my nipple and stared at me wide-eyed as if trying to comprehend what I just said.

Sitting back on his heels, he began to unbutton his shorts.

"Take off your shorts and I'll take off mine."

The idea fear of getting caught with my parents right upstairs was nothing in comparison to the thrill that I'd have skin-to-skin contact with Sage. I was dying to feel Sage touch me where I needed him most.

As we wiggled out of our shorts, Sage glanced over at me and I shook my head, knowing exactly what he was thinking.

"Underwear stays on," I giggled, suddenly uncertain about what we were doing together.

But all that worry disintegrated like ash as he laid us back down; he on his side with his back against the couch, one leg draped over mine as I tilted my body toward his. He pried my legs apart with his hand, sliding his fingers over my belly, to the underside of my breast, and then dipping down beneath my panties.

There are no words to describe how good it felt. The minute his finger pressed that hidden, forbidden spot, I nearly whimpered and trembled in release. I gasped loudly, hoping my parents didn't hear me and come running down to investigate.

Our kisses turned to hungry, open-mouthed tongue-lashing kisses, as he probed and flicked my clit in the same manner with his finger. And when he slipped his finger inside me, the first time in my life something or someone breached that inner sanctum, his palm rubbed against my core and I shattered in a million, trillion bursts of starlight.

"Sage," I cried out, my hand gripping hard at the ridge of his shoulder, hanging on for dear life.

Sage wasted no time at all, rolling on top of me and connecting us in the most intimate of positions. He thrusted against my pelvis, his hard erection pressing firmly in that sweet spot as my fingernails dug into his cotton-brief covered ass, searching for more.

More pressure.

More pleasure.

More Sage.

I imagined what it would feel like to be completely naked and connected, the heat between us. What it would feel like to have him inside me. It was with that thought that I moaned loudly, my legs shaking out another release that I had no idea even existed inside of me. At that same moment, Sage buried his head in my neck, his teeth latching on to my sensitive skin underneath my ear, and he stilled.

His body trembled uncontrollably as he let out a loud exhale of breath.

"Shit."

The wonder and magic of the moment quickly chilled as reality dawned and I felt the wetness of Sage's climax begin to seep out.

He moved quickly, jumping to his feet and heading to our down-stairs bathroom.

Fumbling for the blanket to cover my nearly naked body, I pushed myself upright and sat up, reaching down to locate my shorts and shirt. As I slipped them on, Sage came stalking toward me. I blinked up at him, taking in his beautiful presence, as he bent down and gave me a quick kiss.

"I gotta go. I'll talk to you later."

Confusion and hurt swept over me. I felt a sharp stab of pain in my heart as if he'd used a knife to slice through my chest cavity. It was that acute of a pain; to have him just walk out of there without any other endearment or acknowledgment of what we'd just done together

Even though fully clothed, I was left naked and exposed.

I sat unable to even squeak out a goodbye as he took the stairs two at a time until he was no longer visible, and the front door closed with a quiet *snick*.

This wouldn't be the last time Sage would walk out of my life without a backwards glance, but it was the first time I felt utterly alone.

CHAPTER 7

Our senior year began with a flurry of activities and celebrations that sent the three of us scurrying off in different directions.

In fact, I tried to keep myself busy to avoid both Cam and Sage as much as possible, still confused over everything that happened that summer.

Sage later apologized about that night, citing that he'd felt guilty for messing around with me. But even after we seemed to regain our balance, there remained a rough edge to our friendship. Like it was Humpty Dumpty, an eggshell teetering on the brink of ruin at any given moment.

Cam was in daily, if not twice daily, football practices, as well as his Junior ROTC program. He'd also been active in some student council activities.

As for me, I was back to my twice weekly dance classes, volunteering with my church youth group events, along with the planning committee for both the homecoming festivities and the spring carnival.

We were rarely together, except for one weekend at the end of September. We'd all planned on attending a party being held in the field adjacent to Jace Lambert's house. The nights were still warm enough to wear our summer clothing, but with the bonfire going, the blazing heat made for a sweltering evening.

Cam had picked us both up in his truck, with me in the middle, as always. It gave us the opportunity to get caught up on each other's lives. It felt good, but a little stilted and stiff at first.

I nudged Cam in the side, his muscular arm resting behind my head in the cab of the truck.

"What's this I hear about you asking Hallie Cunningham to homecoming? Why didn't you tell me?"

My voice was light and amused, but inside, a small prickling of jealousy welled up, ready to crash into me like a gigantic wave. After the kiss we shared this summer, I had hoped he'd begin to see me in a different light and would consider asking me. Honestly, I'd hoped to go with one or both of my boys.

Fat chance.

Sage twisted in the seat, leaning over to stare incredulously at Cam.

"He's apparently looking to get laid with a sure thing. Isn't that right, bro? 'Cause we all know Hallie is hot to drop those panties for Cam."

"Fuck off, Sage. That's not the case." Cam stared straight ahead as both Sage and I looked at each other, trying to stifle our laughter.

It didn't work. We couldn't contain our outburst, knowing full well that Hallie had been trying to get Cam for years and would do anything to hook her claws in him, especially if it meant sleeping with him. I'd heard it on good authority, too, that she was quite experienced in that department, having hooked up with half the boys in our class already. Sage had even had a short-lived thing with her.

Cam's hand shot out behind me and shoved Sage's shoulder, whose head was now bent in roaring hilarity as he tried to catch his breath.

The truck came to a stop along the side of the field and it suddenly grew silent. Cam shut off the engine, his hands gripping the steering wheel, his head bent to rest his forehead against it. His own deep, self-deprecating chuckle was all we needed to hear to prove we knew him better than himself sometimes.

"Shit," he laughed, peering sideways at us through his fingers. "I guess that's how it looks, huh? I just assumed the two of you would go to the dance together," Cam explained, looking at both of us for confirmation. "I didn't want to be the third wheel."

None of us had ever even discussed the dance up until now. In fact, we'd never even attended those school activities with other people, either. We'd always just gone together as friends and had a good time. Somewhere along the way, something changed between us. Shifting our roles and creating a different look and feel to our threesome.

I laid my palm against the thickness of Cam's thigh, and then turned and did the same to Sage, turning my head each direction as I spoke.

"I'd hoped you'd *both* take me."

While our friendship made all the sense in the world to us and always had, no one else in our small, back-water town could make heads or tails of it. Now that we were older, it was something that the gossip mongers latched on to and turned it into something torrid and taboo.

Apart from the previous two times when I'd kissed them both separately, there hadn't been any jealousy or deception that I was aware of. Although it did create a little awkwardness for a while, leading to some avoidance, this was the first time we'd openly discussed anything like this.

"London." Cam's voice was hesitant, offering a whiff of condemnation. "People would talk if you went with both of us. I think it's best that Sage take you."

I looked at Sage, who was staring out the window as if he wasn't even paying attention. I squeezed his knee and he turned to me and shrugged.

"Doesn't matter to me either way. Y'all know we always have more fun together, anyhow."

His eyes darkened as he glanced at me and then at Cam, giving us a rare glimpse into the thoughts he kept hidden from us.

The comment threw me off a bit because there was an implication there; a hidden innuendo that hovered just out of reach.

I patted them on the thighs, smiling at them both. "So, it's settled, then. Hallie can find her own date."

Turning to place a kiss on Cam's cheek, I missed it entirely when he moved his face toward me at the last second and our lips smashed together. My eyes widened, as Cam's sprang open, seeking to gauge Sage's expression.

None of us, to my knowledge, had shared anything about our separate and brief intimate encounters with the other. I guess I'm the only one who knew the whole truth.

We'd kept it secret, not because of the potential jealousy that could arise, or because of the potential stigma associated with it, but likely from an underlying uncertainty of what it meant for our friendship.

Whatever the case, it was still this fragile, guarded secret that could go either one of two ways. It could lead to something beautiful that we'd share together, the three of us; or it could shatter the friendship we shared entirely.

The air in the truck cab sealed off like a lid on an airtight container, vacuum sealing our stalled breaths. Cam's hand tentatively wrapped around the back of my neck, his fingers threading through my hair and pulling my mouth to his, stealing the sips of air that escaped my lungs, his lips curving over my mouth. I opened for him, his tongue penetrating and eagerly exploring, reclaiming what had been his all those months before.

Without realizing it, my right hand searched for Sage's, who remained silent next to me. Upon finding it, I clasped it tightly and pulled him in closer. My body screamed for his touch. For the connection. I couldn't bare for him to feel left out.

It felt undeniably good to have Cam on one side of me and Sage curled against my back, his thigh pressed snugly against me. My body was like an inferno, bursting into flames so hot it felt I was coming out of my skin. Sage's breath turned ragged, a sexy sound that expressed his desire at what he was watching. Cam groaned into my mouth in the same manner.

Pulling away from Cam, I licked my lips to find Sage staring at us, his expression a mixture of awe and raw hunger.

"Sage," I whispered, uncertain how to tell him that I wanted him, too.

Instead of words, I showed him. A longing bubbled up from deep inside my belly as I leaned forward and grazed his lips with mine.

Due to our height disparity, I had to lift myself off the bench seat, craning my neck slightly to touch the soft velvet of his lips.

He sat immobile for a moment – perhaps stunned by my boldness. Either way, the crackle of electricity and desire swirled around us, and the sounds of our three breaths in synchronicity and chorus turned into a deafening orchestral concert.

I blindly moved my hand from Cam's thick thigh, while reaching around the back of Sage's neck and grabbing onto the longer fringes of his dark hair, applying more pressure into the kiss. His breath came out in a warm whoosh as if something inside him had burst wide open, and he took the reins from me in one swift motion. His sensuality and confidence spilling over and drenching me with excitement.

Sage covered my cheeks with his hands, his mouth moving solidly over mine, kissing, licking and sucking, as his tongue slid between my lips with a moan.

Everything about that moment was heaven.

It was the first time that the feelings we shared for each other were openly shared between the three of us – opening like a Pandora's box of pleasure – morphing into something more. Something different and special. Something unique and shared only between the three of us.

I allowed my fingers to weave through Sage's soft locks as we kissed, and our chests pressed against one another. His hands moved to my waist, pulling me into him, telling me without words that he wanted me closer. As if to say I was the only thing he ever wanted and that he craved me, my touch and my kisses.

Perhaps it was the love and friendship that Cam and I provided him that held him together most days, as he dredged through an otherwise loveless home life. Where his father would do and say anything to tear him apart. To belittle him and make Sage feel small and weak. And unloved.

Emboldened by my squeak of pleasure that erupted when Sage's tongue swirled deeper, Cam inched closer to our entwined bodies, his hand landing on my knee, trailing up the inside of my thigh, dragging the material of my skirt up as he went.

This was the first time Cam had ever touched me in this manner - scrolling up my bare legs with his rough fingertips. The contradiction of his rough touch and Sage's soft lips felt forbidden and erotic. It dripped with sensuality and carnality.

I wasn't sure where to place my concentration – on Sage's kiss or Cam's delightful exploration of my leg. Cam's face was next to my ear beside me, his breaths rapidly increasing, as his nose drifted up my neck, the action mimicking to the movement of his fingers on my thigh.

Goosebumps danced across my flesh, as Cam's palm navigated toward the juncture between my legs where he abruptly stopped. I jolted from excitement and anticipation.

"Can I touch you here?" Cam's hoarse voice was reminiscent of how it was last winter when he had strep throat. *Deep and husky.*

All I could do was mumble an invitation into Sage's mouth for Cam to continue, as he pressed a finger into the damp cotton covering my sex.

This is all uncharted territory for us. Despite the kiss Cam and I had shared at the river, he'd never touched me so intimately. I knew it wasn't his first rodeo, though, as he'd made out with many girls since hitting puberty. He'd had his pick of any girl in school. It had just never been me before, except for that one kiss.

A moan escaped my mouth when Cam's thumb slid over my core at the same time Sage's fingertip found my sensitive nipple, flicking at it over the material of my shirt. My legs parted wantonly on their own accord, as I leaned back against the seat of the truck to give both boys more access to my hungry, needy body.

Could this be any hotter?

Craving everything and more, I became theirs to do whatever they want with me. In that moment I wasn't worried about my grades, or my upcoming dance recital, or my college applications.

All that fell to the back burner because in their arms I became an incendiary device, with no other goal but to burn eternal.

Unfortunately, the loud slam on the hood of Cam's truck threw a bucket of ice-cold water over our steamy make-out session, as Booker Holden, one of Cam's football buddies, yelled out his warrior cry.

"Let's go get some pussy, dawgs!"

CHAPTER 8

"Oh my God, do you think Booker saw us? Does he know what we were doing?" I practically screeched like a siren.

Flinging the boys' hands off me, I tugged my skirt back into place, brushing at the strands of mussed hair. I took a quick glance at my image in the rearview mirror.

My lips were a nice swollen pink and my neck had a dark, angry red hickey at my collarbone. What the heck? How in the world did that get there?

I snapped my head to where Cam sat, a naughty smirk across his face, as is finger outlined the mark.

"Oh my God, I'm so embarrassed," I mumbled, with my hand covering my face, wishing away the fact that I was just caught making out with two boys.

When neither Cam nor Sage said anything, I looked between them, their cat-that-ate-the-canary smiles telling me they did not share the same sentiment.

Cam cleared his throat and spoke first. "Booker is clearly drunk and probably didn't see a thing. Plus, it's dark and the windows are fogged up."

Sage chuckled next to me and I elbowed him in the ribs.

I glared at him until the smile left his face in a contrite apology. "You…zip it."

Cam, always the sensible one, cupped my cheeks in his hands.

"Don't worry, London. Booker won't even remember his own name in an hour if he even does now." Cam pointed out the window where Booker stumbled down a ravine across the field toward the bonfire. "It'll be okay. I promise. And if anyone says anything, I'll handle it. I won't let anyone say shit when they don't know a damn thing about it."

Always my guardian.

Sage rubbed my back and I purred at the sensation, leaning against his hand. Cam knew how to calm me with his words of assurance, and Sage simply had to touch me with a reassuring gesture and I was calmed.

"Okay. I'm sure it'll be fine."

Cam jumped back into action-mode. "Sage, grab your guitar. I'll bring the blanket and the cooler. Let's go have some fun."

He winked at us both and the doors flew open, but I stopped them both in their tracks.

"Guys, should we talk about what just happened?"

I could feel my face flaming red under the yellow interior light of the cab. I knew boys, in general, didn't like to "talk about feelings" or whatever, but I felt it was important to determine if that was a one-time thing or something we might do again.

Because I knew I wanted that.

"Uh…" Sage rasped, unable to complete the sentence.

I looked toward Cam, who had one foot out the door and his hand tapping at the steering wheel.

When he said nothing further, I bit the bullet and made my desires known.

"I want to do that again sometime – with both of you. I liked it. A lot. But maybe more privacy next time."

I bit my lip and smiled when their mouths dropped open in utter shock. I'd always heard how easy it was to shut up a boy by using your body, but who knew you could drive them speechless with just a suggestive idea?

"Yes, ma'am," Cam politely responded, with just an edge of desire laced within the words.

And Sage agreed, "I'm good with that, too."

Agreements made, we each gathered our things from the bed of Cam's truck and trekked into the wooded area until we came to the open field where at least thirty people drank, smoked, laughed and partied.

Although we each separated several times throughout the night, their sheer presence lingered on my lips, my tongue and my body. The ghost of their touches and kisses consumed me and made me hotter than any bonfire could ever do.

With heated gazes shared throughout the night and friendly touches and gestures given, we remained connected as the evening progressed and people began leaving the party.

At one point, as I chatted with my friend, Chloe, Booker stumbled into me, wrapping an arm around my waist and nearly taking me down to the ground with his wobbling stance.

"*So,*" he slurred, spittle flying out of his mouth with the smell of beer and maybe vomit. "Our own sweet goodie-two-shoes likes to be gangbanged. Isn't that right, London?"

Due to his incoherent speech, it was hard to decipher what he said unless you knew what he meant. Chloe gave him a disdainful glare, probably because she was used to his idiocy when she dated him a few years earlier. I immediately scanned the party to locate Cam and Sage, hoping they'd come to my rescue and dispose of Booker's gross and raunchy behavior.

My eyes locked on Cam's, who was standing on the other side of the bonfire talking with a few of his football buddies. I opened my eyes wide, biting my lip in the hope that he'd get the hint.

There was no way I was going to get Sage's attention. He was sitting on a log, hunched over his guitar amid playing *Stairway to Heaven*, his favorite tune. He was also surrounded by several girls, so he was in his element.

Booker began to cackle in husky, drunken laughter, talking about some porn movie he'd watched and how maybe someday he'd see me in one of those '*sexy librarian*' films. It wasn't until one of his hands landed on my shoulder, a way to keep himself upright, that he tripped on his own two feet, grabbing hold of my T-shirt at the collar and ripping it with the force of his fall.

I screamed in horror as Booker toppled to the ground, my shirt dangling open to expose my shoulder, arm and bra. Chloe jumped out of the way and my head popped up to see Cam charging toward us.

My worried gaze then moved to Sage, who immediately laid his guitar on the ground and jumped to his feet, aiming in my direction, as well.

I sloppily adjusted my clothing, trying as best I could to cover up my nakedness, as my face heated with humiliation. Cam got to me first, confirming that I was okay, Sage stepping in behind me, covering my shoulders with his jacket.

All the tension and turmoil immediately dissipated with just the scent of Sage's warm, leather against my skin. The scent of spice and something just him calmed my nerves and relieved my embarrassment as the gawkers around the fire stared at us and snickered. Like we were some kind of circus, parading in front of them for their entertainment.

In that moment, I hated everyone in our class and couldn't wait until graduation and then I could leave this small-minded town and could get out of here for college.

Although that thought should have made me happy, it turned into a sad realization. I'd not only be leaving a town of gossips and backstabbers, but also my two loves. My best friends and confidants. The two I relied on for more than half my life.

"Get up, you piece of shit," Cam snarled at a confused Booker, who was seriously too far gone to even realize what he'd done wrong. "Don't you ever grab her like that again."

I reached out and placed a trembling hand on Cam's solid forearm, pleading with him through touch to let it go. It wasn't worth it. The damage had already been done and all I wanted to do was go home and leave this crowd of unworthy people behind.

Sage moved to my side, adjusting his arm around my shoulder as I leaned into his embrace – warm and safe.

"Come on Cam, just leave him. He didn't know what the fuck he was doing. Let's just get out of here."

As he spoke, Sage's voice shook. I didn't know if he'd feared for my safety or if it was something else. Either way, when I spoke, my words were meant for both of them.

"I'm fine. Really. I just want to go home."

Without another word, we left the lingering crowd behind us, the heat of the roaring fire, and the whispered gossip and headed back to Cam's truck, side-by-side.

We may have left the bonfire, but the fire between us had just begun to burn. And it would soon blaze hotter than the sun in a Tennessee July.

CHAPTER 9

Sometime over the weekend, Booker's recollection of what he saw in the truck became the town fodder for gossip and the salacious undertones related to the "dirty slut girl who liked to gang bang." Although we'd all grown up in the same town and everyone knew us; it quickly turned scandalous. By the time I returned home Sunday night and checked my social media accounts, it had spread like wildfire.

The following Monday at school, the rumors were rampant. Like a cyclone that had picked up speed over the weekend and now swirled heavily through the school corridors; our classmates the whips and waves and thunder that spread the tasteless tales around.

All I could do was hold my head high as I walked the hallway to my classroom, even though inside my spirit was crushed flatter than the Kansas plains.

The boys had dropped me off at my house on Friday night and I'd kissed them both goodnight. Although it began as chaste kisses, it soon grew fevered. We'd gotten ourselves worked up again, just from the touches and kisses that stoked the flames of that fire.

The rest of the weekend I was out of town on a college visit with my parents. I hadn't yet applied to any schools yet but had narrowed it down to a few. We visited Emory University in Atlanta, which was high on my list of potentials. It was my goal to be far enough away from home to learn to live independently; but close enough to be near my family, Cam, and Sage.

Cam had already been accepted into Vanderbilt, which was in Nashville, and not too far from Atlanta. His father, however, was pressuring him to enlist into the Air Force, something that his father and grandfather had all done. Cam had admitted to me on more than one occasion that he was torn between feeling obligated to his family, and his desire to go to college.

Sage, however, wasn't looking at colleges. It wasn't his thing, he'd said, and would leave to conquer the music world in some way shape or form.

The indecent rumors made it sound like we had some forbidden love triangle going on. That Sage and Cam were fighting over me and that I was their sex slave. It was utterly ridiculous. So, I paid it no mind and kept my head held high.

The same didn't hold true with Cam and Sage. They seemed to crack under the weight and pressure of the heavy implications within the made-up stories. While there was only the tiny kernel of truth to the sordid tales that were sown, the lies were so outrageous and egregious that the boys couldn't turn the other cheek.

And it led us into a heated argument later that week. I had hoped by the end of the week the rumor mill would have died down, but it hadn't. The stories only grew bigger and more vibrant, leaving Cam ready to forgo the football game that Friday night.

"It's utter bullshit and I won't allow people to say the things they're saying about you, London."

Cam paced in front of his truck that was parked in front of my house after school. He'd ditched football practice in favor of meeting up with me and Sage.

Sage sat on the soft grassy yard, picking at the blades of grass that were still brown from the heat of the summer sun. His head was bent, either silently contemplating the situation or to avoid the conversation entirely.

"What exactly are they saying that's so terrible? Who cares what they're saying? It shouldn't make any difference." I softly stated, hoping my bravado sounded believable, even though on the inside I cringed at being the talk of the town. Like I wore the red *A* across my breasts.

Cam scoffed, pacing and pacing and pacing like a caged lion.

So serious. So intense.

"They are all mother fucking lies."

"Just tell me what they're saying, Cameron. If they are lies, then it shouldn't matter one bit."

He bent at the waist, pressing palms against his thighs, huffing out a stubborn protest.

"They're saying you're a slut who likes DP. And that the only reason we hang with you is because you'll let us do anal." He coughed out the last word and I let out a high-pitched squeak.

"What? Oh my God, that's so...*ugh*," I squealed, covering my mouth with my hand. I turned and stomped off two steps before returning to Cam.

Lowering my voice, just in case the neighbors or my mom, who was inside the house watching her soap opera, can hear our conversation.

I didn't want to sound stupid, but I needed clarification. "What's DP?"

Sage choked out a noise, his voice scraping like metal. I looked down at him as his gaze snatched mine, his cheeks coloring with red.

"Double-penetration."

Sage gave some weird hand gesture with his fist and fingers, lifting a shoulder. My mouth opened as I took in its meaning, and the nasty suggestions from small minded people.

"*Oh.*"

It made sense that people outside our circle wouldn't fully comprehend the friendship Sage, Cam and I had together. Or how tightly our bond connected us in ways that were mind-blowing. Maybe we were some odd love triangle or had an unconventional love for one another that others just couldn't understand so they justified it with explanations that weren't accurate.

But to create lies and stories about us was inconceivable to me. How could they do that? Where did they get off casting those stones when they weren't infallible?

The anger bubbled up inside of me and I felt like a volcano ready to erupt, steam rising and climbing from my belly as my fists clenched.

"Argh," I belly-ached with a loud grunt, kicking at the ground with my Sketcher shoe.

And at the same time, both Sage and Cam threw their ideas in the ring.

"We could just do what they claim we're doing…" said Sage, a wry smile across his face, just as Cam said,

"We should lay low for a while until this all fades away…"

I stared at them both, my head reeling, blinking in rapid succession as I worked through their suggestions.

Throwing my hand up in order for them to shut up, I heaved a deep breath.

Glaring and pointing at Cam, I gave him the what-for, stuttering with condemnation.

"I'm surprised that you of all people would suggest we tuck tail and hide like we're guilty of some crime. You would allow their ignorant comments to ruin our friendship? Ruin what we've had together for thirteen years?"

Cam's shoulders drooped in despair. "I don't know. Yeah, maybe. Just for a little while. Give us a break to hang out with other people."

A tear escaped and dripped down the side of my nose. Sage jumped to his feet and wrapped his arms around my back, pulling my head into his shoulder.

I sniffled into him. "I don't want to hang out with other people. I want you."

"Don't cry, sweetheart. You know I can't stand it when you cry." Sage turned to speak directly to Cam.

"That's the lamest fucking thing I've ever heard you say. You're just gonna roll over like some pussy because some people are talking shit about something they know nothing about? Fuck 'em all, I say. They can all go to hell right along with my asshole dad."

I snapped out of my funk and giggled, my body shaking against Sage's chest. Sage slid a hand down my hair and the column of my neck, kissing my forehead sweetly. Wrapped up in Sage's arms, I couldn't care less about what anyone else thought, as long as we had each other and stayed together.

When Sage's mouth landed on mine, I knew he was thinking the same thing. It was the three of us against the world, and this was our last year together before we went off in different directions.

For Cam and me, the future didn't feel like such an unknown, because we both knew where we were going, and we'd always have homes to come back to.

But for Sage, it wasn't like that. His father had been promising him for years that the minute Sage graduated high school he would be kicked to the curb and would be cut-off financially. Not that Sage got anything from his dad that constituted as parental support, anyhow.

Sage's kiss turned drugging, his tongue slipping inside my mouth sending prickles of heat to ignite my body. His palm landed on my backside, grabbing at the flesh of my butt and squeezing hard, a deep, masculine sound exploding from his lungs. I had no more control over myself kissing Sage than I did breathing. It was a necessity. It was pain and beauty and comfort.

I let my fingertips trace the edge of Sage's square jaw, the bristle of his dark short scruff sexy and tantalizing, shooting lightning bolts of pleasure between my legs.

A car drove by and honked, jeering voices of several boys in our class throwing out rude obscenities from the car window. I could hear Cam growl as he called after them, "*Assholes!*"

Sage broke the kiss and we stepped away, me licking my lips and he running a hand through his hair.

"London, it's up to you. I'll do whatever you want," Sage muttered, but I could tell from the glint in his eyes and the tightness of his mouth that he knew we belonged together.

Not apart. Not separate.

Cam stepped beside us and reached for my hand.

"Me, too. I just want to protect you, not lose you."

Our answer was there filling the space between us. Casting a warm glow of affection over us.

We'd tell all the nay-sayers to go screw themselves and we'd continue spending time together for as long as we could.

In the end, we all decided to forgo Homecoming with each other, must to my disappointment because it was the only thing I looked forward to. Although I wanted to, I didn't argue or fight it, and we each took different dates, but all went as a group together. It nearly killed me, though, to see Cam with Hallie and Sage with my friend Chloe.

They should've been dancing with me, where they belonged.

CHAPTER 10

The fall moved into winter and the holidays were upon us before we even knew it. Cam's football season had ended in a big loss, which was bittersweet for him and his teammates, who didn't finish out their last high school game with a victory.

Every year on New Years' Eve since I could remember, my parents would throw a big New Years' Eve party. They'd splurge and order flowing champagne fountains and decadent desserts and invite all their friends, including the ranch hands, and their families, who would come to revel in celebratory fashion and ring in the new year.

For me, it was always a magical night because I spent it with my two best friends eating popcorn, watching movies, dancing and singing karaoke in my basement. Then we'd count down as the ball dropped and the clock struck midnight.

That year was no exception, but in ways, it was very, very different.

"What's your New Years' resolution?" Sage had asked, as he took a large, messy bite of the white chocolate dipped strawberry that he'd plucked from the dessert table. He unselfishly offered me a bite, holding it out to my mouth as I opened to devour it.

When I saw the expression in his eyes – *lust-filled and needy* – my belly flipped in anticipation.

"I've been thinking a lot about this, actually," I replied, dragging my finger and thumb over the corner of my mouth to wipe away the juices left from the strawberry.

It was on the tip of my tongue, but it was difficult to say out loud. I knew what I wanted from them both, but I wasn't sure they'd agree. Or how it would work. Or if my fantasy would even come to reality.

"I know things got a little weird between us, and you know I love you both equally, right?"

They both nodded their heads, searching my face for clues to where my train of thought was going.

If only they knew.

"Cam, I know you lost your V-card two years ago. And Sage, you haven't told me who, but I know you did it with someone last summer."

Sage blushed and looked away, wiping his strawberry stained hands on a napkin before throwing it on the table. Grabbing their hands and laying them on the top of my legs, my fingertips traced a pattern over their hands. Wondering what those hands would feel like touching my body in time with one another.

"*Yeah…*" Cam gave a raspy acknowledgment.

"I *want-*"

"What do you want, London?"

It's now or never.

"I want to lose my virginity to you. With you both."

A gasp filled the room and then it grew quiet.

Cam, always the logical and practical one, asked, "How is that even possible?"

I gave him a coy smile. "You'd take turns."

"*Fuck,*" they both said in unison.

Giggling, I replied. "Yeah, that's the idea."

Cam let go of my hand and stood, pacing in front of the big screen TV. The sounds of the party could be heard above us, no one the wiser as to what we contemplated doing and what I just asked them.

He shook his head adamantly. "*No.* No way."

"You don't want me?" I snapped, challenging his decision with my own uncertainty over what I just admitted.

We'd all been friends for so long, but that didn't mean I didn't hold the power to ruin it with this one greedy and unconventional request.

"That's not the reason," he argued.

"You'd rather I lose it to someone random in college?"

"Fuck no," Sage piped in, squeezing my hand tight. "Absolutely not. But London, are you sure you wouldn't want…I don't know…to have just one of us? Separately? *Privately?*"

I knew this was a titillating topic and one that Cam was trying to sidestep with his refusal. But it was very apparent that the idea of fucking me turned him on by the evident bulge the appeared in his pants.

I decided to use that against him, to hold him hostage until he agreed to my demands.

I rose from my position on the couch and stalked toward Cam, backing him up with my hands on his chest until he was trapped against the wall.

Tentatively, I reached up on tiptoes to Cam's ear, as one hand lowered and squeezed the very hard length covered by his jeans.

"I want this. I want you, Cam. And I want Sage. The three of us. Like it's always been, but different. We've shared everything, and I want to share my first time with you," I kissed his cheek, then looked over my shoulder. "And Sage."

Cam croaked out a response. "*Tonight?*"

Stroking his impressive erection, I licked under his ear, breathing hotly, dragging my tongue against his flesh, tasting his salty skin.

"No, not tonight. I'm not quite ready for that yet. But I do want to…*I don't know*…experiment." I gazed nervously under heavy lashes at Sage who stared at us both with an intensity so hot, it singed like burning fuel.

"Tonight, I think I just want to fool around with you both, if you want. I've been dreaming about that for a long time now."

Fever seemed to take over as I laid out my most private, sexual desires to Cam and Sage, putting it all out there so they could best decide if they wanted to participate.

In that next moment, Sage pressed his body against my back, his hands skimming down my sides and over my hips, landing at my ass. I was sandwiched between him and Cam, and I shivered at the possibilities. Sage's warm, chocolate-scented breath was at my ear.

"We must share the same dreams, because that's what I want, too." He nipped my ear, all three of our faces within inches of one another.

Leaning into Cam for balance, I kept one hand on his chest and lifted the other behind my head to wrap it behind Sage's neck, weaving my fingers through his hair at the nape. I scraped and dug my fingernails into his scalp, turning my head to his lips to give him access to take what he wanted from me.

I would give them anything and everything. I was theirs for the taking.

Cam was still stoically uncertain, standing stiffly against me until he gently pushed me out of the way with a huff. He moved to stand a few feet away against the wall, arms crossed over his chest, indecision ripe and dripping off along with the tension of his body.

I figured he'd either watch Sage and me together and enjoy it - letting go of his reservations to join us - or he'd leave. Whatever the case, I let myself enjoy Sage's perfect kisses and sensual touch. My back arched as my head tipped back against his shoulder, exposing my neck for him to devour, his hand stroking over the front of my body.

An all-encompassing need swarmed in my breasts like birds taking flight, and electric tingles seared between my legs, as I silently begged and searched for something I didn't know how to explain. Instead, I just moaned and ground against his erection that poked into my lower back from behind.

Sage deftly unbuttoned my polka-dot blouse – ironically representing the perfect image of my innocence up to this point – until the flaps of the shirt exposed my bare belly and pink lace bra. He pulled down the cups under my breasts, cupped them in his rough hands, squeezing and plumping them, before dragging a fingernail over the hardened nipple.

It was the sound of Cam's raspy intake of breath that had me opening my eyes to find him lustfully staring at us under hooded eyelids from the far corner of the room where he'd migrated. His beautiful face etched with marvel and heat, his searing gaze reaching straight into my soul.

I held out my hand toward him, yet he still didn't make a move. He remained glued to the floor where he was, wearing a tight, painful scowl.

A small cry burst from my throat when Sage rolled my nipple between his fingers, tweaking it and driving my ass to grind against his cock in a circular motion, one that elicited a growl from Sage. Or maybe it was Cam again, whose voyeuristic participation seemed to increase the intensity in the air.

Cam's frown and voice may have vocalized his unwillingness and uncertainty to join us, but the tension rippling from his entire being said otherwise. He was controlled and restrained…of which I knew couldn't last much longer. He would find that breaking point and lose it sooner or later. Just like any explosive device…once given the mechanism to detonate, it would explode with purpose.

I hadn't realized we'd moved until I fell backward onto the couch, with Sage underneath me, his knees spread wide cradling me between them. The short-flared skirt I wore billowed up past my knee-caps, exposing the creamy flesh of my thighs. I once again dared to look up at Cam and he nearly shook with unrestrained heated-lust, depleting him of his resolve.

My eyes swept the length of his body, just as Sage brushed his hand over the landscape of mine. He closed his eyes momentarily as if the sight of Sage and me was too much to bare, and I stared unnoticed as his hand fell to cover his crotch.

When his eyes opened again, our gazes connected, and I bit down on my kiss-stung lip to keep myself from doing or saying anything that would sway Cam's decision. I knew he warred with himself and had to weigh his options.

Deep inside, Cam wanted this but thought what we were doing was wrong – sinful and incongruent with what society and church had taught us. It was written all over his face. The tight purse of his lips and the clenched jaw told me he was conflicted.

For whatever reason, it didn't feel wrong to me. Being with these two boys felt right. I trusted them with my life, with my thoughts, secrets, and now my body. They knew just about everything about me. It was only natural that my feelings of deep friendship would morph into something heavier. Stronger. Needier.

I wanted them as lovers.

Their bodies.

Their hearts.

Their souls.

Sage continued peppering my neck with wet, lush kisses. Exposed to the cool air, my nipples tightened even more, and everything became overly sensitive to his touch.

I felt the hardening pulse of Sage's cock behind me at the same time he let out a long, exquisite groan.

His voice was husky and deep.

Sage, as if trying to wear Cam's defenses down through deliciously dirty commands, whispered in my ear, but it was meant for Cam to hear it, too.

"Your skin tastes so good, London. Your tits would look so good with Cam's mouth wrapped around them, wouldn't they? I bet you'd cream your panties if Cam sucked on your nipples, making them wet and hard. You'd squirm and scream as you came, wouldn't you, sweetheart?"

"Oh, God." It was Cam's voice saying what I was thinking out loud.

"Cam, get the fuck over here. Take care of our girl. *Now.*"

I blinked up at Cam, as we shared the simultaneous look of, *"who is this guy?"*

This was a side of Sage we'd never truly known before. A dominance that seemed to ooze out of his pores; giving orders like a commanding officer. Cam shook his head like a disobedient child.

My skin was so tight, alive with pleasure, aching for touch and throbbing wildly from the naughty imagery that Sage used to fuel my imagination. Cam's own posture tightened even further, but he didn't relent. He remained solid and steadfast in his stubborn refusal to join us.

Sage continued to add to the torment, plumping both breasts now in his hands, massaging and circling, playfully tugging and pinching, as I cried out for more. Nothing else mattered at that moment than feeling the rough, callused fingers of my guitar-playing Sage, touching and teasing my body. Playing it like his very own instrument and bringing to life the music that was inside of me. Humming and ready to break free in a cacophony of sound.

Sage skimmed his hand down my abdomen, my skin breaking out in shivers, as he fluttered his fingers between the V of my legs, stopping only momentarily before landing at the edge of my skirt. His palm smoothed the length of my leg, pushing the cotton fabric up until my panties were in plain sight. I saw Cam gulp down a swallowed breath, as I inhaled with the excitement of what was to come next.

Adjusting himself under me, Sage shifted his body and toyed with the edge of my underwear, skimming the sensitive skin on the inside of my thigh as I moaned and squirmed at every feather-light touch. I could feel how wet I had become and I'm sure Sage was fully aware of that when he touched me.

It reminded me of our night together last summer, on this same couch, the way he touched and kissed me. But it was so much more intense with Cam's presence in the room. Even though he hadn't moved and wasn't joining in, his presence ratcheted the heat level up to a thousand.

"Cam," Sage roughly commanded again. "Don't you want to find out how wet our girl is? How good she smells? How sweet she tastes? I could find out myself…but I want you to tell me."

Everything that was happening was beyond my wildest fantasies. Over and above what I had ever dreamed would happen if I ever had the pleasure of being with these two boys together.

Perhaps it was the sound of the clock striking midnight or the sound of my gasp as Sage slipped his finger inside my panties and between my folds, that finally brought Cam to a decision.

A decision that was bigger than a kiss at midnight.

One that changed our lives and our future's together.

With just one spoken word, Cam started a down a path that none of us could ever change or return back from.

"Okay."

CHAPTER 11

That night, we kissed and touched and made-out as we marked the advent of the new year, as each of us found a new role in our threesome.

We were three parts of a whole, destined to find a way to close the gaps and learn how our individual pieces could join in a new exciting way to create something special. Something more than the friendship we had built over the years.

Where in the past, Cam had always been the leader of our trio – the one to take action and give orders – it seemed that Sage was ready to fill those shoes in this new role. He called the shots, instructing me and Cam on what to do and how to do it. It was beautiful to behold, my gorgeous musician and angsty boy taking the reins and opening the doors to a new world for us.

As for me, I was simply *"their girl"* and I loved it.

I was the center of their world and craved their physical attention. Being the center of attention had been part of my life in all manner of ways. As a dancer, I came alive when I was on stage and in front of an audience. I was used to the attention.

But this was a wholly different level of focus and devotion. I'd never felt more like myself, someone who could let go and just be free of all the expectations that the world had of me until I found myself in the arms of my two boys.

It was only something that Sage and Cam, together, had the ability to do. I was like a cocoon in their arms, transforming through the physical metamorphosis triggered by their involvement.

I was already on the verge of coming when Sage slid his fingers inside me, finding that sweet spot of desire deep within me. The place that contained every forbidden secret inside me. He unleashed and untethered my hopes and dreams, desires and fantasies with the crook of his fingers.

And when Cam finally stepped toward us, one slow inch at a time, he cautiously bent down to his knees in front of me, careful not to touch us, something unexplainable happened. Like a brilliant supernova bursting in the sky, obliterating everything in its path, that same starburst exploded inside my heart.

With Sage's hand between my legs and the other at my breast, Cam gently placed his hands on my knees for balance, leaned in and took possession of my mouth, sealing our fate with his lips sealing over mine – stealing my breath and my lucidity.

Sage's fingers pumped and thrust inside of me, as Cam's mouth moved lower to latch onto my nipple. Sucking and licking, tasting and tormenting.

"Shit, you two look so hot together," Sage rasped from his position behind me, his hips grinding with deep thrusts against my ass with eager excitement; seeking friction and bucking with pleasure.

Cam moaned around my tight nipple. "You're right, Sage. She tastes so fucking good."

Whether it was the accolade or the fact that Cam was fully participating and in agreement with Sage, my body lit up like the Empire State Building; bright white lights flashing and narrating a story of simmering desperation and excitement.

My hands found the top of Cam's tousled mane, and I ran my fingers through the soft silken strands, tugging tight when he nipped the sensitive skin of my breast, leaving a bruising mark. He swiped his tongue over it in a soothing lick.

I thrashed and rocked, seeking that ultimate gateway to eliminate this throbbing ache inside me. Cam's eyes bored into mine as he pulled away from my breast, licking his lips and then dragging a thumbnail over the wetness he left there. I arched and bowed from the divine tingle that ran down the length of my legs and back up, settling at my spine.

"Unbutton your jeans and pull them down," Sage commanded gruffly, his voice deeper and thicker normal. A baritone that bore deep into my very soul.

Cam's eyes popped wide. "What?"

"I said, take off your jeans and your boxers. I want to see you jack off for us. We want to see that, don't we London?"

The question is so bold. So dirty. So incredibly foreign, I could only nod my head.

"Do you want his tongue between your legs, too?"

Oh, sweet baby Jesus.

Stammering, I watched Cam do as he was told and remove his underwear, still kneeling in front of me, as I responded to Sage's question.

"*Y*-yes."

Sage chuckled darkly. "I thought so. You're so fucking wet."

I watched in rapt awe as Cam took his own swollen length into his fist and encircled the dark purplish crown. He stroked it hard, exhaling a harsh, raspy breath that escaped his lips. Agony and ecstasy played across his features as if he was trying to deny himself the pleasure that coursed through his body.

"Cam," I whispered, drawing his attention back up to me, where he hopefully saw the raw emotion and fevered excitement that bubbled within me over his actions.

I didn't have words to describe what they were doing to me. How watching Cam jerk off and stroke himself, while Sage fingered me, made me lose my mind.

Sage's movement underneath me rocked me side-to-side as he wiggled out from under me, his fingers leaving me empty. He slid next to me, thigh-to-thigh, unbuttoning and unzipping his own jeans, letting himself pop free from the tight confines.

I turned to look at him and the corner of his mouth curved into an apologetic smile.

"Sorry, I have to…I'm dying."

Two things happened at once.

As Sage freed his cock, he reached for my hand and placed my palm around the smooth steel. At the same time, Cam bent down under my skirt, his nose nuzzling at my center, inhaling my scent. He pushed my knees out wider with his broad shoulders and placed his lips at my wet entrance.

I may have stifled my keening cry, or I might have let out the loudest shriek ever. All I know is that it was the best, most erotic feeling in the world.

The dueling sensation of the soft, yet strained, texture of Sage's cock in my grip and the smooth slide of Cam's tongue at my most intimate place had my entire body shooting into the stratosphere. I'd never been so completely transported into that out-of-body type of experience.

I felt like I was lifted above the ground, outside of my physical being, and was floating and gasping, tightening and relaxing somewhere far, far from there.

Sage helped guide my hand as we stroked his length in unison. The sounds of the skin slapping against skin, mixed with Cam's own rhythm and movements, were a symphony of sensuality. Adding in the wet, slick noises as Cam sucked and kissed my body heightened the intensity as we crescendoed higher.

I lifted my hips and shamelessly ground my core against Cam's face, boldly and with no inhibition whatsoever. I delighted in his growl of approval. And when he added a finger, slamming it inside my virginal body, a curse ripped from my mouth as my entire body tightened with awareness. My legs quivered and shook until something inside unleashed a torrent of pleasure, a shockwave of unbelievable sensation.

I'd never orgasmed that hard before, even previously with Sage, much less done it with my pelvis jutting against a boy's face. But goddamn, it was electrifying and out of this world. My body was wrung out, yet wildly yearning for more.

In the climactic haze, I'd nearly forgotten about Cam and Sage. *Nearly.*

Rolling my head to the side, I glanced down to where my hand moved in time with Sage's and then stared up into his face.

With lips parted and eyes closed, Sage held the most serene, yet dire look on his face as he chased his own orgasm. I continued my hand job, increasing the pace and pressure, listening to his labored breaths; gasps and moans and pleas for *faster, harder*.

The same held true for Cam. Although I wasn't touching him, we still felt connected. His eyes bore into me, drinking me in, as his fist flew over his own hard flesh. My inner muscles clenched in response; tumbling and somersaulting, needing to be filled.

I boldly placed my hand between my legs to slide through the wet, springy curls, reveling in the sensation and aftershocks of my orgasm.

"Fuck, that's so hot, London."

As if on cue, they released their orgasms simultaneously. Cam leaned over me, one hand pressed firmly against the couch cushion next to my leg, and very quietly, with just a low guttural roar, his orgasm shot across my thigh and belly.

Sage, still in my own grip, gave a wild, hoarse cry. His hand clenched mine, as I felt his cock strain and pulse, as he shuddered, and the warm rush of his seed shot over our joined hands.

The air was thick with sweat, chocolate and champagne, and the scent of sex. It grew quiet and a blast of cold air from upstairs seemed to blow across our bodies, drying the residual of their climaxes.

My body was a damp rag, wrung out and numb. I felt sated and happy. Completely relaxed and blissed out.

Until the sound of a door opening at the top of the stairs pulled us all out of our perfect, after-sex haze, and brought us back to reality from the insolated bubble we'd just been in.

We scrambled to get dressed, as the voice of my dad grew imminently closer and closer with each step he took down the stairwell.

"Happy New Year, kids!" he called down.

When he finally reached the bottom and rounded the corner, the three of us all put on our dopiest grins from the spots on the couch we'd flung ourselves to.

"Happy New Year, daddy."

My voice sounded like a little girl's, but the three of us knew better.

I'd just stepped into the world of womanhood. My sexual innocence now a thing of the past.

CHAPTER 12

After my daddy had gone back upstairs, leaving us with a plate of cookies and some more popcorn, there was a stir of electricity still buzzing in our bones and blood, as we tried to come to terms with what happened.

Cam was the first to leave, shutting down like he'd often do.

"I told my parents I'd be home before one a.m. I gotta go."

I was sitting cross-legged on the couch and looked over at Sage who had picked up his guitar and was plucking at the strings.

"What about you? You leaving, too?"

Sage tipped his chin up, the soft melodic tune he played momentarily stopped, as he looked up at me through his make-up lined-lashes.

"I'll stay."

I gave him a wan smile and held out my hand to Cam, hoping he'd give me a hug before he left. I didn't want it to get awkward between us, like it had during the school year, even though there was a potential it could get weird.

My naivety about love and sex proved how little I truly knew about the complications that arise when sex is in the picture.

I had no real-world experience to tell me otherwise.

"Cam? Will you come here? I need to tell you something. Please," I begged, unfolding my legs, my panties still wet from his mouth.

Cam sighed, an obvious war going on in his head again about what to do with me and Sage.

I patted the couch beside me and he sat down with an insolent *plop*.

His voice was gruff and impatient. "What do you want, London? I need to get home."

My smile contained a silent understanding of his uneasiness and confusion over what we'd done together, and I wanted to leave him with a reminder for later reference. To ensure he wouldn't doubt what we did and what it meant.

With the speed of a gazelle, I straddled his lap, bending my knees at the sides of his hips and placing my hands on his shoulders to hold him in place. I instantly felt the heat that gathered between us.

Cupping his cheeks, I leaned in so our foreheads connected.

"Promise me you won't overthink what we did tonight."

"I won't," he argued, rolling his eyes like a willful child.

I snickered. "Yes, you will. You already are. I know you, Cameron. And right now, you're worried that you shouldn't have enjoyed this experience. That what we did together is wrong."

My eyes bore holes in his head, hoping I could manifest some sort of brainwashing tactic to change his mind and ease his worry. He'd always been the worrier in the group. Wanting to be perfect and always aiming to please everyone. His parents. His coaches. His leaders and teachers. And me and Sage.

"Oh yeah?" he snipped at my lips, pretending to bite me with a *chomp*. I laughed and wiggled on his lap, which only had him leaning back to avoid any further contact.

"Just tell me one thing before you go, Cam. Did you like it?"

I cocked my head to the side, my fingers interlaced behind his neck to massage the ropey, strained muscle there. He groaned in my touch, or maybe as a result of the question. Dropping his head back, he shut his eyes to the sensation.

"God, London. Of course, I liked it. Kissing you. Being with you like that. Tasting you was the hottest thing ever. I'm going to dream about it for the rest of my life."

I noticed he was careful not to mention Sage's involvement tonight. Which from the sad look in Sage's maple-glazed eyes, suggested he was disappointed in that omission, as well. But it was one step at a time with Cam and there was no sense pushing it.

When Cam's eyes reopened, our connection grew heated, all the memories of our childhood swirling away like liquid being poured through a syphon, sucked through a drain. Those moments now replaced with the carnal knowledge of one another.

I bit my lip, swallowing the lump in my throat and strummed my fingers down the front of his chest, smiling coyly as I say, "Do you know that I've fantasized about being with both of you? I want to do that again sometime. Do you?

Something dark flashed in Cam's eyes as he sucked in a breath, jostling me on his lap. His head snapped toward Sage, who had stopped playing to listen intently to our conversation. I followed the direction of his gaze, Sage now the center of our attention.

Sage shrugged, leaning back against the couch in a sexy, relaxed fashion as if to say, *"You're on your own here, dude. I'm with her."*

Cam's voice was low and raspy, his conflicted emotions evident in his dubious response. *"Yeah."*

"Okay then. If I'm fine with it, and we all enjoyed it, then there is nothing to feel weird about. And it's nobody else's business how we feel about each other and what we do together. Just us. You, me and Sage. Got it?"

I pulled him into my chest and kissed him until we were both breathing hard once again. When the kiss ended, I turned back to Sage, confirming he was on board as well. A warm, daring smile tugged at his lips, his skin flushed and the way his jeans were tented said it all.

Pointing my finger in his direction, I crooked it, beckoning him to join us.

"Come 'ere, Sage. Come say goodbye to Cam."

He carefully placed his beloved guitar next to the chair and stalked over to join us, sitting down next to Cam.

I knew Sage held an unrequited longing for Cam in his sullen and wary aventurine gaze. Sage wasn't one who was quick to trust or love because of his hellish home life. But when he did, it was deep and beautiful, just like the inside of Sage's heart.

Sage had never openly discussed his sexuality with Cam and we'd never talked about his interests outside of that one time in our early teens. But over the last two years, he'd shown aspects of his sexual interest in Cam through longing looks and glances that others may not have noticed, but I did.

Cam was oblivious, which may have been a good thing. He'd likely have a problem with Sage's desire for him. Cam was raised in an ultra-conservative, Southern Baptist home, with a father who'd been in the military and a mother who went to her prayer group every week to pray for the *"souls of those who lost their way."* As in, the *entire* LGBTQ community.

I wasn't sure if Cam shared their views on homosexuality, but he never said otherwise. Although to be fair, he also never put anyone down or slung arrows of righteousness at those different from him. In fact, Cam stood up for those weaker than him. Aside from the incident in kindergarten where he fought with Sage over the toy (which they eventually shared), Cam was heroic in his convictions to help others. To stand up for me and Sage when it was called for.

Cam was my strong superhero while Sage was my tender-hearted, yet tortured soul.

And I loved them both.

I stretched out a hand to cup Sage's scruffy cheek, my fingers lingering over the jawline before I flicked my thumb over his bottom lip. He surprised me by tasting the pad of my thumb with his tongue before he sucked it into his mouth.

I replaced my thumb with my mouth, kissing Sage soundly and thoroughly, as he returned it in kind.

Then I pulled away, leaving Sage with his mouth open and eyes half-lidded, and kissed Cam just as thoroughly.

At that moment, I knew our lives would never be the same, but there was nothing I could do to stop the momentum.

Or the feelings that grew between us.

CHAPTER 13

"I've decided I'm not going to college," Cam announced, as the three of us laid out on blankets by the river.

It was early April, but the spring weather had warmed the earth and kissed the skies with its blazing sun and heat that only the south can give that time of year.

Sage's eyes narrowed, and my mouth dropped open, eyes popping like wide-saucers.

"What?" Sage and I both exclaimed simultaneously, my voice two octaves higher than his.

Cam flopped on his belly, the sheen from his sweat glistening all along his exposed back. He'd filled out so much this past winter, bulking up with weights and getting ready for swimming and baseball season.

His head cradled in his locked arms, face turned toward Sage and me. I openly stared, waiting for him to explain.

"I'm going to enlist in the Air Force."

It didn't surprise me to learn he was going to follow in his father's footsteps, but it was a shock that he'd leave behind a college education, one that he had expressed wanting.

Cam was smart and well-educated and had a scholarship waiting for him. Plus, we had decided we'd be going to the same college. In March, I'd received my acceptance letters to both Emory and Vanderbilt and had chosen Vanderbilt for a plethora of reasons, but mainly because Cam would be there, too.

While Sage wasn't going to attend school, his plans were to move to Nashville to begin his music career. My heart had soared that day when we'd realized we'd remain together even after high school and there was even a possibility of moving in together. The idea had my heart soaring.

But Cam's announcement broke our pledge to one another. And subsequently shattered my heart.

I bolted up from my spot beside him, jumping to my feet, ready to march off toward my house.

"You can't go. You promised me, Cam Lucas. You promised you'd always be there for me."

I began to run, crying as I did. When I stopped just short of my house, I heard footsteps come up behind me. It wasn't Cam who followed me, but Sage. My body was still warm from the sun, and my breathing labored, but I shivered until he threw his arms around me in a supportive embrace.

No matter what turmoil he had going on in his own world, Sage was always the one to calm me down. Soothe my aching heart. He'd sing to me when I was feeling down or depressed. Even though I had everything in life – loving parents, a good home, a good life - and he was born with the short end of the stick to be raised by a hateful man, who didn't know how to love a son, Sage still knew how to love.

"Shhh. It's okay, sweetheart. Let it go. There's nothing we can do to change his mind. He's gonna do what his father wants. It's important to him to make his father proud."

I was crying and in an angry state of mind. My tears streamed over my cheeks, dropping like rose petals onto Sage's T-shirt covered chest.

Gripping onto the soft cotton with my fists, I sobbed quietly, letting out all the anger and hurt that brewed inside, all the while being reassured by my best friend.

"He's made up his mind, London. If he doesn't do this, he'll feel guilty and then *he'll* be unhappy."

I sniffled and snorted disgruntledly. "What about my happiness? Our happiness? How can he do this to us? Leave us like this at the last minute, breaking all his promises and our plans?"

Sage stroked my sun-drenched hair with one hand, the other gently caressing my back.

"I don't know, babe, but I'm sure it wasn't easy for him, you know that. He always weighs all his options before making a decision and I'm sure it ate at him. He has his reasons and we need to support and respect them."

Snorting, I laughed ruefully. "When did you get so wise, Sage Hendricks?"

Pulling back to stare up at him, he shrugged a shoulder and winked playfully.

"How does that stupid phrase go? If you love someone, let them go…if they don't come back, then you're a fucking idiot?"

I hooted with laughter, slapping at his chest. "That's not how it goes, dummy."

Sage smiled playfully, turning us around so we could walk back toward Cam, who remained behind to pack up our gear. He lifted his head, a blanket looped over his arm, a sad, woeful smile pulling at his lips. He opened his arms and beckoned us both in for a hug.

I don't know how long we stood there in that embrace, but the way Cam and Sage's arms locked around me had me forgetting about all the pain. I knew that with them by my side, I could handle anything in the world.

Anything, that is, except Cam leaving us to go into the military.

"Is there anything I can do to change your mind?" I asked, the dare present in my gaze, hoping it would be enough to dissuade him.

Cam chuckled, shaking his head solemnly. "I know you don't understand this, but I have to go. I'm not giving up college entirely. I'll enlist, do my duty to my family and the country, and then I'll go to college later. It's not the end of the world, London. I'm sorry if it hurts you and that I won't be there with you in college, but please don't make this harder for me than it already is."

Burying my head in his neck, I sucked back my tears, hiccupping my response. "I'll try not to, but I already feel the loss. Like a piece of my heart is dying and I can't even take a breath without it hurting."

Sage was quiet for a bit, kind of doing this humming thing that he always did when he was lost in his own head. When he spoke, though, you knew it came from a place of love and conviction.

"Let's not dwell on the what if's for now, okay? There's still two months until graduation. Your eighteenth birthday is coming up and then prom. I say we make the most of the time we have together and do everything we want to do before the summer ends."

A smile broke out on Cam's face, lighting it up and removing the guilt and sadness that had been there only moments before.

Cam spoke first. "I can do that."

When both pairs of eyes landed on me, I pursed my lips in consternation before replacing it with my own watery smile.

"I can do that, too. And I have some things in mind for my birthday."

I stepped out of their arms, slapping them both on their butts before dashing off toward my house, turning to look over my shoulder behind me as I did.

"Be ready, boys. This is going to be the best eighteenth birthday in the history of birthdays ever! Just you wait."

Luckily, the wait was only a few weeks.

Long enough to get up the courage to do what I needed to do.

CHAPTER 14

I didn't tell Sage and Cam about my birthday plans until the night before. I had to inform my parents beforehand, though, since we were going on an overnight camping trip.

Being friends for as long as we had and having gone on similar camping trips together in the past, made my parents comfortable in our arrangement. They knew Cam and Sage and trusted *us* together. We'd never given them any indication, otherwise, that we were anything other than "just friends."

So, when I revealed that the three of us were going camping for my birthday, my momma and daddy hadn't batted an eye.

My daddy did surprise me, however, as I packed for the trip.

"You got everything you need?" My dad had asked me as I shoved an extra pair of shorts into my backpack which was filled to the brim and barely able to zip up.

I nodded. "Yes, sir, sure do."

My dad stood next to my bed, suddenly quiet and reflective. Tugging the zipper up, I glanced sideways to find my daddy staring at me with a faraway look in his eye.

"What's wrong, daddy?"

My dad, a beefy man in his early fifties, had built a business of farming and ranching, turning it into a lucrative farming system that supplied the county and state with fresh meat, eggs, cattle and organic food staples. He also hired and employed many locals who relied on him for their livelihood and had raised a family doing what he loved.

I was always proud to say I was Lee Moriety's daughter. He was a respected member of the community and his legacy wouldn't die now that my oldest brother, Grady, had taken the helm as his right-hand man.

Daddy sat down on the bed, pushing the bag over to allow room for me, as he patted the plush pink bedspread with his rough hand.

Plopping down on the bed, I faced him with criss-crossed legs.

He cleared his throat nervously and I noticed his neck and face were red and blotchy. And it wasn't from the heat of the sun or working outside day-after-day. It was something different.

"I know your momma already talked to you some time ago about…" he gave a long sigh, slapping his jean-clad thighs with his palms. Then he returned his gaze to me.

"Well, darlin, this is a bit more difficult for me than it was with your brothers, so give me some slack, here. I'm fixin' to do my best not to make this too awkward. But I need to make sure my little girl is protected."

Tilting my head up in alarm, I watched as he lifted his butt to the side and pulled something from his back pocket. My eyes bugged out with surprise when he opened his palm, producing three condom packets.

The giggle that escaped me couldn't be helped and my hand flew to my mouth, covering my embarrassed laugh.

"*Daddy…*" I groaned with discomfort, covering my face with my hands. "Oh my God, this is so embarrassing."

He gave a deep chuckle, indicating it was the same for him.

"Darlin, I know it is, but it has to be said. You know that I trust you…and for the most part, have faith in Cam and Sage to do the right thing. But ya see, darlin, I was once in their shoes around a pretty girl, too. Also known as your mother. And boys your age have all sorts of inappropriate thoughts in their heads about girls…

"And if Cam and Sage were any other boys, I'd have my shotgun aimed and ready. But I know Cam would never do anything to hurt you in that way. I'm also not dumb. I've seen how you look at him. So, if you and Cam decide to get serious, I want you to protect yourself. There's too much riding on your future to get knocked up or worse."

Underneath the impossibly humiliating topic of the sex talk with my dad, I found it odd that he pinned my interest only on Cam and not Sage. Did he not consider Sage as a potential love interest for me?

"Daddy, in case you were wondering, I'm still a virgin."

His response was immediate, rubbing his temples in either agony or relief. "Thank God I'm not too late."

We both laughed at his obvious relief.

"You're not too late. And I appreciate the concern. But out of curiosity, why do you assume it's me and Cam? What if I liked Sage in that way?"

Daddy's lips tightened, his jaw clenching.

"Sage is bad news, darlin. If I had it my way, you'd stay far away from him and not let him drag you down. He doesn't belong in your life."

I was stunned at what I was hearing. Since when did my Dad think so unkindly toward Sage, who had never been anything but a wonderful friend to me? I was disgusted with my Dad's low opinion of my best friend, who had overcome so much in his life and was desperate to get out from under his father's thumb, doing everything he could to make sure that happened.

"Daddy, I can't believe you think that about Sage. He's my best friend and has the kindest heart. He's always been here for me and would never do anything to hurt me."

He patted my knee affectionately, with a sorrowful acknowledgment.

"London, you must realize that Sage's life is incredibly different from yours. He's not going to college. He doesn't have the same opportunities that you have. And his father…"

I jumped from the bed, appalled by what my dad was implying.

"You're judging him based on his father? On the way he was raised? That's not Sage's fault!"

My anger flooded my body, my hands tightening into fists and my stomach twisting into knots. I grabbed my bag from the floor and ran downstairs and outside to wait for Cam in the driveway.

My dad followed me out, continuing the conversation with a gentle hand on my shoulder. I kept my back to him, anger seething in the pit of my stomach.

"Baby, I know you only see what you want to about Sage. But there's something dark there. It's bound to shake loose someday, and maybe not intentionally, but he could hurt you. I only want you to be careful. Do you hear me?"

He tried to reach for my hand, but I flung it out of his reach, taking two large steps away from him before spinning to face him.

"Daddy, you don't know him like I do. He's the most loving, caring and sweetest boy I've ever met. He'd do anything for me or Cam. He might not be going to college but that doesn't mean he doesn't have plans for his life. He's such a talented musician and is going to be a huge star someday. I just know it."

My dad's whiskered lips pressed together in a firm line, either begrudgingly agreeing or disagreeing with me, I wasn't sure. Either way, he was so wrong about Sage. He didn't know him like I did and he had no right.

"London, listen to me, darlin. You're still young and don't know the things I know as an adult. Abuse and neglect from a parent can have life-long impacts on young people. One small thing could set him off at any given moment. You may never even see it coming," he warned.

Crossing my arms in a huff, I turned my face away from his accusations and inaccurate assessment of Sage. If he knew about Sage's home life, why hadn't he intervened? It made me angry that he'd let it continue and not do anything to protect him from his father.

We both heard the screen door open and glanced to see my mother walking out carrying a cooler. Her eyebrows lifted at the obvious chill in the air, despite the heat of the day.

The silence was noticeable as she walked down the path to my car, pinging her gaze between the two of us, silently questioning what the tension was all about.

"London, sweetheart, I've packed up some food for you and the boys to take with you," she chirped, her ever-present smile somewhat tempered by curiosity. "I'm sure you're fixin' to do some fishing, but at least you'll have some other goodies with you. And I made Cam's favorite peach pie and Sage's Rice Krispies treats."

My comment was snide and meant to be a barb toward my daddy. "Thanks, momma. I know *you* love Cam and Sage."

My dad sighed and shook his head ruefully.

"I'll let you to it, then, London. Just be careful, ya hear me? I love you and I just want you to be safe."

He stopped in front of me, my body language still very much a broody, moody teenager with my arms crossed at my chest, and he stooped to place a kiss on the top of my head.

I knew he only wanted the best for me and my life. I was his only daughter and understood where his protective nature stemmed from. But not his malign assassination of Sage's character. That was hurtful and unforgivingly wrong.

The corners of the condom packages cut into my palm as I hid them from my mother, who placed the cooler in the back of my car as my dad walked off toward the barn.

"Everything okay, sweetheart? You seem upset."

Shaking off my bad mood, I stuck the packets in my pocket and peeked under the cooler lid, hoping to replace my bad mood with a believable smile.

"Everything's fine, momma. And thank you for putting this all together for us. You're the best," I said, meaning it whole-heartedly.

She stood at my side and put her mother's caring arm around my shoulder, squeezing me to her side.

"And of course, there's something special just for my birthday girl in there, too."

I smiled a genuine smile. "My favorite?"

She nodded. "Yes, your favorite."

There was nothing better than the chocolate chip, butterscotch cookies my momma made, and I would gorge myself on them anytime she made them.

I hugged her with all my might. "Thank you, momma. I love you."

She squeezed me tightly in her warm embrace. "Anything for you, sweetheart. I love you, too. And whatever is going on with your dad, it's only because he loves you so much. You're his only baby girl and he worries about you. And Lord have mercy we are going to miss you when you go off to college."

We pulled out of our embrace and my mom had tears glistening in her bright, sky-blue eyes.

"I know, momma. But he doesn't have to worry about me when I'm with Cam and Sage. They'll always take care of me."

If only I knew then what I know now.

CHAPTER 15

"Your mom made me pie?" Cam beamed with excitement when I told him what awaited us in the cooler.

We'd parked in the overnight lot and had been hiking into the Smoky Mountain park wilderness to find our campsite. The boys were thrilled when I told them where we were going, one of our favorite spots we found two summers earlier. It wasn't often that we got to spend the entire weekend together, especially now that we were late in the school year and with all the pre-graduation activities eating away at our time.

Sage had been working a part-time job at the local grocery store ever since he was old enough to work. His dad never provided him money for anything outside of necessities, so if Sage wanted to leave town after graduation, he had to earn his own way. Cam had been busy with his athletics and school activities, and I, too, had been focused on my studies in preparation for finals.

I knew when I asked them to take the weekend off for my birthday, both boys would do it in a heartbeat. I'd hoped it wouldn't be our last camping trip together, but after graduation, who knew where our time would be spent.

"You know my momma loves you both to death, right?"

"Your mom is an angel," Sage stated, stepping over a fallen branch, his backpack and guitar swinging heavy on his back as he held another bag of supplies in his left hand.

It always hurt my heart that Sage was motherless. And it made me spit nails that my dad admitted his concerns about Sage when he was doing the very best he could, given the horrible home life and circumstances he had been dealing with for years.

"Guess what my dad gave me today?" My voice came out in a hushed excitement, adding to the suspense that drew both of their interests.

"What?" they both asked with curiosity, but not enough to stop our hiking progress.

I giggled. "Condoms."

Cam stopped suddenly in front of me and because of my proximity behind him, I ran into his back, with Sage bumping into me, as well.

"What? Are you serious?" Cam asked incredulously.

"Your dad gave you rubbers? Holy shit!"

I nodded.

Sage huffed out a laugh, but it was laced with worry. "Wait, does that mean he suspects something?"

Before I could respond, Cam added, "If he did, he'd had already aimed his shotgun at us and London wouldn't be on this trip alone with the two of us, dumb shit."

Sage agreed with a laugh. "That's true. But kinda weird, don't ya think? Why now?"

I shrugged, adjusting the straps on my shoulders to avoid their inquisitive stares. I didn't want them finding out what my daddy said when he gave me the protection. That burden and the weight of that secret felt heavier than the bag I carried.

"Well, he did say he's noticed the way you two look at me and if you were any other boys, he'd get his shotgun out with a stern warning."

They both snickered uncomfortably as we started preparing the campsite, setting our packs down and unloading all the tent, camping gear and equipment.

It was mindless work, as we chatted and laughed and joked for the next two hours. The sun was high in the sky by now, the temperature was warm and humid, so after the camp was ready, we got our suits on and hiked down to the lake for a swim.

We'd found this place by accident two years earlier, a little off the beaten path and completely isolated. It was the perfect spot for us where we could goof off, play, sing and laugh 'til our hearts' content.

The water was murky but clean as we swam around, cooling off our sweat drenched bodies after the strenuous hike to camp. The boys splashed and dunked each other as I swam in a circular pattern, floating on my back enjoying the freedom from the responsibilities and pressures of the end of the school year. There was excitement, and nervous anxiety about what was to come, but also a level of nostalgia, knowing we would soon be venturing into the unknown. And in different directions.

"Hey, Ariel…whatchya smiling about over there?" Sage inquired, referring to my favorite *Disney* character and the movie. The one I made them watch at least a thousand times when we were six-year-olds.

I peered over at them, shielding my eyes from the sun's glare, seeing the faces of the boys I'd known for as long as I could remember, and the bodies of the men they'd become. Cam and Sage were so very different, each holding a unique appeal that did something to me every time I looked at them.

I continued my aimless float but answered his question. "I'm just thinking about all the great times we've had together. And how much I'm going to miss you both when school's over."

As if sensing that I needed their comfort, they swam over and surrounded me on both sides, my body floating between them. I became extremely self-conscious of my nearly naked body, the water sluicing between my legs and over my bare belly, my breasts covered only by a bikini top. My nipples puckered against the material, which didn't escape either of their notices, either.

"Nothing's gonna change, London," Cam insisted, his voice raspy and heated as his hand swept up the length of my arm, gliding along with the direction of the swirling water. "Just because school ends doesn't mean it'll change us."

Cam's heart was bigger than the world sometimes, and when he made a commitment, it meant something to him. He'd made a promise to his father that he'd enlist in the Air Force, and although his heart was set on college, he wouldn't back down from what he'd committed to do.

The same was true for his friendship with me and Sage. He gave his all to us and would do anything in his power to ensure we were happy. To him, the bond the three of us shared was unbreakable. Impenetrable. Inseparable.

I wanted to believe him and hold that same conviction, believing that what we shared throughout childhood could withstand anything we'd face in adulthood. Even the distance that would separate us come fall.

Sage, sensing my own uncertainty, leaned down and placed a kiss on my lips. An assurance that we'd all be okay. Cam's hand slipped underneath the waterline and cupped my head as I continued to float. He leaned in and angled his mouth to mine, where Sage's had just been.

I felt Sage's hand caress my leg, his fingertips gently stroking up from my ankle, over my shin and the climb of my knee, until he was at my mid-section. He stopped to swirl a gentle pattern over my belly button and the rise of my stomach, continuing further until he reached the swell of my breast.

I gasped when his thumb flicked at my nipple. I looked between the two, who stared at each other and exchanged a wordless conversation. As if coming to some consensus, Cam leaned down again to suck at my lips, as I opened for him and his tongue brushed against mine. I sighed and felt my body succumb to the intense connection.

Cam's kiss deepened, drawing a moan from my throat as Sage's fingers wandered up and down the path along my body. Every-where he touched made me ache – with pleasure and pain. Cam's other hand dropped underneath the curve of my spine, holding me up so I no longer had to paddle.

It left my hands free and I dipped them under the water to slide over the bulges that had formed on each boy, hidden below the water's surface. Sage growled savagely, and Cam sucked in a breath, both responses bringing out of me something that I've never felt before.

Possessiveness.

Power.

Female pride.

It amazed me that I could bring these two strong, capable men down to their knees with just a single touch.

"London," Cam groaned, his eyes shut tight. "If you don't stop… I'll…"

He didn't finish, because my hand burrowed under his swim trunks, latching on to his very erect, very wet and smooth cock. I did the same with Sage. They both felt incredible in my palms, my fingers fisting around them, gathering them in my hold and stroking with a confidence.

I still didn't know what I was doing when it came to sex, but I figured the boys would direct me if necessary.

It wasn't hard to distinguish their lust and pleasure from the looks on their faces, but I wanted to ensure it was good for them both.

Wiggling out of Cam's hold, I dropped to my feet, feeling the cool, sandy bottom of the lake squishing between my toes. Even upright, I remained sandwiched between their solid bodies, reattaching my grips on their hard lengths, each tip pressing into my thigh.

"Show me what to do," I begged, my palms sliding from base to tip and rolling my thumb over each of the smooth heads. "Give me your hands."

Sage was quick to comply, firmly joining our hands together to demonstrate the rough tug at his erection. Cam hesitated slightly, but I gave him the impetus to help when I stopped and waited, giving him a sidelong glance.

This garnered a response and he huffed out a laugh. "Such a tease."

"Such a hold out," I snipped back.

Cam's left hand entwined with mine to continue our stroking motion. His other hand snaked up my belly and up the crest of my breast, grabbing the wet material of my bikini and yanking it down to expose my taut nipple.

The moment he took me into his mouth was the same moment Sage slipped his hand down my center, fingertips sliding under my bottoms and into my slick heat.

Oh, dear sweet baby Jesus.

Our curses mingled and mixed as I arched into Cam's mouth and sought friction from Sage's fingers. I was on the cusp of something mind-blowing, my body tensing for something just out of its reach.

Sage continued to thrust his finger inside me, adding the pad of his thumb to my pulsing, aching clit which throbbed against his touch.

"I can tell you're close," Sage murmured, his lips caressing the sensitive spot under my ear, tongue lapping at the skin there. "You're so goddamn hot and feel so fucking good."

The water licked my feverish skin, along with his words, as Cam's own tongue flicked at my nipple, drawing it in between his teeth and using his whole mouth to feast on me.

It was sensory overload, as Sage reclaimed my mouth, kissing me wildly. I tasted the mint on his breath, felt the pull and sting of Cam's teeth over my nipple, smelled the masculine scents of each man, and heard the gasps and moans that we all made together.

Heaven.

If it weren't for each of their hands guiding me and reminding me of their needs, I would have been mindless to my own pleasure. My hands tugged and glided along the length of their hard shafts. I marveled at the similarities and differences between their cocks. Cam much heavier and thicker, and Sage's long and robust. It was a heady combination and experience.

A few minutes later, as Sage's thumb circled and teased my sensitive sex, adding another finger to press deep inside me, my legs trembled, a strange and liberating pressure erupting from low in my spine and shooting through my body like euphoric lightning.

I may have whimpered and cried out. *Oh my God Oh my God Oh my God*

The orgasm washed over me until my knees buckled and I was almost too weak to stand. Lucky for me, I had two strong bodies holding me up and supporting my weight. As I came down from my sensual high, Sage and Cam each reached their own individual pinnacles together.

Sage's cock pulsed in my hand and I could feel the rush of warmth leave his body, just as Cam shouted out his own release, head tipped back up toward the sky.

It was serene perfection.

Yet it still only offered me a small taste of what I was really looking forward to later.

My birthday present.

CHAPTER 16

Hours later, we'd long since dried off and replaced our swimwear with our shorts and T-shirts. The boys had a fire going in a fire pit we formed out of stones and rocks, where we roasted hot dogs and took swigs of the Schnapps Cam had pilfered from his parents' bar.

Cam had taken his first bite of my momma's homemade pie and nearly died from a food orgasm.

"Holy shit, this is so good."

Sage and I both eyed each other before erupting in laughter. When Cam loved something, he *really* loved it. Like when the first *Avengers* came out, he went to see it in the theater at least six times. He was obsessed with the movie.

I, personally, was more obsessed with reading my favorite *Harry Potter* books. I loved to read and get lost in the pages of fiction over seeing something on the big screen. Sage wasn't much of a reader or a movie buff but preferred finding new music and bands for us to listen to.

Sage loved most kinds of music, where Cam was a country music fan and loved Dierks Bentley and Sugarland. I listened mostly to Taylor Swift and pop music much to the boys' dismay. Between the three of us, we covered the gamut of music preferences.

"Hey London, can I give you your present now?" Sage had asked, stuffing the final remnants of his third hot dog in his mouth.

"I told you boys not to buy me anything."

I'd meant it, too. I didn't want anything store bought. What I preferred was something physical from each of them, something we'd discussed only once before but had never spoken about since.

I'd initially suggested wanting to lose my virginity on prom night, but as we got closer to the date, it looked like it wasn't going to work out because Sage wasn't interested in going to prom and said he had to work. So, this camping trip was my idea for the perfect setting and alone time with my boys.

And how could they say no to that?

Sage licked his lips with his tongue, flicking away the crumbs from the bun and then bent behind him to pick up his guitar case.

"I didn't buy you a damn thing, just like you asked."

Sage tuned up the guitar, his fingers deftly strumming and fingering the strings, the melodic sounds filling the quiet around us. Dusk had just begun to descend, the crescent moon just a sliver up in the graying sky, the twinkling of lights shining down on our little campsite.

It was magnificent and perfect.

Cam returned from the forest where he'd gone to relieve himself and picked up some more wood for the fire. He smiled at me, a heart-stopping grin, full of the secret acknowledgment of his feelings for me. I smiled back, feeling adored and loved.

Sage cleared his throat and then began to hum for a few minutes to the music until he stopped and looked over the campfire at me, his eyes sparkling with affection.

"I wrote you a song for your birthday. Can I play it for you?"

My hand landed on my chest to cover the wildly beating rhythm of my heart and the pang of adoration that settled and spread there.

"Oh, Sage. Yes, please."

When Sage began to play, the melody enveloped me like an embrace, the beautiful lyrics entwining around my heart like a ribbon.

The day we met,

Was so long ago.

When shadows wrenched,

My heart and soul.

And through the years

You've kept me here

You wouldn't let me go.

Don't let me go, darlin'

Don't let me go.

Although our paths are winding roads.

I will be here, through thick and thin.

You are my world, my love, my kin.

Don't let me go.

Don't ever let me go.

Cam sat beside me now, his fingers wrapped in mine, holding me close as we both listened to Sage's heart being spoken through his song.

When it was over, Sage dropped his head in silence, and I realized I had tears streaming down my face. There had always been a part of Sage that spoke to me. Even without words, I knew when he was happy or sad, conflicted or confused.

But this song, the way he wrote it just for me, broke me in ways I knew could never be repaired.

It was his plea to me. Asking me to always be with him. To never let go of our love and friendship.

Before I knew it, Sage was kneeling in the dirt at my feet, his hands cupping my face as he kissed away the fallen tears. Each one, a reminder of his love and the perfection of the song.

"Happy eighteenth birthday, London. I love you."

Sage kissed my temple, and then my cheek and finally my lips. I could taste my own tears on his lips, as his tongue swept inside my mouth, claiming me and fanning the fires that burned inside my body.

Cam's hand trailed down my hair that cascaded down my back, his fingers playing with the locks and inching down ever closer toward my butt. When their hands were on me, there was nothing I could do to ward off the utter excitement and frisson that turned me hotter than an ember in the fire.

Sage pulled back and Cam began suckling at my neck, immediately finding that sensitive spot below my ear sending sparks racing through my blood.

And then Cam's voice, so deep and rough, turned me into a blazing inferno.

"I want to give you my present now, too, London. But it's not music or lyrics." He was so close to my ear, his warm breath singing my skin. "My present requires you to lay down with your legs spread wide."

My eyes flew open to see Sage in front me, still on his knees wearing a sinful grin. I licked my lips and turned to Cam, saying the only thing I could say.

"It sounds perfect. Exactly what I want."

Cam helped me to my feet and we entered the tent, Sage holding the flaps open for us as he followed behind, closing it again and zipping it up to shut out the night sky.

It had gotten dark, but we had a small LED lantern in the corner, which cast a soft yellow glow across the shadows of the space. My heart hammered in my chest, not from nerves, but the thrill of what we were about to embark on. Over what we were going to do together.

What I was about to give these boys that they would carry with them always and forever.

Although there's never been any resentment or jealousy between the three of us, tonight could easily spur those feelings. Because of that, I was ready to offer a solution that would be the fairest and most unbiased approach in this situation. Although I technically wanted both of them to take my virginity, logically, we all knew only one could do it.

Reaching into my pocket, I produced a coin, holding it out in the palm of my hand. They looked at it curiously, their expressions confused.

"I want to sleep with both of you tonight, but I won't choose between you. The coin will do the choosing."

With that frank decision made, it was either heads or tails.

CHAPTER 17

We all stood there, uncertainty swimming through us, unsure of what to do with ourselves until Sage found his voice of authority and took charge.

"Take off your shirts, both of you."

My tummy fluttered, warmed by the traces of liquor swimming in my blood and the thrilling way Sage became this bold and dominant man in these situations. We were wading into uncharted territories, both exciting and wickedly naughty, and I could barely breathe from the thrill that gripped my throat.

I pulled off my tank and threw it to the ground, my eyes turning up to land on Cam, who did the same. When he caught me staring at his bronzed and bare chest, my lower lip between my teeth, he snickered.

"It's not like you haven't seen this before."

Unbidden, my feet took two steps toward him, ready to reach out for what I wanted, but then I thought better of it, quickly glancing at Sage, looking to gain his approval.

His chin tipped in Cam's direction, as he removed his T-shirt, as well.

"Go ahead, London. I want to watch you touch him."

The idea that Sage may want Cam in the same manner I did, fanned the flames that had been flickering and burning low in my belly for months into a full-on blaze. I stood in awe, my fingertips grazed over the vast expanse of Cam's broad mountainous chest. He was my warrior and a strong competitor with a body made for protecting others.

Close enough now where I could feel his breath on me, I leaned in and placed a kiss on his solid pectoral muscles, being bold and brave to lick the dusty-colored flat disk of his nipple with a stroke of my tongue.

"*Fuckkkkkk*," Cam sighed, his body tensing under my touch. "I like that."

My eyes darted sideways to Sage to gauge his expression. He watched us from a few feet away, his brown orbs darkening with heat and lust. A hungry desperation.

Cam lifted his hands in an attempt to touch me but was stopped by Sage's sharp command.

"No. Not yet. Let her do what she wants."

Tilting my head up to meet his eyes again, I smiled, lifting my eyebrows. My question was for Sage, although my attention was all on Cam.

"I can do whatever I want?" It was a tease. A way to be seductive, even though I really didn't know how.

Sage's response was just as torturous for him as it was for me and Cam. "*Anything*."

Cam groaned as if a bear lived deep inside his chest when my knees met the ground in front of him, my hands gripping his waist.

I only peeked up for a moment to ensure he was okay with what I was about to do. Cam had won the coin toss, which meant he would be the first to have me. To be inside me. To take my innocence that I freely gave and make me a woman.

But Sage called the shots. Guided us on how he wanted this to go and what he wanted us to do. Giving all of us a sense of both pleasure and torment through his directions. It made this experience so much less nerve-wracking and awkward.

My fingers trembled as I worked to unbuckle, unsnap and unzip Cam's shorts, pulling them down past his knees.

I'd felt him in my hand and watched him pleasure himself before this, but I'd never had him in my mouth. Never used my tongue on him to drive him over the edge. I had the intense need to make him go crazy with lust. To make this a memory that he'd never forget as long as he lived. Something for him to take with him when he left for boot camp.

Cam's erection jutted between us, standing bold and straight at attention, its mushroom tip shiny and stretched to a purpling color, straining with need.

As if it killed him to leave me on my own device and not be part of the action, Sage piped in again.

"Lick him. Use your tongue on him, starting at the base and up to his head."

A smirk formed on my face as I muttered, "Yes, *sir.*"

Using the flat of my tongue, I ran up the length of Cam's erection along the bulging vein that pulsed under the skin. When I reached the head, I swirled it around the crown, enjoying the texture and salty taste, and the weight of his hands that he laid on top of my head. They shook with need.

I placed one hand on the back of his thighs, the light dusting of hair tickling my fingertips. With my balance secure, I brought his cock to my mouth and opened wide, sucking him in, getting my first taste of him, the wetness of my saliva coating his dick.

I reveled in the masculine essence of his body, my hand running down the length of his powerful thigh.

"That's it, just like that," Sage encouraged, remaining in the corner of the tent, observing from afar. It was reminiscent of New Years' Eve when the reverse was true and Cam stood and watched. It intensified everything.

Swallowing around the head, I was encouraged to go deeper as his warm hand threaded through my braided hair, silently asking and begging, *'can you handle more?'*

"*Mmm.*"

The moan rolled off my tongue as red-hot lust surged and tingled between my legs. My body ached with a greedy need to be filled. The way my inner walls clenched from the vacancy, needing what I had in my mouth to be buried deep inside my pussy. And then, as if he was a mind reader, Sage dropped behind me, knees on either side of my folded legs.

His lips settled at my ear and he whispered, "You look so fucking hot. I bet you're so wet right now as you fuck Cam with your mouth, aren't you baby? You don't have to answer that because I'm going to find out."

My body stiffened as Sage yanked down my shorts and under-wear, his hand slipping through the crease of my ass, finding the wet entrance of my body and slipped into my heat.

"Such a good girl, aren't you London? You're ours, baby. *This* is ours." Sage's finger thrust through my wet folds, prompting a howl of delight from me, as I moaned around Cam's cock.

The sudden jolt of motion rocked me forward on my knees and I ended up swallowing Cam to the back of my throat. I gag unexpectedly at the intrusion as Cam growls, his grip tightening on my head.

"Oh, Christ. Just like that." Cam's voice is a savage roar, sending ripples of desire zig-zagging through my blood, his words touching every internal cell and space inside me.

I don't know how much longer the three of us went on like that. It could've been minutes or hours. All I know is the way my body responded to Cam and Sage was an all-out out-of-this-world and out-of-body experience.

With every thrust and curl of Sage's finger, with every word he spoke, with every breathy, raspy moan that came from Cam's mouth, I climbed higher and higher. And when Sage reached around my front and palmed the fleshy mounds and pinched at my taut nipple, I let go of Cam's dick, arching my back with a pleasure so strong I felt that I would collapse right then and there. My legs clenched in response and red-hot lust surged through me.

In fact, I shifted backwards into Sage's lap, grinding into his erection with a greedy need to be filled, that empty ache throbbing inside me and becoming unbearable. I clung to him like life support as I tried to catch my breath from the intensity of the climax. As his fingers slipped out me, a new need took up residence between my legs. A stronger, more primitive need to be filled by Cam.

The look of intense need washing over Cam's face told me he felt the same way, as his eyes roamed over every inch of my body while I continued to float back down to earth.

Laying back against Sage, I spread my legs and stretched out a hand to Cam, beckoning him down to the floor with us. "I'm ready for you now."

His dark, denim blue eyes scanned my face and then glanced at Sage, his control gone, but an anxious expression returning to his face.

"Um, I'm not sure what…I mean, how to do this."

Sage gave a husky chuckle. "You mean, how to fuck her? Need me to show you?"

"Asshole," he grunted, a smile pulling at the corner of his mouth, his middle finger in the air. "I know how to do it, just not *how* to do it."

Sage scooted out from under me, prompting me to lay back on the sleeping bags that had been laid out for us. He patted the ground next to me.

"Get naked and come lay down next to us. We'll go from there."

The three of us began to shed our clothing. As I was already nearly naked, I removed my bra, covering my breasts and stomach with my arms, shielding myself from the sudden wave of awkwardness that washed over me.

My skin and body were completely bare to them both, leaving me vulnerable from the exposure.

"You okay?" Cam asked, landing on his side and propping his head up on his elbow, his fingers lightly feathering over my arm covering my stomach. My tummy tumbled with awareness.

Turning my head, I saw comfort and solace in his loving gaze. Felt it in his touch. He wouldn't hurt me, ever. And neither would Sage. I knew this. I had no doubts.

"I'm fine. Yes."

Sage joined us and laid at my other side, his naked warm body curling into my side as he began to place gentle kisses along my shoulder, bicep, collarbone before taking my hand and bringing it to his mouth. He kissed the tips of each of my fingers, moving my hand to my side and then leaning down to place hot, open mouth kisses along the swell of my breast until his lips landed over my nipple and he sucked it in deeply, tugging it into his mouth.

My body arched into him, needy from the pleasure his lips evoked and the sensations he left in his wake.

I dropped my other arm to the side, my hand grazing over Sage's dick. He bucked against me, thrusting his cock into my thigh. And then his fingers trailed down my belly, over my mound and slid into my wetness.

His next words were directed at Cam. "She's ready."

Cam groaned loudly, rolling over me to press his hips between my thighs, spreading my legs wide. The head of his cock met the wetness between my folds as he glided his length up and down a few times. We all seemed to relish in the sensation, even though Sage only experienced it through observation.

"Where's the condom?" Cam croaked, as he pulled away from me, scooting down to kneel between my spread legs.

I pointed toward my backpack, and Cam followed my directive. While he worked to find it, Sage continued to pepper me with kisses, sucking at my skin, over my breasts, down my stomach, over my pelvic bones. One hand weaved through my hair, his thumb stroking my cheek. And when his lips found mine, he kissed me deeply, and I opened for him, just as I would do for Cam.

A minute later, I felt Cam's tongue at my body's entrance.

"Ohhh…" I cried out, the sensation so overwhelming I couldn't bear it.

Cam worked me over with his tongue, teasing, flicking and sucking my clit in an effort to get me prepared for what was to come next. My gaze landed on his latex-covered cock and I shuddered, knowing it would soon be buried deep inside me. His tongue probed my entrance and I nearly sobbed for him to stop.

But Cam stopped on his own accord, his chest rising and moving over mine, as his mouth claiming me in a wet, dominating kiss, stealing my breath and my thoughts and my fears. I tasted myself on his tongue and I was overcome with lust and desire.

"I'm so close, London. I need to be inside you now. Should I stop?"

My response was to wrap my fingers around his cock and guide him to my entrance.

I was faintly aware of Sage's deep inhale of breath and the sound of his fist tugging at his own flesh next to us. The sound of Cam's curse as he panted with labor above me. And the noise in my ears that sounded like waves crashing against a rock as Cam entered me with a push.

Slow.

Slow.

Slow.

I pinched my eyes shut from the sharp pain as he hit my inner barrier. Cam's movements halted, his biceps straining and shaking above me.

"I'm sorry it hurts. It'll go away soon." His concern was sweet but unnecessary.

My hands landed on the rounds of his ass and I gripped him tightly, my nails digging into the flesh as I pulled him into me.

And with one final push inside me, Cam lost the last vestiges of his control.

And I lost my virginity.

CHAPTER 18

I woke at some point during the middle of the night, finding myself sandwiched between Sage and Cam. Sage had his front to my back and my head was in the crook of Cam's neck. Both of their arms were slung around me, heavy and warm.

I was in a cocoon of love, content, just a little sore in all the right places and so very happy.

Not wanting to wake them, but having to go relieve myself like the dickens, I scooted out to find some clothing. Cam rolled over on his back, snoring loudly. Sage stirred and woke up, blinking to adjust to the dark.

"Hey, everything okay?"

I pulled on a T-shirt that was near my feet and shushed him with a finger to my lips.

"Yeah, just have to go the bathroom."

He sat up, searching in the dark for his shorts when I laid a hand on his knee.

"I'm fine, Sage. Go back to sleep."

He ignored me and stood up, opening up the tent flap as we slipped our feet into the flip-flops just inside the tent.

"Grab the light," he said, nudging his chin to the place where the camping light sat.

I took hold of the handle and followed him outside. The night had cooled off, the mugginess dissipating sometime earlier with the light breeze off the lake tickling my skin with its cool touch.

Sage grabbed my hand and we walked toward the tree line in silence. As we reached the small trench Cam had dug out earlier, he dropped my hand.

"I'll be right over there taking a leak. Holler if you need anything."

I squatted and took care of business, listening to the first sounds of daybreak simmering and percolating quietly around us. Being raised on a ranch, I was more than a little familiar with nature and the outdoors. It made me wonder how I would fare in the city when I went off to college. The noise, the crowds, the lack of privacy and quiet. It would be different, for sure, but I was excited about the new opportunities it would present. Even if it meant having to be brave and leaving behind the world I knew and the two boys I loved.

I finished and took a few steps forward toward the clearing to find Sage smoking a cigarette, the scent of cloves and nicotine wafting through the air. He was the only one of us who smoked; a habit I didn't particularly care for and begged him to stop. But he said it was the only thing that calmed his nerves. That and alcohol, unfortunately.

His propensity to fall into the same patterns as his father worried me. From what I knew of Mr. Hendricks, he was a mean asshole who didn't have a heart. Sage was so very opposite of him in that respect. Sage had heart, and love and acceptance and soul for days.

"All good?" He threw the butt in the firepit and stamped it out.

"Yep. You?"

He hummed a response and sat down on the log facing the water, patting the spot next to him for me to sit. As I did, he wrapped his arm around me, pulling me in close, my body shivering with his warmth.

"London," he whispered into my ear softly like a hummingbird fluttering there. "Tonight was…*holy fuck*. It was fucking amazing, better than I could have ever imagined. You were perfect. And so was Cam."

His voice was wistful with the last part of his confession and I knew that he kept his true feelings for Cam hidden deep, not wanting to rock the boat or upset the applecart when it came to his secret desires.

"Do you think you'll ever tell him how you feel?"

Sage scoffed sarcastically. "Not if I want my nose to remain in the same place it is right now."

I laughed softly but saw the true fear through his joke. Even last night, with the three of us together in a variety of ways, Cam was very careful not to purposely touch Sage intimately when we were together – maybe a brush of a hand or foot, but that was it. He avoided Sage's body as much as he could.

I placed my palm on his thigh, staring at his side profile. His perfectly sloped nose and strong jawline accentuated his full lips. Those lips that touched every part of me last night. And his eyelashes fanned across his high cheekbones, the moonlight giving them shadows and making them look even longer.

Sighing, I snuggled closer, breathing in the scent of his skin. Spicy and smoky.

"Are you okay with what we did together? I mean, it's not exactly…*normal* to do that."

Lifting my chin, I kissed at the base of his neck. "It was perfect for me. I'll never forget my first time. You two gave me everything I needed, wanted and more."

Sage shifted toward me, reaching his hand up to the side of my face and cradled my cheek in his palm before kissing me soundly. My lips automatically parted, granting him access, never wanting to deny him anything.

We made out for a little while longer, our breaths turning into pants, bodies arching into each other, hands clinging and fingers brushing over heated skin. Sage slipped a hand up my T-shirt, his fingers skating over the curve of my breast with its taut nipple begging to be plucked. His thumb swept and flicked at the sensitive tip, sending bolts of desire and need coiling in my belly, where white-hot pleasure shot to my clit.

"Do I get to fuck you now?" His question was needy and laced with longing.

"Mmm…yes. I want you, too, Sage."

This would only be my first time with him. After Cam took my virginity, Sage orgasmed into his own hand and we fooled around some more and then fell asleep side-by-side. A little while later, I gave Sage a blowjob and Cam got me off with his fingers.

But I hadn't had Sage inside of me yet. And I wanted it so badly. I wanted to share that same intimacy with Sage as I had with Cam.

Realizing that we might wake Cam, although he seemed sound asleep, I stopped Sage with a touch at his elbow.

"What about Cam?"

It was now light enough for me to see the way he bit the corner of his smile that tugged at his mouth.

"If he wakes, he can watch," he grinned. "Or join us."

I felt a titter of excitement and giggled as we stepped inside, zipping out the increasing light of daybreak with the closure of the flaps.

Sage reached for the hem of my T-shirt and tugged it over my head as he kissed his way down my shoulders and collarbone. My skin brushed against his solid flesh and wanted to mold myself into him, like clay in the potter's hand.

We were limbs and mouths, heat and sex. I gasped against his open mouth as his fingertips skimmed through the wetness between my legs. I coasted my own fingers over the smooth and ridged muscles of his chest, circling down until I felt the straining mass trying to break through the top of his shorts.

He bucked against my hand as I wrapped my palm around his throbbing length, our kisses becoming less gentle as we both sought more friction in any way we could find it.

Our tongues dueled and explored one another's mouths as we rocked into each other's hands, his thumb pressing and adding just enough pressure and circular rhythm to make me beg for more. A hot ache grew and built between my legs as I neared release, but I wanted him inside me when I came.

"I'm ready, Sage."

"You're not too sore? Will you be okay with me?"

Pulling away from his touch, I smiled, crooking my finger suggestively at him. I laid down next to Cam, who was still sleeping with his back to us. I gazed up at Sage who shucked off his shorts and began stroking his hard cock.

The sight of him touching himself, his hand lassoed around his swollen length, still gave me a twinge of embarrassment. But it was overshadowed by white-hot sparks of heat racing through my blood.

"Where's the condom?"

I nodded toward my bag and he made quick work of finding it, handing it to me as he knelt between my legs.

"You do it. Put it on me."

I was clueless, having never rolled one on before and only having seen it demonstrated just once last night. Honestly, I hadn't even paid much attention at the time, simply caught up in the moment of anticipation of my first time.

Sage nudged my palm open and I took the foil packet with shaky hands. I pulled it out and discarded the wrapper, examining it for a moment to decipher which way it rolled on. Sage chuckled and flipped it over for me as I placed the slippery ring over the top of Sage's crown.

My hands stopped their movement when he sucked in a deep breath and I thought I'd hurt him. But when I peered up at him, he was staring down at me with heat in his gaze.

"I want to remember this moment. The way you're looking at me. I don't deserve you. The way you look at me makes me feel like I've hung the moon and the stars or something. And I'm nothing without you. But fuck if I'm not going to take what you're offering me."

Licking my lips, I spread my legs wider, my toes hitting the back of Cam's calf next to me, hard enough to cause him to stir. My eyes widened in alarm, but my concern was short-lived as Sage's body moved over mine, positioning himself at my entrance and making me forget everything else.

"I love you so much, London."

Sage took my mouth, his tongue opening me up, in the same manner his cock did as he entered me, thrusting inside hard enough that I let out a loud breath. A slight sting remained from earlier that night, but as he rocked and lodged deeper inside me, my inner walls began to ease and adjust.

It was either the noise that tore through our lungs or the sound of our bodies slapping rhythmically together, but Cam slowly roused from sleep, turning over and mumbling in a drowsy voice.

"Am I dreaming?" he asked, his hand reaching out to touch Sage's backside before palming my breast. The dual sensations – Sage pumping inside me and Cam's dreamlike perusal of my skin – shook me to the very core.

Upon realizing that he was awake, along with the awareness of his hard arousal, Cam scooted closer to the action, lifting my hand from Sage's ass and positioning it on his own dick as Cam and I began to jack himself off together.

"This is better than any dream watching you get fucked by Sage as you hand-fuck me. Holy shit, it's unbelievable."

Every entry and subsequent withdrawal of Sage's cock from my body hit me at my core, each time nearly blinding me from the pleasure that erupted there.

"If only you could see what I see right now. How fucking sexy you both look," Cam marveled, as Sage's breaths became more labored, turning into breathless pants as his thrusts pushed deeper and faster into me.

I could no longer concentrate, my sole attention was centered on the tingling sparks at the bottom of my toes, that began to vine through my legs, settling at my clit.

"Doesn't our girl feel perfect, Sage? She's so fucking tight and slick…I can hear how wet she is. Fuck, it makes me want to come. I can smell her, too."

Oh, my God. The words coming from Cam's mouth were so explicit. So dirty and wickedly sexy, they brought me closer and closer to my breaking point.

As our entwined hands jacked him off, I turned to face Cam and brought my lips to his, kissing him roughly. Passionately. With greed and physical need.

"I'm coming," Cam moaned against my lips, just as I felt a rush of heat on my hand and between my legs. My body tensed, and I thrashed my head from side-to-side, crying out in my own pleasure.

"*Ohhhh….*" That word was on constant repeat and seemed to be the only thing I was capable of getting out.

And then suddenly I was airborne as Sage lifted me up in his arms as he sat back on his heels, pulling me into him like a limp ragdoll. This position gave him leverage to pump harder and faster, and so much deeper, as I straddled his legs and joined in with undulations, bouncing up and down and writhing against him.

And then Sage tightened his arms and buried his head into my neck, my hair curtaining him as he came long and hard, pulsing inside me in synchronicity with his grunts.

"You look so beautiful, sweetheart. I think I'm going to cry." My momma gushed from where she stood behind me in the full-length mirror, her hand covering her mouth.

She lifted her other soft, motherly hand over my hair gently glossing over the top, playing with the strands that had fallen loosely from the updo I had done at the salon just an hour earlier.

She smiled, her eyes glistening with unshed tears, leaning in as she placed a sweet kiss on the tip of my nose.

"You're going to be the most beautiful girl that Lancaster High has ever seen. And wait until Cam gets his first look at you."

A sudden sadness swept over me, even though I should've been thrilled for the night's events ready to take place. My senior prom had finally arrived, a rite of passage I'd waited so long for. Unfortunately, I wasn't going to be attending with both my boys.

I wasn't happy about the way things had turned out for tonight's events, but Sage insisted that he had to work and couldn't attend the dance. We'd agreed, though, that since Cam was the Prom King, he would take me to the dance and we'd meet up with Sage later that night at the hotel room Cam had booked over in Williamstown, the town next to Chester Fork.

Sage's excuse for not attending was financial limitations. He'd said there was no way he'd be able to afford a tux rental if he was going to be able to have enough money to move to Nashville after graduation.

How could I argue that?

Although, I did try to loan him the money from my college savings, Sage flat out refused and there was nothing I could do to change his mind. I tried to remind him how fun homecoming was, but he argued that things had changed too much and if anyone got a whiff of our situation now, it would cause an uproar in the town.

I begrudgingly agreed, only for the sheer fact that I knew things were not going well at home between Sage and his dad. All I wanted was for him to get out of town as soon as he could. The dance wasn't as important as Sage's happiness and well-being.

Momma lifted my bent chin with her finger, eying me suspiciously.

"What's wrong, sugar plum? Aren't you happy that Cam's taking you tonight? You two look so good together."

I nodded, smoothing down the gorgeous blue taffeta gown that flared out from my hips. It was a strapless dress that hugged my upper body like a glove, with the top being satin and sequence. I knew Cam would die at seeing my cleavage peeking out from the top and that thought brought me some joy.

"I am. Of course, I am, momma. But I hate the idea of Sage missing out on this night. I wish he could come, too."

My momma had no earthly idea what had been going on under her nose over the last few weeks between Cam, Sage and me. If she knew, she'd have locked me up and gotten out my daddy's shotgun herself.

My body had become a sensuous wonderland with the new territory being explored and mapped out each time I was with Sage and Cam. We'd made a promise together after my birthday camping trip that we would be faithful to one another, and if any one of us weren't around, then we'd remain chaste.

It was a tough promise to keep because we were hungry for each other all the damn time. Just a look from either one of them in class or across the school cafeteria or the brush of a hand against my skin in the hallway made me wanton and itchy for more. I was in a constant state of arousal and I wanted them all the time.

All I had to look forward to was prom night. When we'd get to spend the entire night together – the three of us – kissing and touching and fucking. I was so excited I could barely stand it, had it not been Sage not attending the dance with us.

"I just don't understand why he didn't ask someone to go with him. He's such a sweet boy, any girl would be lucky to go with him."

She sat down on the edge of my bed and patted the spot next to her.

Reaching for my hand as I snuggled into her shoulder, she clasped mine tightly with hers, wrapping her other hand around it.

"You know how important it is for Sage to move out as soon as possible, so he really didn't want to spend the money on this. You know him. These traditions are frivolous and mean nothing

to him. I don't even think he plans on showing up for the graduation ceremony."

You'd think someone had just slapped my mother across the face
with the force of her gasp.

"What? Why in the world not?"

I gave her the look that implied, *"are you serious?"*

My parents…well, anyone in town who knew about Sage's home
life shouldn't be surprised that Sage wouldn't be there to accept
his diploma. It wasn't just the pomp and ceremony that Sage
detested, but it was for fear that his dad would show up drunk
and make a scene.

In fact, over the last few weeks, since we'd returned from our
camping trip, Sage's dad had been thrown in jail several times
for drunken and disorderly conduct in public, as well as threat-
ening to kill one of the local bar owners who refused to serve
him one night.

And truth be told, I was worried for Sage every single day that
he lived in that house. He claimed it was nothing and that he
could take care of himself, but I saw the bruises on his arms and
neck in the past. I knew how important it was for Sage to get out
of that house as soon as feasibly possible.

Luckily, Sage was at an age where he could finally stand up for
himself and wouldn't take a lickin' if he could help it. The last
time it'd happened, Sage just shrugged and said, *"The old man
has bad aim when he's fucked up."*

"Momma, you know his life isn't like mine. And I won't push
him to do it if it makes him uncomfortable."

My momma thought about this for a moment, strumming a
thumb over my hand. I stared down at our joined hands, seeing

the similarities but differences between them.

Her's were roughened and aged from years of raising children and working in the kitchen and outdoors in her garden. Mine, still soft and feminine, were unfamiliar to the exposure of weather and conditions. Sure, I'd worked with my dad's horses and livestock since I was just itty-bitty, but I hadn't raised three children or taken care of a home and family for nearly thirty years.

I wasn't sure what my future would hold or where I'd end up, but I knew one thing for certain – if I were to ever be a wife and mother, I wanted to be like my mother. She had shown me how a woman can carry strength and dignity through the love she projects to her friends, family, and neighbors. And to my best friends, Sage and Cam.

"Would it help if I talked to Sage? Told him that we are his family and we'll be out there in attendance, cheering for him?"

"Ah, momma," I sighed, leaning up to kiss her cheek, a watery smile across my mouth. "You are so sweet. I'm sure he'd love to hear that, but it won't change his mind. But I'll invite him over tomorrow and you can tell him then."

I stood up and wobbly-stepped into my high-heeled shoes, turning in a circle to show off my dress.

"Oh baby, I'm so proud of you and the young woman you've become. And I love you to the moon and back. And just make sure that boy of yours is respectful and treats you well."

We finished up with a hug and then went downstairs to find my dad already sitting in the family room with Grady, talking to Cam.

A low whistle escaped my brother's lips and I rolled my eyes, waving him off with a flourish of my hand.

"Stop it, you idiot."

He and my dad chuckled, as Cam stood and turned to face me, his eyes popping wide, jaw going slack and his mouth dropping to the floor.

I blushed at his expression. "Wow, London…you look…you look…"

My brother, momma, and daddy all helped him out.

"Beautiful."

"Like a girl for once." This from my brother.

"Untouchable."

The last comment was my daddy's and I couldn't even look at him for fear that he'd know exactly how much Cam had already touched me over the last month. The blush across my cheeks was probably a dead giveaway.

I sucked my lower lip between my teeth, with my momma scolding me to stop.

"London, you'll smear your lipstick. Now, come and stand next to Cam so I can take pictures of you both by the fireplace."

She ushered me over and Cam, seemingly still struck dumb at the sight of me in a gown, gave me his arm and we stood shoulder to shoulder in front of my family. Posing for pictures that would last a lifetime and would someday be cherished memories.

But it all felt so incomplete without Sage. Like a phantom limb, it was a painful memory of what was missing at my side tonight.

My life had always been filled with moments where they both were next to me. If one pulled in one direction, the other naturally gravitated.

They were my bookends. My anchors. My compass.

And right now, I felt unbalanced. Off kilter.

Doing my best to give a natural smile, I looked up into Cam's eyes, who gazed down at me. And in his own wan smile and simmering blue eyes, I saw the mirror image of my own thoughts.

Cam bent down and whispered in my ear. "I miss him, too, baby. But we'll see him later tonight. I promise."

I nodded and reached up on my tiptoes to kiss his cheek, hearing the snap of my momma's phone as she caught the moment.

"Ah, you two look so adorable together. Don't they Lee?"

My daddy grunted, stuffing his hands in the pockets of his worn jeans and giving Cam the death glare that clearly stated, *"don't mess around with my daughter."*

We finished off the photos, stepping out into the garden for a few more before we finally left for prom.

A piece of our hearts was missing as we went through the motions of enjoying our senior prom together.

All the while, something in my gut kept sending me warning signals. Roadside flares to alert me of danger. A shift in the universe that told me something wasn't right.

An uneasy feeling crept through my veins like vines on my momma's garden arbor trellis.

It screamed for Sage to stop.

To run.

To hide.

CHAPTER 20

"How's it feel to be king, your majesty?" I teased Cam, as he held me by the waist and spun me slowly around the dance floor, where we'd been dancing over the last two hours.

He'd been crowned Prom King, along with Cecily Peterson, the school Prom Queen. Cam was pissed off that I wasn't nominated for the prom court, but I had no interest or desire to be part of the ceremony or school tradition. It'd never been my aim to be voted for popularity. I was happier as valedictorian, performing on stage in with my dance crew or enjoying my time with Cam and Sage, not with people who were superficial and insincere.

I had my close circle of friends and if others thought that was strange, I was okay with it. They would all be distant memories when I left for college. This town would always be my home, but my heart was with my family, Cam, and Sage. The rest was irrelevant to my future happiness.

Cam tickled my ribs to get me back for my comment and I wiggled against his hold, giggling in a fit of laughter.

"It feels good, but only because I have my rightful queen in my arms."

His comment melted me in his embrace. Everything about the evening had been perfect, from the dinner we ate out under the stars to the way he held me while we danced and never let me out of his sight. It was rare to be touched by Cam in public and outside our bubble we'd created with Sage.

Sage.

Although the night with Cam was something out of my dreams, I still couldn't shake the strange feeling that continued to niggle in the back of my mind. It made me anxious and ready to leave almost as soon as we arrived at the dance, hours before.

"I'd like to go soon so we can see our prince."

Cam placed a kiss on the top of my head, his hand at the small of my back, pressing me closer to his warm body. He smelled so good. Like the scent of warm apples on a fall day. Spicy and something just Cam.

"Me too. But I kind of like having you all to myself right now, too," he admitted against my ear, as we slow danced to Lady Antebellum's song, *Need You Now*. "But we can go after this song. It's almost time to meet up with Sage, anyhow."

It felt so good to be held by Cam. In his arms, I always felt safe and cherished, and most certainly, loved. Although Sage would say it to me more often, I knew Cam loved me. He just expressed it in a different way.

The song ended, and we stood holding each other for a long moment. Peering up, our eyes connected, and I felt something so strong, so indelible, that my body trembled in response.

"London, tonight was … it was perfect. This whole year has been perfect and it's because of you and Sage. You're my best friends…and, well…" The words stalled at his lips and he cleared his throat. "You're more than that. You are the love of my life."

My heart shimmied inside my chest from his confession. It meant everything to me.

"Let's go, Cam. I want to be with you and Sage tonight more than anything."

We drove in relative silence, our hands clasped together, the windows of the truck rolled down as we road through the countryside to the next town. The room Cam had booked was at a small and intimate out-of-the-way motel that we knew wouldn't be crawling with any of our high school friends. Most of them were staying in town or going to someone's kegger party out in the woods.

The plan for us this evening was relatively simple: do things to each other that made us feel good. And I couldn't wait. My body was tight with anticipation for what I knew would happen with them. I'd been daydreaming about the two of their naked bodies with mine and all the sensual things we did together for weeks, longing for their touch.

As we pulled into the motel lot, my intuition was on high alert. Cam, sensing my concern, eased my worry.

"He'll be here. He's probably just running late. He had a shift tonight and said he'd be here as soon as he could get away. In the meantime, I have this."

Cam's mischievous smile pulled me out of my funk as he reached around behind the seat and pulled out a bag.

Setting it between us on the seat, he opened it up and removed a bottle of champagne. After having some for the first time on New Years' Eve, I was a fan.

"And it's pink, too," I gleefully exclaimed, kissing him quickly on the cheek before turning toward the truck door.

His hand landed on my arm. "Whoa there, little missy. Hold your horses. Let me get the door for my queen."

Aw, such a chivalrous gentleman.

Waiting impatiently for him to come around to the passenger side, I peeked at my phone in my purse, just in case my parents had tried to reach me. Or maybe Sage had texted to let us know his expected arrival time.

Sadly, no texts or direct notifications, but I made sure to turn the volume up just in case.

I closed my purse just as the door swung open and Cam appeared to help me down. Jumping into his arms, he picked me up and swung me out the door, grabbing the bottle and collecting our overnight bags with our change of clothes.

He'd already checked in before he picked me up earlier and had a card key to open the door.

"After you, pretty girl," he winked, motioning me into the room.

My eyes darted around the room when he flicked on the lights. To my amazement, there were rose petals and flowers strewn across the floor and all over the king size bed comforter, and soft music played in the background.

"Oh my God, Cameron. This is so beautiful." I swung around and wrapped my arms around his neck, hugging him tightly. "It's so romantic."

He lifted a shoulder. "Can't take credit for it. It was Sage's idea. I just did the dirty work."

I wiggled my eyebrows at the word dirty. Regardless of the romantic notion, I knew things would surely get a little naughty tonight. Our group texts were a testament to all the possibilities and potential.

"Well, the two of you together make the perfect team."

Cam set down the champagne on the table, his bag on the floor and loosened his bow tie. He stepped toward me, crowding me against the side of the bed as he did.

"*We* make the perfect team."

The first brush of his lips on mine nearly buckled my knees. It took my breath away. I missed touching him in this way. I dug my fingers into his scalp, as electricity rippled through me. Cam's hands cupped my butt, squeezing and plumping as he pulled me flush against his very hard length.

My body sizzled, and my legs clenched together, as I squirmed against him searching for friction.

"I've been dying to get this dress off you all night," he admitted, placing wet, open-mouth kisses along my shoulder, my collarbone and landing at the top of my cleavage. "And holy fuck, the sight of these got me so hard, I was worried your parents would see exactly where my thoughts were and lock you away from me upstairs."

I laughed with mirth and brazenly slid my hand down to his trouser zipper, palming the bulge that had lengthened and thickened with our kisses.

"Do you think we should wait for Sage?"

He choked out a masculine rumble as I edged along the material over his straining erection, which told me what I needed to know.

"I'll do whatever you want…but maybe I should get you out of this dress first. You know, so you can be more comfortable while we wait."

"You're so thoughtful," I teased, stepping back to give us some room.

Cam's fingers stroked over the sequined ribbing of my corset, flicking over the taut nipple that strained against it.

I moaned my agreement. "Mmm…maybe you're right."

His fingers found the zipper in back, deftly unzipping me out of the confines of my gown, brushing the bare skin of my back. Shivers ran down my spine at his touch, as his fingers latched to the edge of the dress, pulling it down to my waist to expose my breasts.

He cupped them reverently, plumping and squeezing. "Is it okay to tell you that I want to fuck these sometime soon?"

His words made me breathless. Made me want more. Want it all.

"How about tonight?" I responded, lacing my fingers over his as we massaged my breasts together.

"Shit, London. You have no idea how much I want to push you down on that bed right this instant and do that to you."

Smiling decadently, I pulled him down on top of me as I stretched out wantonly across the bed.

"Do it, then."

"Fuck yes."

Sounding like a savage animal, a growl erupted from his lungs as he moved with lightning speed, unzipping, removing, and throwing our clothes to the floor until we were both left in only our underwear.

Just as he was about to slide my panties off, our phones began chirping incessantly with incoming notifications.

One.

Two.

Three.

Until the sounds of our phones drowned out the music and our own heavy breaths and pulled our concentration away from each other.

Cam looked down at me expectantly.

"Maybe it's Sage."

I nodded and we both reached for our phones at the same time. I had to get out of bed to grab my purse and Cam bent down to fumble for his from his pants pocket.

He was first to reach his phone and began to scroll through his messages that continued to beep, beep, beep. The moment I opened the first text, I was paralyzed with fear. I collapsed to my knees, clutching my chest where my heart had just surged through a red light and crashed into a fiery, painful explosion.

When I looked back over at Cam, he stood frozen as well, pinning me with a hard look.

"This has to be a mistake. It's a fucking lie."

"What does yours say?" I hesitantly asked, my voice quivering from my throat. If his messages were anything like mine, I was scared to learn the truth. That we'd received the same horrific notifications.

The same life-changing and horrible news.

Cam's strong jaw clenched in anger as his eyes clouded over with raw pain.

"Sage's dad is dead. Sage has been arrested for murder..."

PART II

Cameron

CHAPTER 21

I hold the gun in my hand in front of me, cocked and loaded.

It trembles from my shaky nerves and it makes me seethe with anger.

I can't even pull the goddamn trigger because I am a coward.

The same coward I've been all my life. The same one that walked away from the girl I loved and his best friend because shit got too real and I couldn't deal.

The same boy who turned into a man, hiding in the military because he was too fucking scared to face his guilt. The same one that made piss-poor decisions that had a ripple effect on the rest of my life.

The consequences that would unfold.

The mistakes that would be made.

If I could take back some of the things I'd done in the last ten years, I would. Without a doubt. All but one.

But that's not how life works, is it?

And now here I sit, overlooking the Smoky Mountain range, my feet dangling off a dock at my parents' lakefront home, regretting almost everything. Regretting all the stupid things I've done, the decisions that can't be undone and the things I couldn't save.

I couldn't save my friendship with Sage.

I couldn't save my sister from the cancer that ate away her insides. Or my mom from having to suffer through the deaths of her only daughter and her husband.

I couldn't save those on my watch and in command, who died and left widows and fatherless children behind.

I couldn't save my doomed-from-the-start marriage.

And I couldn't save myself from breaking London's heart when I left her, kneeling on the ground, tearing out her heart through her tears. The pain to see her like that was so great it cost me a piece of my soul.

I was a coward then and I'm a coward now.

The gun in my hand is the only thing that reminds me that I'm a man and I have courage. That I'm doing the right thing and will save my son from looking up to a man he calls Daddy and finding out later the devastating truth. That his father is a lying piece of shit and a no-good, worthless man.

My breath is stilted as I lift the cold, metal gun and press it into my temple, as I have to consciously drag air into my lungs.

The irony in all this is that London once called me her protector. She thought I was some goddamn hero. As did my family and friends, and those in my pararescue unit in the USAF that I served with. And now my crew in the Tennessee forest fire rescue squad. All those men and women who thought the pins, stripes, medallions, and plaques that have been bestowed upon me over the years prove that I was meant to be revered.

If only they knew…

I'm nothing but a shell of a man, hiding behind a made-up heroic façade.

Closing my eyes, a myriad of memories flash through my head. Like the explosions in the night sky that I escaped countless times in missions in my special ops pararescue unit.

In a blink of an eye, the last ten years appear, at first bright and bold and then clouded with the black stain of death, regret, and guilt.

Everything changed that prom night ten years ago. Every moment and step I took after that was marred by the stupidity of my youth. My ignorance and arrogance. My recklessness. And my naivete of how people – and hearts – can change in a single moment.

My heartbeat ramps up, beating wildly on a collision course as I waffle back and forth over what I must do.

If I want to save my son – the *only* one that I can honestly save at this point in my life – I must take control of this one final decision.

I mentally count down my last seconds on this earth.

Ten.

Nine.

Eight.

Seven.

I breathe in through my nose, inhaling the crisp, fall scent of the land and earth around me. The fragrance of my childhood.

Come on you coward, just do it already.

Everyone will be better off without me.

Six.

Five.

"Daddy! Daddy!"

The small, excited voice of my son, Taylor, reverberates off the water, as I hear him calling me from the top of the hill close to the house I grew up in.

Shit. He was supposed to be gone with my mother in town. I was supposed to be alone.

Dropping the gun to my lap, I quickly snap on the safety and slide it in the holster between my thighs. Turning to look over my shoulder behind me, I place a smile on my face, reserved solely for my son. Shielding my eyes from the direct sun to see the shadowed and silhouetted body of Taylor running down toward the lake dock.

Fuck, what if he would've found me?

A sick feeling of despair rumbles inside my stomach, retching to climb out. He wasn't supposed to be here. I'm a selfish prick. What was I thinking?

Taylor flies toward me, his five-year-old spindly legs leaping in gigantic strides and arms flailing in all directions from his sides. He looks like a crazed octopus from one of those cartoons.

Standing and sliding the gun into my back pocket, I stretch my arms out wide and welcome him home.

"Hey buddy. You're home. What are you doing back so soon?"

He slams into my body and I pick him up, swinging him around in the airplane toss he practically lives for. His joyful giggle worms into my heart and eats away at my guilt.

"Hi Daddy! We came home 'cause Nana brought someone to see you."

I'm sure confusion is etched across my face. Our trip home was an unexpected visit and I can't imagine anyone knows I'm here or would stop over to see me. I don't have any friends left in this town anymore and the ones I once had…well, I burned those bridges a long time ago.

"Who is it, buddy? One of Nana's friends?" I inquire, thinking maybe it's Helen or Marjorie, my mother's church friends.

Taylor shrugs his bony little shoulders at me, wiggling from my grasp and jumping out of my arms and onto the wooden dock. He runs toward the edge of the platform and I have to grab his wrist and pull him back with a hard yank to keep him from barreling into the water.

My son is fearless. Like I was at that age.

But that trait is long gone for me.

Taylor grins widely, crinkling his nose up and laughs.

"I don't know," he giggles, running back in the other direction. "Some lady named London."

My legs nearly buckle from the weight of that name. In fact, I have to sit back down on the dock to keep from falling over.

London.

CHAPTER 22

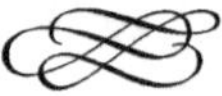

Ten Years Earlier

MY FIRST REACTION upon hearing the news that blared from our texts and messaging apps was how to comfort London.

Sage was arrested for murdering his father?

It was unfathomable. Like one of those stories that start with a small grain of truth and then spreads like a wildfire, picking up more crazed ideas until this is its distorted reality.

I looked from my phone to London's face, her expression riddled with panic, horror, and alarm. Her face was white as a ghost and she teetered on her heels, still half naked.

Jumping into action, I gently pulled her down to the bed and wrapped a blanket around her shoulders. Her body trembled violently, as if in shock, as she slumped against me.

My voice had an oddly serene and calm resonance to it. "I'm sure it's all a very big misunderstanding. We'll find out the truth."

She vehemently shook her head to the contrary. "No. I knew something like this was going to happen. I didn't do anything, Cam. I let it happen."

I'd never heard sobs as gut-wrenchingly loud and pained as I did in that moment. It was as if a torrential rain was pouring through the room, so loud and destructive. Flooding us with grief.

"Baby, you know there is nothing we could've done." But even as I said the words, I knew they were a lie.

Over the past few years, we'd both claimed witness to the bruises and black eyes that appeared on a regular basis on Sage's body. He'd blow it off any time we asked about it, but we knew. It was so obvious they were from his father. The SOB was a nasty drunk and it wasn't often when he wasn't drinking. If Sage wasn't careful to avoid him, his father would beat the shit out of him.

I wasn't sure when it all started or how long it had gone on, maybe his whole life, but Sage never talked about it. Not even to me when we were alone together. If I said anything that sounded even remotely like a question about his home life, he'd tell me he was fine and to "let it go." And I did. Because who was I to say anything? What could I have possibly done to help him against the brutality of an abusive, alcoholic dad?

Sage's dad was infamous in our small Tennessee town for being a public disturbance and a regular in the town jail. I don't know why everyone turned a blind eye to the possibility that if Merle Hendricks was such a menace in public that there was a proba-bility he was twice as bad to his kid in private. But nobody dared to get involved. They simply looked away and "prayed for the little Hendricks boy" in church on Sundays.

Fucking hypocrites. Fat lot of good that did.

I searched around for our clothes that had been scattered around on the floor of the hotel room, handing her the beautiful prom dress she wore not twenty minutes earlier. I felt a stab of fear and anger pummel me in the stomach, which churned with the possibility of what might have happened if everything had gone as planned that night.

It was supposed to be a celebration. The three of us together. Sequestered away together in a small hotel room in the neighboring town where we'd be able to do the things we wanted with each other. Our last night together before we graduated and took the world by storm.

BUT THOSE PLANS came to a screeching halt the minute we were notified about Sage.

Not knowing what to do or where to go, we dressed in relative silence, just the occasional sniffle and tear coming from London. The evening shouldn't have ended this way. It was supposed to be a perfect night for the three of us.

My thoughts drifted back to Sage and the conversation we recently had over our futures.

"You gonna leave for Nashville right away, man?" I'd asked him as we sat in my dad's fishing boat and fished for crawfish in Pitney's Pond – which was more of a lake than a pond.

I should've known things weren't good by the way Sage gave me an unnerving sidelong glance and smirk.

"As soon as I fucking can. Wouldn't you?"

I'd shrugged my shoulders, uncertain of what to say in response to that.

But Sage let me off the hook with a chuckle. "The only things here for me are you and London. No other reason to stick around this town any longer than I have to."

His voice is forlorn and lost. I knew his childhood was riddled with pain and adversity. He lived in a run-down trailer off Marsh Road, just past the Gleason's farm. His dad had a beat-up old truck that only ran half the time, and Sage had to get around to and from his job at the grocery store on a second-hand bike.

Where London and I shared a commonality of two sets of parents that loved us and provided us good homes, Sage had nobody but us.

We'd always been friends. Different people with different upbringings, but something bound us together. The three of us. Although we all had our own interests and lives outside of school – I had sports, London with her dance and academics, and Sage had his music – we just gelled. People thought we were an oddity, the three of us. Like peanut butter, jelly and mayo. You wouldn't think we'd work, but it just did.

I'd also come to know over the years, since maybe our early teens, that Sage liked me as more than a friend. It was in the way he'd smile at me, his brown eyes glinting with something darker and needier. Heavier than a way you'd look at just a bro-friend. He'd always be careful not to touch me, but his gaze would linger when he thought I wasn't looking.

Sage had never come right out and told me he was bisexual, but I knew. Maybe that should've bothered me that he didn't confide this in me since we were best friends and all. But I was too much of a coward to ask, afraid of what he might say. I didn't love him in that way. But I still loved him as my friend and I stood by him no matter what.

London's terrified voice shifted my thoughts back to the present, as I buttoned the last buttons of the rumpled tuxedo shirt I'd worn to prom that night.

"What should we do, Cam? Go down to the jail and ask to see him? Should I call my dad? We need to help Sage. We *have* to be there for him. He needs to know we're there for him."

Wrapping my arms around her trembling body, I kissed the top of her head, the fruity scent of her shampoo wafting through my nostrils, her hair now soft and wavy, streaming over her shoulders.

"Let me call my dad first and see what he thinks. He knows a few attorneys and was in the military long enough to know a little bit about the judicial system and process."

I wasn't worried that my dad wouldn't know, but I worried he would hold me back from getting involved. And that just wouldn't do. *No sir.* I'd do anything to make sure Sage was okay and wouldn't need to spend even one night in a jail cell.

We gathered up our remaining things and walked to the door. Glancing back, I took one last wistful sweep of the room, mentally giving a good-bye to the night we had planned. Sage and I had wanted to make it perfect for London. He'd even written her a song he was going to play for her on his guitar.

It wasn't supposed to end like this. It was supposed to be a final farewell to the three of us. Our send-off before I went to boot camp and joined the Air Force, Sage went off to Nashville to start his music career and London went off to college.

But sometimes the universe tips you on your side, shaking loose any semblance of control you thought you had, and knocking you on your ass. Those earthquakes are meant to remind us that we have no fucking control over anything.

CHAPTER 23

Present Day

"Hi," London says with that soft lilt that always had a way to melt my insides. "I'm sorry to have just shown up like this, but I ran into your mother in town and she said you were back. I had to come see for myself."

I don't know if I should laugh, cry or hug the shit out of her. Of course, my mother would mention I'm here. She was always a fan of London's and always thought of her as one of her own children.

I lift a shoulder. "Gotta love small town news. It travels faster than the FedEx truck on speed."

She laughs at this, out of commiseration or something else, and tucks a piece of her blonde hair behind her ear. The sun silhouettes her from behind and she has an ethereal glow; as if an angel or one of those shimmering oasis images you see on a hot, paved highway.

"I heard about your sister, too. My mom called me when it happened. I'm so sorry, Cam."

Now her voice is laced with sympathy and condolences. I turn back to stare at the lake to avoid her penetrating eyes. She would see right through me.

My younger sister, Jeanine, recently passed away. I wasn't able to come home for her funeral a month earlier because I was fighting a wildfire ripping through the Smoky Mountain national forest. I had to leave my mother alone with no one else around, to deal with the shitty circumstances of burying her only daughter.

I sense her approach and feel the prickle of her heat as she closes in on my space. The scent of her perfume – peaches and cream - that I would recognize anywhere surrounds me and transports me back to my youth. I hide the gun underneath my thigh and fist my hands on my lap to refrain from reaching out and touching her. Keeping myself from drawing her into my side and burying my head in her neck.

"Thanks. But you didn't have to come all the way back home. I know you're busy."

London lays a hand on my shoulder and I nearly jump out of my skin. It's been way too long since I've felt that touch. Since our time together as lovers and friends.

Two things we aren't any longer.

Not after all that's happened between us.

London slips off her sandals and sits down next to me, dangling her feet over the dock, kicking at the cool water underneath.

"Cam, don't be stupid. Of course, I'd be here for you and your family. They are…" She stumbles over the words. The lie. "They've always been like family to me."

My head snaps sharply to the side, as I glare at her with undeserved blame and persecution. It's easier to pitch my anger in her direction rather than at my dead sister, her disease or the world. London is here, in the flesh, and the source of my discomfort.

My voice is venom. "They haven't been your family in a long time."

She gasps like I've just stuck a knife in her back. And maybe I have with my hurtful remark. In reality, we know it wasn't London who caused the riff. It was me and the decisions I made.

The decision to marry someone else. And to hurt London and my family in the process.

I'd always been a people-pleaser, trying to do right by everyone involved. Yet the moment I made a choice solely for myself, I hurt everyone. My parents were wrecked with disappointment knowing I was marrying a woman I really didn't love when it was so obvious I still loved London. So, I did what any gutless, spiteful prick would do. I forbid my family and London from coming to my wedding.

London closes her eyes and inhales deeply, allowing me a moment to look her over. So much has changed in ten years but everything about London is the same. Her golden sun-kissed hair, dewy skin and soft, lush lips that I've tasted and kissed and had wrapped around my…

Pushing the inappropriate thoughts away, I steel my resolve to avoid those topics all together.

"I'm sorry. I didn't mean that."

Her remorseful smile is still gentle and kind but gilded with pain. Yet it still holds the solace I seek.

She lays her hand across my fist, gently unfolding my fingers and slipping them through hers. Only London could bring me to my knees like this. To shed the 100-pound guilt guerilla that weighs me down every day. For the last ten years.

Our fingers interlock, palms touch, heartbeats in sync once again. As if they'd never lost their connection or timing or beats, even when mine felt it died a thousand deaths over the years.

"Cameron, your son…Lord have mercy, he is the spitting image of you when you were his age."

I chuckle because that's exactly what my mom says about Taylor. She says he has my gumption, stubbornness, and spirit. And energy. Holy crap that kid is a cyclone on legs, constantly in motion.

London flips my hand over in hers, a long, tapered fingernail tracing the lines of my palm. All the lives that I have lived in my twenty-eight years. All the mistakes I've made and the decisions – good, bad and indifferent – that have brought me to this place. To this moment of reconciliation.

This is the first time London has ever met or seen Taylor. And it hasn't been for her lack of trying, but simply my unwillingness to allow her back into my life in that way. I just couldn't. Not after how I walked out on her. Changed the direction of my life – *our lives* – with the biggest mistake I could have ever made.

I never should have let her go. Or left Sage.

I thought I was doing the right thing - what was right for all of us.

I thought it was best. I thought we could move on.

I was wrong.

I thought I could stop loving her. Or forget about him.

I didn't.

I could never stop.

Like an avalanche barreling down the mountainside at full speed with nothing in its way to halt its progress, so was my love for London and Sage.

Strong. Unrelenting. Powerful.

But with catastrophic endings.

London and Sage broke my heart first, in very different ways, but I shattered theirs. I abandoned them both when I should've stayed and protected them. Decimated any chance to later salvage even a fragment of our friendship.

Yet the universe is giving me a second chance.

Because here she is. Our hands entwined in forgiveness. In comfort. In unconditional love that I don't deserve.

"He deserves a better father than me."

London's mouth gapes open and she smacks the top of my thigh.

"Cameron Taylor Lucas. Don't you ever say that! In just five minutes of meeting him, I can see just how much he adores you. He wants to be just like you. He's so proud that you're his daddy."

I scoff. She has no idea what she's talking about. He's just a kid and doesn't understand how flawed I am. Looking up to me is a waste of his time and energy. He'll find out soon enough that I'm not as brave as he thinks I am.

"Whatever. He's a good kid, though. Not sure who he gets that from."

It's a barbed remark aimed at me and his mother, Lisa. She's a fucking piece of work and no more fit to be a mother than I am a father.

London lifts an eyebrow skyward, glancing at the house behind us over her shoulder. "Is Lisa here?"

"As if," I bark, unable to contain my condemnation toward my soon-to-be-ex-wife. "She saw this as her chance to have a free week at the beach."

A soft frown lines her mouth and she pats my leg again. It's a compassionate gesture – yet my mind goes elsewhere whenever London touches me. Her touch does something to me that no one else has ever been able to replicate.

Certainly not Lisa.

When I met Lisa, she was everything that London was not – which was what I thought I wanted at the time. Lisa was wild and promiscuous. Always looking for a party. She helped me escape the pain of missing London and Sage, but led me into more misery than I could've ever conceived. *Because* she conceived, and then I was trapped into a life with her that I hadn't planned. Or ever really wanted.

London tried to warn me. Did her best to try to convince me to stay away from Lisa. She knew…even though a thousand miles away - just by the way I described Lisa and her clinginess toward me when we initially began dating - that she was a bad influence on my life. That Lisa was looking for only one thing – stability through a child and a military husband.

And that's exactly what she got because of my recklessness and arrogance.

And my stubborn pride.

CHAPTER 24

T en Years Earlier

THE COURTHOUSE in our small town of Chester Fork is the county seat for our farming community. It rarely sees much action with the exception of marriage licenses, divorces, and drivers seeking to contest vehicular violations.

Sage's initial court appearance is the crime of the century in our sleepy town. Within twenty-four hours of his arrest, word spread throughout the county, as far as Nashville, about the son murdering his father in cold blood.

As soon as London and I left the hotel, I called my dad, who jumped into action and contacted his friend, Geoff Custer, a criminal defense attorney from Nashville. They had been in the Air Force Academy together and Geoff later went on to law school. Within hours, Geoff had arrived at the Chester Fork county jail and had already met with Sage, signing on to be his attorney.

The hard part for London and I was the waiting. We arrived at the jail but were told we couldn't see Sage. It was against the rules. Thankfully, after Geoff and my dad arrived, Geoff was able to give us some details.

London and I clutched each other's hands in solidarity and worry, sitting in a small conference room across the table from Geoff and my dad.

Geoff lets out a deep sigh, his hands folded in front of him on the table, nodding his head up and down without a word. I'm not sure if this is a good sign or a bad one. My stomach clenched and my throat gathered dust as we waited for him to sift through all his paperwork on the desk.

Geoff cleared his throat. "Well, I can tell you that Sage is okay for now. He received some medical attention before he was placed into custody."

London gasped loudly, clutching at her heart and I squeezed her hand. "What? Is he hurt? Please tell us he's not hurt."

Geoff held up a hand, prompting her to quiet herself and let him finish speaking.

"He suffered a broken rib, nose and wrist in the scuffle. All will heal in time and no permanent physical damage," he reassured, making some notes on the pad of paper in front of him. Then he flipped through the yellow legal pad, stopping at a page with a bunch of chicken scratch on it from what I saw.

"The timeline leading up to the death of Merle Hendricks can't be verified by anyone else, as there are no other live witnesses at the time of the event, with the exception of Sage, of course." He lifted his bushy gray eyebrows skeptically. Fucker didn't look like he believed Sage's account of what happened. Which we have no idea what that was.

Geoff rubbed his temple as if he's the one that has something to lose out of this whole ordeal.

"We'll hopefully receive the coroner's report soon to establish the cause and time of death."

My dad jumped in, agitated and pissed off. "What does that mean and why is it relevant? If Sage is beaten that badly, there was obviously an altercation that was provoked by his father's drunken state."

My eyes darted to my dad, who sits with military-straight posture at the end of the table, lines creasing his forehead and between his brows. He's never been a fan of Sage, nor understands how our friendship has lasted all this time, but thankfully he's not going to turn his back on him. Not when everyone else in Sage's life has and not when he needs us most.

Geoff continued. "It's pertinent because it establishes the timeline of events leading up to the altercation and will either confirm that Sage is telling the truth about what transpired, or if there are holes in his story. And when this goes to trial, which for obvious reasons it will, that information will be key in the testimony and case. Now, let's see…"

As Geoff reviewed his notes, I took the opportunity to give a sidelong glance toward London, who sat to my left. Her tears have long since dried up since we left the hotel, but now she just appeared shell-shocked and scared.

I rubbed my thumb over the top of her hand, hoping that it would give her some piece of mind. Trying to assure both of us that if we hold on tight, it'll all work out.

London's voice sounded timid and so quiet you could barely hear her.

"Can we see him tonight?" Her pleading tone stabbed me in the chest like a knife.

The attorney's head popped up, his tired eyes staring at London from above the frames of his reading glasses.

"We need to see him, sir. Please." I emphasize.

Geoff sighed and dropped his pen on the paper, folding his hands in a steeple to prop up his chin.

"Unfortunately, not tonight. He's being processed right now."

"Processed?" I had no idea what that meant, so I clarified, unnerved by the sounds and smells of the jail. It sounded like they were putting Sage through a meat packing factory like they have over in Watertown – all the metal-clanging of the cold steel gates.

"Yes, there are procedural steps when a perp…I mean, an individual who is booked and charged for this kind of violent crime. And he won't be able to step in front of the judge until tomorrow morning's bail hearing."

My dad spoke up, saying what we're all thinking. "Will they release him then?"

Geoff cleared his throat again, taking a sip of his coffee on the table next to his stack of papers. "I honestly don't know. Typically, with any crime of this magnitude, there will be a review of his criminal history, his flight risk, the nature and circumstances around the crime, and any history of violence."

London stared at me, her eyes glistening with unshed tears, the make-up she'd worn for prom now smeared and smudged. Her head snapped suddenly back to the attorney.

"He's only eighteen and has no criminal history. Will that matter?"

"I wish I could give you the answer you want, but the truth is, he will be tried as an adult. Now, if he pleads Not Guilty at the arraignment hearing, it'll be months before anything moves forward. I just want to prepare you all, that if the judge denies bail tomorrow, which could be likely as a man was murdered tonight, Sage will be looking at spending the length of that time incarcerated in the county jail."

"Oh my God!" London wailed, her head shaking back and forth in frantic denial.

"Fuck No!" I said at the same time.

My dad slapped a hand on my shoulder, trying to reassure me with his physical presence. But it didn't work. I was sick to my stomach thinking that Sage could be stuck in that place – with all its horrific noises and musty, urine-scented hallways.

And I thought his living conditions at home with his dad had been bad. This was a thousand times worse.

"Son…London," my dad interjected. "Do not get caught up in the what-if's right now. Let's get through tomorrow and we'll do everything we can to ensure we are there for your friend."

I noticed my dad doesn't use Sage's name. It made me angry and that frustration, already brewing on simmer, bubbled up from the pit of my stomach. I wanted to hit something. Destroy anything in my path that was separating us from Sage.

This night couldn't be happening. It was supposed to be such an amazing night to remember but turned into a nightmare. A horror movie of epic proportions. And it had to be a thousand, if not a million times worse for Sage.

The attorney interjected. "Okay, let's turn our focus on how you can help Sage. I need to get some information as to the last time you saw him, spoke with him or heard from him. What his state of mind was during that time leading up to tonight's events. Can you both do that for me?"

London and I nodded our heads in unison and we begin regurgitating everything we remembered as it related to Sage over the last 24-hour period.

Everything except for the reason the three of us were planning to meet up at the hotel.

That might not have gone over so well in the grand scheme of things.

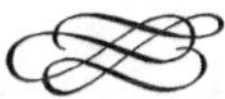

Present Day

LONDON and I sit outside a while longer, reminiscing and talking as the sun begins to beat down, reflecting off the water and heating us up with its hot rays. I can feel the prickle of sweat beading in between my shoulder blades and at the base of my neck.

Or maybe that's just from the burn I feel under my skin anytime I'm around London.

Fuck, I screwed my life up so bad.

Why did I ever think it would be a good idea to leave London?

It was because I was a coward. I was scared of my feelings that had developed toward Sage and what happened between us. London was just in the cross-hairs and a collateral victim.

"Hey, what's going on in that head of yours, Mr. Lucas." London taps me on the temple with her finger. "You've always been the thinker amongst…"

She stops herself before saying any more, but I know what she was going to say. She was alluding to the way the three of us were together. Me, Sage and London.

"I know what you mean. You don't have to say it. Honestly, that was partially what I was ruminating over. All my past mistakes. The direction my life took. Yours. Sage's."

I blink and look away, suddenly uneasy about where the topic of Sage might lead to. Things were already difficult for me with Lisa and Taylor, now my sister's death and staying with my mom while she sorts things out. It's just all a lot to process.

My dad died five years ago. Heart attack. I was stationed in Italy at the time, but when it happened I was on a mission in Afghanistan and couldn't get leave to return home. In fact, it was three days after my father's death that I'd actually received word. It fucked me up in the head and that's when I concluded that I wasn't cut out to remain in the military. Another one of my regrets in life, but something I had absolutely no control over and couldn't take back.

Thankfully, my mother knew the score, as she'd lived it with my dad, who had retired just right after my fourth birthday and they returned to their hometown to raise their family.

Although when I returned to Italy and had made the decision not to re-enlist, that was the beginning of the end for me and Lisa. When I asked if she could take Taylor home and spend some time with my mother, she flat out refused. Said she didn't want to travel overseas with our young son because it would be a hassle and she didn't know how she could possibly help my mother since she barely knew her.

As if she knows I'm thinking about that, London asks, "You want to tell me what happened between you and Lisa?"

I snort uncomfortably. "Let's just say you were right."

"Cam," she says, her voice soft and remorseful. "I'm so sorry. For everything. I only wanted the best for you. I should've been a better friend."

After that summer and everything that happened between me and Sage, I was so confused and mixed up and angry at myself and the circumstances, I did everything I could to ruin the friendship we had. Nothing London could have said or done would have changed anything, and it eats away at me that she thinks otherwise.

I place my hand at the small of her back. "London, stop it. You were a good friend and flat out told me I was making a mistake. You were honest and that's what friends are. I just didn't want to listen. I did what I did out of anger and confusion. It felt like everything was spinning out of control and I just needed something – *or someone* – who was there to help stop the madness. Someone other than you or Sage. Lisa just happened to be the first person I grabbed onto. I was young and made a rash decision. I was stupid."

"No, you weren't. We were in an impossibly difficult situation. You were off at boot camp, and I know that was so hard for you. I was away at school trying to come out of my shell a little bit and figure out who I was when I wasn't with you or Sage. Plus, if you'd done something different or gone a different direction, you wouldn't have had Taylor."

She turns and looks over her shoulder at the house. We can hear the distant laughter of my son, who is singing along to my mother's favorite Elvis song, *Blue Suede Shoes*. London returns her gaze to me with a grin on her face.

"At least he sings better than you." Her joke is emphasized with a quirk of an eyebrow and I nudge her shoulder with mine.

"Yeah, well you know I have many other talents," I reply, but the innuendo falls between us like a lead balloon.

That's a topic of conversation we steer clear of since that fateful night.

I quickly recover with a question of my own. "Tell me what you've been up to these past few years? Are you still with Clay?"

Clay Christopherson was the guy that swept London off her feet her third year in college after she'd transferred to NYU. I never asked or found out the reason why London moved to New York and left behind Nashville. She would never tell me, except for the fact that she wanted to study sociology and felt the program at the bigger school was better and aimed more at the work she wanted to do in the future.

Because we'd lost touch, I had no idea what was going on in her life now. All I knew was she'd returned to Nashville and began work as a social worker, helping and guiding foster children who were being pulled out of abusive homes and abandoned situations. Although she's never said so, I think it's based out of guilt for never stepping up and saying something about Sage's abusive father. Maybe things would've been drastically different had that happened.

But none of us did that. And we all have to make amends in different ways.

London shakes her head, scrunching her nose like she smells something rancid.

"Um, no. Clay and I broke up a long time ago. He hated Nash-ville and returned up to his hometown in Connecticut. He's practicing law there now and I think he's married." She shrugs her shoulders, as if uninterested and couldn't care less about his whereabouts in life.

I'd never met him, just like she'd never met Lisa, but he sounded like a stuck up, conceited douchenozzle. He wore collared polo shirts and loafers, for fuck's sake.

Now I'm curious if she's dating anyone else.

I give her the eyeballs. "Well then? Anyone else in your life right now?"

The air between us grows heavy as if a thick fog descended and created a murky film in the space between our bodies.

She clears her throat. "I see Sage every once in a while when he's in town."

My jaw drops to the floor like an anvil.

"What? Where?"

She breaks our gaze and looks off into the distance, her fingers toying with her lips. I reach out to grab her wrist, drawing her attention back to me.

"London, how is he?"

The unshed tears glisten like crystals in her eyes, her lips quivering uncontrollably.

"Being on the road doesn't help him…I've tried, Cam. I really have. I love him so much, but I don't think I'm good for him, but I know I'm the only stable force he has. Everyone else around him – his manager, his agents, the music producers, fans…they all bring out the worst possible environment for him. I know he loves me too, but it's just hard for him. I think I only serve to resurface all his pain and past suffering when I'm with him."

She lowers her head in despair. "And I think he's using again and I can't do anything to help."

I loop my arm around her shoulder and draw her into me. Just like I would've done in the past when we were together. Friends. Confidantes. My only aim is to shield her from more suffering.

There's one thing I know just as plainly as London does. And it's that Sage can bring out the best in us and also the worst. After everything he's been through, that pain manifests itself into an armor that repels love and kindness. We tried to help Sage. We were young and foolish and thought our love could get him through it.

We were naïve to think that the three of us together would be enough to make things right and help Sage sort out all the shit his life and that dreadful ordeal lumped on him.

But as that summer drew to a close, and London and I went off in opposite directions, we lost that final connection and hold we'd had on one another. And the ties were eventually severed between me and Sage over something I still feel guilty over.

London held on a little longer, though. Until Sage finally cut those strings, as well. I didn't even know that they had reconnected again.

"Shh," I murmur against her ear. "You've probably saved his life more times than we can count. You've shown him more love and more compassion than anyone else has ever done, just like you always have. He just doesn't know how to reciprocate. Maybe, London, it's time to let go."

She looks up into my eyes, her green eyes sparkling like gems, and I can clearly see that's not an option.

"Cameron, will you help me?"

My eyes go wide because I don't know what she's asking. "Help you with what?"

"Help me prove to him that he is loved and worth something. That he means something to us and we need him. He won't listen to just me. I sound like a broken record with him. It has to be you, Cam. It *has* to be you."

CHAPTER 26

T en Years Earlier

SAGE'S ATTORNEY had contacted my dad to let us know that the bail hearing was scheduled at ten a.m. the next morning. London came with her mom, who sat in the front row of the courtroom. I sat on the left of London, her hand clasped tightly in mine, with my parents sitting right behind us.

Geoff, the attorney my father retained, indicated there was really no reason for any of us to be at the bail hearing because it would take all of fifteen minutes for the proceeding to occur. But nothing and no one was going to keep us from seeing Sage for the first time in three days.

Geoff spent a few minutes outside in the hallway when we got there explaining the process, but I spent that time holding London in my arms, trying to comfort and reassure her that it would all be all right. My dad had promised to do anything he could to post bail for Sage if it was granted.

Geoff warned us that in cases like murder and domestic violence, bail was normally denied by the judge unless there was no previous criminal history and there was little worry over Sage fleeing. In that case, the typical bond could be from a hundred thousand dollars up to a million dollars.

A million dollars in this small, redneck town was unheard of. And no way could my dad come up with that kind of cash. And neither could London's family, even if her dad was willing to contribute.

None of that mattered, though, the first moment we locked eyes on Sage.

When he shuffled into the courtroom, his eyes were cast downward, avoiding our eye contact altogether. I'd half expected him to be in a bright orange jumpsuit and handcuffs behind his back. Instead, he wore his tattered jean jacket, an old concert t-shirt, old worn jeans with the knees ripped and his Converse.

The sight of him, his face bruised and purplish from the broken nose, his arm in a cast and the exhausted circles underneath his eyes had London immediately crying out.

"Sage," she gasped, as I wrapped my arm tighter around her waist to hold her up as she swayed into me.

I leaned in to whisper in her ear. "We need to be strong for him, sweetheart. He needs that from us now more than ever. Can you do that?"

It was like seeing one of those inflatable balloons that was withered and collapsed, inflate with air and stand tall as London found her resolve. She stood up straight, shifting her shoulders back and nodded in agreement.

Because we were in the front row as the attorney and Sage sat in front of us, London bent down, stretching out her arm to reach for Sage. She touched the top of his shoulder, squeezing him with a reassuring gesture.

"We love you, Sage. We're here for you."

Sage ignored her, his head bowed in defeat and defiance, his exterior shell and armor in place for all the world to see. It was his "*fuck all*" attitude that he gave to the general public. The one that protected his heart from being hurt.

London and I were the only ones who really knew the true Sage. The light within him that would shine bigger and bolder than even a harvest moon in August.

The guy sitting in that courtroom, ignoring us with his steely aloofness, was not our friend Sage. This one was the product of a mean, abusive drunk and a system that didn't care about boys who are beaten by their own fathers.

I watched as my father chatted quietly with Geoff and London blotted her eyes with some Kleenex her mother had handed her. I could feel the tension ripple off Sage's shoulders. The anger and hostility that brewed just underneath the surface. The pain that lingered there like a thousand-pound boulder that he'd been carrying around for years.

I was so pissed that this is how things landed for Sage. Could this all have been prevented? Hindsight being twenty-twenty, the guilt ate away at my conscience. We should've spoken up before. Done something to get Sage out of his house and away from that cruel man.

"All rise for the Honorable Judge Bettencourt."

There were close to twenty people in the courtroom, including those who work in the court system and other attorneys who were awaiting their clients' hearings. I stood up on shaky legs, assisting London with a gentle grip on her elbow. The room suddenly felt like the air had been syphoned from it and I found it hard to breathe.

If Sage didn't get bail, or my dad couldn't afford to post his bond, I didn't know what we'd do. Or how London would be able to handle it. Or how Sage would survive it.

If Sage was remanded to jail, I couldn't bear it.

He was part of our lives for thirteen years. I didn't know who I was without Sage and London in my orbit. I knew I couldn't live without him. I'd suffocate and die without them.

The gavel's harsh *thud* rang out and snatched me from my reverie. We sat down and I kept close tabs on the back of Sage's head. Geoff leaned over to Sage and whispered something in his ear and Sage gave a curt nod. From the angle in which his face was visible to me, I could see the tight-lipped expression demonstrating his mood.

Solemn.

Angry.

Scared.

Alone.

Goddamn it. Had I pushed for Sage to come to prom with us, this would never have happened. The only reason I didn't was because I was a selfish bastard and I'd wanted London all to myself at the dance. I didn't want to share her that night and wanted her alone for as long as I could have her. So, when Sage told us he had to work that night and that he would meet us later at the hotel, I was thrilled because it meant London would be mine alone for a few hours.

I loved Sage – maybe more than I'd ever admitted to him. When we'd all been together sexually, it turned me on to greater heights with just the way he looked at me and watched us with that unapologetic heat in his gaze. Or the brief brushes of his skin against mine. Or the way he allowed me to let go when he took charge. It was so fucking hot.

But I also wanted to know what it was like to be one on one with London. How it felt not to have to share her with Sage.

I blinked and cleared my mind of the hot thoughts and memories that swirled in my head, covertly adjusting my dick that had grown semi-hard with the erotic memories.

All I knew for certain was that the outcome of that hearing better be a positive one so that Sage could come home with us.

BECAUSE I WANTED MORE time with him before I had to ship off to boot camp.

CHAPTER 27

P resent Day

WHAT THE FUCK was I even doing here?

I'd literally just been grieving the death of my younger sister the last week, offering my mom what little comfort I could give as we mourned together. Holding her as we stood at her gravesite where Jeanine's body was buried next to my father's grave.

And now here I am, sitting next to London in my old beat-up truck outside the gates of a beautiful historic mansion twenty-minutes outside of Nashville. Sage's home for the last three years, according to London. The one he bought with his first earnings after making it big as an alt-country crooner.

It seemed like a far-fetched fairytale, one of those *Lifetime* movies where the convicted felon turns into a big-time rock star in the course of ten years. But it's reality, as if the time Sage spent in the state penitentiary was completely expunged and ignored by his legions of fans and it didn't matter to any of them. He was revered like a modern-day Jonny Cash. The man in black.

But Sage wasn't in Folsom, he was locked up in the Smoky Mountain state correctional facility for three years. An inmate in a prison full of murderers, rapists and child predators. All of which he was not.

It still makes me sick to think about it. All the while he was locked up and unable to live his life in freedom, I was far away fighting for freedom and doing a great job messing up my own life.

After begrudgingly saying yes to London's favor to visit Sage in Nashville, I left Taylor with my mother for the night as London texted Sage and asked if she could stop by and see him. He'd responded within an hour giving her the green light. What London conveniently failed to mention was that I'd be tagging along with her.

I can't wait to see how this goes down.

Landscaping lights illuminated the heavy wrought-iron fence – likely there to keep creepers and stalkers out of his home – as we idled at the front waiting to be buzzed in.

"You sure about this?" I asked, turning to London who stares out the front of the truck. "We still have time to back out."

Her beauty strikes me like a right hook to the jaw, the shadows dancing across the slope of her nose and the slight subtle curve of her forehead. She is flawless, and it stuns me that she doesn't have a boyfriend or husband. Some lucky bastard who by now should've swept her off her feet and treated her like the Queen that she is.

On the other hand, I'm selfishly thankful she isn't attached to anyone. Mostly because jealousy is an evil beast that tears through my gut with its sharp talons and fire-breathing breath whenever I think of her with someone else. All the feelings that I never let go of and harbored over the years have resurfaced with a vengeance. It's made me realize that maybe under different circumstances, we could start something together. Rekindle our old relationship.

That is, of course, dependent on her feelings toward Sage and vice versa. She'd told me about their casual hookups over the years. How she fell into a pattern she called, "hopefulness and lies," where she'd hoped that Sage would stick around and love her the way she knew he could and believing his promises to remain sober and faithful.

It made me seethe with hatred and anger that Sage had had London all these years and yet he was so careless with her love to throw her away like that. Hypocritical, I know, considering I did the exact same thing when I left for boot camp. Leaving her to think she wasn't enough for me when really it was my feelings of inadequacy. Knowing I wasn't good enough for her and didn't want her holding on to something I couldn't give to her in the long run.

London nods her head as if convincing herself she is ready for this reunion to happen.

"Yes," she confirms emphatically. "I just want you to be prepared for what you might find. Sage's different now, Cam. He's changed. A lot. That delicate softness that existed in the past is long gone. He's been hardened by his experiences that we can't even begin to comprehend."

She shifts in her seat, nervously clasping and unclasping her hands in her lap.

"He'll never be the same boy you once knew."

My gut clenches in guilt. The way we left things between us. The things I said to him when he was at his most vulnerable. I knew he was hurting and scared and so angry with the circumstances back then, and yet, I crushed him with what I did to him.

Running away, even though I concealed it through boot camp and later my tour overseas and time in Italy, was just a coward move. I left him when he needed me the most. I could've been there through letters and visits when I came home during my leaves. I could've answered his calls.

I could've apologized for my reckless abandonment of him.

But I didn't.

If Sage even lets me into his home, it'll be a miracle. I don't deserve it.

Running a hand through my short-cropped hair, I exhale a breath.

"Sage is not going to be happy to see me."

London laughs, a sound I love to hear. Sweet and naughty in equal measure.

"Probably not. It's a wonder he's even agreed to see me. The last time he left…we had a big fight. He was so angry at me."

I enfold her hand in my palm, closing it in my fist.

"Sage is angry at life. At himself. At the universe. Not you, London. Never you."

The corners of her mouth upturn into a small smile, full of grief and appreciation, as the gleam of the gates as they open in front of us catches my eye.

I take the truck out of Neutral and slowly drive down the long, curved driveway toward the gigantic house. A far cry from the trailer he grew up in.

Parking behind several cars – all expensive, high-end luxury models – I'm greeted with the first glimpse of a life that in a million years I never would have expected Sage Hendricks to be part of. Rich. Famous. Opulent.

It just didn't fit with his childhood. Most days when we were kids, he wore tattered, dirty clothing and his hair and face were rarely washed.

Rounding the front of the truck, I open the door to assist London out of the passenger's side. We step up the gray-stone steps to the front door and ring the bell.

From inside we can hear loud music pumping through speakers and the sound of laughter, singing, and people. Lots of people.

I bend my head so my lips are at London's ear, squeezing her hand in mine as I say, "It's showtime."

The door opens and a half-naked girl, maybe nineteen or twenty at most, opens the door. She has a beer cup in one hand and she leans against the door with her hip jutted to the side, her midriff exposed between a bikini top and short cut-offs with the pockets visible from underneath the jeans material. She stumbles a little to the side, catching herself on the door before she falls over.

"Hey, you guys. Are you the ones with the coke?"

London gasps as I cough a chuff of surprise. London composes herself quickly, responding to the young girl's question.

"Um no. We don't have any coke with us, sorry. We're here to see Sage."

The girl gives a disinterested shrug of her bony shoulders and turns to walk away, leaving us standing in the doorway slightly amused. And a little worried.

"Okay then. Lead the way." I extend my hand to allow London to head in first. Since she's been here before, I assume she knows her way around the house.

A brief glance down the long, marbled corridor shows the back exit to the patio area and the area I assume is the pool. A few people meander around out there, drinks and cigarettes in hand. London grasps my hand and pulls me to the left and then to a large room with a couple of white and black couches and chairs, a big stone fireplace along the back wall, and the other walls decorated with gold and silver records.

It reminds me that while I was in Italy, Sage was nominated for and won Best New Artist of the Year through the Country Music Association, as well as Billboard Music. He even graced the cover of Rolling Stone two years ago.

I'd seen a copy of the magazine in the base commissary one day and had to do a double-take when I saw the headline and the picture. It read, *"From Felon to Fame: Sage Hendricks Rises from the Ashes."*

It hadn't looked like Sage at all, and I'd honestly not even recognized him when I first saw it – therefore, the reason for the double-take. His cheeks had appeared sunken and concaved, eyes lacked their usual brown effervesce, his dark olive skin a dull, paler hue. His entire facial structure and body looked emaciated.

And even now, as we emerge further into the room toward a group of people, my gaze skips completely over Sage, who sits on the couch, strumming a guitar, sandwiched in between two scantily-clad women who hang on him like he's their savior. The only reason I know it's him is because when he lifts his gaze first to London, a smile of recognition alights his face and eyes, and a sense of nostalgia swirls through me. He places the guitar down and stands on wobbly legs, opening his arms to give London a hug.

I stand a few feet behind her and observe – as if I'm not even in the room and just watching it through a TV screen – as he encloses her in his arms and then whispers something in her ear to make her laugh. It's not a *"ha-ha, that's funny"* kind of laugh, but a sad, humorless laugh.

Just as he begins to pull away, he lifts his gaze and his eyes land on me.

Everything I deserve and have avoided in the last ten years can be easily read in that wounded expression as Sage's eyes flitter with recognition.

And then the words I absolutely deserve to hear are muttered from his intoxicated mouth.

"What the fuck is he doing here?"

My sentiments exactly.

Ten Years Earlier

Sage's bail bond was set at one-hundred-fifty-thousand dollars.

It could've been a lot higher, Geoff had said. As if that was going to make that type of money appear so Sage could be set free.

My parents and London's parents each contributed a combined hundred thousand and through various donations through the local church community (who had never done anything to help him in the past, even though they knew he was living with a monster) ponied up the remainder.

It took over a week to collect all the donations and pay the bond company, so during that time, Sage remained in the county jail, right alongside drug dealers, child abusers, meth addicts and various other life-long criminals. London was sick and broken-hearted, and I was just numb to it all, barely eating or sleeping while I knew Sage was living through a hellish nightmare.

Thankfully, with a little coaxing, Sage agreed to allow me and London to visit during the visiting hours every day. It broke our hearts to see him trying to act strong and unscathed when deep inside we knew the truth behind the steely mask he wore.

He was broken. And not just his body.

The system was in place to supposedly protect children from the hands of monsters, not throw a young man, whose scar tissue was still raw from years of abuse, behind bars. Alone and without the people that loved him there to watch out for him.

The only decent aspect of being raised and living in a small community and county was that our jail wasn't high tech like the state penitentiary, which enabled us to visit regularly with Sage in the small, but relatively open environment. The cinder-block walled room housed four different tables, with an armed prison guard at the only door in and out.

Sage wasn't even cuffed when he was led into the visitor room the first day we showed up to see him.

But he was wearing the god-awful red jumpsuit with his arm in a cast, a bright blue and purple bruise on his cheek and jaw nearly reaching his eye.

London was the first to speak, her voice a shaky quiver when he walked toward us.

"Oh my God, Sage. Are you okay? Are you in pain?"

Sage waved her concerned inquiry away with his arm that wasn't in a cast, lifting it with a slight wince of pain that only I seemed to notice. We couldn't hug or touch him, so we all sat down at the table, an uncomfortable moment passing by and between us.

"It's fine. It'll heal."

"Hey."

I had rehearsed what I was going to say to him the minute we sat down, but instead, all I could get out was the lame, generic greeting.

He nodded to us, pulling a loose cigarette from behind his ear, and placing it between his too-dry lips that looked cracked and a little swollen from the beating.

"Got a light?"

Both London and I snagged questionable looks at one another, confused by the question. Neither of us smoked. She shook her head and I glanced around the room to see if anyone else might have one. I noticed a man and a woman at the table next to us, both smoking, and decided they might be a good option.

Standing, I moved slower than I normally walked, and stood at their table.

"Excuse me, but could we bum a light?"

The guard from the corner of the room was at my side immediately, towering over me with his imposing figure. Although I was only eighteen, I was a tall guy at six-two, but this guy was NFL-massive, his body build, and size of his limbs thick as a tree trunk.

"Get back to your table. You're to refrain from speaking with anyone else while in here otherwise, I will escort you out. Got it?"

My body jerked at his loud and intimidating voice. I hung my head in apology.

"Uh, yes sir. Sorry. I was just…"

"I don't give a fuck what you were doing. Go sit the fuck down." A large finger poked me in the chest and I staggered back a little.

Swallowing hard, I turned and returned to the table where London and Sage looked on with wide-eyed, nervous expressions. London's face showed fear, where Sage's was more amusement than anything, his teeth clamping down on his bottom lip to keep from smiling.

"Well that's not something I've ever seen happen before," he mused, the cigarette dangling haphazardly from his mouth. "You're not used to getting the smackdown from anyone."

Realizing it was useless, Sage pulled the unlit cancer-stick from his lips and shoved it back behind his ear.

London leaned forward, her breasts pushing against the lip of the table, her voice quiet as a whisper. "Are they all like that? So hostile and mean?"

Sage's eyes darted toward the guard, then to me and back on London. "Some are better than others. But it's all relative. To keep the wild animals in here subdued, the zookeepers don't put up with any shit. I've just tried to stay off their radar."

He glanced away, but not before I saw the weary look in his eyes. The sadness and fear in them.

London's eyes filled with tears, slowly cascading down her pretty face. I could tell Sage was trying hard to refrain from reaching over to catch them with his fingertips or move to comfort her. He steeled his composure and sat back against his chair, propping a foot over his knee. As if he didn't notice or have a care in the world.

I cleared my throat, flipping through my rolodex of appropriate topics I could bring up in conversation. Honestly, I wasn't sure what I could or couldn't say or ask Sage. How the hell do people do this?

I wanted to know about what happened. How it got to the point where he ended up killing his dad. What pushed him that far? London and I were still pretty unclear on the events that transpired that night, and no one had told us much more than the little Geoff originally divulged. We wanted to hear it directly from Sage. *Needed* to hear it from our friend.

"Can you talk about what happened?" My voice croaked like the question was trapped in my throat, clawing to get out.

When Sage's eyes met mine for a brief second, I saw everything he'd kept hidden from us for far too long. The turmoil and pain that had built up over his lifetime. The abusive environment he was made to grow up in, the unfairness of it all. London and I were blessed to grow up in loving households and Sage got the short-end of the stick the moment he was born into this world and the parents that he was given. The cards he'd been dealt were shit.

While my family wasn't perfect by any means, I always had a loving home. Although my dad had been strict because of his military background and was extremely hard on me, pushing and pressuring me to get straight A's and be the MVP in football, baseball, and track, I still knew he only wanted the best for me.

Whereas Sage's dad, Merle, was a fucking abusive asshole who only cared about where he'd score his next drink or fix. Merle was never a father or role model to Sage. He only proved that some men are not meant to be fathers and should never have procreated in the first place.

Sage realized his mistake the minute my discerning gaze met his and he glanced away, scanning the room as if looking for somewhere else he'd rather be. He rubbed a hand down his face.

"Attorney Geoff told me not say anything to anyone until the arraignment hearing." He lifted a shoulder, his attention now centered on the scuffed table, his hand wiping away at invisible crumbs.

"But it's us," London argued softly, garnering a sympathetic smile from Sage. "You can't say anything even to your best friends?"

He pursed his lips tightly and let out a long exhale. "I don't know what to say. It was just like every other night in the last decade. The old man came home drunk or high, I don't know which, looking for money to go score some more. When I got home from work, I found him ransacking my room, throwing shit around and yelling at me to give him some. He knew I'd been saving my money to leave and he wanted it, but I wasn't stupid enough to hide it in my room. And I told him that, which he didn't appreciate hearing. He called me an ungrateful worthless shit."

Sage laughed sardonically with a roll of his eyes as London hiccupped a soft cry. I cursed.

"I was trying to stop him, pulling at his arms to get him out of the room when he turned on me and hit me in the face. It wasn't more than a slap, but I turned to protect myself, covering my face with my bent arm. That's when he turned the tables on me, and he picked up a bat and slugged me in the ribs, and then connected with my wrist, as well." Sage pointed to his middle and his casted arm, indicating his broken body parts.

"Mother fucker." I spat. "If he wasn't already dead, I'd kill the asshole."

Sage snorted, but then winced in pain. "I fell to the floor and before he could hit me again, I grabbed his legs and yanked him off balance. When he fell, his head hit the corner of my bureau.

That was that. He hit it at just the right angle and he died. Fuck, my dad was an ugly bastard on the best of days, but the look on his face as he laid there dying in front of me, with blood pouring out of his skull, was pure evil. It still gives me nightmares. Knowing that bastard, he'll probably haunt me the rest of my life. I'll never get rid of the fucker."

He laughed mockingly but it was plain to see how much it bothered him. The memories, I'm sure, would live on in his head forever.

"Remember when we saw that movie, *Unfaithful*? It was just like that. Fucking creepy. The dude just laid there, staring up at me with wide-opened eyes. I think he took a piece of my fucking soul." He shivered.

London gasped loudly and dipped her chin to her chest, as if in prayer. But I knew she wasn't praying for the soul of Merle Hendricks. That cock sucking bastard deserved to rot in hell.

"Jesus, man. I don't wish death on anyone, but I hope he died painfully."

"Yeah, no doubt."

"What happened then?" London asked, knowing there's still more to the story after all the shit went down.

Sage rubbed his chin, the dark stubble beginning to grow in from the last few days without a shave. I assumed the prisoners don't get razors.

He leaned forward, pressing his chin into the heel of his unbroken hand and palm. "I got up, checked for a pulse and then called 911. Waited for them to arrive and then was arrested. Probably right around the same time you were being crowned prom king. Ironic, right?"

I scoff angrily, uncertain where the hostility came from. "Yeah, real fucking hilarious, man. Why the hell didn't you call us? Text us? We had no fucking clue what happened and had to fucking hear about your arrest from kids at school."

London rested a hand on my thigh and I shook my head indignantly. Sage's response just proved that deep down, despite all the shit he dealt with growing up and throughout his childhood, he had the biggest heart of anyone else I knew, with the exception of London.

Sage closed his eyes, a smile formed across his mouth.

"I didn't want to ruin your night together."

Present Day

SAGE'S EYES fill with something I don't recognize, but they turn dark as a barrel of rye whiskey as he glares at me, seething with hatred.

I deserve to be hated by him.

I deserted him when he needed me the most.

I called him vile names. I turned my back on the best friend I'd ever had in my life.

London returns to my side and grabs my hand, pulling me into her so she's tucked into my side as we stand in front of a crowd of people we've never seen before and probably will never see again. Part of me wants to bail and say, "fuck it, this isn't worth it."

But then again, that's what the coward in me would do. I need to face him like a man and let him take a swing at me if that will make Sage feel better.

I know it would make me feel a hell of a lot better.

"Sage, can we all go somewhere to talk?"London begs. I know she doesn't want witnesses around when she says what she has to say to him.

Sage's eyes leave mine briefly and land on London, his expression softening just slightly, but only for a moment. A sneer begins to form across his mouth and a jeering scoff leaves his throat.

"Fuck, no. Not with him," he nudges his chin toward me, his nose scrunched as if he smells sour milk. "He's not welcome here. Only you, London. And right now, I'm not even sure I want you around. You're both ruining my chill vibes."

I can't help the vitriol remark that comes out of my mouth.

"Oh, you mean your coke high?"

His eyes narrow into a death glare and then he smiles, shaking his head.

"Forever the Golden Boy. Perfect in every way. Somethings never change."

He bends down to pick up the discarded guitar, motioning with a flick of his wrist to the girls to follow him and then they walk down the hall and up the stairs.

The chicks laugh and giggle, moving in front of Sage as they begin to ascend the stairs, their hips swaying for attention. Sage stops halfway up, returning his attention to me and London, as we stare after them. London's eyes are misty with unshed tears and the hurt bleeds from her body so visibly that I can practically feel it.

My gut churns with guilt and anger. I didn't expect a warm or receptive welcome, but I didn't think he'd turn his back on London. For someone who had once expressed his undying love for this woman, he certainly has changed his tune.

His voice is icy-cold. As cold as the marble floors our feet stand on.

"I expect you to be gone by the time I'm up tomorrow. You're good at leaving, anyhow, aren't you?"

The comment is aimed at both of us when the blame should be focused on me. Not London. She's never left his side to my knowledge and has been there every step of the way.

I won't allow him to direct his anger toward London when she's remained by his side through thick and thin. Been the only constant in his life. The only loving presence.

"Sage, wait. *Please.*" I swallow my pride, taking a step toward him, as he watches me like I'm a predator to be feared. Or killed.

I can tell he wages an internal war as to whether or not to give me the courtesy and hear me out. His knuckles turn white around the banister he grips tightly. Maybe to keep him upright or maybe to keep him from lashing out more. I'm not sure. Either way, he at least gives a minute to express my regret and to apologize.

I glance around the room, where people still linger and are clearly eavesdropping to hear what's going on between us. I wouldn't be surprised if someone was taking video of this confrontation, in hopes it turns into a physical fight and they can sell it to TMZ for some cash.

But it doesn't stop me from saying what I need to say. What I should've said years ago but was too dumb and stupid to cop to.

"I'm so sorry, man. You have every right to be angry at me. We were so young and dealing with such enormous circumstances. I didn't know how to deal with the feelings…" I taste bile in my throat. Bitter regret. I swallow it down and drop my eyes to the floor.

"I was confused about how you felt about me. What I felt for you. I panicked and lashed out at you out of fear. Shame. But I always loved you. I know that now. I know that I made a grave error and hurt you. Hurt you both," I nod my chin over my shoulder toward London. When I return my gaze to Sage, his expression has softened, but not enough to turn this thing around. *Yet.*

But if it's one thing I remember and know about Sage, it's that his heart has the capacity to love bigger and bolder than anyone else I've ever known. He accepts others who are different than him for who they are and never makes them feel less-than. Unlike me, Sage has never shied away from who he is or what he is. He's owned up to everything he's done in life.

Maybe that's why his star shines so brightly.

I just need to get him to accept me for my past grievances. To recognize that who I was then isn't the same man standing in front of him now.

Sage inhales a breath and closes his eyes. It's a concession. A start.

I continue, taking a step closer to the bottom of the staircase, dismissing the audience in our midst who linger and loiter to get a whiff of what's happening. If Sage doesn't mind the lack of privacy in his own home, then I can deal with that, too.

"I want to make amends. However long it takes for you to forgive me, I'll keep working to earn your trust back. To earn your forgiveness. I just don't want you to shut her out because of me and my failures to be a friend to you. Whether you believe it or not, I do love you. I always have."

London slowly moves toward Sage, taking cautious steps and reaches for him with an outstretched hand.

"Please Sage. Let us talk to you. We love you."

Sage turns his head away, considering his options. This is his home and he has every right to kick me out for just showing up unannounced and *"ruining his good vibe"* like he said. Maybe we should've given him a heads up, but what's done is done. I'm here now and I'm here for them.

As if he's just elected to have a root canal, Sage grimaces and shrugs.

"Whatever. Stay the night," he concedes, looking at us both. "We can talk tomorrow. Tonight, I've got other plans." He tips his chin up the stairway in the direction the two chicks went off in, which I presume is his master suite.

A part of me feels like that's a slap in London's face to flaunt his sexual proclivities in front of her like that. A woman he's been on and off with for years. But it doesn't seem to phase her at the moment. It seems par for the course. Her only established agenda for coming here tonight was getting him to listen to reason and getting him to commit to getting help.

A smile bigger than the Grand Canyon alights London's face and she kisses Sage's palm that she still holds in her hand. As if he's the king. Or her sweet prince.

"Thank you, Sage. Thank you for giving us a chance."

As he continues up the stairs that curve over the foyer, he corrects her assumptions.

"I'm doing this for you, London. *Not him.*"

Well, at least it's a start.

Just like the fairytales we all read as children, the door has been opened for us to find a way to change the story's ending. So that the Princess and Prince can have a life free from tragedy and live happily ever after.

CHAPTER 30

Ten Years Earlier

THE DAY SAGE'S bond was finally posted, London and I waited for four hours outside in the county jail parking lot.

Apparently even in a redneck county like ours, releases of inmates only happened once a day without a real concern for people's lives or schedules. Geoff originally told us to be there at nine a.m., but it wasn't until after the lunch hour when Sage finally appeared.

He walked slowly behind two larger, scruffy men who looked like they hadn't showered in weeks. Sage himself was looking pretty haggard and shitty, even though he'd only been in custody for five days.

I didn't have to be in jail to know it wasn't a garden party. Although he hadn't mentioned how bad it was, there's no way Sage would ever want to return there. Who would?

With every step closer to us, we watched Sage transform; the deep lines of worry in his forehead slowly dissipating and erasing the closer and closer he got to my truck.

London, unable to hold herself back any longer, jumped out of the cab and ran toward him, arms thrown wide open as she launched herself against him and enveloped him in a tight bear hug.

Staggering back slightly, he reciprocated with his own hug, lifting her up in his arms so she could swing her legs around his waist. Sage buried his face into the curve of her neck and even from where I stood, I could see his body shaking with emotion.

I moved in until I was just inches from them and I swung my arm around his shoulders, pulling them into my embrace.

"I'm so glad to see you, Sage. We missed you so goddamn much."

His long, thick lashes were wet when he reluctantly peered up at me.

"Get me out of here, man."

Dropping London to her feet so she could walk on her own, the three of us wordlessly walked back toward my vehicle, London sandwiched between us, her hands clasping ours on each side of her. *Always between us.*

As we situated ourselves in the cab and I turned on the engine, the air flicking on to eliminate the heat, the atmosphere was atomic. It was still – the way the sky gets moments before the funnel cloud sweeps down out of the sky and annihilates every-thing in its path. It felt both the same as it had always been and yet wholly uncomfortable. Like wearing an ill-fitting pair of jeans that you've grown out of but don't want to throw out. We still wanted to make it fit between us, but the dynamics had changed.

Everything had changed since that prom night just a few days before.

We had changed.

I should've fought harder for him to join us. But instead, I was a jealous asshole who wanted London all to myself. Had I not been so selfish, that night would've ended differently. His father would still be alive, and Sage wouldn't have to go to trial for charges of involuntary manslaughter.

Sage stared out the window, completely still, London holding his hand as we drove toward my house.

As a condition of his bail, and approved by my parents, it was required that Sage was to live at my house. It was no big deal, considering he'd been a fixture at my home since we were kids. This time, however, he didn't have a real home to go back to. No mother. No father. No family.

Just London and me. *We* were his family.

It was like a kick in the gut knowing that Sage's life would never be the same again. Starting now – and dependent on the outcome of the trail – he would always carry the weight of his father's death on his shoulders. The blood on his hands.

"You hungry, bro?" I asked him, figuring he was probably starving after having to eat prison food and would want something to eat.

"Nah. I just want to sleep."

I could feel the weight of London's stare as I glanced to the side where she gazed at me with a deep-green eyed, fragile look. I knew she felt exactly as I did – hopeless and useless. Uncertain what we were supposed to do for him. Unable to change the situation or make things better. Walking on eggshells with Sage because the circumstances were so tenuous.

But I wasn't about to let him wallow in this depression or state-of-mind. So, I pushed him. "Come on, man. How about we stop by Pete's Burgers for burgers and shakes? Your favorite. My treat. We can take them back to my place if you want."

"Whatever." His response nearly broke me. Nothing could cheer him up if his favorite food didn't work.

"Or how about pizza?" London added hopefully, her voice overly chirpy.

"Jesus Christ!" he exploded, startling London so that she jolted back against my shoulder. "I said I wasn't fucking hungry and just want to go to bed. Can't you two mother hens just give me that? I just need some fucking sleep."

It wasn't the tone of his response that surprised me so much as it was the way he immediately shut down and didn't say another word the entire ride home. Sage turned away from us, leaning his head against the passenger side window, crossing his arms at his chest and closing his eyes to shut us out completely.

"Sure thing, honey. Whatever you want." London stroked his thigh reassuringly, the tension vibrating off his body so intense, even I could feel it from where I sat. And London's normally sunny disposition suddenly became clouded with sorrow.

The minute we parked in my driveway, Sage flung the door open and was already jumping out of the cab before I'd even turned off the ignition.

"Sage, wait." I demanded, jumping out of my seat and rounding the truck hood.

He turned to stare at me with a far off look in his eye, as if he heard me but wasn't really present.

I walked toward him slowly – to avoid startling him – and held open my arms. Before he could protest, I pulled him into me and squeezed him tightly.

We'd shared bro hugs in the past, but never one of this magnitude. I wanted him to really and truly know I was there for him. That I loved him, even if I couldn't necessarily say it out loud.

"We're here for you, man. Always. No matter what…"

The rest of that sentence died on my lips. I couldn't bear to say them. The implication that he could lose the trial and be given a prison sentence was too heavy of a reality. A weight that could easily bury us in the coming months. Or years.

We had to find a way to keep Sage's spirits up.

To help him live his life fully in the event the worst possible outcome occurred, and our world would be turned inside out and upside down.

CHAPTER 31

P resent Day

THE PARTYGOERS BEGAN to dwindle and clear out around
four a.m.

I roll over on the bed and gaze down over London's sleeping
body, her hands formed in a prayer position near her cheek
against the pillow. Her blonde hair spills out and I can't stop
myself from petting the silky locks. It brings back a flood of
memories – her hair in pigtails when she was six. Her tight,
dancer bun when she danced a solo in her ballet recital at twelve.
Her cascading waves that fell over her shoulder as she straddled
me and road me naked at eighteen.

So many moments, many of which we reminisced about last
night.

After Sage departed upstairs, London and I'd hung out by the
pool for an hour or so, catching up over a few beers, as people

came and went, watching us with a mild curiosity. We didn't quite fit the rock and roll scene, both of us dressed far more conservatively than the others. But I didn't care about any of those people. It was just nice to sit and catch-up with London.

I hadn't realized how much I'd truly missed what we had once shared.

Over the last ten years, I'd seen and done so much, lived a thousand lives. But nothing – with the exception of the birth of my own son – made me feel as whole and complete as I did when I was with London.

My heart felt fuller. My burdens lighter. My smile bigger when she was around. She just had a way of bringing that out in me.

Or maybe it was also knowing that Sage was in our presence. That the three of us were together once again – at least under the same roof – it lifted my spirits and comforted me with some kind of peace.

I shake my head at my own sentimental stupidity as I quietly roll to the side of the bed, careful not to wake London. We'd only gotten a few hours of sleep, and I wanted her to continue resting because last night took its toll on her. I could see the sadness in her eyes, even when she tried to pretend it was all good. Sage's behavior hurt her.

Slipping on my jeans, I leave them unbuttoned and quietly open the door into the hallway, seeking out the nearest bathroom. The house looked different in the morning light, brighter and sunnier, with the rays of morning sun slipping through the cracks of the closed bedroom doors.

Seeing nobody around, I close the door behind me with a soft *click* and turn to head downstairs, the same direction we came up last night when I bump into someone.

"Sorry," I begin to say, but lose my train of thought when I lift my eyes to see that it's Sage.

His nostrils flare as he takes in my shirtless torso and he takes a step back as if avoiding a venomous snake. He runs a hand through his messy bedhead hair.

"Morning. I was just coming to find you two." His voice sounds gravely and thick like he swallowed rocks. "I wasn't sure if you took me up on my offer and stayed the night."

I lift a shoulder and watch his eyes track the movement.

I have never been attracted to another man in my life. I enjoyed women. But something about Sage – some unique element of his being – always attracted me to him. The way I felt about him scared and *scarred* me. It made me doubt who I was. Who I was with him and without him.

And it was for that reason that I did what I did to him.

Clearing my throat, I nod. "Yeah, we found a room. She's still asleep."

Sage's eyes land on the door and then reconnect with mine, the dark brown simmering with curiosity. He lifts an eyebrow skyward.

"Did you fuck her? Make up for lost time?"

Anger seers through me at the implication and his obvious jealousy. He's the one who's had her on and off for years, keeping her dangling from a string and pulling her in only when it's convenient for him. When he's lost and needs her light to help him find his way. Otherwise, from the sounds of it, he couldn't care less about her.

And yet here he stands, angry with me because I slept in the same bed with her?

"Fuck you, man. You're a hypocritical asshole. You practically broke her heart last night when she watched you leave with those two hoes, flaunting it in her face. How could you do that, you prick? I thought you loved her?"

Something I say strikes a chord with him, and he heaves a heavy sigh, dropping his head, his fingers threading through his hair.

"Fuck, I know. I'm an asshole of epic proportions. I was just so angry when she showed up with you. I was wasted and high and then pissed off that she didn't give me any advance warning. It's a bad combination that prevented any good decisions on my part. I'm sorry."

Something in the way he says it and the genuine regret over what happened last night makes me accept his apology. Plus, it'd be mighty hypocritical of me if I want him to forgive me and I don't do the same for him.

Before we can say anything more, our conversation is interrupted by a sleep-riddled woman who saunters down the hallway from what I assume is his master bedroom. She scoots between us, leaning in to whisper in Sage's ear, her voice tinged with a smoky, southern accent.

"Thanks for last night, darlin'. I had fun. Hope to see you again soon, baby." The girl reaches up on tiptoe and kisses Sage's cheek, her hand sliding over his ass to give it a hard squeeze. Then she turns to me and eyes me up and down, giving me a wink before turning to leave.

"Yeah, see ya."

I watch her walk off, my jaw dropping open at the blasé and completely casual nature of their exchange. Especially if they'd fucked each other last night. It floors me to see how nonchalant their exchange was. I've never been a guy who was into casual. I hooked up once with a woman after I'd learned of Lisa's cheating, and felt disgusted with myself after that.

"Girlfriend?" I ask, even though it's obvious she isn't anything to him.

Sage coughs, leaning around my body that's blocking his view of her retreating form.

"Nah, man. Don't even know her name. I think she's the daughter of one of my producers. She offered, I accepted. Although, I have to admit, I'm not even certain we got to the fucking last night. She may have blown me before I blacked out."

Okay, then.

I stand in awkward silence, remembering that I have to take a piss.

"Hey, I need to use the bathroom. Where's the nearest?"

Sage points two-doors down. "It's right in there. I'm having some coffee made and brought out to the patio. Why don't you come and join me when you're finished? We can talk then."

I'm stunned at how open he is right now. Like everything is right in the world and last night didn't even happen. Nor did anything in the past.

But that's Sage for you. His heart can't stand hate or ill-will. His temper is a flash in a pan and then it burns itself out just as quick.

He pats me on my shoulder before heading down the hallway in the opposite direction the girl went and leaves me there scratching my head in confusion over the weird turn of events.

As if he can read my mind, Sage turns and says with a dirty smirk, "I'm still fucking pissed at you, if that's what you're wondering. It'll require some groveling. Maybe even a blow job while you're down on your knees. I seem to recall you owe me one."

I choke out a cough, my jaw hitting the floor and I hear his deep chuckle from around the corner where he disappears from my sight.

That motherfucker.

I can't tell if he's serious or not, because the truth is, there's always been a possibility that I might do it for him. I just never had the opportunity because of the way things ended.

But that doesn't mean he hasn't done it for me.

Once before. A very long time ago.

And it was the best head I'd ever received.

It was also the start of the end between us.

CHAPTER 32

T en Years Earlier

"HEY, I was thinking. Maybe we should go camping this weekend?"

I'd already been up for an hour and completed a workout and a run when I walked into my bedroom, a towel wrapped around my waist, fresh from my shower. Sage was in the same spot he was when I left, but now he was awake.

He'd been sleeping an inordinate amount since getting out on bail. Not that I blame him. His life had taken a bad turn and gone to hell in a handbasket after his arrest. He'd no longer had a job because Stu the grocer fired him while he'd been locked up. Regardless of the fact that Sage had worked there since he was fourteen, he cited "attendance issues" as the reason. Disloyal motherfucker. It left Sage without a job, with no prospects for anything else and no other way to earn money until his trial started.

Although the justice system says an individual is innocent until proven guilty, this back-water town felt otherwise, and no one would hire a guy who'd been arrested for murder. Even if it was the murder of a man everyone knew was a nuisance and a child abuser.

London and I were nervous about Sage's state of mind and what he would do when we left. I was set to head off to boot camp in less than two weeks and London would be off to Nashville to start school in mid-August. We wouldn't have much more time to have fun or to be together.

Although fun wasn't an adjective to describe this summer. It was also clear Sage wanted little to do with us and would leave the house and not return until late in the evenings well past the curfew my dad had set for us, smelling of cigarettes, weed, and booze.

Graduation night was a shit show, with Sage getting completely trashed at an after-party where we all celebrated our graduations from high school. Sage didn't attend the ceremony with the class of one-hundred and eighty kids but he still earned his diploma.

It was like living with a ticking time bomb for weeks and I tiptoed around him, either looking to appease him and make him happy or having him ditch us and completely ignore us.

I didn't know which Sage I would get that morning when he rolled over, eyeing my attire with a lift of his brows, reaching for a cigarette.

Propping himself up against the bedframe, he stuck it between his lips and lit up. He'd been smoking like a chimney, but what could any of us do? He was a loose cannon and rightfully so. I tried to remain empathetic to his plight, but it just got harder and harder.

I had no idea how to cheer him up or make things right for him. None of it was in my control.

He blew out a smoke-filled breath, finally answering my question about camping. "I don't really feel like it."

After trying for weeks to be there for him, my anger got the best of me.

"Well, what do you feel like, then? Come on man, you gotta do something…you can't just sit around and mope and smoke and get high. You need to get out and…"

He snarled, his dark eyes narrowing in on me. "And do what? Enjoy life and my freedom while I have it, you mean? In case I get locked up for the rest of my life? You want me to go live my best life while I have the chance?" He used air quotes to emphasize the phrase.

I whipped off the towel and threw it to the ground, picking out a pair of clean briefs from the dresser. Our eyes met as I pulled them up, and then I watched Sage's hungry and interested perusal of my body. I quickly looked away but not before the heat of his stare created a tingling sensation in my balls. Fuck me, my dick took notice as the blood poured south.

No. That's not gonna happen.

I turned my back to him, running a rough hand through my wet hair and opened my dresser drawer to pull out a T-shirt and shorts. I felt oddly exposed and yet instantly turned on.

I chose to sit down on the edge of the other twin bed opposite him. Over time, the former bunk beds I had as a kid, extremely useful for sleepovers with Sage, had been removed and converted into two twins. I bent forward and placed my elbows on my knees, steepling my fingers underneath my chin as I faced him. Smoke hung in the air and the scent of nicotine cloistered heavy between us.

"That's not what I meant. Fuck, no one knows what's gonna happen with your trial. But regardless of that outcome, London and I are leaving soon. We won't be around much longer, and we want to spend as much time with you as possible. We want you to be happy. We'd do anything to make you happy. You get that, right?"

Smoke rings swirled from his move and above his head, one arm propped behind him against the pillow. Anyone else witnessing Sage would think he's the picture of calm and serenity. I, on the other hand, know him and could read the apprehension and anxiety written across his features.

Suddenly, Sage leaned forward, swiveling his legs around over the edge of the bed, stamped out his cigarette and stood in front of me. He towered over me in a posture made to intimidate me, but as I was bigger and weighed more, I wasn't threatened in the least.

I was, however, curious. His dominating stance sent a thrill up my spine. He placed his hands on my shoulders, pushed me backwards, and got right in my face. We were nose to nose. Breath to breath.

"Oh yeah? You'd do *anything* for me?" The corner of his mouth lifted in a saucy antagonistic snarl.

I swallowed thickly, my dick plumping and filling under the weight of his stare and the intensity of his brown, half-lidded eyes.

He may not have been bigger than me, but when he wanted to, he turned into a dominating opponent. I'd learned enough about him in the several sexual encounters we'd experienced that past year with London that Sage had an innate ability to make me do things I never thought I would do. Like jack off in front of both London and him as they watched. Or eat out London's pussy under his lustful scrutiny.

Time seemed to stand still as he hovered over me. We were so close, I could smell the spicy and intoxicating scent of the soap he used and something else that exuded masculinity.

I'm not into dudes.

In my mind, it was one thing to be with Sage when we fooled around and fucked London. Watching each other fuck was the biggest turn on there was. But it was an entirely different ball-game when we're alone. I knew Sage was into both girls and guys and had known he was bisexual for years. But me?

I was into London.

I liked *fucking* London and *watching* Sage fuck London. Or having Sage watch us.

I didn't want to fuck *Sage* or vice versa.

Did I?

My erection grew stiff as my balls filled with the need to release. Just his surly attitude, like a captured bear, and the aggressive position over me had me spreading my legs, opening my knees wide to accommodate him in. So, he could move closer.

"You know what would make me really happy, Cam?" Sage whispered hotly in my ear, his light growth of whiskers brushing against my earlobe.

My throat went bone dry and I lost the capacity to speak. I couldn't breathe. I needed to give myself room, so I leaned back, pressing my palms into the bed behind me.

The only response I was able to give was a grunt.

Sage snickered wickedly and tipped his head down, staring at my package, which was expanding by the second under his watchful eye. His hand landed over my cock, my dick straining on its own accord against the confines of my zipper and shorts. I could already feel the beads of wetness that clung at the tip from the pre-come gathered there just from the zing of excitement over this encounter.

I didn't say anything when he squeezed my junk and his hand glided down my length, cupping my balls in his hand.

I couldn't help but groan.

This is wrong, this is wrong, this is wrong.

My brain warred with my body, jockeying for position.

Sage is my best friend. We shouldn't be doing this.

My body demanded action as my thoughts kept centering on the indecency of the situation, even though the same thing happened between me and London. She was my best friend and yet I'd fucked her. No, my problem wasn't that we were friends, me and Sage. It was that he was a dude and doing this alone together meant we were gay.

Under his ministrations and on its own volition, my body took over and shut down any other consequential thoughts that dissuaded me from acting upon that urge. I closed my eyes tight, trying to block out the negative thoughts running through my head. The sensations from the heat of his hand and the friction he created was more than enough to give my brain the smackdown.

"Stop thinking…just feel," Sage demanded, tugging the edge of my shirt up and placing soft kisses along my belly, his tongue popping out to taste the thin line of hair leading down to my waistband.

It's as if Sage were inside my head. He knew me too well.

It happened lightning fast as I reached the point of no return, where I no longer cared or gave a damn about anything else because it felt too good. Too perfect. Too much. I stopped fighting it and I let Sage take over. He unbuttoned and unzipped my shorts, urging me to lift my ass. He pulled the material down past my knees, removing one foot at a time from my long legs.

I peeled open an eyelid just to peer down and see what he looked like between my legs. My hard cock stood at attention, throbbing with a deep ache to be touched, hitting against my belly. When I lifted my gaze further, I noticed Sage's dreamlike expression. Like he couldn't believe what he saw in front of him. As if it were Christmas morning and his favorite gift is under the tree.

It was like our first time together on London's birthday when I woke up from a dream to find Sage fucking London, sliding in and out of her with long, smooth strokes. Their bodies slapped against each other in an erotic dance. Fuck, I was so turned on, I just watched and let it happen – helpless to the sensations swirling through my body. I watched, breathed in their scents…

And then the memory vanished and everything else faded away the instant Sage fisted my cock and sucked me into the back of his throat. I let loose a strangled groan.

He hummed around me like I was the best thing he'd ever tasted, and his eyes looked up wildly in admiration when I gripped the top of his dark head of hair and tightened it in my fist. That seemed to spur him on, his fingers sliding under my balls and locating a spot no one had ever touched before.

"Oh fuck," I shouted.

It took me about two seconds and two licks of his tongue and I came harder and faster than I'd ever come before.

And the minute the euphoria of the post-climax high wore off, and I came back down to earth, I pushed him off me. He landed with a hard *thump* on the floor, his lips swollen and shiny, and his mouth covered with the sheen of my release.

That's when I said the words that would forever haunt me. The words that would ruin our friendship.

"Get off me, you motherfucking faggot. Don't you ever touch me again, you queer."

CHAPTER 33

Present Day

THERE ARE certain aspects of my life that I look back on and immediately feel a sense of pride. The first and foremost is making the decision to serve my country in the Air Force, which is my crowning achievement and one of the highlights of my life.

I had my doubts at first. I yearned to be home and with my friends but instead was homesick for the first few weeks. Although my last encounter with Sage was a breaking point for us, I still missed him terribly and I knew I'd been the worst friend in the history of best friends.

During my time in the USAF, I'd made mistakes that I'll take to my grave – ones that had life and death consequences. College would have been easier, less complicated and led me into a completely different life, but I wouldn't trade it for the world.

Nor would I trade my other proud accomplishment. While the reason for his birth is somewhat of a mess, there is nothing I would change about bringing my son into the world. Taylor is the best thing that ever happened to me and the light of my life. He came into the world at a time where I had let love go and didn't want it again. Another reason I chose to stay with Lisa. It was safe to be with her because I didn't love her, nor did she love me.

But having a child and holding a newborn in the crook of your arms for the first time does something to a man. His cherub face, pouty lips, and the sweet coos that he emitted while asleep reached into my ragged and torn heart and rebuilt me. Restored my faith in mankind and love.

And through the years, it helped me to come to terms with the love I had buried deep inside me for both Sage and London. It helped me recognize some things about myself that I'd never allowed myself to think before then.

But there is still that low point in my life that will forever fill me with regret. And I need Sage to know how sorry I am for the way I treated him and the things I said before I left.

I ponder all of this as Sage and I sit outside on the huge patio overlooking his property and the huge infinity pool he has in the backyard. I'd returned to the bedroom after speaking with Sage in the hallway to find London awake and getting ready to go out to the stables. Sage had bought her a quarter-horse a few years back and she wanted to go for a ride this morning before breakfast.

Sipping the cup of strong, Italian coffee that one of his house staff poured for me, I stare off over the lush green valley of his property, toward the horse barn out in the back acreage where London went off to ride. Blows my fucking mind that he has the kind of dough now, considering his poor upbringing. Knowing where Sage came from and where he was raised, I never in a million years expected his life to turn out this way. A bigtime recording star and celebrity with a million-dollar estate. It's insane and so incongruent with who he was the last time I saw him.

"You're sure living the good life and have it made here, man."

Sarcasm drips from Sage's tone. "For a fuck-up, ex-con you mean? Or for a kid who once had nothing and now seems to have it all?"

Shaking my head, I take another sip from the hot mug and remain silent. He's been raring for a fight since last night and I'm not about to give him cause to kick me out. Not yet, anyway. I came here at London's request to get Sage some help. And hopefully make amends. I'm not about to fuck it up by losing my patience and falling for his bitter attacks.

I try the lighter approach. "Nah, for a guy who sucks at guitar playing."

Sage knows I'm joking because his lips quirk up at the corners in a smile and he flips me the middle finger.

"Hardee-har-har. You're so funny for a dumb ex-jock."

The air turns a little lighter with the humor injected in and we watch London off in the distance riding around in the penned corral. I want so badly to bring up the topic that still mars the space between us, but I'm not sure where to begin.

From the looks of it, Sage hasn't lost any sleep over it.

I steer the topic to something less brittle for the moment, hoping to save face and ease into our conversation and the apology I need to make at some point.

Over the years, once I realized and hashed out my feelings toward Sage, I'd rehearsed over and over again what I would say to him when the time came. When I got up the courage to tell him that I'd screwed up all those years ago and never meant to hurt him.

But there was always something preventing our reunion from happening. I'd be back stateside for only brief moments while I was enlisted and only had time to visit my parents. And then when my enlistment period in the Air Force was over, I moved to Georgia for a while with Lisa and then decided to go to the smokejumper academy for forest firefighting. I was stationed in several locations until I returned to the Smoky Mountain area.

This career decision was a huge source of contention for me and Lisa and was really the last straw in our marriage. It really didn't matter what caused it, because the relationship was bound to end sooner rather than later. The only thing that mattered now was making sure Taylor was loved and cared for and we could figure out the co-parenting shit.

And figuring out a way to repair and salvage the relationship that I once had with Sage.

"You've stayed close to London," I hedge, checking out his reaction with a side glance over the rim of my coffee cup. "I'm glad you two could remain together."

Sage makes a loud scoffing noise. "You're such a liar, Cam. Get real. You're fucking jealous that we've had a thing all this time and it's had nothing to do with you. And I bet you're dying to know whether I fucked her with another guy who wasn't you."

I inhale through my nose, counting to ten like I learned so many years ago in my special ops training when working underwater. It helps you to remain calm and in control of your anxiety and fear. Or in this case, my anger.

He's just trying to get under your skin.

I lift the corner of my mouth in a smirk, rolling my eyes.

"You're so wrong it's not even funny. I'm not jealous, Sage. I'm relieved."

My comment seems to throw Sage, whose mouth gapes open wide in surprise. His face scrunches and tightens in disbelief.

Quirking my eyebrows, I turn in my seat to face him.

"I'm serious, man. I walked away and left her hanging. I was an asshole of epic proportions. And I'm glad that once you got out, she had someone who was there for her. To take care of her and be there for her through everything."

Sage chuckles and he stands, walking toward the edge of the pool, his back to me.

He looks pretty good from every angle, especially his backside – considering all he's been through. Still tall and lanky, but bulkier now with tattoos wrapped around his arms and calf. I haven't seen his bare back, but I've heard he has a full masterpiece in vibrant colors across his shoulder blades.

I'm struck with a sudden desire to see him naked and find all the tattoos he has hidden from the world that the casual observer wouldn't know exist.

"If you think I was the one to take care of her, you obviously don't know me at all." He replies heartlessly. He stares off toward London who is now brushing the horse's coat near the stable.

Sage's voice turns wistful. Nostalgic. "She was the only one who ever loved me no matter what. And I fucking pissed all over that. She's a tough girl, though. She knew her mind and never gave in just to placate me."

He grows silent and bends his head as I stand up and move behind him. Placing a hand at the nape of his neck, I squeeze gently but firmly, feeling the bristle of his hair over my fingers. Unable to stop myself, I tip his head toward me, closing the distance between us.

My lips land at the top of his head and I kiss him once. He resists for a moment, but then gives in with a sigh. It's my way of telling him thank you for being with her. For his perseverance in digging himself out of the hole that was left behind in his life and making something of himself. It's a kiss that says, I'm sorry I hurt you and fucked up. I love you, still.

My lips move down the side of his face, over the bristle of his jawline until they land on the corner of his mouth. Neither of us move for a moment, scared of what happens next. Worried it will open Pandora's Box and the history of our lives will come barreling out.

I cover his mouth with mine, a kiss to say all the things I can't tell him. His lips infuse with mine and our breaths are labored. There's no tongue and it's not overly lustful, but the kiss packs enough punch to prove to him that I truly mean what I say. As I pull away to a wide-eyed Sage, the words to tumble out of my mouth.

"Sage, I'm so sorry for the way I ended things. How I treated you and left you when you needed me the most. You have absolutely every right not to forgive me, but I hope someday you will consider it." I stop for a moment and purse my lips together tightly. "I was young and stupid and scared."

"Yeah, fucker. You and me both."

I swallow, trying to get out all the words that have lived inside my heart for years.

"I know. But I was scared of you. Scared of having you. Losing you. Loving you. It was never my intent to hurt you when you were going through the worst ordeal of your life. Especially when I loved you so fucking much."

He yanks his head back and out of my grasp, glaring at me with malice.

"You loved me? You're a fucking asshole," he spits, pushing me away with a hard shove at my pecs, stepping out of my reach. "You sure had a funny way of showing it."

I rub a hand down my face with disgust. Sage is absolutely right to resent me for being such a dick to him. I'm just about to say more when London appears and interrupts us.

"Good morning, boys."

Her megawatt smile washes over us and casts a magic spell, making the last ten years disappear into thin air. "How about I go wash up and meet you two in the kitchen in fifteen and we can make some breakfast and get caught up."

She waves at us both and heads into the house, turning to give us a flirty wink.

"And don't you think I don't remember how good your pancakes are, Cameron Lucas."

My eyes dart from London's retreating form to Sage and back again when he pivots and follows her.

"You heard the lady," he calls over his shoulder, with a chuckle and a shrug. "Better not keep her waiting. She's a bitch when she's hangry."

I guess I'm on pancake duty. And the rest of our conversation will go on the back burner, along with that kiss.

CHAPTER 34

T en Years Earlier

I'D AVOIDED the calls and texts and other attempts that London had made to reach me for two days straight. I was still seething with pent-up rage and confusion over what I let happen with Sage. With the way I just let it happen.

What the fuck was I thinking?

Oh yeah, that's right, I wasn't. Sage had done some gay erotic voodoo magic on me the minute he touched me.

At least that's what I thought, anyway. And thankfully, he'd been kind enough to find ways to avoid me and had slept on the couch the previous two nights, only coming home when I was already asleep in my bed. I should've felt guilty for acting like a prick when he was the one who was going through so much turmoil. It made me sick to my stomach to know that once he went to trial, there was a really good chance he'd be sentenced to prison.

I'd be heading to boot camp to learn combat skills to fight for our country's freedom, and he'd likely be locked up for an unknown period of time without *his* freedom.

My head throbbed with the constant reminder and the possibility we'd lose him.

Laying in my bed, I covered my eyes with my forearm, blocking out the sun peeking through my blinds. I didn't want to get out of bed or do anything today. I just needed some downtime, so I could figure out what the hell I wanted to do about Sage.

A knock on my door had me swiveling my head to the side and dropping my arm against the bed as London's voice echoed softly through my room.

"Can I come in?"

"Sure," I agreed, although inside I was wishing her away. Hoping she'd leave me alone and not ask any questions.

There was no doubt in my mind that she didn't know about the riff between me and Sage. I just didn't know if she knew what caused it and she was sure as shit here to talk about it. So, I beat her to it, attempting to slam the lid on any potential inquisition.

"I don't want to talk about it if that's what you're here for. Go away."

She sat down gingerly on the side of my bed and sighed. She never did heed my warnings and was stubborn as a mule. So, instead, she launched right into it.

"I don't know what happened, and if you can't tell me, I guess I'll have to be alright with it. But please don't do this to him, Cam. He needs us. He needs *you* in his life. You're his best friend and I know he's hurting inside and we're all he has in this world."

"Goddamn it, London," I cursed, swinging my feet off the edge in the other direction and bending over my knees to cup my aching head in my hands. "You wouldn't understand. Just leave it alone."

I stood up and made my way to my dresser, pulling on a pair of shorts and a fresh shirt and haphazardly combing through my bedhead hair. When I turned back around, I found her lying on her side, chin resting in her palm to prop her up. A sweet cherry-red grin across her lips.

Even though worried for Sage, she looked sexy as fuck. Gloriously tan, smooth skin, freckles dotting her shoulders that are visible under the straps of her tank top. Her long blonde hair cascaded over her arm and down her back. She looked like the All-American girl. The girl-next-door.

An angel who is currently my adversary.

"He didn't tell me what happened, but something obviously happened. He's all surly and combative when I ask him about it. And if you don't want to tell me, that's fine. But Cam, we're running out of time. I know you'll regret it if you leave without making peace."

Deep down, I knew what she said was true but there was just too much at stake for me. It was one thing to have fooled around with both Sage and London in our previous encounters because Sage and I were careful never to touch. We didn't kiss or play with each other. And he certainly never had my dick in his mouth. I knew where things stood when it was the three of us. I was a hetero dude.

But now, I was just fucking confused.

Maybe I could chalk it up to "experimenting" or some shit like that. It happens, right?

I'd be stupid to say I didn't have feelings for Sage. Of course, I did. He'd been my best friend for as long as I could remember. Not a day had gone by where we hadn't been together. He knew everything about me and vice versa. I loved him in ways that best friends love each other.

But there was never any dick touching 'til now.

And that freaked me the fuck out. It changed the definition and dynamics of our friendship. Now it felt murky and fluid with no shape or box to describe it.

If he identified as a bisexual, and he blew me, did that mean I was one now, too?

I'd never given any thought to my sexuality before now. Never figured I'd have a reason to label myself anything other than heterosexual. I was straight, and I liked girls. I loved fucking London. Plain and simple.

On top of which, my parents held very strict religious beliefs that held no room for gay or queer or trans or anything outside of sex and marriage between a man and a woman.

I tugged at the end of my short-cropped hair, not yet buzzed for boot camp regulations. "London, it's messed up. I'm confused, and I need to straighten it out on my own, apart from him. I can't be around him right now."

When I looked down at her face, it about killed me.

"I'm sorry. It's just the way it has to be."

I landed on my knees beside the bed and pulled her into my arms. She rested her chin in the curve of my neck, swallowing her sorrow behind wet tears.

"I'm going to lose you both, aren't I?"

Pulling away so I can see her face, I answered her with a flat-out lie. A refusal to believe that it would come down to that. I had no idea how it would turn out, but still had some sort of hope for the best. Even if I was lying to save both of us.

"*No*. No. Absolutely not. Like I've said before and I'll say it again. I've got you and I will always be here for you."

CHAPTER 35

P resent Day

"YOU EAT THIS STUFF? Turkey bacon...really dude?"

I wave the packet of bacon in my hand, garnering over-the-shoulder looks from London and Sage who have their backs to me at the counter. They are slicing up fruit and making fresh orange juice in Sage's state-of-the-art kitchen as I work at the commercial grade stove.

London pipes in. "I bought it for him. Sage needs to start eating healthier. Don't you, honey?"

From the corner of my eye, I notice the look Sage gives her, sticking his tongue out as she bumps him in the hip with hers playfully.

It reminds me of how things used to be. The fun we had together. How we'd joke and laugh and tease each other unmercifully. We had good times, and this is just a small glimpse into our past life.

I see the meaningful look that passes between them and for a moment I feel like an interloper. And for the most part I am, having been out of the picture while they've been together over the years with stories to share and relive with one another. It creates the tiniest of cracks in my heart.

On the drive here yesterday, London shared a little about her history with Sage and all the ups and downs they've been through while I've been gone. London had returned to Nashville after graduating college and leaving New York, Sage's star had just begun to rise, and he was touring for months at a time. Sometimes she'd get calls from him well into the middle of the night when Sage was lonely, drunk or high, barely discernable, pleading for her to come and join him on tour.

The few times she did, however, they'd get in a fight and she'd return home with a broken heart and a promise to herself that she'd never be that weak again.

And I was never there to ease her pain.

Yet London never gave up on him. Even now, she wants him to get back on the healthy track. To eat better. Drink less. Or better yet, get sober altogether.

Sage speaks to me over his shoulder. "It's times like these that I really wish I had a dog to feed all this healthy foo-foo food to."

London smacks him on the ass with a ladle. "You had a dog once if I recall and you were never at home for him. Poor Ralph had to go live with another family."

"Well, it wasn't my fault. I couldn't take him with me on tour because he farted all the time! No one could be on the tour bus without wearing gas masks."

I chuckle at the story as London giggles and adds to it.

"You blamed that poor dog for his flatulence, but we all know it was probably you or anyone of your bandmates. Ugh, that bus stunk to high heaven. It was dirty socks, beer, and pizza. That's why we need to get you back to eating turkey and lean meats. Your gut needs it."

Sage laughs with mirth as she jabs him in the stomach with a nail. He twists around, grabs her wrists and pulls her into his chest as she giggles with delight.

"You know I'm a sausage guy," he remarks provocatively, with something dark flashing in his maple-brown eyes as he turns toward me and nods. "But maybe Cam will eat your bacon."

The comment is so heavily-laden with innuendo that my body tenses with a mixture of arousal and anger, blood surging in my veins as I watch his hands roll over London's ass, his fingers flexing and tightening and exploring the lush curves there.

My eyes remain fixed on them, unable to shift my gaze, as Sage places a hand on the back of London's head and claims her mouth in a kiss. She squeaks loudly, her posture stiffening before relaxing against him, tilting her head to the side and throwing her arms around him. The ladle hangs loosely in her hand, dangling behind his back, swinging like a pendulum as they move together.

I'm caught between desperately wanting to watch this unfold and needing to get the hell out of Dodge. My heart hammers in my chest, my body yearning to take part. But then my jaw clenches, in the same manner that my fists tighten at my side, and I look away for a moment before returning my gaze to them.

I should use this opportunity to walk away and allow them privacy.

That's what I should do, but I don't.

Sage lifts his chin toward me, covered with a mass of dark stubble, a sated and lecherous grin fixed on his mouth. The same mouth I kissed earlier.

"You remember how good her bacon tastes, don't you Cam?"

He slowly unravels from London's arms, leisurely leaning against the edge of the countertop, fingers spread at the rounded granite ledge. The position makes it very clear how turned on he is from the kiss and PDA.

London feigns disgust, slapping his shoulder. "I am not one of the four food groups, Sage Hendricks."

And then I remember that he slept with some random chick last night, yet here he stands so casually offering up memories of sex with London and kissing her like…like she's just a piece of meat to him. My blood boils in my veins and I can't contain my disdain for his actions.

"That's enough, Sage. It's not funny. You're being a rude asshole and degrading London."

Sage straightens and stalks toward me. As a grown adult male, he's a little taller than average, but nothing compared to my size. I've been in the Air Force for six years and now a full-fledged forest firefighter. I'm massive and could overpower his too-lean frame in a second. I could have him sprawled out on the floor with my hand at his throat in a flash.

And yet I'm slightly intimidated. Or maybe turned on when he wedges up against me with his thigh and chest, pushing me back into the stove.

"My house. My rules. You're the guest. I have the right to be a rude asshole if I want."

I roll my eyes. "Yeah, I noticed. Very mature of you."

Brushing past him, I return to the pancakes to ensure they don't burn, flipping them over and hoping to hide my erection from Sage. The low, baritone timbre of his voice, smoky and arrogant, has a way of wiggling under my skin. It's potent and mercurial as it sends sparks of heat racing through my blood. And it obviously turns me on when he talks dirty and nasty like that.

Sage backs away and resumes what he was doing, as I open the package and start frying the bacon.

"Why are we making breakfast, anyway? Don't you have a shit ton of money for cooks to do this for you?"

My gaze meets his and he shrugs. "Yeah, I normally do have a cook and housekeeper on staff. But I sent them home."

It has me curious about his lavish rock and roll lifestyle. In the last five years since his star has risen, touring with the likes of other alt-country, folk-rock stars like The Avett Brothers, Brandi Carlile, and Ryan Adams. He's been on a plethora of magazine covers, some touting his music-writing genius and crooning voice and beautiful face that have women young and old wanting to drop their panties.

He's also had stories and pictures published of his conquests. Both men and women. It wasn't news to me, but certainly made for titillating headlines when he'd have some young hottie doing the walk of shame outside his hotel or home.

Sage's rock star lifestyle doesn't make me envious but makes me angry for the way he's gotten away with treating London. It pisses me off that he's so cavalier with his sex life with others, flaunting it in front of London who has allowed for that disrespect to go on. My mother raised a southern gentleman and I'd never do that to her. Ever.

You did when you left her.

I shake my head free of the internal smack talk and return to their kitchen PDA. Sage kisses her liked he owns her, like she is his property, when just a few hours earlier he had two other women slipping out of his bedroom and out the front door. Who the hell does that?

I turn the burners off and grab the plate on the counter next to me, filling it up with the bacon and pancakes. A few blueberries for London. Her favorite. My ire grows the more I think about how badly he is disrespecting London.

My London. *Our* London.

"Just like you sent those groupies home this morning before London woke up? *Fucker.*" I grumble the last word quietly to myself.

Sage's brow lifts skyward as we sit down in the dining room adjacent to the kitchen. It's a table that could seat sixteen and I wonder if he has ever hosted a dinner party. Or if it's simply a house to host pool parties for groupies to attend, their sights set on hooking up with Sage Hendricks, lead singer of *Crenshaw*.

"You got something to say, Cam? Just fucking say it."

My nostrils flare and I let loose all of the hostility that's been building all morning and just came to a head when he kissed London.

I glare at him, then my eyes meet London's, her brows furrowed in question. Goddammit, I'd promised myself to keep my anger in check and follow through on my promise to London to get Sage help.

"London doesn't deserve to be treated like some two-bit mistress. She deserves so much better than that."

"Cameron." London howls like she's been scarred by a hot poker.

Sage sniffs, glancing between us both and then landing back on mine.

"Yeah, you don't think I know that? You don't think I've wanted her to be mine alone and vice versa? But here's the kicker, Cam. She's turned down my proposals to marry me three times. And she won't live with me either. I ain't got any other leverage, Cam. So, unless you have any better ideas, why don't you just shut the fuck up? Since you don't know what the fuck you're talking about."

I'm too stunned to say anything as Sage pushes back from the table and stomps off, leaving me to stare over the table at London, speechless and disappointed.

CHAPTER 36

Present Day

I LAY in bed staring at the ceiling, looking for answers that I know aren't there. My mind keeps replaying the events of the day and everything that happened between the three of us.

Once again, I've fucked things up for London. She'd asked me to come with her in hopes of convincing Sage to check into rehab or at least see a therapist. And within less than twelve hours, I've gotten into a heated argument with Sage and been shocked to learn that while I've been out of the picture, Sage had asked London to marry him.

Marry him.

And she declined. Not once, not twice, but three times.

Poor Sage. No wonder he seems so lost and dejected, the woman he loves has rejected his proposals. That fucking hurts for any dude, but when it's someone you've been with your whole life, it takes on a completely different meaning.

After I'd been slapped with that little piece of historical trivia, Sage got a call from his producer, agent, or someone in the music business and he left to attend a meeting. He'd gotten dressed and left the house indicating he'd be back in a few hours, but by the time dinner rolled around, it was still just London and me. Alone. And I was feeling mighty awkward.

She'd been out by the pool most of the day and had remained quiet, obviously not wanting to discuss what happened between her and Sage, so, I didn't pry. But goddammit, I was curious as fuck. I wanted to know why London turned him down like that, even though she admits to loving him. And for what reasons.

Having been in the whole loveless marriage situation myself, I wasn't the foremost expert in the sanctity of vows, touting the benefits of marriage or the expert on being in a committed relationship. Lisa and I were a marriage of convenience for the sake of my son. It wasn't a relationship rooted in love or even respect, sadly.

But London and Sage loved each other. I wasn't justifying his actions, because I still thought the way he handled it and flaunted his sexual conquests in front of London was shady as fuck. He did seem somewhat reluctant about sleeping around with other women when the real woman he wanted to spend his life with kept rejecting him.

After showering and freshening up from her pool time, London and I ate a small meal from Sage's well-stocked fridge. As I pulled out some sandwich items and shut the fridge door, I decided to take the opportunity and ask her what I wanted to know.

"Will you tell me what happened between you two?"

She wrinkled her forehead, her brow furrowed in contemplation. Grabbing a tomato to slice, she sighed.

"It's complicated."

I laughed out loud because honestly, Sage was always complicated.

"That's a given."

I busied myself with piling on meats and cheeses onto the Artisan bread that was available, quietly waiting for her to open up.

"You want a beer?" she asked, dodging my glances.

"Yeah, sure. I'll take one."

Handing me a bottle, she took a swig from her own and swiped at her mouth with the back of her hand.

"I couldn't marry him or give him what he wanted."

I'm surprised by her admission because as an outsider looking in, they were perfect for each other. They loved one another. Knew each other's secrets. Understood each other's quirks. And London didn't care about Sage's stardom, his wealth or his past.

"Seems to me like all he ever wanted was you. Although, I can't say I like his philandering ways, but from the sounds of things, he would give all that up in a heartbeat just to be with you. Seems like he's just doing it to get a reaction from you."

London fidgeted with the beer label and sat down on the kitchen stool.

"Oh Cam, you've always been a little clueless."

Sniffing at her remark, I sat down next to her, running my fingers through my hair that's slowly grown out since my last cut.

Keeping it short and cropped while in the Air Force was a necessity. Now that I'm a smokejumper, it's not a requirement but sure makes things easier.

"Maybe I'm a simple guy, but if you love him and he loves you, then what's the problem?"

She cocked her head to the side, pinching her lips in a tight frown, staring at me like I just rolled in dirt.

"The problem is that there's always been someone else in the picture for both of us, even when he wasn't in the picture," she divulged, as I slowly blinked to catch up. "You can't give your whole heart when you only have half to give."

&

I GRAB my phone from the night table and check the time. A quarter past one a.m. and I'm wide awake.

Figuring I'll go take a piss and maybe get some fresh air, I head out into the hallway in only my unzipped shorts that I'd pulled on for decency sake. As I take a few steps out into the long corridor, I hear quiet whispers.

Actually, it's more than just whispers. It's the sound of heavy breathing and exhales. Moaning and panting.

I stop in my tracks and look at the doors down the hallway. The one to London's room is closed, but Sage's master bedroom door is slightly ajar and a soft light shines from under the doorway.

My first thought is that maybe Sage is watching porn. From the sounds of it, that's an easy assumption.

But it doesn't sound like it's coming from a TV or computer speaker. It sounds live.

Maybe he brought another groupie chick home with him tonight.

None of my business.

I turn toward the bathroom when I come to halt with the one word that would pique my interest enough to investigate what was going on in the bedroom.

His voice is low and smoky.

"London."

I pull in a straining breath.

"Please, baby. I need this tonight."

CHAPTER 37

P resent Day

My own breath and heart rate accelerate a whoosh of blood to my head, creating a crashing wave effect in my ears.

Holy shit, they're fucking. Or at least, getting ready to fuck.

I can't stop my feet from moving me forward any more than I could stop an avalanche down a mountainside. My feet propel me toward the cracked door and like the voyeur I am, I peer in.

Sage sits on the edge of the bed facing the door at an angle, London straddling him as he peppers her neck with kisses. Her hands strum through his thick mess of dark hair, yanking his head in the place she needs his lips.

"I've missed this so much, baby."

She hums with satisfaction, arching her back as his lips move down to her collarbone. London has on a short nightie, flimsy enough to see through in the soft light of the room. The skirt is hiked up so I can see the gentle curves of her ass, one of Sage's hands spread out and cupping her flesh.

He pushes the nightie material up as he explores the skin of her backside. It's smooth and shimmery, the golden tan hidden only by the waves of her hair cascading down.

"*Mmm…I just wish…*"

Sage stops his assault on her neck, tilting his head up to stare at her. I notice the crinkles at the corners of his eyes no longer lined with make-up. At least not tonight.

"What do you wish for, baby?" he urges, as she slowly rocks into his groin.

It's a word that spears me in the heart. Brings me to my knees. Gives me hope and longing so great that I believe in miracles, in fairies and ghosts of the past.

The one word she murmurs has my cock filling with blood, thickening with need.

"Cam."

Perhaps I let out a noise, or maybe it is intuition, but suddenly Sage's eyes peg me and bore into mine. He notices me standing there, my hand over my groin, half naked as I watch them without permission. His gaze heats and burns through me.

He smirks, speaking the words directly to me even when he says to London, "Should we ask him to join us, baby?"

I shake my head, but he crooks a finger behind London's back to beckon me forward. She still has no idea that I stand there, on the precipice of making a monumental decision. My mouth is dry and I'm in need of…*fuck*.

I need them.

Never letting his eyes leave me, he drags his mouth across London's lips, sucking at her, making me yearn for her delicious taste. It kills me to watch and not partake. But it'll hurt me even more not to join in. To take what they're offering.

He wraps a hand around her hair, pulling it back with a hard tug. "Answer me, baby. Tell me how much you want Cam here with us right now. How long you've waited for him to fuck us again. Isn't that what you want? For Cam to fuck your tight pussy and come inside you?"

London grinds on top of Sage's lap, wrapping her legs around his waist. The sound she makes – a soft, sensual mewl – has me taking my first step into the room.

Her head snaps in my direction when she hears my first steps.

Sage chuckles knowingly. "Your wish is my command."

I'm not the same boy I used to be. I'm a man, with life experience, and I no longer hesitate when it comes to something I want. I am savage desire and wild longing and I know what I want now.

Them.

In three short strides, I'm next to the edge of the bed and I fall to my knees in supplication.

Because of my height, my lips are inches from her shoulder and I lift my hands to cup her face, pulling her down to meet me.

"London…I need you," I plead, my voice raw with hunger. And then I look to Sage, who has dropped his hands behind him on the bed to lounge in a lazy as fuck position. "Can I have her?"

His lips curl in sinful delight, a smile worthy of the devil himself. It's as if I'm making a deal for my soul.

But I already gave up my heart and soul ten years ago. No sense trying to win them back now.

Sage shrugs with one shoulder and cocks his head. "I don't know. She's not mine to give. You'll have to ask her."

I nod like a kid who's been asked if he wants a present from Santa. My head snaps back toward London.

"May I?"

London's smile vanishes as she looks between Sage and me, a myriad of questions and desire darkening her eyes.

She lays a hand against Sage's rough jawline, and the other on my cheek. She slowly leans over to place a gentle kiss on my lips. It's soft and perfect. A consent. An agreement. A desire.

Before she turns to do the same to Sage, she stares into my eyes, reading something there.

"On one condition."

I will give her anything and everything. Whatever she wants. Just to be here with them tonight. She bites the corner of her lip. I'm fascinated with her tantalizing mouth as I stare between her mouth and down into the V of her nightie, noticing the peaks of her nipples that poke through, eliciting a thrill of excitement to my cock. My hand reaches out unbidden, my fingernails scoring over the tight bud.

"Anything. Name it."
She doesn't give me an immediate answer but palms her hand over mine to massage her breast, the silk of the material slipping down to expose the nipple. My mouth waters to taste it.

"Let him touch you, Cam. I want to watch."

Sage and I both let out simultaneous curses.

"Oh fuck," I say.

"Fuck me." Sage sits up, no longer lazy and carefree, and grabs for London's face, claiming her kiss with a fiery passion and heat. I hear him speak something against her mouth between kisses and he murmurs, *"Thank you."*

I drop back to sit on my heels, a little shell shocked by her request.

The last time I let Sage touch me, it ended our friendship.

It ruined everything.

Maybe this is what redemption looks like. Forgiveness of my sins.

Giving in and giving up the ghost of past mistakes.

Coming to the realization that life is about letting go of guilt and anger and learning to love in any shape and form to find fulfillment.

CHAPTER 38

Present Day

I DIDN'T NEED to give her a verbal answer. I simply stood up and curled over their bodies so they both fell to the bed in a heap.

Our hands and lips are everywhere all at once. I am so lost in them that I don't know who is touching or kissing who.

London rolls off Sage's lap and lays down on the bed, sandwiched between us, as we lay on our sides. I drag a finger at the bottom edge of her silk shift and slowly trail it up over the flat of her belly, nudging the material past her full breasts. I groan with admiration and reverence as London's feminine curves are exposed to me. To us.

"You may have the honors," Sage offers, winking at me seductively. "I'll just busy myself down here."

He slips down and off the bed, pulling London's panties with him and flings them aside. Positioning myself so I have more leverage, I lean over and lap at her nipple. It has been so long since I've tasted her peaches and cream skin. She'd certainly filled out since our teens, where she'd once been smaller and less than a handful.

Her proportions are now more generous, offering me a banquet of flesh to feast upon. I plump at her lush, firm tits, flicking and circling my tongue around the smooth, taut nipple.

I'd forgotten how sexy it was to make London squirm under our ministrations. It only heightens the intensity with Sage's participation. Based on London's reaction to our touches, she appears to be in heaven, enjoying the attention we are lavishing on different areas of her body.

London's hand lands on top of my head, grabbing hold of the hair, her grip inciting an almost painful pleasure. She reaches her other hand for Sage, her fingers sliding through his hair, as the wet sounds of his sucking at her delectable center fill the room.

"Just like that," London sighs, her body shifting and flexing underneath my mouth. "Oooh yes…you both feel so good."

My cock strains violently with the need to be touched, as I grind into her bare thigh. I need so badly to be inside London's tight pussy again. I feel just like that high school kid the first time we were together when I stripped her of her virginity. I barely made it three minutes before exploding gloriously inside her tightness. It was one of the best nights of my entire life.

Sage must notice that I'm getting punchy. He stops eating London and lifts his head.

"Getting a little antsy there, Cam?" His gives a lusty chuckle, nodding at my thrusting motion into the bed. "I'm sure London'd be happy to help you out. Unless…"

Sage stands, pushing his shorts to the floor, his entire body now plainly visible. My eyes scan the work of art scattered across his torso and arms. He's like a living, breathing Picasso painting; vibrant and colorful. I yearn to touch his inked skin.

When our eyes connect, I see it there. I see the longing and the need. All the emotion that I tried to ignore all those years ago and pushed away for fear of being labeled something I felt wasn't me.

But now, with time and experience, I realize it doesn't matter. Labels mean nothing. It's people that matter. It's Sage that matters. Who matters to me.

"Unless what?" I urge, my eyes remaining on him while I nibble at London's ear.

I can feel her smile grow, her cheeks expanding against my lips.

She crooks a finger at Sage, beckoning him back down to the bed.

"*Unless* he gives me what I want."

I plead ignorant, just to hear her say it. "And what's that, London?"

She points first to Sage and then to me. "I want to watch you two together."

I shouldn't be excited by this prospect. But I am. I didn't think my cock could get any harder, but it does. It thickens exponentially, and I have to pinch the base hard to keep from coming. Because no matter how hard I tried to forget what happened with Sage all those years ago – my one and only time with a dude – my dick remembers it quite well. It remembers the intensity of that orgasm brought on by Sage's wickedly talented mouth and tongue.

Sage cocks his brow. "Would you like to watch Cam fuck my mouth, baby? Watch me suck him back so far that he's shooting and seeing stars?"

She nods her head with a coy grin, her fingers dancing over her own nipple.

"*No.*"

My voice is raspy and gruff, but adamant, and their eyes pop wide open with shock.

And then I clarify. "I owe Sage. I need to return the favor from a long time ago."

The expression on both of their faces is like a cartoon animation – almost comical - as they process what I've just said. But my actions brook no debate, as I slide off the edge of the bed and position myself over Sage, who's now laying on his back, his surprised shock now turned into a sexual consent by the look on his face.

London shifts to a sitting position and Sage places his hands behind his head.

Suddenly, the nerves jumble together in my stomach like a highway loop in LA. Tangled up in a weaved mess.

"You'll have to forgive my lack of finesse," I admit, heaving a sigh and inhaling a deep breath.

"Do your worst and it'll still be the best thing I ever had."

The tone of his voice – almost reverence – along with the softening of his brown sugar eyes, calms my nerves. I reach for his cock, grasping it in my palm, and take my first lick.

The sounds that our three groans make is a mix of pure lust and pleasure. I may not have ever done this to anyone else before, but I know what I like. It's pretty simple to send a guy to the moon and back when you have his dick in your hands and mouth.

Swirling my tongue around the tip of Sage's cock, I get my first taste of the salty beads of his pre-come. It shoots waves of tension into my own balls – his heady taste. And then I see movement from London out of the corner of my eye. Her fingers are poised at her wet entrance, and as she pushes a finger inside her wet cunt, I swallow Sage to the back of my throat.

Never in a million years would I have ever considered doing this. Giving a guy head. But it's not just any guy. It's Sage.

I've never been attracted to another guy. Never had the connection with anyone strong enough to make me want to do this.

But with Sage and London, it just feels natural. There's no question in my mind that the three of us make sense together.

It only took me ten years to get to this place again.

Ten years, countless mistakes, a failed marriage, losing my grip on life and who I was and feeling unworthy and not good enough for anyone.

But here we are, rediscovering each other once again.

And finding myself in the process.

CHAPTER 39

P resent Day

"Cam," Sage murmurs softly as he lays his head back onto the bed. A sexy smile tips the corners of his mouth as he turns his head to the side and his eyes connect with mine. He seems at a loss for words, so I help him out.

"Not bad for a beginner?"

He chuckles and shakes his head. "Nah, man. It was fucking fantastic."

We both grin like giddy fucking teenagers, as a very naked London crawls up next to us. From the sounds that she made as she fingered herself, she'd gotten herself off just before Sage let go of his own release. I'd chosen at the last minute not to swallow and let him come over my hand and his belly. I figured he'd forgive me since it was my first time giving head.

His praise over the experience sends a thrill through my body and into my still aching, full cock.

London traces the muscles of my back, swirling around in an infinity pattern until her hands slides below my belly, her nails scraping through the coarse hair that leads to my erection. I suck in a large gulp of air when her fingers slip around my length, squeezing me and stroking me slowly.

Her voice is wispy. "Remember our first time, Cam?"

I stand at the edge of the bed looking her over. She's positioned on her back laid out across the bed, as Sage went to clean up in the bathroom. She spreads her legs and reaches for my cock, bringing the tip to her entrance. She glides my length through her wet folds and I growl with hedonistic pleasure, tipping my head back and closing my eyes.

The words are like gravel from my throat. "I remember every-thing, London. The way your tight pussy squeezed me as I thrust inside you. Fuck, it was heaven."

She squirms, brushing our pelvises together and the head of my cock somehow manages to find its ways inside her cunt. Just barely enough to feel how warm and wet she is, but I do, and it feels fucking marvelous.

London gazes up at me impishly, almost shyly. "Would you consider going bare? I have an IUD. I want to…but only if you're safe and you're okay with it."

The wires in my brain seem to crisscross and go haywire for a second. Fucking London bare without a condom is a lifelong dream. After I found out Lisa had been fucking around on me, I got tested for everything.

"Oh shit, baby. Yeah, I want that. And I'm good. Was tested recently."

She nods, confirming our decision. "Good."

I lean over, my hands at the insides of her thighs and press her back against the bed, pushing inside.

"Oh fuck."

It's overwhelming. The heat. The pleasure.

I think the curse word comes from my mouth, but instead, it's Sage's voice, who has returned to the room just as I enter London's body. He stands behind me, his half-hard dick coming back to life, and lays a hand at my lower back. I tense for only a second, his calloused hands foreign to my skin.

"You two have always looked so fucking sexy together. Especially when you're fucking. So perfect. It gets me so hard."

Sage rolls his hand over the curve of my ass. His touch, rough and firm, sends shivers up my spine and his hoarse voice goes directly to my cock.

"Mmm…what I could do to this ass." He snickers when my head snaps to the side, my mouth gaping open. He just grins. "Well, maybe not tonight."

Nodding my head, I turn my attention back to London and stare down into her eyes, which are glazed over from the attention my cock is giving her pussy – thrusting in and out in a timed rhythm. Her inner walls stroke and choke my dick with every entry and withdrawal.

"Come here, Sage. Let us see how hard you are again."

London crooks her finger at Sage, her other arm slung around my waist, gripping my flesh tightly. Just as tightly as her cunt sucks my cock inside her so deep that I'm practically hitting her womb.

I close my eyes briefly, enjoying the incredible sensation of being inside her and realizing that I'm getting closer and closer to climax. The thought of coming inside London without a barrier sends lightning bolts of pleasure through my blood.

Sage kneels at London's side, leaning down to massage a breast and then lick her nipple as she arches into his mouth. The movement has her shifting, and I slip my hands underneath her ass, lifting her up to gain better leverage for us all.

London agrees with the position and the deeper intensity with a keening wail when I hit a spot inside that has her clenching her inner walls around me.

I continue pumping, my own breaths and groans blurring my vision the closer and closer I get to letting go. But I want to make sure London gets there first.

"Sage," I order. "Make our girl come."

A flash of recollection floods my memory of the first time we were all together and the way we took turns making each other feel good. Realizing at the time that London was ours. She'd always been ours. As friends and then lovers. A woman we craved and loved and shared together. Sage and me.

The difference between now and then is that before, while Sage called the shots, I steered clear of any potential male on male interaction. It was strictly hetero sex.

But now?

After letting go of my inhibitions and ideas of what love should look like and just give in to my desires, it's opened me up to new and incredible experiences with Sage.

His reply has my cock growing even bigger and harder inside London.

"Yes, sir."

His hand brushes against the hair above my groin as he slides a finger between London's wet lips. I look down at the place that we're connected – me, Sage and London - and I'm jolted with an unfamiliar notion. One I haven't felt since the last time we were together like this.

Home. I'm home.

Sage wedges another finger inside, and I can feel it rub against my cock. I hiss out an explicative, the pleasure so incredible and foreign, I'm surely going to come.

"Oh shit, I'm getting close. Keep doing that." My words are choppy at best as I try to drag in air to my depleted lungs.

Sage continues to pump and slide his finger in and out of London's pussy, jamming it against my foreskin and the sensitive spot under my crown that has me seeing stars.

I know Sage has already orgasmed, but I have a selfish need for him to come again. The three of us coming together would be epic.

"Can you take him in your mouth, London?"

She smiles. "I like that idea."

London wraps a hand around Sage's cock and brings him to her open mouth, sucking him in.

Although her supine position doesn't allow her the best access, her head against the mattress and her ass in my hands off the bed, I can still see the swallowing motion of her throat and based on the vocal reaction from Sage, it must feel fucking spectacular.

With one hand in her pussy, he cradles London head with the other to give her further leverage. When she moans around his cock, I can feel it in mine from the vibrations making their way down her body.

London's pussy clenches around my cock and I know the minute she's coming.

As if a chain reaction is set off from the explosion inside her body, her limbs trembling and tightening from the intense waves of pleasure, both Sage and I become completely lost in the sensations. Or at least, I do.

Sage removes his fingers and is about to swing his arm away when I grab his wrist, pulling his hand to my mouth, slipping his fingers along my tongue and then clamping around him, sucking them in deeply.

The taste and essence of London and the salty taste of Sage's skin is all I need to push me over the edge.

The orgasm bursts unrestrained from the bottom of my toes up through my spine and back down again.

"I'm coming…fuck, I'm coming." I throw my head back and shout.

Everything I have in me is released inside London's pussy, as I come, and come, and come until I've emptied myself inside her.

She shutters again as she moans around Sage's cock. His head tilts forward and he releases a deep, gruff noise that sounds like a wolf howling at the midnight moon.

I pull out of London, the remnants of my orgasm spilling out and filling me with a deep male pride. Sage carefully dislodges from London's mouth and the look on his face says he's been thoroughly pleased.

And London.

London's golden hair fans out across the bed, her face and neck flushed from her own climaxes and the heat we made together.

She looks like a goddess.

A sated and well-used, goddamn beautiful goddess.

Our goddess. Our queen.

CHAPTER 40

P resent Day

"WHEN DO you go out on tour again?" I ask, taking a sip of hot coffee.

The three of us sit outside on the patio watching the sun rise over the hills and valleys of Nashville, coffees in hand. We've been up for the last thirty minutes, still unshowered with freshly rumpled bedhead from the night before.

The night before. Holy hell was that insane.

Best night of my life.

It's ironic to think that I've experienced both the worst night and the best nights of my life with London and Sage at my side.

Last night, while incredible and memorable, will be a fleeting memory all too soon. Not something meant to last before we all go back to our normal lives. Sage had mentioned earlier that he's about to embark on a 15-city U.S. tour and London will return to her job as a social worker and I'll go back to fighting forest fires.

For obvious reasons, the summer months are the worst and require nearly all my time and effort. When called upon, smoke-jumpers can be away from home between two-days or two months, depending on the severity of the fires. I've been assigned outside of Tennessee to assist in other national fires several times in the last four years, especially in the west. I've been to Montana, Colorado, and California several times, serving with my brothers and fellow smokejumpers to preserve our natural resources.

We'll be going our separate directions in the next 24-hours and that thought grips me in the heart like a vice.

Sage runs a hand through his dark, thick hair, the edges long enough to cover the nape of his neck.

"I have a show on Tuesday night in Philadelphia, then we tour around the east coast, down to Florida, and into Texas, I think."

London makes a noise that encompasses both a sadness and a wistfulness, reaching to entwine her fingers through Sage's. She peers up through her lashes and meets my gaze with a look of meaningful recognition to remind me of the reasons we came here in the first place.

Bending down, I place my elbows on my knees, cupping my chin in my hand.

"Sage, I know touring can't be easy. Long hours. Endless nights. Probably some boredom. Bad influences." I quirk an eyebrow at him in question, hoping he understands where I'm heading with my inquisition.

He shrugs noncommittally. "Yeah, sure. I guess."

I lock eyes with London's who stares me down with a pleading look. I know she wants me to say something more but it's outside my comfort level. I've had opportunities to talk to firefighters in my crew about dealing with the devastating PTSD effects that come with losing their partners and crew members, but never about this with Sage.

In fact, there's a lot of emotional baggage we've just swept under the rug during this impromptu weekend together. Things we really should clear the air about in the future. But one thing at a time.

"Okay, man. I'm not gonna beat around the bush here. Time's short and I want to get it out in the open. We think you need some professional help."

Sage's eyes go wide and he snaps his head toward London, untethering his hand from hers and jumping to his feet.

Taking two steps forward, he swings back around, his ire directed at London.

"So that's what this visit is about? You bullied him into coming and intervening on your behalf?"

I stand up, ready to defend London's actions, but she beats me to it.

London reaches out with both hands toward Sage unconcerned with his hostility and anger. She wraps her arms around his waist and presses her head against his chest. I see him visibly relax, his body turning from stone into a mass of whipped butter.

She whispers softly against his shoulder. "Sage, we love you. And I'm scared for you long-term."

He straightens his shoulders. "I've told you before, London. I'm fine. There's nothing to worry about."

I interrupt. "Then now's the best time to get some help and support, while things are fine and you're not dealing with all the pressure of the road. That's all we want."

Sage glares at me over the top of London's head. "What the fuck would you know about the pressures of the road? And why suddenly are you so concerned over my well-being,"- he uses air quotes - "when you haven't been around in ten years? You just wanted to get back into London's pants and this was the best way to do it, wasn't it? Through me. Per the usual."

If he'd had punched me with a fist in the face, it wouldn't have hurt as much as his words did. Or hit the mark so square on. I haven't been around and have no business giving him advice on his life when I have made a fucking mess of my own. And because of my coward tendencies, I probably wouldn't have slept with London had it not been made easier due to Sage's presence and his participation.

But he is wrong about me not understanding the road. I've been there – in the Air Force when I was out on missions for long periods of time, leaving Taylor and Lisa on their own. Having him grow up from baby to toddler to little boy all the while I was gone. It sucked.

My tone is even and subdued. "You're wrong about one thing. I *do* know what it's like to be gone. I was away from my son so often that he'd cry when I came home because he didn't recognize me. It was also one of the reasons my marriage ended. I've lost men on my crew from wildfires that took their life without any thought to what they were leaving behind. The same holds true for addictions, bro. If you don't do something to stem the fires, it'll blaze out of control, killing everything in its path."

As if the universe wants to ensure it plays a part in the conclusion of this reunion, my phone alert blares from inside my jeans pocket.

It stops the conversation between the three of us as I pull out the bat-phone, as my son calls it, and look at the incoming message.

Alert: All smokejumpers on deck. Smoky Mountain Forest Fire in progress. Uncontained. Evacuations required. Report to base within two hours.

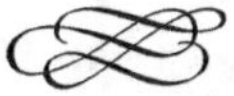

CHAPTER 41

P resent Day

"CAM, WHAT'S WRONG?" London asks, fear in her voice as she reads me with a wide-eyed expression.

I type in my text reply to my Commanding Officer, Luke Trenley, and check the time on my phone.

"I've got to head out to work. There's a large wildfire in progress that we need to contain."

London steps up in front of me, reaching her arms around my neck, stepping up on her tiptoes to get closer.

"What about Taylor?"

"I'll need to let my mom know and ask her to drop him off with Lisa. I'm not going to have time to go home to get him."

"Do you need me to pick him up and drop him off?"

I scoff and shake my head. "Lisa would blow a fucking gasket if you showed up with our son. She's already jealous enough as it is and if she met you now…"

There was a time long ago when I had first met Lisa that I spoke about Sage and London all the time, and shared with her how much I missed them. She'd wigged out on me, convinced that I didn't love her and that I was still in love with London. I'd let it slide then because she'd been six months pregnant at the time with the crazy pregnancy hormones raging through her head.

But after Taylor was born, it got even worse. She accused me all the time of cheating on her, even though I never laid another finger or even a roaming eye on another woman.

But I know deep in bones that Lisa would remember London and would take issue with her bringing our son back home to her.

"Nah, I got it. But thank you. I appreciate it. But maybe Sage can drive you home?" I look behind London at Sage, who nods his head.

"No problem at all. Go get your stuff and go do your thing. We can talk when you get back."

Our eyes connect, and something passes through them that I can't quite comprehend. His gaze clouds over and he steps into my space. We're inches apart, his head only an inch shorter than mine as he leans in, his hands cupping my jawline.

"Be careful. I want to see you after my tour."

I'm stunned into silence when his lips claim mine. He sucks my bottom lip into his, tugging it, and then biting it, before I feel his tongue brush along the seam as I automatically open for him.

The kiss isn't long but packs a wallop. My knees buckle when he pulls away, leaving me disoriented and slightly fuzzy in my brain.

"What was that for?" I ask, my voice raspy with arousal.

"I've wanted to kiss you like that for years, but I was scared you'd fucking hit me. I guess you could call it a Cam bucket list item."

I chuckle. "Consider it marked off."

Sage swats my ass and winks. "That ass of yours is on the list, too. Just so you know."

I choke out a cough, swinging my backpack over my shoulder and turning toward London.

London's broad smile comes into view as she moves in close, encircling us in her open arms.

"Whatever happens," she says, staring up at us both, her green eyes flickering with light. "I'm so glad we had last night. It just reaffirms the feelings I've always had for you both."

She reaches up and kisses Sage, long and deep. My cock jumps and demands attention.

And when she finishes, she turns to me, wrapping me in her arms.

"I want you to come back to me in one piece. I need more of what we had together last night." She looks between me and Sage for confirmation, which we both give her in the form of a smile from me and an eyebrow raise from Sage.

"Cam, do you know the reason London gave me each time she turned down my proposals?" Sage asks, turning to look out the window to avoid my direct eye contact.

"No, what was that?"

He turns back and stares between us and a remorseful smile appears on his lips. "You. You were the reason, Cam. She said she couldn't marry me because it wasn't fair to either one of us. She loved both you and me. And she also knew I was in love with you, too. We were only two-thirds whole without you."

I nod, not surprised by the confession. I know it's true with everything in my being.

As if the world is on fire and spinning out of control, I lean in and kiss him again, and then kiss London. I need their love as the forcefield around me to protect me from all the shit the world has thrown my way. And the fire that rages in and around me.

"I love you both so much. I never stopped," I murmur against London's lips and then turn to look longing at Sage.

We say our goodbyes and I agree to call them once I've returned home.

CHAPTER 42

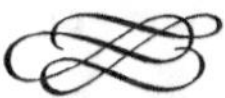

The smoke is thick.

It surrounds me.

Chokes me.

Blinds me.

I've been cut off from the rest of my crew except for Mullins, who stumbles behind me, as we try to outrun this thing. It's a flash of an inferno that rages like an angry monster – a fire-breathing dragon that wants revenge.

I drop to the ground and begin digging the trench that I've taught many recruits after me to use in situations like this. When you're surrounded and trapped, this is how you hope to keep yourself safe. Protect yourself from the harsh, hot death of the blaze.

I note my coordinates and contact the lead dispatch on the team.

"Get down, Mullins. Help is on the way."

I lay down and close my eyes, praying for that to be true – the bleak reality that we may not be rescued a severe threat to our lives.

My life flashes before me as the heat grows so hot that the hair on my arms singe.

My last thoughts are of Taylor, Sage and London. Crying. Saying goodbyes. Begging me not to go, but if I must, to come back to them.

I told them I loved them. It was all I had to give.

And then I inhale my final breath.

PART III

Sage

CHAPTER 43

P resent

I WAS eighteen when I wrote my first hit single from the inside of a jail cell.

It didn't become a hit until years later after I was released on parole. After I'd served my three-year sentence for voluntary manslaughter for killing my father.

As you can imagine, careers and jobs are slim pickins' when you're a convicted felon, and there's not much opportunity for a guy like me. Born and raised in a small-town, a high school diploma, and no living family to speak of.

With no one and nobody to go back to, I moved to Nashville and did what I had always dreamed about doing before my shitty life came to a screeching halt and I was imprisoned. I formed a band.

The fact that I became a famous alt-country singer after I was paroled is a gigantic what-the-fuck moment and something I'm still scratching my head about. I never dreamt I'd become an award-winning, highly sought-after musician. My dreams were never that big.

The crazy ups and downs of my roller coaster life could easily fill ten amusement parks. The lowest point being my years in prison.

Getting out and starting over, without London and Cam, definitely another low.

But the highs of stardom, of being a revered celebrity and musician, is pretty fucking high.

As was the unexpected opportunity I recently had to spend a weekend with London and Cam.

For once in my life, things seemed to finally be turning around for me, giving me hope for something good to last. Something that will endure and make me feel whole. Lord knows I'd give up this crazy, chaotic rock-and-roll lifestyle in a heartbeat if I could spend the rest of my life with Cam and London. To be with them in the manner in which I've always wanted. To love them like a family – a forever home within my heart.

"Yo, Sage. We gotta roll, man. Bus leaves in five minutes and you need to get your ass on it."

I heave a sigh and stamp out my cigarette butt on the cement with the heel of my boot. My tour manager, Cliff, steps down off the tour bus and gives me the hurry the fuck up sign with a flick of his wrist. He's a good man and has been with me since I started on this crazy-ass journey. He keeps me on a short leash when we're on tour, which is probably a wise thing to do. And possibly something London tapped him to do.

The exhaust from the retro-fitted bus that has my band's name in big bold print across the side filters through my nostrils and a cough escapes my throat. I hesitate, glancing sideways in both directions, wishing for a miracle. Hoping to see the two people I love – the two people I've given my heart to - walking toward me.

No such luck.

They don't love you like that anymore.

I check the phone I've been clutching in my hand for the last hour to see if I've missed any notifications from either Cam or London. Maybe they're simply stuck in traffic or running late and will be arriving any minute?

It was a long shot to invite them to come on tour with me. But after the incredible reunion and weekend we spent together last week, I couldn't bear to say goodbye for the next two months. My lonely and reckless heart needs them by my side.

Just thinking back on our night together – the sex, the laughter, the memories – and the possibility of having more of that has my dick perking up in an uncomfortable manner. It was a night that my dreams were made of, with the two most important people in my life.

I stare off, unseeing, at the car that pulls up in front of me. While it's a long-shot that it's either Cam or London, my heart hammers loudly in my chest, growing tight with anticipation that they'll step out together and into my arms.

But I'm left disappointed when Deg, my drummer, hops out of the back, dragging me from my wistful thoughts. He stumbles out, throwing a wave in the air at his girlfriend, Madeline. Ducking down, I peer into the car, realizing I'm wrong. It's not Maddie. It's an entirely different chick.

I shake my head, watching as he staggers toward me, dripping in leather and not much else, a pair of drumsticks shoved in the waistband. Makes me queasy to consider what else may have been stuffed down there. My body shivers unbidden.

"Sage, you're here on time, man. That's a first." He gives me a one-armed bro-hug, smelling of booze and weed, his voice hoarse from too much whiskey.

Lifting my eyebrows, I pin him with a snarly smile. "I think you have me confused with *yourself*, dude. And who the hell was that?"

Deg shrugs with a quick look over his shoulder. "Dana? Danni? Deena? I don't know man, not a clue. You know how it is. Me and Maddie broke up so I'm a free man now.. You of all people should know how it is since you're the king of snatch, bro."

He's not wrong there.

I've had a pretty wild past and been notorious for my conquests with groupies, both men and women. While I made it look like I was having fun, it was really only a way to block out my past. To shut down those memories with sex, booze and drugs was the only way I could survive.

Inside my heart, I only ever wanted Cam and London.

But the boy I loved hated me and left me without a single good-bye. I hadn't heard from him in over ten years until recently.

And the girl. London kept me dangling on a string, with all the pull and leverage to do so. She never let me keep her close and gave me ultimatums that I couldn't abide by; I couldn't be who she needed me to be.

I hated myself for that. If I could've been the man she needed, I would've pulled out all the stops.

But we both knew that wasn't possible.

I wasn't enough for her.

She needed Cam, too.

Regardless of that tear in the fabric of our relationship and my unforgivable behaviors, London would still come every time I called. Anytime I needed her loving arms and her warm body to make things right again. No matter where I was in the world – and I've been everywhere – she's been just a phone call, a text message, and a Skype chat away.

But she'd never stay long, claiming her job and life demanded her attention back home. And her answer was always "*No*" to my proposals.

We both know I never deserved her love. This was just the universe's way of righting that fact. There is no doubt that London is my grace and salvation, always quick to save me when I've been down and lonely and needing rescue.

Lord knows she should've left me long ago.

Just like Cam did.

He left me the moment I was locked away and my freedom was taken away. She should've hightailed it out of my pathetic life, too, while I wasted away in that jail cell for three years.

Yet, she never truly let go.

Just like a kite on a string, she kept hold, even through the windiest and harshest years of my life. London never strayed far but lived a separate life without me, while I was on the road, living my pathetic excuse of a rock star life on the road.

I shrug and chuckle at Deg's comment. "Just make sure to make good life choices and wrap it before you tap it."

Deg laughs loudly at my advice and swings his thick, beefy arm around me as we walk side-by-side toward the bus, where our other bandmates and tour personnel await our arrival. I inhale a deep breath before stepping on, the anxiety steeping inside the bowels of my stomach. Scratching and clawing to get out.

It happens every time I go on tour. Being on this bus affects me in the way only being locked inside four walls can do. The only difference between the bus and prison is that I'm not surrounded by felons when I'm on tour.

The similarity, however, is that I don't own my life when I'm confined to this bus – just like I was without my freedom in prison. When on tour, I'm told where and when to go, how to get there, and what I'm supposed to do when I'm there. The next two months will be a test to my strength and willpower.

And the only thing I have to look forward to is the moment I can have both London and Cam back in my arms.

CHAPTER 44

P ast

The cell door clanged behind me with a loud metallic *thud* as I land on my ass on the barren and cold cement floor, shivering out of fear and dread.

Everything is cold and metal in this fucking god-awful place. I'd been led to believe as a child that Hell was fiery and hot, but it's not. It looks, feels and smells just like this jail cell. It's a stench of bodies – still living, but dead on the inside - along with my butchered heart. It used to beat with the warmth of love and blood, and now it only serves as a reminder of everything I've lost.

Everything that happened to me in the past six months was akin to living out a nightmare.

A nightmare that never goes away.

I'm gripped with sadness over what my life has become. Eighteen years old looking at three years in this god-forsaken place.

Why did this happen to me? What did I do to the universe to make her hate me so much? To be given a childhood so fraught with abuse and neglect and shame that it's a touchstone of my future, branding me with a bleak existence. Why was I born into a family where hatred was as prevalent as the booze and pills that littered the home I lived in?

The night I accidentally killed my dad still feels surreal. As if I'm looking through a pair of 3-D VR goggles and my life is shown in slow-moving, distorted animation. Not real, just a version of reality.

There was no disputing what I did. I murdered my father.

I watched him bleed out and take his final breath, all while he stared up at me with unseeing eyes. But his death wasn't in cold-blood. It wasn't premeditated or planned, even though I'd wished him dead too many times to count throughout my childhood.

It was an accident, plain and simple. But in the state of Tennessee, it's still manslaughter, a Class D or E felony. The question is whether my attorney can get the charges dropped down to a lesser sentence, not that a jury would ever let me off the hook. I only hope I can plead to the lesser crime of criminally negligent homicide, involuntary manslaughter instead of first-degree.

Either way, whether it's reckless homicide or criminally negligent homicide, I'd still be facing hard time with a two-to-twelve-year prison sentence.

While my two best friends would begin their adult lives in college and the military, becoming model citizens, I'd be locked away, chains around my hands and shackles at my feet, as well as my soul.

I hung my head in my hands, wallowing in self-pity over the circumstances that led up to this pitiful existence. I put myself in this position by being stupid. By making the wrong choice.

Prom night was supposed to end with me wrapped up in Cam and London's arms – our bodies melding together in perfect harmony. Instead, I ended up being handcuffed and tossed in jail.

That night and the decisions I made, will haunt me forever.

I was supposed to go directly to the hotel after work to meet Cam and London, but I had to run back home to get my clothes and money. I should've brought everything with me when I left for work that day, but I was in hurry and my head was in the clouds, thinking about what it would be like that night. Would Cam let me touch him like I'd been dying to do? Would I let him fuck me while London watched? There were so many possibilities, and my imagination was full of all of them.

None of that happened, though, because the moment I got home and got a whiff of the wretched stench of my father, I knew I wasn't going.

I found the old man in my room, wildly ransacking and turning it inside out and upside down in search of my money. The hard-earned, "get me the fuck out of Dodge" savings that I was going to use right after graduation. He was yelling and screaming at me in a way I'd never heard before. He'd gone mad.

There was no way in hell I'd even give him a wooden-nickel from my savings. I didn't owe that fucker a goddamn red cent. I wasn't stupid enough to hide my money anywhere in that house. I'd been very careful over the years, knowing something like this was bound to happen one day, so I'd hid it in old lady Manoff's backyard. She paid me to mow her lawn once a week since I was thirteen and I kept the money in a box underneath a loose floorboard in the shed where she stored her lawn equipment.

Needless to say, it didn't go over well with my dad when I called him stupid.

"What'd you call me, boy? You're a worthless piece of shit." He stumbled back on drunken legs, catching himself with an unsteady hand against the wall, spittle drooling across his chin.

Merle Hendricks was once again wasted. An addict who'd lost everything when his wife, my mom, died. The way he saw things, it was all my fault. Her body wouldn't have given out like it did had she never gotten pregnant with me. I was the constant reminder every time he looked at me of how shitty his life had become.

I scoffed, sneering at my dad. "Apple doesn't fall far from the tree, then, I guess."

Stepping back to keep my distance, I crossed my arms defensively, eying his movements carefully, puffing out my solid chest appear more intimidating, like someone he shouldn't fuck with. Merle was known to fly off the handle without cause and backhand me on more than one occasion.

It was then that I saw his half-lidded eyes track across the floor to the corner of the room where I had a baseball bat and my guitar. *My beloved guitar.*

The look in his eyes told me exactly what he was thinking.

"No," I shouted, lurching across the bed and wailing on him, just as he picked up my guitar. "Don't you fuckin' touch that."

My guitar wasn't just an instrument. It held sentimental value. It was the only thing I owned that was mine and had nothing to do with my dad. I got it for my fifteenth birthday, bought and paid for with the birthday money that London's mom gave me. It meant everything to me and I loved making music with it, hearing the chords chime and feeling the strings vibrate under my fingertips. It was an escape from reality when I wrote and played my music on that guitar.

I shoved my dad out of the way, grabbing the guitar neck and swinging it out of his grasp. That's when he tackled me headfirst in my stomach, like a line-backer on the football field. He charged me, sending me reeling back on my ass, the guitar flying from my hands and dropping to the floor with a harmonic *thud*.

I scrambled to get up and gain my footing, but he threw a few quick punches, hitting me in the kidney and jaw. It had been a while since he'd beat me up, mostly because I'd grown taller and stronger than him over the previous year. He was a chickenshit and coward and knew he was outweighed by his opponent.

But whatever he was on that night – a cocktail of booze and drugs – made him feel invincible and powerful, so he'd gotten the surprise attack on me and all I could do was defend myself by holding my hands up to cover my face.

That didn't stop me from kicking, though. I shot my foot out into his groin and he fell backwards, giving me just enough time to jump to my feet. All I wanted to do was get the hell out of there and leave him to pass out and sober up.

I turned toward the door and was almost across the threshold with guitar in hand when something hard and solid connected to my side. The sounds of shattering bone stunned us both, as my hand dropped the instrument and clutched at my ribs. I stared at him with shocked, wide eyes. Dangling in his hand at his side was the baseball bat, his own blood-shot eyes blinking in confusion over what he'd done. Neither of us could believe

he just pummeled me with the bat. That was a new low
for him.

"I think you broke my ribs, you fucking asshole," I shouted
loudly, gritting through clenched teeth as I doubled over, my bent
arm wrapped around the pain, knowing I'd need to go to the
hospital. "Get the fuck out of my room, now!"

For a second, I thought he'd comply. The bat hung limply from
his hand, ready to drop to the floor in defeat. But just as fast, the
fury and hatred that simmered inside him always boiled over and
his eyes grew dark as Brazilian coffee. They became dark with
rage, as he fixed his sights on me, lifting the bat to take aim.

My bent arm instinctively covered my face as he swung,
connecting with my arm. I heard the bones splintering underneath the weight of the wood.

Somehow summoning enough strength, I moved out of the way
and dodged the next blow. Gaining my balance, I charged hard
and barreled into my dad's body.

His head whipped backwards, his eyes bulging out in drunk
surprise that I'd fight back. The fucker didn't know me at all if
he didn't think I'd stand my ground. He staggered back, falling
over and hitting the base of his head on the corner of the
nightstand.

Blood leaked out from behind him, dripping down the cheap
Ikea particle board and onto the carpeted floor. Confusion
grabbed hold as I landed on my knees, sagging against the pain,
dizziness clouding my brain.

He stared at me, his cruel, black eyes still bugged out, unblinking
and unmoving. It was a snapshot in time capturing him with
parted lips, as if he had one final thing to say before he just...
died.

I bent at the waist, wincing from the pain, to get a closer look. I nudged him with the heel of my trembling, bruised hand.

"Hey…you okay?" My voice shook weakly.

His body didn't move. It remained slumped over to the side, caught on the edge of the nightstand, the dark-red blood staining his grimy T-shirt.

"Dad?"

Nothing.

With reserved strength and resolve that I didn't know I had in me, I calmly did the only thing I could think to do in that situation. I dialed 911 and waited.

Knowing nothing would ever be the same again.

CHAPTER 45

Present

THE BUS RAMBLES along the interstate as we head out from our third show of the tour. Tonight, it was Albany, New York and tomorrow night we'll be in Hartford Connecticut, making our way down the eastern seaboard toward Florida and then eventually Texas.

My band and I just recorded a new album and this 15-city tour is just a warm-up until the album releases, as we test the waters in front of an audience. Performing in front of an audience is the only time I really lose myself and put my past behind me. I put everything else out of my mind, leaving those emotions to slowly unravel across the stage like a giant ball of string as I work through the set song by song.

Plucking at some fruit and cheese that's been left out on a tray by our chef – no more Cheetos and pizza for us – I eat a handful of grapes. London took care of that when she appealed to the band manager, Aimee, requesting healthier food options for me while on tour. I swallow down the fruit and take a swig of my beer.

It's been a long night, and my body is exhausted as I toe-off my cowboy boots, swinging my legs up on the bench and close my eyes for a brief second. I'm so tired.

Someone plunks down at my feet and I lift a drowsy eyelid. It's Aimee, with what looks like a shit-ton of paperwork she needs me to review. So much for getting some rest tonight.

"Go away, Aim. I'm tired and need a quick nap and then some peace and quiet to work on a few songs."

She drops the folder on her lap and swats at the bottom of my feet with an evil twinkle in her eye. Aimee's been the band's manager from the beginning, originally meeting me first after I finished a three-song set at the Blue Bird Café. She walked up to me, all female confidence and sway, handed me her card, winked and said,

"I don't want anything from you except your talent. And maybe your soul."

That was five years ago, and she hasn't stopped since. She helped me find a recording studio and my Crenshaw bandmates that I have today. She's the brains, beauty, and brawn of our operation.

Aimee opens the folder and thumbs through a few sheets of paper before landing on what she's looking for.

"No rest for the wicked," she snorts, sticking out her tongue at me. "You've got to look over these contracts and the licensing agreements for Stuart."

Stuart's my agent and has done an amazing job getting my unrecorded songs out in the hands of the bigger stars like Chris Stapleton and Eric Church. I've always maintained that I'm a singer-songwriter first and foremost, and the lead singer of Crenshaw second. While I love the audience energy and high I get when I'm on stage, I'd much rather be behind the scenes writing hits for other singers.

I guess old habits die hard. It was what I'd become accustomed to while in the slammer day after day for three years. The words and music pouring out of me, even without the instruments needed to perfect a song. It was the only bit of happiness I'd had since before prom night; when I could write down my feelings and experiences on paper.

"Fine, let me see them," I grumble, bending at the waist to grab the pile from her. Aimee generally doesn't ride with us on tour and certainly doesn't stay on the bus with the boys, but she'd mentioned going as far as our New York gig for a meeting she had lined up with a new producer.

"Is Emily meeting you in New York when we get there?"

At the mention of her girlfriend's name, Aimee's face lights up and she blushes, smiling sweetly. The smile only those in love can understand. It's the same smile I wore a week ago surrounded by London and Cam.

I sign them wistfully and return the document to her awaiting hand.

"Yeah, we're celebrating our one-year anniversary this weekend. Can you believe it? So much has happened in the last few years."

"You can say that again." I lean back against the couch cushion just about to close my eyes again for some rest when my phone vibrates on the table.

"Will you grab that for me?"

Aimee leans across the table and checks the caller-ID before handing me the phone.

"It's London."

Aimee obviously knows all about London and understands the heartbreak I've been through with her over the years. Aimee and I spent many nights talking through our situations, commiserating with our own similar experiences.

Before she met Emily, Aimee was married to an NBA basketball player who broke her heart with his cheating. But after the divorce finalized, she met Em and it changed the course of her life forever.

I nearly skyrocket off the couch, ripping the phone out of Aimee's hand, her mouth left agape in surprise, as I rush back to the one bedroom on the bus. I close the door behind me and exhale a whoosh of air that I've been holding in for days.

When I left three days ago, I messaged London and hadn't heard a thing back yet except a few brief texts. As a public social worker, she keeps herself very busy with more case files than she can handle. But that's because she gives her heart and soul to those kids she works with, trying to get them out of abusive situations and into foster care. Her level of empathy for those in foster homes is unparalleled. The depths of her unconditional love vast and unending.

My voice sounds winded as I answer. "Hey, darlin'. I've missed you."

There's a pause on the line so big and vast that I can feel it swallowing me whole.

"London? What's the matter, baby? Are you okay?"

She sniffles and hiccups, a sure sign she's been crying.

"Sage…it's Cam."

My heart stops. My breath is strangled like it's been lassoed and squeezed tight, the grip sucking out the remaining air in my lungs.

"What about him? What's going on?"

Every single possible worst scenario runs through my head. A week ago, Cam was summoned to the Smoky Mountain National Forest where a forest fire raged and had to be contained. It's Cam's job now and one I know he is exceptionally good at. But even strong and experienced firefighters still face bad situations.

Cam told us how he became a smokejumper after he was decommissioned from the Air Force. How in three years he's been promoted to a crew leader and is responsible for six other men.

He knows the risks and consequences and would never do anything to jeopardize his life because of his son, Taylor.

No one can ever prepare you for bad news. Even when you're someone like me, who's been the recipient of some pretty rotten shit thrown my way. Like hearing from the judge that you're remanded to a sentence of three-years for reckless homicide.

Or being told by a prison guard that you're being thrown in the hole for a week. It should be easy for me to deal with this because I'm used to it.

But hearing London's words across the line has me stunned silent.

Her voice is so soft I can barely understand what she says. I strain to hear it over the raucous laughter and chatter on the bus. But then wish I never did.

"Cam's been medivacked to the Nashville Trauma Center with second-degree, possibly third-degree burns and life-threatening injuries. Doreen just called me and I'm meeting her there as soon as I get dressed. Sage…" She can't finish the sentence through her anguish and tears.

Oh my God.

No. This can't be happening. Not after things just resolved between all of us. Cam can't leave us like this.

Shaking off all the negative thoughts that run through my head – like, is he going to die? What will happen to us? Or to Taylor? – I clear my throat and with more confidence than I actually have, respond to her.

"London, please don't worry, babe. Everything will be fine. I will make sure of that," I promise, knowing I have no way to ensure this or protect any of us from this tragedy. But until I know the extent of the problem, I need to keep London calm and protect her from this pain.

"Listen to me, darlin'. You just sit tight, and I'll find the nearest airport and come home tonight. Just give me some time to make the arrangements. I'll be there soon, baby. I'll be there for you and for Cam. Because he's not fucking leaving us. You hear me?"

The increased volume of my voice and my loud tone must have alerted Aimee of my tension, as I find her in the doorway when I lift my eyes. Concern etches at her features and I just shake my head and stab my index finger in the air to ask for a minute. She nods and steps out of the room, leaving me once again standing here in utter disbelief.

"Okay," London quavers, sounding like she did when she was a little girl. "Please hurry. I need you."

It's those words that do me in and I fall to my knees, my head hitting the floor. I've lost my way more times than I can count, and I've always relied on London to pull me back up. But now that the roles are reversed, and London needs me to soothe her worries, I know it's what I was made to do. If Cam can't be there to protect her this time, then it's up to me.

And right now, it looks like I need to find a way to help them both.

CHAPTER 46

P ast

As an inmate at the state pen, there were few things you can actually look forward to on the regular. For me, one of those activities was getting out in the yard and breathing fresh air.

As a man who grew up on the outskirts of the Smoky Mountains, the outdoors was something I craved. I needed the sunlight and the humidity in the summertime. The mist in the spring and even the first bite of winter cold to make me feel alive.

I also enjoyed my rotational visits to the library and music therapy sessions. I'd check out books on writing music and recording to learn everything I could about the industry. I was also extremely lucky to meet Drew Vanguard, a local music teacher who came in once a week to provide group therapy to inmates through the study of music.

Over that first year, Drew became my mentor and friend. He taught me how to play the piano with the small electric unit he'd bring with him and fine-tuned my guitar technique. He even taught me how to pick the banjo. Music took me out of those four-walls and kept me sane.

But the most prized days were visiting days. Every other Thursday and Saturday.

London continually showed up during those first few months. During the lowest parts of my life. I was not fit for company and was bitter as fuck with her, but she never gave up on me. Until I betrayed her.

"Hendricks, you've got a visitor. Hurry your ass up before someone else grabs her."

The guard rapped on my cell with a clipboard, the intent in his voice meant to rile me up with jealousy.

I'd been sitting at the small desk in the corner writing some lyrics down for a song I'd been working on. Somedays that was the only way I could come to grips with what had happened in my life. The only method of letting my feelings out to prevent me from going crazy or getting in a fight.

I pushed back the rickety stool and moved to the front of the cell. Unless you were in for aggravated or first-degree murder, we weren't handcuffed when we went into the visitor rooms. It really didn't matter much, since we were enclosed in a room with posted guards and there was a plexiglass, shatter-proof window between inmates and visitors.

As I stepped out of the cell into the cell block, the guard – Cosworth – made a display of sniffing in the air as I walked in front of him.

"Mmm, mmm, mmm. Smells like fine, fresh pussy out there with that visitor of yours, Hendricks. I think she might need herself some big black cock to fill her juicy sweet cunt."

My back stiffened, and I seethed through clenched teeth, as I glanced over my shoulder to see Cosworth lewdly grabbing at his crotch. This was how it always went in here. Whether guards or prisoners, nothing was sacred, and everyone was trying to find a way to catch you off-guard to get under your skin. To expose a weakness and molest and compromise your sanity. Tear you down and then tear you apart.

I hummed the tune I'd been working on, repeating inside my head my mantra. *"It's not worth it. It's not worth it."*

Shuffling toward the locked door to the visitor room, I pushed back all the murderous thoughts I had about Cosworth and some of the nasty comments he'd made about London and steeled my emotions as I stepped in through the door, unlocked by another guard.

What's ironic about being locked away in prison is that not only am I locked up, but I learned fast to keep all my feelings and emotions hidden from everyone.

Especially London.

But it had gotten so fucking hard to keep doing that. Every time I saw her, I cracked a little more inside. The brick wall I'd erected chipped away piece by piece by her loving presence. It wasn't just her appearance – all beauty and light – that did me in. It was the way she had about getting me to open up and share what was going on.

Writing about it was one thing – but sharing these atrocities of prison life with an innocent like London was unconscionable.

I had to put a stop to it. To end it once and for all so that London could move on with her life and quit torturing both of us.

The thought of doing it slayed me, but knew it was the only way.

I sat down, careful to avoid her eyes and picked up the phone on the cubby wall.

Just the sound of her voice – *sweet and wispy* – nearly broke my resolve.

"Hi, Sage. I've missed you so much."

When I finally looked up at her, I saw my life in the graceful features of her face and the love shining in her clear blue eyes. She wasn't just beautiful. She was mine. Always had been and always would be. Even if it meant I had to let her go.

"Hey."

I didn't have the confidence in my ability to say anything more, for fear I'd fall into the abyss and let all my black thoughts bubble up to the surface.

I shifted my view, turning a bored eye in the other direction, hoping she'd get the hint.

"Have you gotten my letters?"

Fuck. Those letters were my downfall.

They were like a drug and I waited daily for the fix from London – holding out hope that I'd also receive something from Cam one day. Devouring every letter and sentence she wrote; the loopy, feminine script of her handwriting jumping off the pages and entwining around my heart as if she was gripping it with her own two hands.

I shrugged with boredom. As if unaffected by her spirit and generosity and beautiful soul.

"Yeah. Thanks."

Her face fell, and she sniffed. "Okay, good. I'm glad. I may have mentioned that I heard from Cam."

Swallowing the lump in my throat and feeling it drop like a lead balloon in my stomach, I nodded.

"How's he doing in bootcamp?"

She smiled stiffly, cupping her chin with her palm. God, what I would've given to be the one touching her like that.

Instead, I made a fist and gripped the phone tighter in my hand. Crucifying the need in me to soothe her worried expression.

"He doesn't write much. Just a few details here and there. Mainly about his drill sergeant and a few guys he's become friends with in his unit. But he graduated and is now completing his specialized training. Something about special ops. And…" She stopped abruptly, her voice growing weaker. Sadder.

Cocking my head to the side, I squinted discerningly. "And what?"

She worried her lip, biting down on the flesh that I'd once kissed and fucked. Loved and worshipped.

"Cam's met someone."

My body jerked and jumped as if I'd been electrocuted.

"Who?"

London shrugged as if it pained her to talk about it. As if she knew she would be hurting me with the details. And fuck, it hurt either way.

I waved my hand in front of my face. "Never mind. Don't tell me. I don't want to know. Cam's free to do whatever he wants with whomever he wants. That part of my life is over. We need to move on. You need to move on, too."

The shiny strands of her blond hair cascaded over her shoulders, dangling softly as she shook her head.

"I can't Sage. I love him. I love you. Nothing will ever change that."

I hissed sarcastically. "You're so fuckin' naïve, London. Get over yourself. Nothing will ever be the same again and you need to accept that and move the fuck on. In fact, I can't do this anymore."

I gestured between us with my index finger and glanced away, avoiding her gaze knowing she'd see all the truth behind my lie.

The truth was, I'd never be over either one of them. They could lock me away for a lifetime and throw away the key, but that love was rooted too deep to ever leave me. It'll be there until my dying day, even if both Cam and London are no longer in my life.

"Don't you say that, Sage. I will never give up on you. I will keep coming here, every week. I. Won't. Give. Up."

She poked the window with her finger, emphasizing each syllable and her fury lighting up her words.

I stared at her for a minute – or maybe it was an hour – memorizing the lines in her brow, the soft curve of her cheeks, the lush fullness of her lips. Capturing every detail of her face and pocketing it in my heart before I stood up, pushed the chair back and hung up the phone.

As I walked out the door, my back to London, I made a peculiar observation.

Living without a heart wasn't that hard at all.

What was difficult was living with a lie.

And knowing you just killed any joy and happiness you'd ever known or would ever have again.

CHAPTER 47

P resent

"Is he alive?" I pant out in a rush of exhaled breath, rushing toward London and Doreen Lucas, Cam's momma.

They sit like two mannequins in the plastic hospital waiting room chairs at Nashville General Trauma Center, until London hears my voice and jumps into my open arms.

She comes willingly, her slight frame dropping into my embrace like a stone being pulled down in a raging river, the weight of the water drowning her. Over her shoulder Doreen's head is bent in silent prayer, clutching a Kleenex in her hand.

"Baby, I'm here. Everything will be okay. I promise."

These are obviously words that hold no meaning and are only meant to placate. She and I both know it, but she nods into my chest anyway, because to think otherwise right now has too many implications.

Loosening my hold, I cup her jaw and lift her face to meet my gaze. London's eyes are red-rimmed from all the tears, puffy bags under her lids. It still doesn't detract one ounce from her beauty. She has naturally sun-kissed, dewy skin that is flawless even without makeup. A face I've kissed goodnight for years and awoken to even when I didn't deserve to be laying beside her.

I owe London so much for being there for me through all the difficult times. Now is my chance to be strong for her. Hold her up when she needs me most.

"What's the status? Do you know anything more? Should I go talk to the doctors?"

She grabs my hand and pulls me toward Doreen, who finally lifts her head to stare at me. She blinks a few times and then her expression turns white – as if she's seen a ghost.

"Sage? Is that you?"

She hasn't seen me in over ten years. Not since I was handed down my sentence and remanded to the state pen.

Although Doreen and her husband, Mike, tried to visit me a few times while I was locked away, I turned them away. They had been more of a parental influence growing up than my own mom or dad, which made my shame even greater. Therefore, I chose to stay away.

They gave up after the second year of my sentence and then even the letters from Doreen stopped coming. I understood why. Her own son was overseas fighting a war and her husband had just passed away.

Slowly dragging my heavy-guilt-laden feet toward her, I bend to hug her gently. Her bony-body trembles under my touch and I fight back tears that threaten to spill.

"Hi, Dori. It's been a while. I'm so sorry…" The words catch in my throat. I swallow thickly. "I'm sorry about everything."

London steps around us and sits on the opposite side of Cam's mom and I sit down on her right, clasping her petite, aged hand in mine.

"I can't lose my only living child," she wails in anguish, and I squeeze her hand tighter, meeting London's concerned gaze over Doreen's head.

Swinging my arm around her shoulder, London lays a hand on top of mine, as together we try to comfort her the best way we know how.

London's voice holds an authority of conviction. "You won't, Doreen. Cameron Lucas is the strongest man I know."

"Can you tell us what's going on? What information has been given to you by the doctors and staff?"

She sniffles and weeps. "Not much. Only that the first responding ER doctors indicated that after their initial assessment, the burns looked to be second-degree and they've put him into a medically induced coma to keep him sedated for the next few days while they assess his situation. They've checked his lungs for soot and smoke inhalation. They have intubated him to help his breathing and will be doing some scans to see what internal damage may have occurred. A burn specialist is being called in and that's all I know."

Goddammit. How the hell did this happen?

"He'll make it. Don't you worry. I'll make sure he has all the best medical care there is. He's not going through this alone." My voice is firm and unwavering.

London's lips curve up in a slight smile and she nods her head. Then her body seizes in panic.

"Where's Taylor? Does Lisa know?"

Doreen begins to cry harder, an inconsolable grief that cuts me to the bone.

"The paramedics initially called Lisa who didn't answer, so they called me. I called her when I arrived here earlier tonight, and she said she wasn't going to bring Taylor to see him. That it was Cam's fault he's in this situation because he wanted to go into this career. She's such a horrible woman. I just can't believe Cam ever fell for someone like her."

Doreen's sobs bring me back to the day I was sentenced in the courtroom ten years earlier. Cam had already shipped off to boot camp and London was at school in Nashville and couldn't get back for the sentencing, but Doreen, Mike, and London's parents were there all seated in the front row. I heard Dori crying from behind me as she wept over the injustice and unfairness of it all.

And here we are again, and she's still fighting the universe's injustice but this time it's her own son. Her only living family member, aside from her grandson.

I was absolutely floored when Cam told me about his failed marriage to Lisa and his son, Taylor. It just seemed so strange to me that he had this whole life outside of what he'd shared between me and London. But I could tell how happy Taylor made him – and how *unhappy* Lisa made his life during their divorce – yet he still smiled, saying the best gift life had ever given him was Taylor's birth.

Then I remember something else Cam had shared with me that morning on the porch. He'd admitted to almost ending his life. He was ashamed of his weakness and felt that some guardian angel had been looking out for him that day, sending both Taylor and London out to him on that dock. Cam realized he hadn't wanted to die. He had too much to live for.

And now he's in a hospital room close to death.

The cruel irony of our fates.

It seems the same punishing forces had a hand in my life, as well, when I was sent to prison.

CHAPTER 48

P ast

I KEPT HAVING A RECURRING dream about them.

Every night once I allowed my body and mind to relax and fall asleep, they'd come to me in the best, most erotic dreams. Ones where I was with London and Cam, together.

Touching, and kissing, and fucking. It was hauntingly beautiful.

And then somewhere in the middle of all the hot stuff, it would turn violent. All the colorful images of bodies and sex would be inked in black and red. Blood and death. I'd wake up and want to scream but would instantly remember where I was and stifle it back down, racked with tremors from the excruciating horror of the nightmare.

I'd lay back down on the top bunk, throwing off the flimsy, scratchy sheet, and shiver in the cold sweat that drenched me from head to toe. This happened every night for months.

It was worse when I'd picture Cam, decked out in his boot camp fatigues that I'd never see him in, sweaty from his drills, as he'd step into the empty bathroom where I'd be waiting.

In my imagination, I'd be right there to help him. Naked and hard for him. I'd watch as he removed his combat boots, then his socks and whip off his T-shirt, sweat-stained and smelling of him. A perfect combination of perspiration and masculinity.

"Let me help you," I'd murmur, my hands landing at his belt buckle and slowly unclasping the metal buckle, pulling it from the loops and throwing it to the ground. "I want you in my mouth."

Cam would wiggle his eyebrows and smirk, flexing his muscular biceps and arms as he'd lift his arms at his sides, allowing me room to maneuver.

Kneeling in front of him, I'd unbutton and unzip his camouflage pants, pulling at the flaps and dragging the material down and over his heavy erection. His hard cock would spring free, standing at attention like the soldier he was. My fingers let go of the material at his ankles and trail up his calves, enjoying the sensation of the coarse hair tickling at my palms, as I mapped out the terrain of his thick thighs.

I'd tease him mercilessly, enthralled with every sigh and moan out of Cam's mouth, as I placed kisses everywhere other than his dick. He'd growl with displeasure and frustration and I'd chuckle at his impatience. Because I knew that deep down, Cam wanted me to make him feel good. He longed for me to take him in my mouth. To cup his balls. To make him come down my throat.

Even if in real-life he rejected me. Turned against me when all I wanted to do was to love him. I'd fallen in love with Cam when I was thirteen years old. That love had to be disguised and kept hidden in the dark recesses of my heart out of fear of losing his friendship. From the sheer panic over losing him as my best friend.

"You're such a faggot ass queer, boy."

My father's icy-cold voice hits me across the jaw as forceful as if he'd taken a swing at me with a fist.

His dark, imposing figure hovers over me in my childhood bed. I'm fifteen years old again and he's in my room, stumbling drunk.

I'd never come out to my dad, or anyone other than London. She just knew it instinctively. Understood that I found both girls and boys attractive and didn't have any preference. But I never knew how my dad determined I was queer. I'd read up on the terminology, and found I identified more as a bisexual boy than gay, liking both girls and boys.

One boy, in particular.

Cam.

Maybe my dad just thought his insults were a way to hurt me verbally rather than being bound in truth. Who knew? My dad was never someone I'd understood or figured out.

He was just a drunken loser who failed at life, yet his voice rang out in my head as if he were still right there in front of me.

"You call this succeeding, boy? You're in a fucking prison cell for killing me. You're no better than me, you little shit."

He'd always be there, taunting me from inside my head. Laughing sardonically at my circumstances.

I woke with a start once again, gripping the edges of my hair in my sweaty palms, my breaths loud and staggered.

Knowing I wouldn't be able to get back to sleep, I jumped out of the bunk, careful not to wake Clem, my cellmate, a sixty-year-old lifer. I sat down at the desk chair, sifting through a stack of letters I'd never intended on opening.

Letters from London.

It'd been a year. A fucking wasted year since I told her to leave me. To move on with her life. The irony of it is that she took my advice and did just that. She moved on and I stayed in the same hell hole.

London had told me about a guy she'd met at school named Clay. He was two years older, a senior about to graduate. He was attending Columbia Law School in New York in the fall and London was considering transferring to NYU to be near to him.

And away from me.

My heart had been sliced open, the pieces like ribbons, dangling precariously in my body. Cut to shreds from her announcement.

She'd written about how she enjoyed his company and how he was from the East Coast, which I read between the lines to mean he was from a wealthy family. Of course, he was. And goddammit if I didn't feel a strong hatred for him. Clay could not only offer London something that I never could, but something she deserved, to be treated like a queen.

Cam wasn't around to do it, and I would never be able to offer her that kind of life. Even once I'd served my time and out on parole, what the hell kind of life could an ex-con offer her? Not a home, a family. Nothing. She was right to heed my advice and write me off.

I was a worthless, no good piece of shit, just like my dad had always reminded me.

The funny thing about prison is that it's supposed to give you time to come to terms with what you did and to make amends; to redeem yourself and make reparations to those you hurt when you committed your crime.

The only ones I ever regretted hurting, the ones who deserved my apologies were Cam and London.

Ripping a piece of paper out of my notebook, the memory of my dream lingering in the forefront of my mind, I began to write a letter. I addressed it to Cam. It was a letter that would never be sent or shared, but I knew if I didn't get out what had to be said, it would eat me alive.

Dear Cam,

I know you hate me. I guess there's a part of me that hates me a little, too.

I don't regret kissing you or doing what I did to you. It was one of the best things that could've happened to me. I only regret that it cost us our friendship.

My life is so fucked up right now it doesn't even feel like my own. Prison is everything you've heard about it and worse. It's a stink-tank of the worst people you could imagine. Men who kill out of cold blood. Who abuse their wives and girlfriends. Who abduct and hurt children. Who buy and sell drugs and women.

I don't think I belong here. My heart doesn't bleed the same dark poison that runs through most of these men. It scares me to think that maybe someday, maybe even soon, I could end up like them. Unapologetically savage and evil. Hating the world and everyone in it.

I'm grateful, I guess, that my sentence is fairly short. It scares me to think what I might become if I have to be in this place for more than three years. Lucky for me, my cellmate, Clem, is a pretty decent guy. Doesn't talk much. Just grumbles to himself a lot about "this mother fucker or that mother fucker" but otherwise he leaves me alone.

It's hard, man. I'm scared. I'm so alone.

I need you.

I can't see London anymore. It hurts too fucking much. I told her not to come back and it broke my mother fucking heart. I didn't want to. I swear to God, if I could take it back, I would. Take back everything about the night and everything since then.

But life doesn't work that way. I'm just glad I had the time I did on the outside to spend with you and London. I still dream about those nights together. Camping out in the mountains. You, me and London fucking and loving each other.

I want that again someday. I need to have something to hold onto and to hope for in my life. Otherwise, it's just unbearable.

The pain of not talking to you or seeing you right now is killing me. But not as much as it would if I didn't have the belief that someday in the future, we'll all be together again. And all will be right in the world.

I just know it.

I love you, Cam. I always have, and I always will. You and London. Forever.

All my love,

Sage

As for London…my letter was short and to the point.

Dear London,

Good luck in New York. Be happy, that's all I want for you.

Love,

Sage

CHAPTER 49

P resent

I_{T WAS} touch-and-go for the first three days Cam was in the hospital in the intensive care unit, with round-the-clock care.

Although the doctor's assured us that their assessment of his burns was labeled second-degree and treatable, they were still worried about his lungs and internal organs.

His specialist, Dr. Sun Kim-Lee, indicated that most fatalities with firefighters weren't from the burns themselves but from internal injuries and trauma or cardiac arrest.

The doctor gave us hope that due to Cam's size, his health and fitness, and the fact that the burns were contained to his back, side and a small portion of his torso, he'd be able to make a full recovery after undergoing skin grafting surgery, scheduled for today.

London and I were only allowed in Cam's room for a few minutes after the first day while he was still heavily sedated and in a semi-conscious state. His eyes fluttered open once or twice as both London and I held his hands and whispered our prayers and thoughts into his ears, but otherwise, he was out of it.

Thankfully.

While London drove Doreen back to her apartment to take a nap and shower, I remained behind to be available in the event there was any news. That's when one of Cam's crew members, Benito, stopped by with a gift basket and get-well card from the other crew members. I'd never met that man before but could tell he was worn and haggard from days of exhausting work.

From what he shared with me about the incident, I seriously hoped Cam would wake up with little or no memory of what happened. It was too brutal otherwise. Another one of his crew members named Dominic was found lying on top of Cam and died at the scene.

"How's he doing?" Benito asks.

I shrug. "As good as can be expected, I guess. How long have you worked with Cam?"

The guy scratches his forehead in recollection. "I started with the Smoky Mountain team two years ago. He wasn't my supervisor then, we were just crew members together."

A wisp of a smile pulls at his lips. "Cam was always a ball-buster, man. He was one helluva guy."

As if realizing what he said, he corrects himself.

"Aw, man. I mean, Cam's a good guy and we're all pulling for him to make a full recovery. He's one of the best there is, and we need him back." Benito shakes his head in disbelief. "It's hard to understand why or how this even happened."

I stand there alone with this stranger, feeling the exact same way. Trying to make heads or tails out of this tragedy and uncertain by how this could've happened.

"What did happen out there? Do you know anything?"

Benito runs a hand through his thick, dark hair, staring off into the distance.

"We usually work independently or in small groups of two or four. We had our morning briefing at base camp, got our gear ready, then our pilots flew us up and we parachuted in. It was a successful jump. Each team landed according to the scheduled coordinates and began our mission of surrounding the fire on all sides to extinguish and contain. The last we heard, Cam and Dom were on the west side and were cornered. It took us less than fifteen minutes to get to them, but by the time we did, we found them in their trench."

Benito's dark, empathetic eyes connect with mine and he swallows.

"When we got there, Dom's body was atop Cam's. He must've shielded him from the blaze. We don't know why."

My stomach clenches at the thought. "Jesus. Did Dom have a family?"

Growing up with a fucked-up father was one thing but I can't imagine any kid going through this – knowing their father died protecting another man. In the line of duty. It's the true act of service, but sad for a kid to lose a father like that.

Benito throws a look over his shoulder as someone walks by us in the corridor and then replies.

"Nah, Dom was a young kid. Twenty-two and single. But his parents…"

I place a hand on top of his shoulder and squeeze. "Please send me the details of his funeral. I'll make sure that London and I attend on Cam's behalf."

Benito nods appreciatively. "You bet. Thanks man."

He cocks his head then, mouth opening and recognition seemingly sparking in his eyes. "Holy shit. Wait, aren't you the lead singer of Crenshaw?"

I lift an eyebrow and place a finger at my lips. "Shh. I'm trying to remain incognito and keep things quiet while we're here. But yeah, I am. Sage Hendricks. Nice to meet you, Benito. And thanks so much for stopping by and checking in on Cam."

Benito shakes my hand vigorously, a huge grin covering his mouth. "Ah man, my wife, Camilla will die when I tell her I met you. She loves your music, man. Wow, what a trip. Are you and Cam *family*?"

I can tell by the way he hesitated and enunciated the word that he assumes something entirely different. The world knows about my sexual tastes in relationships and I've never shied away from talking about my bisexual proclivities. But Cam identifies as a straight man, and I'm not going to be the one to out him in front of one of his coworkers. I don't know or trust this guy.

"Cam and I go way back and grew up together. I love him like a brother."

All truth. No lies hidden there, even if there's more to the story than that. But it's all this guy is gonna get.

I extract a black Sharpie from my back pocket and sign a Crenshaw photo card I always carry with me exactly for times like these.

"C-A-M-I-L-L-A? Is that how you spell your wife's name?"

He nods enthusiastically, and I hand him the card for him to take home to his wife.

"Here you go. It was nice meeting you, man. And thanks for your service. You're doing good stuff out there."

Benito suddenly seems starstruck, stumbling over his words.

"Thanks man, I really appreciate this. I'll send you the details once the funeral arrangements are made. Nice meeting you, Sage. And give my best to Cam."

"Will do. Take care."

I watch him walk off down the hallway, stopping to say something to the nurse at the station about the basket, and then I sit down, dropping my head back to rest against the wall. I suddenly feel like I haven't slept in years. I'm so tired.

My thoughts float to Dom, a man I've never met, but who was a guardian angel to Cam. Without him, I would've lost my best friend once again.

And that's one time too many times.

Fate has really fucked with my life once again.

But at least this time, I won't have to go through the bad stuff alone. London is here with me and there is a good prognosis that Cam would recover and be practically good as new in a few months' time.

And hopefully, we'd be able to pick up where things left off.

CHAPTER 50

T hree Months Later

"JUST LEAVE ME ALONE," Cam bellows from the upstairs bedroom, his frustration evident in the way he shouts at London. There's a thud against the wall and then something lands on the floor. From the sounds of it, Cam threw his ointment bottle in a tantrum huff.

That wouldn't be the first time he's acted like a stubborn two-year-old.

While Cam has always been the more stoic and reserved of the three of us, this ordeal and his recovery process has drawn on his last reserve of patience and brought out the worst in him. He's ornery as fuck and the worst patient. Not that I blame him one bit.

I hear some faint whispering and then the soft click of the door latch, followed by London's footsteps padding down the staircase.

Swiveling on the piano bench I've been perched on for the last thirty minutes, trying to come up with a stanza for a song I'm working on, I see London walk into the kitchen and set down her basket of medical supplies.

From across the hall, I can see the stress and despair in her body language as her head tips forward and her shoulders droop.

Cam has been staying here since he left the hospital after the successful skin graft surgery of his back and side. For the first month, he had a physical therapist and a nurse that I'd hired to come in daily to change his dressings, clean the surgical sites, and get him stretched out and moving so the scars would heal properly.

Unfortunately, one man can only take so much pain and agony. And now poor London has been making sure his back is staying moist by adding the topical ointments and keeping it clean and free from infection where the skin begins to heal.

It hurts to know Cam is still struggling with the pain, and that he inadvertently and unintentionally takes it out on London. I suppose it's human nature to take it out on the ones you love.

Walking into the kitchen, I come up behind London and begin to gently massage her shoulders. She moans in pure pleasure.

"Oh Sage, don't stop doing that. *Ever.*"

I chuckle and lean in to kiss the curve of her neck. She smells heavenly, a soft fragrant perfume scenting her skin. Although she stayed here with Cam after he was discharged, while I returned to tour to make up the two weeks of shows I'd missed while he was in the hospital, she refuses to live here full-time. She stays over every weekend and tries to stop over a few nights a week, but she claims her apartment is easier because it's closer to work.

My body and cock grow hard as I continue to touch her, wedging myself behind her, my full erection pressed into her ass. London's head drops back to rest against my chest and she sighs.

I can't help myself around her. London is the sexiest woman I know and my senses are flooded with arousal whenever she's near. Like a beacon signaling to a sailor, she's my light and my salvation.

"Are you okay, babe? Can I do something to make you feel better?" I murmur into her ear, nipping at her earlobe and trailing my fingers down her arm.

She stretches on tiptoes, her arms wrapping behind our bodies to clutch my ass, which she greedily squeezes.

"You know, maybe we can do something to help our patient relieve some of his own pain. What do you think, baby? Should we go see if he wants to join?"

London shifts her head to the side and I capture her smile with my kiss. She tastes of her vanilla latte and cream. My tongue spears between her lips hungrily, taking everything she has to offer.

Her moan has my head spinning and body shaking with pent up need, my cock thrusting against her ass crease. We've fucked a few times together while Cam has been convalescing, but it's usually quick and rough to get our rocks off. And it hasn't been with Cam.

And I miss him desperately.

He's been angry and surly during his recovery, which I can completely understand. London and I have been patient and sympathetic, knowing it will take time. It's not just the physical wounds he's healing from, but also the emotional ones left behind. But tonight, we need to show him what he's been missing. He needs to get back to his old self again. To remember what it's like to feel good.

London swings around in my arms and kisses me soundly, her hands sliding through my hair, tugging hard, just the way I like it.

"Yes," she says breathlessly. "Take me upstairs so we can make him whole again."

Dr. Kim-Lee was very adamant about what he told us about recovery. He said that the psychological healing normally takes longer than the physical recovery time because of the emotional upheaval that caused the injuries in the first place. That, along with the body image issues that a burn victim will typically deal with and have to learn to face.

It's obvious Cam is knee-deep in self-loathing over his looks, and hasn't left his room once without a T-shirt covering his torso. Except for the times London or I have slathered the ointment and massage the tight, raised and rippled skin on his back, he refuses to let us see him naked or shirtless.

I reach for London's hand and pull her behind me as we ascend the staircase and up to the door of Cam's room.

Knocking quietly, I open the door to find Cam laying on his side with his back to the door.

"We brought you a present. Can we come in?"

Cam throws a quick look over his shoulder and sees the grins on our faces and lifts an eyebrow.

"A present, huh? I don't think I deserve one."

London and I walk around to the side of the bed and I glance around the room. It's a bright, sunny Saturday afternoon yet his room is dark and bleak, the drapes closed tight on both floor-length windows. Dragging over a high-backed chair to the bedside, I order London to sit down as I open the window, allowing sunlight to waft in.

"What the fuck, bro? I like it dark." Cam grumbles, shielding his eyes from the light cascading over his bed.

I smirk. "That's too bad, because you're gonna want to see what we have for you."

"Whatever. Just make it quick."

Rubbing my stubbled whiskers across my chin, I quirk an eyebrow.

"Mighty impatient there, Cam. But this is a gift I think you might be interested in savoring a bit. Don't you agree, darlin'?" I turn my head and land my gaze on London, who's sitting primly in the chair, her feet crossed at her ankles, her dainty hands in her lap.

The way the sun casts a glow over her hair, she looks like an angel. Ethereal and other-worldly.

"Baby, are you ready to give Cam our present?"

She nods her head excitedly, a touch of naughtiness attached to her smile.

"London," my voice lowers, deep and baritone. "Why don't you show us your pussy."

I don't see it, but I hear it.

Cam's sharp inhale of breath. I feel the temperature in the room change around us, the electricity zipping and crackling. The chemical reaction boiling and bubbling as it readies for an explosion.

Sitting down at the edge of the bed, my ass bumps up against Cam's legs. While my gaze remains on London in front of me, I notice every little thing that happens within Cam's body. The quick pants of air; the tightening of his thigh muscles; the darkening of his hooded gaze.

While he might try to deny it, he's not unaffected by this.

Not at all.

My plan is to make sure he's reminded of how good the three of us are together and how pleasure can overpower the senses and eliminate pain entirely.

And we know just how to do it.

CHAPTER 51

P resent

"GO ON, DARLIN'. Take off those little shorts of yours that have been making me hard all day and give us a peek at your sweet pussy. You want to see it, don't you Cam?"

I'm taunting him to get a reaction.

He needs this more than any man I know. He needs to forget about what he's been through – with his on-going divorce, the custody battle, the fire, his burns, the death of his friend – and just be in the present.

"Fuck you." He seethes, but it only makes me smile knowingly.

"Ah, Cam. You know how much I'd love for you to fuck me," I tease, *tsking* at him with a waggle of my finger in the air. "I've been dreaming about it for years. It was the only thing that kept me going in prison."

I land my palm on his outstretched leg beside me and absently run my fingers through the wisps of hair. He stills under my exploration, and possibly from my honest admission. It's rare for me to mention anything about my time in prison. When he doesn't wiggle out from under my touch, I know he's interested.

Progress.

London, meanwhile, begins to unbutton and unzip her shorts, lifting her ass to shimmy out of them and kicks them across the floor with a flick of her foot.

Her fingers slide into the top edge of her panties and I stop her there.

"Leave them on. Open your legs and show us." My voice sounds hoarse and throaty as she tilts her head up to look at me, worrying her lip in that sexy way that turns me on.

Foreplay with these two has always been hot as fuck. There's something inside me that finds its alpha voice when I become a dominant in the bedroom. It only serves to spike my blood hotter when I'm with Cam and London. It gets me hard as steel to know that just the tone of my voice and direction I give gets London wet and Cam hard.

London does as I instruct, spreading her long, tanned legs and dragging the lacy panel of her panties to expose her wet pussy.

"Like this?" she purrs seductively, knowing full well that's exactly what I wanted.

My head snaps to Cam, enjoying the first signs of his arousal through the bulge clearly visible in his shorts. "Cam? What do you think? Is that good for you? Or would you like to see more?"

Cam practically chokes out his word. "More."

I wink with a salacious smile at this game we invented years ago. Our cat-and-mouse chase. Our own version of a sexy Simon Says.

Turning back to London, I look her over from head to toe, narrowing back in on her naked center.

"Finger yourself. Let us watch."

She quirks an eyebrow but doesn't protest, simply complies with my command by sliding a long, tapered finger inside her beautiful pussy. As she does, she tips her head against the back of the chair and moans a delicious sound.

"That's it, darlin'. Get yourself nice and wet." My eyes drift back to Cam, whose own focus is clearly on London, the tip of his tongue curled up behind his front teeth and his eyes glazed with arousal.

"Cam, would you like our girl to show you how wet she is?"

His response is in the form of a guttural growl and a nod of his head. Now firmly invested in this sensual game, Cam sits up and throws his legs over the side of the bed, maneuvering himself to make room for London.

Her moan fills the room as she withdraws her finger from her juicy center and holds her finger up in the air in a triumphant display.

I shake my head and bark out a mocking response. "Now how is Cam supposed to know how wet you are when you're way over there, darlin'? You need to present him with the evidence. He needs proof."

As I watch London stand and walk toward Cam, I remove my clothing so that I'm left only in my briefs. My dick is a throbbing and tormented muscle, dying to be touched and played with. I rub a palm over my shaft to get some relief just as London offers her wet finger to Cam.

The tip of her finger disappears slowly inside Cam's opened mouth and his lips close around it as he devours her flesh. They both moan simultaneously – he from her taste and her from the action of his suction. And I groan with the possibilities of how fucking hot this is about to get.

If there's one thing I know beyond the shadow of a doubt, it's that when the three of us start something, it's not going to end until we are all happily satisfied.

I bend at the waist, leaning over so that my face is nearly touching Cam's.

"I want to taste her on you."

London removes her finger from Cam's mouth and I replace them with my lips. Cam's mouth is blistering hot, my tongue sweeping through the heat, London's taste melting inside against my tongue.

I deepen the kiss, my hand slipping behind Cam's neck, taking pleasure in the way he sighs with relief. As if it's the balm to his pain, relieving his symptoms.

With one hand at the nape of his neck, and careful not to touch any of his scarred skin, the fingers of my other hand travel down his chest, swirling around his collarbone, his mountainous pectoral muscles, and then trailing over the ridges of his abs. When they land on his belly, he sucks in a gulp of air and I bite his lower lip.

"Let me touch you, Cam."

My body is antsy to touch him. I've missed this for so long. While he's been in recovery, I've wanted nothing more than to wrap him up in my arms to show him how much I love him. To prove to him that he makes me complete. They make me whole when everything else in my life has left me in pieces.

"Sage," he whimpers into my mouth. It's a plea.

I let go and run my lips over his cheek, his jawbone, relishing in the scrape of his whiskers against my sensitive lips. When I find the shell of his ear, I murmur,

"You're going to fuck me tonight. And I'm going to take London's pussy while you take my ass. It's my gift to you."

The air in the room shifts, like the current in the river back home in Chester Fork. It's thick and flowing, dense and weighty. Full of anticipation and movement.

"London, get on the bed, baby. We're gonna get warmed up."

CHAPTER 52

Londen spreads out over the bed as I reach into the
bedside table to grab the lube and condoms. Cam
remains perched on the edge of the bed with a glassy-
eyed stare. Looking uncertain and a little shell-shocked.

Seems like he's either ready to bolt or to bust a nut. Could go
either way.

We've given him the time to heal and recover. Over the course of
the last few months, he's seen a therapist for his mental health, as
well as the physical therapists to assist in his healing. But
enough's enough.

What better way is there to get his head back into the game than
to remind his body how good he can feel.

"Cam? You in with us?"

His denim-blue-gaze stares up at me in the same fashion they did
when we were teens. With a nervous longing and greedy need.
As if snapping out of a trance, he looks down at London's
nearly-naked body and skims her inner thigh with his fingertips.

"Where should I begin?"

His question is more to himself rather than either London or me, but I decide to answer for him.

"I want to watch you make her come on your tongue. You were always so good with that."

He flashes a dirty grin and begins peppering kisses along London's leg, starting at her ankle and working his way up past her knee, venturing toward her pussy.

London moans with pleasure when Cam reaches his intended destination, yanking the panties down and off her legs. She smiles lazily, stretching her limbs like a cat in a beam of sunlight, her arm reaching out in my direction.

"Come here, Sage. Let me touch you."

I won't deny any of us the satisfaction and do as she requests. Kneeling on the bed beside her, I take her hand and place it on my cock, her palm rubbing my erection through the cotton of my briefs. The friction feels so good, but so will her mouth.

Sliding down my underwear, my dick pops free, London's hand enwrapping it in her velvet touch. As she's being pleasured between her legs by Cam, she pleasures me with the stroke of her hand along my hard shaft, licking her lips seductively.

I chuckle at her not-so-subtle hint. "You hungry for something, darlin'?'

"Mmm-hmm."

Her lips slide over the head of my cock, tongue sweeping around the tip and rim, as I nearly spasm with relief when she drags it across my slit.

"That's it, darlin. You know how much I love your mouth. And you," I speak to Cam as I lay a hand on top of his head. "I want to feel her gasp around my cock when you slide a finger in her pussy."

Cam lifts his head momentarily, his lips puffy and wet, and then inserts his finger into London, who moans so loudly around my cock that I feel the vibrations all the way to my toes.

London squirms against Cam's face as her cheeks hollow out with the suction around my dick. I can tell she's getting close to orgasm because of the intermittent pauses as she breathes in deeply through her nose, her mouth stopping its movement while she's momentarily incapacitated by pleasure.

Then suddenly, she lets go of my cock and a string of garbled words coming tumbling out of her mouth.

"*I'mcomingI'mcomingI'mcoming…*"

I can feel her body spasm, my hand on her breast, pinching her nipple hard between my thumb and finger to intensify the reaction. As her climax begins to wane, Cam shoots a look up to me, tipping his head in delight.

"I've still got it."

We all laugh at his smugness, and I hand him the lube and condom.

His voice trembles and catches me off guard. "You sure, man?"

Cupping my hands around his jaw, I press a hard kiss to his lips, relishing in the mixed taste of Cam and London.

"I've never wanted anything more."

Letting him go, I lean down to London, kissing her in a much gentler fashion.

"You okay with just me tonight, baby?"

It's always been important to the three of us to be open about our feelings and reservations. Without it, it leaves too much room for resentment and jealousy.

London bites her lip with a coy grin and nods. She looks like a sinful goddess laid out like this and my cock aches to be inside her.

Cam sits up and sheathes himself in a condom, slathering himself with lube. My dick twitches and my hole throbs with greedy anticipation.

He tilts his head. "Um…how do you want me to…"

Strumming a hand down his chest, I enclose his fat cock in a fist, stroking a few times, my gaze volleying between them both. They are naked and gloriously sexy, and I deem myself the luckiest man alive to be able to be with the two people I love more than anything else in the world.

I position London on the bed, moving Cam's body behind me, quirking a brow at him in challenge. "You comfortable with this?"

Cam shrugs a shoulder. "I guess we'll find out soon enough."

London opens wider, inviting me into her wet, slick heaven.

I adjust myself over her naked body missionary style, my tip seeking her entrance as I thrust inside. She envelopes my cock in warmth and I groan with pleasure, knowing there is still so much more to come.

The heat of her body mixed with the heat of Cam's from behind insulates me in a tight cocoon. From behind me, I feel Cam drag his hand over the curve of my ass, as he ventures toward my asshole. The contrasting cold of the lube that he drizzled in my crease and the sizzling burn of his hand is almost too much to handle. I still inside London, who stares up at me dreamily, her hands digging into my shoulder blades.

"I don't want to hurt you," Cam acknowledges sweetly, as I stifle a laugh.

"Dude, the waiting hurts worse. Just do it. I want you inside me."

I grit my teeth, holding myself compliant and lifting my ass higher while Cam peels open my ass cheeks and presses the tip of his cock at the entrance. I know London is waiting for me to move, but I can't. I'm enraptured with divine pleasure as Cam slowly inches his way in until he hits the muscular ring that's meant to keep him out.

Baring down, I lift my ass a little higher, positioning myself at a better angle for him to take me. And take me he does.

Cam grips the sides of my ass with both hands and thrusts his cock inside of me. The momentum forces me down onto London's chest, as I'm now securely wedged between both my lovers.

"Holy fuck, Sage..."

He withdraws with a growl, his dick sliding out and up my ass crease leaving a trail of slippery wetness in its wake.

London and I lock lips, our tongues dueling with one another, tasting and fucking. I rear back when I feel Cam at my entrance again, his fingers spreading me open as he thrusts in. My body adjusts quickly to the intrusion and I feel my balls tightening with the need to release.

Beneath me, London wiggles and moves, seeking her own climactic eruption. Because of our positions, I'm unable to use my hands much or work my fingers at her clit.

"Touch yourself, baby. Make yourself come."

She does as I suggest, wedging her delicate finger at her swollen nub in much need of attention. She closes her eyes in euphoria, working herself hard and fast as I continue to pump inside and Cam pounds me from behind.

It's the most beautiful thing I've ever experienced.

We're connected in ways so much greater than just physically – our hearts are in sync with our bodies. We're wrapped up in a bubble of warmth, saturated with a shared history and a love so strong it's withstood the test of time and distance, tours, deaths, and estrangements.

I feel the first trembles of London's orgasm, her face tightening in ecstasy as she shatters beautifully underneath me. Throwing a look over my shoulder, I see a similar expression on Cam, a light sheen of sweat glistening over his chest and flexing muscles.

His grip on my hips tenses and on the next thrust his cock head hits me in just the right spot, as I unload spectacularly inside London's pussy. Behind me, Cam's jerking movements stop, his dick slamming into me one final time, as he shudders out a roar of climax.

His weight and heat leave me feeling bereft and incomplete as he withdraws from my body.

"I gotta go take care of this," he explains, his voice raspy and deep.

Checking to ensure London is okay, I kiss her cheek before sliding out, my semi-hard dick wet from the remnants of my release.

She sighs happily, and I reach for a tissue next to the bed to clean her up. My hands brush over her mound and between her lips, my gaze returning to her mouth, which edges up in a satisfied smile.

"Thank you for taking care of me."

"Always, baby. I love you. Thank you for sharing in this gift with us."

I bend down to kiss her forehead, then her nose and finally her soft, luscious lips. "You mean everything to me. Even when I was an asshole of epic proportions and pushed you away…I never stopped loving you."

Her watery smile doesn't quite meet her eyes. "I've already told you I've forgiven you for that. I understand it now. I didn't back then, but I do now. You had your reasons. It was just so hard to be away from you."

I brush away the stray hairs from her face, cupping her cheek lightly in my palm.

"London, will you please marry me?"

CHAPTER 53

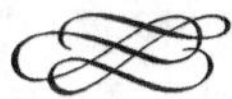

I don't know where the words come from, but before I can stop them, they pop out of my mouth, a surprise to us both.

I'd been very intentional over the last year to shut down the possibility of her ever saying yes since she's rejected me three times in the past. But something about this moment just feels right. Now that Cam is back in our lives, we can figure out our future together.

While it's not possible for the three of us to legally marry each other, and Cam hasn't finalized his divorce and is technically still married, it shouldn't prevent London and me from marrying. And if he's open to it, we can hold a commitment ceremony with Cam when he's ready.

We've never discussed this with one another. The topic of our future hasn't been raised since Cam's returned and has been working at recovering one day at a time. Maybe it's just my simple dream of a future together – sharing one another, sharing a home and our bed and the responsibilities of raising Taylor as a family.

A family is something I never had unless it encompassed London, Cam and our friendship. Their love was more intimate and bonding than anything I'd ever felt with my own parents.

And all I want is for that commitment to be made publicly and forever.

Cam strides into the room, picking up his scattered clothes that were strewn about in our earlier frenzy and puts them back on. As he does, he seems suddenly closed off and distant.

In the past, Cam liked to cuddle afterwards, but now he sits alone as he buttons his shorts, his T-shirt hanging loosely over the waistband.

"Sage," London drawls, an uncertainty lingering in the sweet sound of her voice.

I'm ready for her rejection to my proposal, steeling myself against the sharp cut it'll make in the wound that still hasn't healed from her previous rejections. But I'm also hopeful for the answer I've longed to hear all these years.

"Do you not love me, London?"

I'm layering it on thick, hoping she'll come to the same conclusion I have years ago. We're perfect for each other and I have so much to give her now. Unlike when I was fresh out of prison.

"Of course, I love you, silly man."

She sits up, adjusting the sheet to cover her breasts. Her eyes shine with a touch of sorrow. "But you know I also love Cam. I can't choose between you two. I never have, and I never will. It's impossible."

Reaching for her hand, I bring it to my lips, kissing along her knuckles with reverence.

"Darlin', I'm not asking you to choose. And that's why I think the three of us should marry each other."

Cam scoffs from his seated position, running a hand through his hair, mimicking London's words back to me. "That's impossible."

I beckon him over to the bed with a wave of my hand as he stands, reluctantly sitting down next to me.

My hand slips behind his neck, grabbing hold of the scruff so he feels the honest truth behind my words even if he won't hear them.

"Maybe not in the conventional sense, sure. But we can make London's and my marriage legal on paper and then hold a private commitment ceremony with the three of us. We can do whatever the damn hell we want. Because this feels right. Like is too fucking short not to seal the deal between us. I only now feel like my life is finally on track when I'm with you both. Don't you feel the same way?"

I hold my breath as I wait for their response. London replies first, snuggling into my neck with her face, the scent of her lightly lemon-fragrance shampoo filling my senses.

"You know I do. My life has always been about you two even when I wasn't with you. Everything I am is because of you and Cam." She kisses me on the lips and then moves to kiss Cam, who remains stoic and skeptical by my side.

"What do you think, Cam? Do you want us forever?"

Based on the apprehension written in his expression, you'd think I'd just held him down with a knife to his throat.

He jumps to his feet and paces next to the bed, worrying his lip between his teeth, rubbing a hand over his tense neck muscles.

"I need to think about Taylor and how this would affect him. He's already been through so much with this divorce. I can't thrust this in his face and expect him to just accept it. It's not normal." He uses air quotes and then turns away from me and London.

I search London's eyes for an answer, hoping she'll know what to say to make Cam see differently. Hoping he'll want this as much as I do.

Cam has always been the thinker. He needs to ruminate on something before making a decision. Whereas I've always been too impulsive for my own good.

And London. She's the most logical, practical and yet most sensitive between the three of us. She thinks and acts with an open heart. She bleeds love for the world – for the foster kids she works with in that god-awful foster system, for her family, and for us.

She shrugs her shoulders and scoots out of the bed, unaffected by her nudity, stepping behind Cam to wrap her arms around his middle. She drops her head against his back, careful not to touch the scarred side, reassuring him with her touch.

"Cam, I want to say yes to Sage so badly. But I can't do that without your blessing. Without your acknowledgment that it'll be the three of us together in this arrangement. It's the only way I can live. I need and love you both so much."

I see Cam's broad shoulders tense, his frame so imposing and massive compared to London's lithe body. We've all lost so much in our lives and Cam continues to deal with the shit that's been lumped on him so unfairly.

As I stare at my two lovers, a song title pops into my head, the lyrics flying around like fall leaves in the wind.

Holding on.

I hold on to you so tight,

so scared to let you go.

You're the only one who can make this right.

You're the only one who makes me whole.

Without you, I'm just no good.

I'm just another lost and hurting soul.

Cam turns around in London's arms, capturing her in his own embrace and plants a kiss at the top of her head.

"Let me think about it. It's a lot to take in. I mean, I just fucked a dude in the goddammed ass for the very first time and you expect me to talk about marriage?" His tone is sarcastic with a touch of amusement evident in his voice.

Our laughter fills the room and Cam returns the hug to London. I get up and join in on the embrace, wrapping my arms around both of them.

This is exactly how I want the rest of my life to be.

Wrapped up in of the arms of my two best friends.

My two lovers.

And hopefully, my two forever life partners.

CHAPTER 54

The next six months fly by, our lives having returned to some kind of normal and Cam's healing progressing along nicely.

While there are still some kinks to iron out, I'm the happiest I've ever been because both Cam and London now live with me full-time. Just like I've always wanted them to be.

We moved London out of her apartment after her lease expired and Cam, who is still on a leave of absence from his smoke-jumper duty, has remained here. Cam heads to Chester Fork some weekends to stay at his mom's house when he has Taylor so she can see him, too. But mostly Taylor stays with us here.

That kid is the spitting image of Cam. But way more obnoxious and funnier than Cam ever was when he was a kid, which we make sure to razz Cam about every chance we get. Because Taylor spends every other weekend here with us, he has his own room and he decorated it in a race car theme. We spoil him beyond belief, but Cam is a good father and is strict when he needs to be.

The custody-battle and his injuries, however, have taken a toll on Cam. The divorce has been acrimonious, as is the ongoing custody-battle. Lisa had broached the subject of moving to Florida and taking Taylor with her, but Cam put his foot down. No way was she taking their son away from him or to another state where he couldn't share custody.

He rarely opens up about his feelings over the divorce, keeping much of it to himself with the exception of his anger, but this morning he seems more than willing to share. Proving that he's finally trusting in the relationship that we've worked hard to rebuild.

"I'm just so pissed at myself for ever hooking up with Lisa in the first place. None of this would've happened had I not been so eager and stupid when I went into the Air Force. And now Taylor is stuck with a flake for a mother," he laments, scraping a pile of scrambled eggs on his plate.

Cam loves to cook for us. We never go hungry when he's in the mood to whip something up. "Did I tell you she's dating some hippie-surfer-dude? And I know she's involved with drugs."

His eyes flash to mine with a knowing glare. We have very different takes on that lifestyle. London and Cam have been on my back to lay off the hard partying, which I have, and I've stayed away from the people in my past who have pushed it on me. But I don't agree with their concerns that I might have a problem.

The only reason I ever used in the first place was because I was trying to fill the void and emptiness of not being loved. Classic psychology 101.

Now that I have them both back in my life and bed, I feel whole. No other high required.

I lift a shoulder, setting my phone down on the table that's been blowing up for the past hour. Being a successful musician means always being in demand. It gets old, fast. There are times when all I want to do is to walk away from the spotlight and work from the shadows as a songwriter, so I can have the normal family life I crave.

"Don't give me that look," I scold him, rolling my eyes when he quirks a brow. "Like I'm the devil because I've experimented with drugs. And you know for a fact that I'd never have them in the house with Taylor around. Lisa, however, is another story."

"Don't I know it. I have no idea what she was doing when I was overseas or away for work. When I was gone, she always found excuses to leave Taylor with her mother or ask my mom to watch him. She was probably partying and sleeping around. And when I was home, she'd go out with her friends and leave him with me."

I silently commiserated with Taylor's situation with a neglectful and addict parent. Although when I was a kid, my father, when he was around was just drunk and abusive. I would have rather been on my own.

"Thank God he has you and Doreen."

A phone vibrates on the table, but the call is coming from Cam's phone this time. He wipes his hands on the napkin and answers.

"Hello? Oh, hey Curtis."

It's the divorce attorney Cam hired. I leave him to his conversation and bring my plate to the sink, cleaning off the remnants of my breakfast when Cam's roaring voice grabs my attention and I swing back around to see what's going on.

"She wants to do what? What the fuck does that mean?"

Cam stands, pushing back the chair as it scrapes against the wood floor, and begins pacing. The next few minutes all his replies to the attorney are in grunts and *"uh-huhs"* but the agitated movement continues.

"Are you fucking serious? She has stipulations? That fucking bitch."

He gruffly stomps off into the living room, asperity in his tone, as London comes around the corner, dressed in her business slacks and blouse, ready to head off to the office. Her eyes grow wide with curiosity.

"What's going on?" she whispers conspiratorially, accepting the coffee cup I hand her. She smiles and mouths a *"Thank you."*

Wrapping my arms around her, I bring her in for a morning hug and kiss. Although we had quite the frisky make-out session this morning in the shower while Cam still sawed logs in bed, I can never get enough of her.

"I'm not sure, but it doesn't sound good."

She glances over her shoulder at where Cam went off and lifts the mug back to her lips. A grin of pride forms across my mouth as I hone in on the ring London wears on her finger.

An engagement ring.

The one-of-a-kind, Neil Lane 3.5 carat radiant-cut diamond engagement ring, surrounded by round diamonds, adorns her finger. The ring that I gave her when she finally accepted my proposal to marry me.

I flew the three of us on a private jet to Cabo two months ago and popped the question on the beach the last night of our vacation. Things had been so good between the three of us, Cam being the missing link all those years, and solidifying our love.

I'd told Cam in advance – he helped me design the ring in the first place – and asked him if he would propose with me.

On a beautiful star-filled night, in a private secluded beach, we had champagne and dinner, listened to music, talked and then Cam and I popped the question.

Unconventional to say the least, but it was perfect for the three of us. And even more perfect was the sound of "yes" falling from London's lips.

"You want some breakfast before you leave?" I ask, opening the fridge and grabbing the yogurt and fruit she usually eats.

Nodding, she takes a seat and I place a spoon and her food in front of her.

I watch her as she eats, in awe every day that she's stuck with me for so long and loves me the way I love her. This morning she has pinned her hair up in an intricate up-do, wispy strands hanging past her ears, framing her soft cheeks that are pink and rosy from her earlier shower.

"Have I mentioned lately how I can't wait to marry you?"

London blushes and grins, guiding the spoon between her lips. I groan when she closes them around it, recalling how she did the same thing to my cock earlier in the shower.

"You may have mentioned it a time or two." She giggles softly and I place my palm over her cheek.

"You are going to make us so happy…" I begin to say, when Cam bursts into the kitchen, irritation dripping from his voice.

"Goddamn Lisa!" he roars, startling London so much that her spoon flies out of her hand and drops into the bowl with a *clang*.

"She wants to give up the custody fight. She's willing to give me full custody of Taylor, on one condition."

London and I both turn to stare at him, our mouths lifting in enthusiastic smiles because this is what he's wanted for so long. But our smiles quickly fade when we see the hopeless and helpless look of defeat across his face.

"I can't be with you. Either of you."

CHAPTER 55

My jaw drops, and I shake my head in disbelief, trying to string meaning together from the words he just spoke.

"I'm sorry. Come again? What do you mean, you can't be with us?"

Cam leans heavily against the wall of the kitchen, slumping down like a weighted stone onto the floor, head hanging in defeat.

"Lisa," his voice thick with emotion as he clears his throat audibly. His face has turns ghost-white, with almost a grayish hue. "She wants to travel the world with this surfer dude."

Okay…that doesn't come as a surprise. I suppose in her mind that can't be easily done with a young child in tow. And from what we know about Lisa, she wouldn't want Taylor compromising her fun.

London sits down next to Cam on the floor, a hand placed on his forearm that rests on his bent knees.

"Lisa is giving up her parental rights? Is that what it means? So, Taylor will live with us full time?"

His lips thin in a scowl and he shakes his head, his eyes cast downward, avoiding our gazes.

"Not us. Just *me*."

London's eyes flash up to me and then return to Cam. "I don't understand what you're trying to say."

Cam scoffs impatiently. "Lisa's condition is that for me to have custody and for her to drop the suit entirely, I can't raise him in this relationship."

He points an accusatory finger in a triangle between us.

While not many, except for Cam's mom, Doreen, and London's family, know about our unique polyamorous relationship between the three of us and our plans for the future, it's pretty easy to assume that Lisa has figured things out. And is pissed.

Whether it's out of jealousy or spite, or just plain hatefulness, she's trying to keep Cam from living the life he wants. The life he deserves. How very hypocritical of her.

"That bitch!" I shout, slamming a hand down on the table, the vibrations flipping over the salt and pepper shakers and rattling the mugs of coffee. "She's an evil, backstabbing bitch. We can fight her on this, Cam. Don't let her have this control over you and Taylor."

I'll beg and plead and get down on my knees to make him see how manipulative this woman is being and that there are other options for keeping things status quo with Taylor. He doesn't have to give up his right to love the way he sees fit because she's an envious evil witch.

Cam plays with the phone in his hand, flipping it over back and forth as he works through the logic of my words.

"I don't know. I detest fighting. I had enough of it overseas."

London jumps in, uncharacteristically adamant. "You *have* to fight this, Cam. Don't let her take everything from us. From you. From Taylor. We love him, as much as we love you. He deserves to have everything. I've seen far too many kids in such bad situations, where their parents don't give two-shits about their well-being. I know you aren't like that and you want to protect him. But Lisa is just plain wrong and is asking for something you shouldn't be willing to give up."

"I know. I just need some time to think this through." Cam looks up, his stare unseeing as if looking straight through us.

His mouth tips down in a frown as he presses his lips in a flat line. I know he would do anything for his son, as he should. But that doesn't mean giving up his own life and love in order to comply with a crazy-bitch's demands.

He rises to his feet, helping London stand with a hand at her elbow. Everything seems to move in slow-motion as if this is a fleeting moment and one that will take us down a road that we can't come back from.

Cam gestures for me to stand up and I step toward them. He wraps us in his warm embrace – his hug like an apologetic farewell - the contact sending shivers down my spine. His touch is so familiar; just another extension of my body. And it feels like I'm losing a limb.

Dropping his hand from where it was wound behind my head, he places his mouth over London's, his tongue sweeping over her lips and surging into her mouth. I watch with a hungry thirst, desperate for my own taste.

She is his, and mine, and he is ours. We are one.

Cam releases London and moves onto me with a sad smile, planting his calloused hands over my jaw, his thumb flicking at my lips that part to taste him. I suck his thumb into my mouth, my cock growing thick and hard at the sensation. He slowly withdraws it and replaces it with his mouth, which I kiss greedily. I want to linger and enjoy the feeling of his wet lips on mine for as long as I can. The full pressure and glide; the minty taste of his tongue against mine. I fear that once he walks out of this house, it could be the last. And it terrifies me.

The kiss ends too soon as he backs away, his hands dropping to his sides with weighted decision; as if retreating from a predatory animal. Eyes weary and conflicted with regret.

"I'm going to go up and pack and head to my mom's. Please let me figure this thing out on my own, okay? Don't interfere. Just…"

His gaze snaps away from us as I slip my fingers through London's, squeezing her hand in an unspoken solidarity. It's so hard to let him go through this hell Lisa is putting him in alone. Our instincts tell us he should be with us, so we can support him. To be his buoys when he's drowning. He thinks he has no control in how this situation with Taylor plays out, but what he doesn't realize is that London and I will help him. If he just lets us.

Cam stubbornly refuses help when he most needs it. I saw that struggle within him when he was going through his recovery. He denies our help and is obstinately inflexible.

The same way he's acting now by walking out that door alone.

Three is better than one.

What I learned through his recovery process, however, is that Cam needs to come to his own conclusions on his own time; but he'll always come around sooner or later.

He just needs to be in the driver's seat and takes the long and winding route before he gets there.

CHAPTER 56

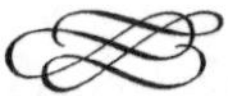

"How do you think he's doing?" London asks me a week later as we lay in bed together watching a movie.

It's obvious she's referring to Cam, who we haven't heard from since he left, with the exception of a selfie text he sent us of Taylor's huge gap-toothed smile showing us that he'd lost his first tooth.

I sigh, pulling her flush to my side and kissing the top of her head. To say we've been lonely without Cam is an understatement. The bed feels ten sizes too big with just the two of us. Every time I walk by Taylor's empty room I feel a pang of grief. Another hole in my heart has been carved out and is MIA.

We didn't just lose Cam in this god-awful situation, but we lost a little boy who we'd fallen deeply in love with. Who felt like our own. A boy I could envision us raising together as a family as we watched him grow into adulthood.

Nuzzling at her ear, I answer honestly. "I really don't know. It kills me that he feels this is the only way to make this work. I disagree with his decision, but what can we do?"

London turns in my arms, her freshly-washed face blooming with natural beauty, the color of her cheeks a dusty pink and her lips plump and shiny.

She lays a soft hand against my cheek, gazing up at me with intensity flashing in her green eyes.

"He'll come back to us. I know he will."

Placing a kiss on the tip of her nose, the light dusting of freckles there that I've always loved, my lips work their way down until I meet her lips. My palm glides over the delicate flesh of her shoulder, guiding the strap of her nightie along with it.

Our kisses transition from sweet and soft to hard and urgent. She wedges a hand between us and massages my already turgid length, straining between my legs.

"Do you imagine him here with us when I fuck you?" I ask, not out of jealousy, but out of hungry interest.

Her hand burrows underneath the fabric of my boxers, and I thrust into her palm. She makes my body come alive with a needy greed to fill her up; to make this empty ache and longing we both have disappear.

"I miss him so much, Sage. You know I want him here with us just as much as you do. But I enjoy being alone with just you, too."

A smile tugs at my lips knowing how good we are together, even when it's just the two of us, as I let my fingers wander over the silky skin of her arms and to her full breasts. I push to my elbow and wedge a thigh between her legs, settling at her center.

Tugging the nightie down, I expose her plump tits, her nipples darting upright, in need of being worshipped.

My thumb strokes against her taut nipple, as I follow it with a swipe of my tongue as she gasps out a needy breath.

We rock against one another, our desire becoming urgent and uncontrollable. I claim her lips again, licking the corners of her mouth and then sweeping between the seam, swirling inside as I catch each moan and sigh between my lips.

With simmering desperation, I slip a hand between our wedged bodies, rolling enough to make room and push the nightie to her waist. Looking down to where our bodies will soon be joined, I see she's pantyless and I groan.

"I'll admit," I murmur against her tit, pressing hot, open-mouth kisses there as she arches into my mouth. "I enjoy having you all to myself sometimes. You're so perfect, darlin'."

My fingers land at the juncture of her pussy and I part the wet flesh there, flicking the nub of her clit with my thumb. Her body cants upwards with pleasure as I continue my ministrations. Teasing and torturing her with my fingers.

I allow my fingernails to skim over the dewy entrance, her pussy slick with desire, thrusting two fingers inside her. The heat of her body is unbearable. She's slippery and hot and it was all I ever thought about during my time in prison. The scent of her arousal and the tightness of her cunt that envelopes me when I'm inside her.

My cock thickens, reminding me he has work to do, and I wiggle out of my shorts, kicking them off the edge of the bed.

With the wetness coating my fingers, I paint a slick swath over her nub, rubbing her in tight circles as she grinds against my hand.

"Right there, Sage....*oh God*, right there." She cries out huskily, her fingernails digging into my shoulders.

There is nothing better than watching London come apart in the throes of passion. She's always been uninhibited, even when we first took her virginity all those years ago. She's insatiable and daring in the bedroom and makes my blood heat with desperation every time we fuck.

Using my thumb and finger, I spread her folds open and rub tiny circular motions around her clit, as she tenses beneath me and throws her head to the side, shouting out her climax.

"Oh God, Sage. Sage. Sage."

I barely let her take a breath before I thrust inside her heat, my cock immediately coated with her slick desire.

Groaning loudly at the insane pleasure, my body begins pumping, pushing and driving into the hot inner sanctum of London's body. Her walls clench around me, as I thrust and withdraw. Thrust and withdraw.

If Cam were with us right now, I'd want to feel his cock thrusting against mine inside her, as we fucked London together. We've discussed it with London, who has been a bit hesitant but hasn't ruled it out. I've taken Cam in the ass, and Cam has fucked London anally, but we haven't crossed over into double penetration territory quite yet.

The thought of taking her simultaneously with Cam has my balls tightening and the telltale sign of orgasm barreling down my spine, as I throw my head back in release. Her ankles cut into my waist, her hands squeezing my ass as I'm seized with white-hot pleasure. I shoot so hard, white-stars flash in my vision.

Panting through harsh and labored breaths, my weight drops over her, depleted and sated, as I leisurely enjoy the sensation of being wrapped in her embrace.

Yet I also miss being held in the much stronger, bulkier arms of Cam.

London's fingers slide through the damp ends of hair at my neckline, caressing me gently as I slowly recover from the aftershocks.

"You were thinking about him, weren't you?"

I rear back, my eyes connecting with hers beneath me. Cocking my head in question, I ask, "What makes you say that?"

She chuckles softly, running her hand along my neck until she's cupping my face. I slip out of her and roll to my side, allowing her room to breathe.

She arches a brow. "Because you said Cam's name when you came inside me."

Oh fuck. I wince.

London notices my expression and she shakes her head.

"It's okay, baby. He's here with us even when he isn't. He's always here." She points between our bodies with her index finger, illustrating the noticeable void.

I softly trace a figure eight around her belly, smiling with the thought of one day seeing it grow fat and round with a child of our own.

In the meantime, we'll proceed with our wedding plans and start our married life together. All the while hoping Cam decides to return to us where he belongs someday soon.

CHAPTER 57

"**I**'m not sure I want Don Caldwell on the guest list. He skeeves me out."

We sit in the back of the limo on our way to the All American Country Music Awards show, stuck in traffic and creeping along the Vegas strip leading to the MGM Grand where the event is being hosted.

Our wedding date is set for a month from now and the only thing we have left to do is finalize our list of invites. London and I agreed that we'd keep the list small and intimate, considering we were holding the wedding ceremony on our property.

But being in the entertainment business, it is nearly impossible to invite some people and neglect the rest, especially in the case of Don, the President of my band's record label.

I shift around to face her in the seat beside me, her sequined emerald dress sparkling in the low interior light, the deep cut of the material emphasizing her plump cleavage. We've been photographed together too many times to count and the public was shocked to learn that London never modeled. I don't blame them for being skeptical. She's a natural beauty, but with the brains and heart to surpass any other woman, model or otherwise.

I watch her face as it transforms with anxious worry, the wheels spinning in her head as her lips pinch in thought.

"I was thinking…what if we just scrapped the whole ceremony and just had my parents, Cam and his family and that's it. Not even the boys from the band or anyone."

Leaning into her, I cup her cheeks gently, staring at her with admiration and love.

"It's your wedding, darlin'. I'm just there to claim what's mine and I don't really care who's there to witness it. In fact, I'd be just as happy to get married in Vegas tonight." I throw this out with a sweep of my hand out the car window at the flashing lights and luxurious sights along the Strip.

London quirks a manicured eyebrow. "That's not a bad idea. I mean, I am already dressed to the nines. Might as well take advantage of it."

I'm dumbfounded by her response, because honestly, I was only half serious with my suggestion. While I've waited years to marry my beautiful girl, there's something about doing it without Cam that doesn't feel right.

As if he knows I am thinking about him, my phone lights up with a text.

Cam: Wishing you a good luck tonight. We'll be watching.

I smile with pride and tip the phone in London's direction so she can read it herself.

Over the last two months, we've slowly re-asserted ourselves back into Cam's life with the help of his mom, Doreen. She'd reached out to us in a desperate plea to help straighten Cam out because he had fallen into a depression so deep she didn't know how to help him.

London and I had met up with her and London's mom, Cora, one day earlier last week for lunch in Nashville.

"Oh, my word, it is so good to see you two," Doreen had gushed, hugging us both tightly as we walked into the crowded waiting area of the restaurant. "And London, honey, you are positively glowing. You are going to be the most beautiful bride. Cora has been filling me in on all the details. I'm so happy for you both."

London blushes and waves her hand dismissively. "Oh stop, Dori. You're embarrassing me. And momma is probably exaggerating about everything, aren't you, Momma?"

We got seated at a booth, the two of us on one side and Doreen and Cora on the other, as the waitress provided us the menus and waters. We immediately segued from wedding into asking about Cam and Taylor.

"Is everything okay with them? Is Taylor adjusting to school? And is Cam back at work?"

Doreen nods her head sadly at my barrage of questions, her lips pursed in a slight frown. "Taylor is doing wonderfully. He just received the weekly class award for Kindness Giver. I was so proud of that boy! He reminds me so much of you when you were that age, Sage. You were such a sensitive boy that cared so deeply for your friends."

She patted me on the hand across the table, her wrinkled hand soft with a mother's touch, flooding me with nostalgia of our childhood. Doreen was always so sweet and generous to me, loving me as if I were her own son.

London heaved a wistful sigh. "That makes me so happy to hear. I miss that boy so much."

I kissed her cheek, laying an arm around her on the back of the booth.

Doreen nodded. "He misses you both, too. He always talks about his cool race car bed, all the toys you've spoiled him with, riding London's horse and all the fun he has with uncle Sage and aunt London. You've been such a positive influence on him."

Cora leans over and wraps an arm around Doreen's shoulder, smiling broadly at the both of us across the table.

"He loves you both so much. So does his dad."

Doreen smiles warmly at Cora and nods in agreement.

"He's so lucky. While he's too young to realize everything that's happened, and the difficulties that Cam had during his recovery, I know his mother leaving has had a profound effect on Taylor. How could it not? But the two of you being there for both Taylor and Cam when they needed that love the most is so appreciated. I can't thank you enough."

Doreen pulled out a tissue from her purse and wiped away an errant tear in her eye.

London and I glanced at each other briefly, exchanging a sorrowful look between us.

"I know from experience how much it hurts to miss a mother when you're young," I admitted, growing reflective. "But some-times not having a mother is far better than having a bad mother. And when you can substitute it for someone like you, Doreen, it makes up for the pain."

Dori smiles a crooked and appreciative smile. "Sage, you have gone through hell and back. I look at who you've become, and it boggles my mind that you turned out to be such a good man when you could've easily slipped into a dark place."

I raised my eyebrows at her comment, flicking my gaze to London. "Believe me, I've been in my share of dark places in my time. Had it not been for my girl, here, I might not be here right now."

A stretch of uncomfortable silence descended over the table as the waitress returned to take our orders and then walked off, leaving us to quietly ruminate on the deep topic.

Doreen cleared her throat, her hands laced together on the table and spoke in a hushed tone.

"Cam's just not the same. Even after he was granted full custody and the divorce finalized, I think the closer we get to your wedding, the deeper he spirals into this hole. *Listen…*" she turns her head and lowers her voice in a conspiratorial tone.

"I know what the three of you share isn't conventional by society's standards and not a lot of people understand it. Heaven knows Cam's father, Mike, never would have given his blessing. But I don't care about any of that. I want what's best for my son and my grandson. I know that Cam loves you both deeply and he needs you both in his life. He's just too stubborn to admit it. And I think that going through what he did with Lisa and her black-mailing threats…"

My head jerked back in surprise. "What? What are you talking about?"

Doreen's eyes grew wide as if she can't believe we don't know. I looked to London who was as equally confused and shocked as I was.

"Blackmail threats?" London repeated.

"He didn't tell you? Oh Lordy, that man." Doreen hung her head and shook it in frustration.

"Lisa indicated she knew about the three of you. She'd apparently seen texts or some video on Cam's phone. And it was revealing."

Oh shit.

Let's just say we may have made a video of the three of us at one point. It was just for our eyes and was hot as fuck and was never meant to be seen by anyone else. We'd all promised each other that we'd guard it and keep it safe from any potential leakage.

"She was holding it over Cam, saying she would go to the press with the details and would ruin your career, Sage. But especially yours London, seeing as you work in public service with children. Lisa was always so jealous of you, knowing Cam never got over you while they were married."

London's mouth dropped open. "Oh my God. He never mentioned any of this to either of us. How did he resolve it?"

"He paid her off. We used the life insurance from Jeanine's policy, as I was the beneficiary, and paid her fifty-grand to make her go away."

"Holy shit." I mumbled in disbelief.

I could've cared less if a sex scandal had been revealed about me and gone public. But I know exactly how Cam felt wanting to protect London's reputation. I would have done the exact same thing he did to protect her.

He was always protecting her.

And now he needed us to step up and be there for him more than ever.

CHAPTER 58

P^{ast}

THE YEAR I got out of prison was pretty fucking bleak. Not as bad as my time in prison, but not great, either.

While freedom living outside the walls of a jail cell was a thousand percent better, I was still remanded to live in a half-way house for a few months at the start of my parole. I had to show effort in establishing a job and contacts that weren't known criminals.

That part wasn't so hard, considering that before going to prison, I didn't associate with criminals. Unless you counted the idiot thugs I smoked pot with back home in high school. But those guys were long gone, and no longer in my life.

And the only other two people that I could've been with were long gone, as well.

By then, Cam was married and in the Air Force overseas some-where, doing pararescue missions to save lives. Heroic as ever.

And London. My angel had just recently graduated from NYU with a degree in social work and sociology. I knew this from her letters. She never stopped writing. And being the sap that I was, I could never keep myself from the torture of reading them.

The only bright spot in that year was my music teacher from prison, Drew. He and his wife, Candace, and their kids lived outside of Nashville, where they were both teachers – she an art teacher and he, of course, a music teacher.

Drew and Candace were my life-saving angels during that year. When I could've fallen down, they picked me up and showed me where I could use my talents.

"Hey, I want you to meet a guy I know. He's a drummer and he was in my band class two years ago."

Drew sits down at the coffee shop off of Maple Street where he asked to meet me. I had nothing else going on that day, and it was always good to hang with Drew. I'd share with him the music I'd written and sometimes we'd go down the street to a music shop and pump out some chords, playing around with the melody.

I lifted my gaze off the notebook that I'd been jotting down some lyrics in to meet his smiling eyes.

"Um, okay. Hello to you, too."

Drew laughed jovially, a booming and boisterous sound. "Good morning, bro."

He thumped me on the back in a quick bro-hug and looked down at the coffee sitting in his spot on the table.

"What's this?" he pointed at the cup. "You didn't have to buy me coffee."

I rolled my eyes incredulously. "I'd buy you the whole damn place if I could. You know I can't repay you enough for all you have done for me."

He waved me off, removing the lid of the cup and emptying a packet of Stevia inside before replacing the lid and sipping it with unrestrained pleasure.

"Oh God, that tastes so good. I need this. I don't think I've gotten two full hours of sleep this week."

I snickered sarcastically. "I assume it's not from hot, all-night sex."

He scoffed. "Pfft. I wish. No, it's the little screamer that was an outcome of all-night sex."

Drew was referring to their newest baby, Dixie, who was their third child and apparently giving them the most trouble with her sleep habits. Or lack-there-of.

Drew scrubbed a hand down his scruffy, unshaved face, the dark-bluish circles underneath his eyes a telltale sign of his seri-ousness.

"Shit, she's gonna be the death of us. Candi is ready to castrate me for knocking her up again with devil-baby."

Heaving a heavy sigh, Drew sipped his coffee and then plunked down a slip of paper in front of me.

"This guy's name is Chris Deggart, but he goes by Deg. He's looking for a band."

I stared at the paper, the handwriting clean and precise, with the name and number of this guy. Cocking my head to the side, my eyes scrunched in curiosity.

"Uh, a band? What band are you referring to?" I whipped my head side-to-side, shrugging my shoulders. "I don't see no band."

Nearly knocking me off my seat, Drew punched me in the chest with a thick knuckle. "Your new band, man!"

I nearly spat out the coffee from my mouth. "My band? Dude, are you high right now?"

Drew laughed like that was the most hysterical thing he'd ever heard. But then his expression grew serious and he leaned over the table, whispering in a hushed voice.

"I am not high. But I am absolutely serious. You my friend, have talent and are the real-deal. You have the music, the lyrics, and the voice. And I suppose by some standards, the look," he said with a flourish of his hand and a roll of his eyes. "Now you just need some back-up musicians to get you started. And Deg is an excellent rhythm section and a great harmonizer. Add a couple other instruments and you can start something pretty fucking phenomenal."

The thing I loved most about Drew was the ever-present internal happy-meter he had. Aside from the sleeplessness, the guy was always plugged into positive. High on life, his family and his passion for music. And for helping others. I'd never seen Drew without a wide smile across his ruddy-face, his ginger hair sticking up in all different directions, and his reddish-brown eyebrows lifted in amusement.

I shook my head and grumbled. "Thanks, but they wouldn't want to play with a convicted felon."

A roar and a loud smack on the table jarred me, my shoulders jerking back from the noise. People at the table to the right of us gasped.

"Don't you ever think that about yourself. Sage. That shit doesn't define you. What happened in your past is over with. You've paid your dues and served your time in reparation. Now it's time to move on. Your whole life is in front of you. You're still a young man, barely twenty-two-years old. You can make something out of your talent. Trust me. You just have to believe in yourself."

What Drew wouldn't understand was that I had never had a belief in myself. After years of hearing my father cut me down and tell me I was worthless, it became a matter of fact. Regardless of how many times Cam, London or now Drew said otherwise.

I hefted my cup in a cheer. "Good speech, man. Thanks."

A sad smile curved at the corners of his lips and he shook his head in a seemingly disappointed gesture.

Tipping his head back, Drew looked skyward and muttered, "When will he ever see his potential?"

I drew my gaze up to the ceiling where he stared, uncertain of who the hell he was talking to.

A split second later, he sternly tapped the paper on the table. "Call him. If not for you, do it for me. Because while the coffee was a nice treat, this would be your real gift to me."

CHAPTER 59

P resent

THE BAND DIDN'T WIN any awards tonight, but I did pick up Best Songwriter of the Year for the song I wrote for Chris Stapleton. That was more of a career highlight for me than anything else.

London and I also didn't get married last night.

After attending three different after-parties at various hotels, hob-knobbing with other musicians and artists into the wee hours of the morning, we wound up chartering a private jet back home instead of staying overnight.

As we sit in the leather-clad airplane seats, I try to justify my reservations about getting married in Vegas. Maybe I was a fool not to take her up on the offer to just do it. And now I'm second-guessing my intentions.

London's bare feet are my lap, as I massage the balls of her feet, her moans over my therapeutic touch sending bolts of electric desire to my cock.

"Oooh…my poor aching feet love you right now," she purrs, the red-soled Louboutin's kicked to the side of her seat, her dress hiked up to her knees. "You can do this all night."

Digging my thumbs into the cushions of her feet, she relaxes, her lids close and a dreamy expression fixes across her face.

"I'm at your service, darlin'."

An eyelid pops open suspiciously. "Hmm…what else would you do for me?"

I catch the suggestive innuendo in her tone and wiggle my eyebrows.

"Anything you want." I lean over and teasingly touch the tip of my tongue to her lips as she giggles, shooing me away with her palm smooshed into my face.

"Everything but marry me, that is."

She sticks out her lush bottom lip in a pout, batting her eyelashes at me.

I stop rubbing her feet and grab underneath her ass to scoot her up on my lap, cradling her in my arms.

"You understand why, right? God knows how much I want to marry you. I've waited for years to make you my wife, but I just can't do it without Cam by our side. It would feel…"

"Incomplete," she supplies, threading her fingers in my hair and kissing my neck. "I understand, Sage."

Her warm breath in my ear sends shivers skittering down my spine. Her words hold so much meaning because we've been in this situation before when we've both been with other people. The wrong people. Partners that were simply placeholders for the right ones.

Our long history of on-and-off again has taught London and me heartbreaking lessons on fidelity and commitment.

I went off the rails the year after I was released from prison, knowing London was in another man's bed and life. I used drugs, alcohol and loads of women to try and erase the ache inside my chest that felt like a crushing meteor.

It was too much for me to take knowing I pushed her away – *threw her away* – and into the arms of another man.

And when she returned to Nashville without Clay, I did what I could to hurt her. Punish her for the way my heart and soul still loved and needed her. I was cruel and heartless, yet her arms remained open to me every time I asked for her help.

I hated myself for the way I treated her.

Every time I knelt on my knees in front of her, begging to be taken back, to be forgiven, she would. I was a worthless user, but she still found the capacity to love me even at my worst.

Those were tough years that we've tried to forget and move past. If she were any other woman, she might've left me without a backwards glance. Tossed me away like the garbage I was. It was only by the grace of her forgiveness and love that got us through that time in my life, until I finally realized I could never love another woman besides London.

Yet a portion of my heart was still carved out with the name of the man I still loved equally as much.

Cam.

Now, in this moment, I had to fess up to what I did. Confess to playing a part in Cam's ten-year absence from our lives. And what I recently did to hopefully win him back.

"London, I need to tell you something."

She stops the pecking against the sensitive part of my neck with her lips and pulls back so she can see my face. I flatten my lips in a thin line, warring with how to tell her all that transpired was my fault.

London gazes at me lovingly, her eyes shining with adoration. She places her hands on my cheeks and gently kisses my lips.

"I know all your secrets, Sage, and I've forgiven every last one of them. Nothing you can say or do will stop me from loving you."

I flatten my palm against her heart, feeling the light *thud* of her heartbeat against her chest.

"I was the one who ruined things between Cam and me. When I was out on bail, I was so angry. So conflicted. So scared and confused."

London places her finger at my lips, shushing me.

"Shh. That is ancient history. It no longer matters."

"But our lives could've been so different had I not done the one thing I knew I shouldn't have done."

London slides her legs over my lap, straddling me and pinning me with a hard, yet consoling stare.

"Baby," she whispers. "What you think you did wasn't wrong. Maybe the timing wasn't perfect, but you set the course, the direction, that he needed. Our fate was sealed that day, don't you see? We needed for our lives to unravel – for that fork in the road to take us in opposite directions – in order that we could meet back up along the way."

She kisses my forehead, then my temple, moving down to my stubbled jawline, her fingertips grazing the skin as she goes. When she's finally at my mouth, she smiles against my lips.

"Don't you see, Sage? Our journey isn't over. I feel it here," she affirms, grasping my hand and placing it over her heart where it had been moments before. "I don't know when, or how, but we will all be together again. A love like ours can't be denied forever."

CHAPTER 60

Our flight landed in Nashville just as the sun came up over the horizon. I woke London who was asleep with her head on my shoulder, with a kiss to her temple.

"We're home, darlin'."

My driver was waiting on the tarmac for us and drove us back toward our house in the hills of Nashville.

I turn on my phone that was powered down since the awards ceremony last night and see an explosion of text messages popping up, all good luck or congratulatory messages. As I scroll through, I see Cam's pop up.

Cam: Congratulations! You deserve it. You're a helluva songwriter.

Cam: Taylor went apeshit when he saw you on TV. He said he liked your boots.

I smile broadly at this because I was wearing a pair that I'd actually gotten a smaller version of for Taylor's upcoming birthday.

He's always stomping around in my cowboy boots like a goof.

Cam: I miss you. You and London. Your speech was…it was…*fuck*. It meant a lot to me. I need to see you.

My heart skips a beat as I recall my acceptance speech last night in front of millions of TV viewers. It was short and sweet but said everything I meant from my heart.

"Thank you to the AACM Association for this honor. Thanks to my manager, Aimee, for busting her ass for me. Drew and Candi, thanks for your guidance and faith in me all those years ago. And most of all, I accept this award on behalf of the two constants in my life. My two best friends. The loves of my life. Cam and London – you mean everything to me. I wouldn't be here tonight without your love and support. My heart belongs to you. I love you both."

I glance over to where London is slumped against the side of the car, having fallen asleep again on the ride home.

I hold my breath as I type out a quick reply and then roll down the glass divider between the driver and me.

"Benjamin, there's been a change in plans. Take us to Chester Fork."

THE CAR SLOWS down as it drives down the long gravel driveway leading up to the Lucas home. London slowly awakens, likely from the jostling of the car and crunching of the ground under the tires.

She's hazy from sleep and rubs her eyes as she peers out the window.

"Where are…wait, what are we doing here?"

She positions herself upright in the seat and stares at me incredu-lously. I give her a devious smirk and show her the text messages Cam had sent, along with my response.

It said, "*Don't move. We're coming home.*"

Her green eyes widen and shine through tears that threaten to spill over. She covers her quivering lips with an equally shaking hand.

"Sage…oh my God, Sage. I love you so much." She throws her arms around my neck and peppers me with happy kisses.

The car pulls to a stop in front of the old farmhouse that was like my own childhood home. Every happy moment was spent either at Cam's or London's homes, memories that I cherish more than anything in this world.

The door swings open and I follow London out of the car, just as I look up to find a little boy running at top speed toward us. I open my arms and catch him, swinging him around in the air.

"Sage! Sage! Did you bring your twophy? Did daddy tell you I liked your cowboy boots? Did you get to talk to The Wock?"

I laugh at Taylor's enthusiastic questions and inquisition, answering each one of them.

"Yes, my trophy is in the trunk and I'll show it to you later. And I'm glad you liked my boots. Maybe you'll get some new ones for your birthday. And yes, Dwayne Johnson was the one who presented me with my award on stage, and I may have gotten him to sign his autograph for a little boy that loves his movies."

Taylor squeals excitedly and jumps out of my arms, doing the funny little arm-swinging, floss dance that's all the rage right now, and then pumps his arm in the air with a "*yes!*"

As he jumps into London's awaiting arms, I lift my gaze and meet Cam's sorrow-filled eyes as he stands on the porch, his arms crossed at his chest, leaning against the post. It feels like it's been years since I've seen him, even though it's only been months.

He's put on some muscle and some additional weight, probably from his mom's home cooking, and it looks really good on him. His T-shirt fits tightly around his pecs and biceps that strain in their crossed position.

I only hear a portion of the animated conversation going on between London and Taylor as I walk forward toward Cam. Each step filled with regret, hope, longing and the need for his love. He steps down the front steps and we meet halfway.

He scans my still tux-clad evening attire appreciatively and winks. "Never thought I'd see you in a penguin suit. It looks good on you."

"Sometimes you gotta blend in with the crowd."

I stand stiffly, nervously watching him, uncertain of what I should do with my hands, which hang at my sides uncomfortably.

One minute, I stand alone, shifting from one foot to the other and the next I'm hauled up against Cam, who smashes his mouth to mine and kisses me hard.

My breath whooshes out of my lungs as my lips part for him, giving him an all-access pass to kiss the ever-living-fuck out of me.

Voices flitter somewhere around me, but I'm too enthralled in the heat and passion between our mouths to care. My hands wrap around Cam's trim waist and slip underneath his T-shirt, where I nearly convulse at the feel of his taut back muscles that clench and tighten against my touch.

I groan loudly as his tongue sweeps inside my parted lips. He tastes of orange juice and sunlight. His fresh outdoorsy scent fills me with unbridled lust, our thickening cocks straining against each other, seeking friction and release.

Taylor's burst of laughter has us losing contact, each of us taking a step back.

"Daddy's kissing Sage!" he shouts, his body wiggling and jumping up and down.

"*Shit,*" I mutter, embarrassed that I let myself get so lost in his kiss that I forgot where I was and who our audience was.

I search Cam's face for any threat of reprisal, but his mouth turns up into a satisfied smile, as he opens his arm to throw it around London's shoulder, bringing her into us for a hug.

He kisses her just as passionately, swooping up her lithe body in his arms as she laughs and giggles. The sound is pure heaven. This entire homecoming is something out of my wildest dreams.

"Put me down you big ol' bear!" she complains, punching him softly on his back with her fists.

Cam teasingly yipes but obliges as he places her feet back on the ground. She doesn't disconnect from his embrace entirely instead, slides one arm through his bent elbow and the other through mine.

"Come on boys, we have a lot of catching up to do."

Cam's and my eyes lock, and a shared smile and wink pass between us.

I agree. "We have a lot of catching up to do."

CHAPTER 61

Doreen returned from town where she'd been running errands about an hour later to find us all talking in the living room, discussing the previous night's events, Taylor playing at our feet on the floor in the center of our triad where he was building a tower with his Legos.

It reminded me of the cities and buildings that Cam and I used to create when we were his age, always trying to one-up one another and me laughing when Cam would get frustrated and end up destroying his entirely. I'd then jump in to help him start over with something new.

It feels awfully similar to the way things have changed for us. The way our lives crumbled and fell without each other and without the support of one another – the infrastructure we had come to rely on that kept us together.

And now here we are, having weathered the tempestuous storms in our lives, ready to start again and build something anew.

Dori took one look at us, and with a broad, unabashed smile, said with a wink,

"It's about damn time."

And then promptly told Cam to pack his bags and said she'd watch Taylor the rest of the weekend.

The minute we enter my house– *our home* – my mouth and hands are on Cam. I catch him by surprise and back him against the wall, my thigh lodged between his strong muscular legs, pressing into his already hardened length.

It sends a rush of satisfaction through me when he opens his eyes with a dazed expression. I search his eyes, reading the guilt and pain that had been buried there. The sadness they convey.

"You're a stupid motherfucker for leaving us," I grumble, letting my hand drift over the bulge in his pants. "This belongs to us. You belong with us."

"I know. I should be punished accordingly." His sexy smirk lifts the corners of his lips and I hear soft laughter behind us.

Slowly angling my head over my shoulder, I find London unzipping the bodice of her dress, the silky, sparkly material left to dangle wide open, offering a tantalizing view of her cleavage.

Her mouth quirks in a naughty grin. "Or, we could reward you for coming home."

My gaze flicks back to Cam, adding pressure at his groin, enjoying his swift intake of breath, his pleasure and pained response.

"I'll take whatever you want to give."

Clasping his hand in mine, I drag him away from the wall, reaching for London's with my other and we ascend the staircase toward the master bedroom.

The bedroom that has been missing the three of us for months.

The bedroom that I plan to label as ours again tonight.

Entering the room one after the other, I head for the deep-backed leather chair in the corner facing the bed, taking a seat. With a flourishing gesture, I make my desires known.

"Undress our girl, Cam. And when she's good and naked, remove your own clothes."

Cam whips his head toward me and lifts a brow high. "It's gonna be like that, huh?"

I laugh mockingly, crossing my arms and swinging one leg over the other in a posture that brooks no argument. "I deserve this. Now do as you're told, or your punishment will be my dick in your ass."

London chuckles as Cam chokes out a throaty, husky grunt. He begins to slowly undress her, teasing and tormenting me as he does, his fingers toying with her body with each layer he removes.

As he pulls down the dress further, he ducks his head to kiss the lush curve of her breast, the tip of his tongue darting out to lick at what I know is her sweet-scented skin. Cam's thumb swirls around the hard nipple and the sound of her breathless sigh seers straight through to my balls. They tighten and my cock strains to be touched.

London begins to reach down to remove the dress, but I stop her with a harsh command.

"Don't. Make him do it. Make him grovel and beg to touch you."

Goosebumps adorn her flesh and I'm rewarded with that sexy bite of her lip, her tongue sweeping out to ease the sting.

Cam does as instructed and removes the dress, letting it fall to the floor. He lands on his knees in reverence next to the discarded garment, cupping her firm breasts in his palms and plumping at her fullness as she arches into his touch.

Cam turns to me looking for further direction and my own voice sounds raspy with desire.

"Worship her with your mouth."

His lips slant up and his eyes grow dark, as he parts his lips to suck in her nipple.

Our groans are in simultaneous triplicate and I'm unable to stand it any longer. My body yearns for their touch, to feel their skin on mine.

I stand and remove my clothes in haste as I move toward them, their eyes closed and lost to their own physical sensations.

With London standing in front of a kneeling Cam – a queen with her subject - I press behind her, relishing in the skin-on-skin contact with her heated flesh. Reaching around her, I slip my hand inside her panties, toying with her swollen nub before submerging my fingers through her wet folds.

I latch on to her earlobe and nip and bite as she squirms against me, Cam's hands still perched at her breasts.

"I think it's time we fuck you together. Are you ready for that, darlin'?"

There had been so many times in the past when we'd discussed the possibility of fucking her at the same time, our cocks pene-trating simultaneously and pumping in tandem inside her pussy. But it hadn't happened up to this point.

Something about this moment, though, seems far too right. Joining us in a way none of us have ever been united. The true testament of our love.

London breathes out a keening sigh. "Yes. Yes, I want you both."

She hoists one arm behind my neck and slips the other around Cam who is bent in front of her peppering her with open mouth kisses. He crouches lower still so his mouth is centered where my fingers are toying with her pussy.

Cam drags the tip of his tongue across the surface of her panties and my fingers twitch inside her. Our connection is combustible.

"Remove her panties," I command, as Cam nods, his eyes greedy with desire, never leaving the sight of her bare pussy as he pulls down her underwear.

Spreading her folds with my fingers, I open her up for Cam to fuck her with his tongue.

"Make her come. Show us how much you missed this. Missed us both."

CHAPTER 62

We moved to the bed the minute London shattered under the weight of her orgasm, slumping against me as her knees shook and her body went limp as a ragdoll.

With Cam being the bulkier of the two of us, he laid down on his back after divesting his clothes, with London laid out on top of him in the same direction.

Generously lubing his cock and priming her pussy, I watch from my advantage point at the edge of the bed as he thrusts inside her, viewing the most erotic vision I'd ever witnessed. My own cock wept with jealousy at the sight before me.

"Oh shit, Sage…you need to get in here now. Don't know how long I can last." Cam pants out, grunting with each thrust.

There's nothing I want more but I know that we need to make London comfortable. To ensure this is pleasurable and not painful for her.

I pour the lube over my erect length, pinching the base tightly to keep myself in check and kneel over the bed – over my lovers' bodies.

"I'm going to use my fingers first, baby," I coach London, who appears to be lost to the sensation of Cam's movements.

She moans as I press two fingers at her vaginal entrance, sliding them inside her tight walls. I feel her clenching around me and I stop.

"Talk to me, darlin. You okay? Do you need me to stop?"

"Mmm. No, it's good. I like it."

I smile down at her, my gaze shifting to Cam who's face lights up with acknowledgment.

Continuing my pumping, I thrust and withdraw my fingers, each time the friction causing Cam's cock to jerk and throb. Realizing we're on borrowed time, based on the pained look and the intensity of Cam's furrowed brow, I remove my slicked fingers and wrap them around my cock, stroking a few more times.

Cam's legs are stretched forward, London straddling him with her knees opened wide, revealing everything to me, as I climb over his outstretched legs, the fuzz of his hair tickling my balls.

"I dreamed of this every night while I was in prison. You got me through my hell and this is my heaven."

The head of my cock poised at her entrance, I cautiously maneuver in, inch by agonizing inch. I feel the stretch of her pussy welcoming me and the skin of Cam's cock glancing across my own slick cock.

"*Ohhhh…*" London wails and both Cam and I instinctively halt our movements.

"You okay?" I ask with concern, my throat constricted with emotion.

She nods, her lips parted, tipping her head back against Cam's shoulder, his hands at her waist to keep her upright.

"*Yeeeesss*…I just feel so stretched…so full."

I grin, catching Cam's half-lidded gaze over her head.

"How's it feeling for you, Cam?"

He doesn't even need to answer me because I know how it feels. It's a wholeness that can't be described. The broken pieces of our lives, renewing and mending back together again into a complete, living and beating heart.

"Fuck, man. I'm so close. You both feel so fucking good. I can't even…"

The bump and grind of his dick against mine shoots paralyzing sensations up my spine, my body fighting and straining against the rising tides of my pending orgasm.

"Cam, use your finger and get her off. Our girl deserves it for giving this to us."

They both moan and he does what I say. His finger fits snuggly between London's and my bodies, pressing into her swollen clit, circling it with purpose. She pants and moans, her pelvis pushing forward as Cam and I continue pumping inside.

There's no doubt this is a tough position. The three of us are in tight, small, hard movements that jostle London with each thrust. I can't even reach her to kiss her because of the angle. But as I stare into her eyes, I watch them close and then flutter open as she releases a long, purring sigh and her pussy spasms around our cocks.

"Oh God, Sage. Can you feel that? So tight…"

"Mmm-hmm," I reply, surging forward, my hands pressed on the mattress next to Cam's shoulders.

"I'm gonna come," he sputters, throwing back his head and growling out his release. "*Fuuuuck*, it's so good."

The throbbing ripples of his cock, mixed with the hot surge of his release, does me in. My balls tighten, and I shoot my own load inside of London, pulsing past the point of oblivion.

"I'm dead." I choke out, a light-hearted laugh tagged on for good measure.

Cam's body lays limp against the mattress, London's lax form pressed on top of his. I pull out of her pussy, the wetness of our releases seeping out between her legs.

Easily the hottest thing I've ever seen or done. It's indescribable the emotions that swirl in my head and heart as I move off the bed into the bathroom.

I make quick work of washing and cleaning up and return to the bed with a wet washcloth in my hands. London is on her side curled up against Cam, whose eyes are shut in quiet reverie, but is kissing her hair, neck, and shoulders.

I place the warm cloth between her legs and she sighs.

"You doing okay, baby? We'll run you a bath later to reduce the soreness."

She pats the pillow next to her head, gesturing for me to lay down.

Tossing the used cloth over the side of the bed, I lay down, facing my beautiful girl. And then my eyes latch on to Cam's, his flashing unsaid emotions and feelings, all of which I am all too familiar with.

Desire. Contentment. Grief. Longing. Serenity.

But most of all, love.

"Welcome back home, Cam."

S age – Three Months Later

THE WAVES of the ocean lap up against the white sandy shore of the excluded beach I'd rented out for our honeymoon.

We've been married three days – London and I – and married life has been nothing short of perfect. Perfection only for the sheer fact that our wedding also included a commitment ceremony between me, London and Cam.

The three of us joined together – maybe not under the law – but decreed by our hearts and souls.

Our wedding and commitment ceremony were intimate, held on our property in Nashville, including our only witnesses of Cam's mom and London's parents. And of course, our ring bearer, Taylor.

London wore a strapless white gown, her long blonde hair twisted in a braided crown, the rest flowing down her back, a few white flowers adorning her head. The three of us stood side-by-side at the altar, London sandwiched between us, arms linked at the elbows, as we recited our vows of life-long commitment and love.

There was no bouquet, or lavish dinner reception, or the standard wedding gifts given. We had no need for any of that. What was important to us was that we spoke our vows to one another in front of our families – and yes, they are my family – and promised to love one another through sickness and health, richer or poorer, good times and bad.

And we pledged our faithfulness to one another for as long we all shall live and pledged we would honor and respect our united bond forever.

It was simple and beautiful and the best moment of my life.

But these past three days have certainly given that day a run for its money.

"Baby, can you rub some more lotion on my back? I feel like I'm sizzling from these rays out here."

A topless London sits up from where she is lying face-down in her chair and hands me a bottle of SPF lotion.

Squirting some in my hand, I rub my palms together and run my fingers over the heated skin of her back. She moans under my ministrations and it brings back memories from earlier this morning when I fingered her in the outdoor shower after we rinsed off from our morning swim.

Or last night as Cam and I double-teamed her, one in her pussy and the other in her ass, sending her to the moon and back with an out-of-this-world orgasm.

Yeah, married life is pretty freaking fantastic.

Finished with lotioning her back, I sneakily wind my hands around to her front where I cup her breasts in my hands.

"Hands off pal. Those are mine to play with today. She promised."

I smile broadly as Cam appears in front of us, returning to our secluded spot with a tray of tropical drinks in his hand. He sets it down on the small table next to us and sits on the opposite side of London, licking a nipple that I've pinched between my finger and thumb.

Then he leans over her shoulder and kisses me flush on the mouth.

Hard.

Demanding.

My lips part and his tongue runs the corners of my mouth, exploring greedily.

London pushes at Cam's chest, pressing him away with a laugh.

"Now boys, you know you're supposed to share. I thought I taught you that very valuable lesson on our first day of kindergarten? Remember?"

Cam and I roll our eyes and snicker at her memory.

Twenty-five years earlier, three kids met on the first day of school.

Two boys battling it out over a toy and one sassy little girl who got between them to break up their fight.

That little girl grew up to remain the center of their lives – their queen.

She is and was the center of their universe.

And hopefully someday, the mother of their children.

Making us the happiest men to ever live.

The End

Want more of this epic romance? You can read an additional bonus scene from Cam's pod by signing up for my mailing list. Just go here:
https://BookHip.com/JTVFRPL

ACKNOWLEDGMENTS

In no particular order, here are the people I need to thank that helped me during the writing, editing and production of this book.

Debbie and Nicole – thanks for being such lovely editors to work with. Debbie, you've become one of my biggest cheerleaders. I appreciate you!

Christopher John – I love working with you and loved this gorgeous cover photo of you, Gus and Lauren.

I needed some legal insight while writing the scenes related to Sage's trial and subsequent imprisonment. Although fictional, I wanted to get the details regarding the legal process correct and reached out to a lovely attorney based in Nashville. Thank you, Nichole Dusché, Attorney at Law, for your expertise and for the time you provided me.

To my friends, both of whom I've known since I was in my teens, Melanie and Sarah, thanks for the information on the Air Force and burn victims and healing times for those with burn wounds.

ABOUT THE AUTHOR

Sierra Hill is a 2020 RONE Award-Winning author of **Game Changer**, as well as over 30 novels, including the award-winning college sports series, **Courting Love**, and the twice award-finalist erotic ménage serial, **Reckless – The Smoky Mountain Trio**.

You can stay connected with Sierra through her newsletter, website and other social media sites. Find all her books listed here: www.sierrahillbooks.com/books

I am pleased to also announce that I've begun writing MM gay/queer romance under a new pen name of K.C. Kassidy.

The first book under this name is now available and is entitled **C*ck Blocked**.

If you like the RomCom movies Leap Year and Notting Hill, you'll enjoy this book set in Ireland featuring a grumpy Irish sheep farmer and B&B owner and the American actor who turns his world upside down.

Subscribe for more information here:

https://www.subscribepage.com/authorkckassidy

And find K.C. Kassidy on these social sites:

FB page: https://www.facebook.com/k.c.kassidyauthor

Instagram: https://www.instagram.com/k.c.kassidyauthor

Website: www.authorkckassidy.com

BookBub

Goodreads

Bio:

K.C. Kassidy is the LGBTQ pen name for Sierra Hill, an award-winning author of 30+ books.

K.C. Kassidy loves a good romance where the most unlikely characters will have their meet-cute and end up with HEA's, regardless of their gender or sexual orientation.

ALSO BY SIERRA HILL

The Puget Sound Pilots (Sports Romance)

The Girlfriend Game (Book #1)

The Wife Win (Book #2)

The Rival Romeo (Book #3)

Change of Hearts (A College Campus Series)

Game Changer (Book #1)

Change in Strategy (Book #2)

Change of Course (Book #3)

Courting Love (College Sports)

Full Court Press

The Rebound

Pivot

Fast Break

Jump Shot

Hockey

Offside (A Vancouver Vikings Series)

Playmaker (A World of True North Moo U novel)

College football - Co Written with SE Rose

Falling for the Fake Boyfriend (CFU)

Falling for the Roommate